LITTLE DARLINGS

Praise for Hannah King

'*The Blindspot* is a stunning and thought provoking novel'
Heather Critchlow, author of *Unsolved* on *The Blindspot*

'With her magnetic prose and unforgettable characters, Hannah King's sophomore novel secures her place as a master of small-town suspense' **Anna Bailey, author of *Tall Bones* on *The Blindspot***

'Not one to miss!' **Cailean Steed, author of *Home* on *The Blindspot***

'Not only beautifully written but gripping and full of soul' **Sarah Pearse, author of *The Sanatorium* on *She and I***

'A nifty fusion of psychological thriller and police procedural' ***Sunday Times* on *She and I***

'Gripping. Thoughtful. Lyrical … It's got all the right shades of Tana French. This writer is going places' **Imran Mahmood, author of *You Don't Know Me* on *She and I***

'King really understands suspense' **Holly Watt, author of *To the Lions* on *She and I***

'A heart-racing, addictive read' ***Woman's Own* on *She and I***

Also by Hannah King

The Blindspot
She and I

LITTLE DARLINGS
Hannah King

First published in the UK in 2026 by No Exit Press,
an imprint of Bedford Square Publishers Ltd,
London, UK

noexit.co.uk
@noexitpress

© Hannah King, 2026

The right of Hannah King to be identified as the author of this work has been asserted in accordance with the Copyright, Designs and Patents Act 1988. All rights reserved. No part of this book may be reproduced, stored in or introduced into a retrieval system, or transmitted, in any form or by any means (electronic, mechanical, photocopying, recording or otherwise) without the written permission of the publishers.

Any person who does any unauthorised act in relation to this publication may be liable to criminal prosecution and civil claims for damages.
A CIP catalogue record for this book is available from the British Library.
This is a work of fiction. Names, characters, places, and incidents either are the product of the author's imagination or are used fictitiously, and any resemblance to actual persons, living or dead, businesses, companies, events or locales is entirely coincidental.

ISBN
978-1-83501-544-5 (Paperback)
978-1-83501-174-4 (eBook)

2 4 6 8 10 9 7 5 3 1

Typeset in 11 on 13.75pt Garamond MT Pro
by Avocet Typeset, Bideford, Devon, EX39 2BP
Printed and bound in Great Britain by
CPI Group (UK) Ltd, Croydon CR0 4YY

The manufacturer's authorised representative in the EU for product safety is
Easy Access System Europe, Mustamäe tee 50, 10621 Tallinn, Estonia
gpsr.requests@easproject.com

Beyond call or bird-call,
Fever or fright,
No light in the twilight,
No footfall at nightfall[…]

In the twilight no light,
At nightfall no footfall,
No fever… fright,
No call, no bird-call.

       – Louis MacNeice,
          'Falling Asleep'

Chapter 1 | January 2023 | Dromary, County Down

I wake up thirsty from my dream, feeling like I have a raging hangover. I've never had a hangover, raging or otherwise, but I've seen enough actors on screen portraying the morning after the night before. Steve has refilled my water bottle and I chug it gratefully, the last memories of my bright, vivid dream trickling away as the bottle empties. It was sunny in the dream, but I can feel the imagined heat fading from my face as the reality of winter in the cottage bites at my nose. I unplug my phone from its charger.

My pulse quickens. Three missed calls from a number I don't have saved.

Charlotte, it must be Charlotte.

The most recent of the calls I've missed by only four minutes.

I am about to tap the number to call back when I hear the distant trill of the landline somewhere in the depths of the house. I haven't heard that landline ring for… must be years. The house phone is something to be dusted weekly and then put back and forgotten about until the following Sunday.

A giggle from Daisy. Steve's big feet plodding to answer it.

We converted our tiny loft space into a master suite a few years ago, replacing the trapdoor with a small flight of wooden steps and a little landing at the top. Steve's friend did it for us. We're not sure it's been done to any sort of building standards, but as Steve has said many times, 'That's only going to be an issue when we come to sell… and that won't be for fifty years.' The door is closed, but the phone is directly below me on the hall table, so

I can hear it as loudly as if it were under my pillow. Were house phones always so loud?

Ringing.

Ringing.

It stops and I know Steve has answered. I can hear polite interest in his tone, then polite concern, then polite agreement. I think I could probably read him from across a room, even if he had his back to me. Then Steve's feet are coming up the stairs to our bedroom two at a time. One creak. Two creaks. Three creaks. I imagine his navy slippers, size thirteens – a Christmas present from me, same as every year – barely able to fit on the wooden, spaced-out treads. Why is he going two at a time?

Something's happened.

It's Charlotte, it must be.

Despite his rush upstairs, I hear him hesitate on the landing. His knock, when it comes, is barely audible. A tentative tap, tapping.

I don't know when I sat up, but I did, clutching the quilt in one hand as if relying on it to tether me to sense.

Don't overreact.

It could be anything.

He opens the door.

'Are you awake?' Steve whispers, though he is staring at me.

I nod.

'Phone for you.' He crosses the room towards me, tap tap on the wooden floorboards, then his slippered steps are muffled by the thick rug under our bed. He is holding out the bricky white landline. There is a cling of dust coating the back of its curved surface that I notice when I take it from him. Maybe we don't dust it as often as I thought.

Steve waves his hand and I look at him. 'It's Tony,' he mouths.

'Tony?' I ask the phone, my voice a little croaky.

'Hello, love.' Then Tony adds, completely unnecessarily, given how I answered, 'It's Uncle Tony speaking.' As has always been his style, he is shouting into the phone, not quite comprehending the fact that we can be eighty miles apart and still able to hear one another without effort. 'I must have dialled the mobile number wrong,' Tony continues to shout. 'The one Audrey's written here—'

'You didn't,' I say. 'Sorry, Uncle Tony. I just missed you, that's all.'

'Still in bed at this time?'

I don't answer right away. I'm thinking too hard, I'm too confused. It's not Charlotte. Can't be about Charlotte. If it was about Charlotte, it wouldn't be Tony calling me. But what reason could Tony have for bombarding me with calls on a Sunday morning?

'I— Yeah,' I say finally. 'Yeah, I was working late.'

I have no idea what Uncle Tony's idea of late is these days, and no idea why I've thought to lie. It's just after eight on a Sunday morning and it's still dark outside, so in my opinion I'm not even having a lie in.

Steve is hesitating in the doorway, caught between wanting to give me privacy and wanting to show he's there if I need him. His round face is full of concern, and he's straightening the leg of his pyjamas unnecessarily, the way he does.

Uncle Tony gives a sigh. For a man who is coming eighty-eight in the autumn, he sounds healthy. Very together, with perfect diction. On the rare occasions when Audrey has passed him the phone to say hello – birthdays and Christmases mostly – I have never known Uncle Tony to be in any way confused or doting. Never known him to even have a cold, actually. Impressive. I can forgive him shouting down the phone, considering—

'It's Auntie Audrey, love.'

'Oh.'

It's not Charlotte.

That's the only thing my brain will let me feel. The slow relief, my heartrate normalising, safe in the knowledge that whatever has happened, whyever he is calling, at least it's not Charlotte.

I meet Steve's gaze and he makes an eye-narrowing, head-shaking gesture. I nod a few times, so he knows I'm okay.

I imagine what he is seeing.

My hair will need brushed, but at least it's clean. My cami top clings to my stomach and digs in just a little bit too much at the shoulders, but Steve has always liked my size, and has said it so sincerely that I think I might actually believe him. The covers aren't sticking to me like they sometimes are after I've been dreaming, so it must have been something nice. I'll see if I can remember it later.

'She's gone, love,' Uncle Tony says simply. If there is emotion in his words, I find it impossible to tell. I'm not good at being able to read anyone who isn't Steve, and Tony Wolfe is, after all, an award-winning actor. Nobody can read him.

'Are we still going to the park?' Daisy asks when I come downstairs ten minutes later, caution in the round face that is so like her dad's. 'Or shall we – shall we give it a miss?'

'Daisy,' Steve says. It isn't an admonishment, more of a quiet warning. 'I explained to you what happened. The park probably isn't at the top of Mummy's list today.'

'No, we'll go,' I say decisively. The park is one of the few places I can go without hours of planning and panicking. It's got to the point where I actually almost enjoy it, so I'd hate to miss it.

Now that I'm downstairs, with both of them just standing there in the hall, looking at me with tentative smiles and eyes full of concern, waiting for me to set the mood, I wish I was back upstairs again, alone. Which Mummy am I today?

'You run and get your shoes on,' I say to Daisy, to make her stop looking at me. 'And I'll sort myself out. Make myself presentable so I don't scare anyone.'

'You're lovely,' Steve says automatically as Daisy runs off to her room, laughing. 'Are you sure you want to go? It's a big shock. I can take her myself or we can all stay in, if you like?'

'No,' I say. 'I'm fine. Honestly, I am. Fresh air might be nice.'

My aunt, Audrey, is being buried in three days' time. A nice enough woman, a perfectly fine aunt, an average actress whose only misdemeanour was thinking she was slightly better at acting than she actually was. Someone quite eccentric and a bit strange, but not a bad person. I don't think. I will likely feel something about her death, but for the moment I am numb about the whole thing.

It wasn't Charlotte.

Audrey was fifteen years younger than her husband, so even for him it's more surprise than anything else. A heart attack, apparently. He woke up next to her a few hours ago to find her motionless, cool to the touch.

'The best way to go,' Tony murmured in my ear on the phone. 'Least she wouldn't have known what was happening.'

I wasn't sure I agreed. I've heard all kinds of pleasant things about drowning.

But sure, at least she didn't suffer or get old enough or sick enough to need a carer. She'd have hated that.

I go into the kitchen to find Steve has already made me a coffee, perfectly. He makes it better than I do even though he doesn't like any hot drinks. I always turn the machine on and forget about it and come back to hot coffee spilling over the side of my mug and onto the counter. I take a long sip.

'When is the funeral?' he asks. After I had quickly explained what had happened, hand covering the receiver, Steve had nodded sadly and left me to my phone call.

'Wednesday.'

'Oh.' He straightens his T-shirt and watches me steadily. 'How do you feel?'

I look out of the kitchen window at the bird feeder we set up. The little cages of peanuts are swinging in the breeze. It is bright, now that the sun has come up, and I watch as two robins peck at the fatballs, trying to poke something off for themselves. The feeder was Steve's idea, and Daisy loves it too. I'm less enthused but time and time again I find myself, without conscious decision, doing anything and everything that I think might make them happy.

How do I feel?

I've seen Audrey a few times a year since I was ten. Always in Dromary, or somewhere close to it; she always came to me. When was the last time I saw her? I try to think, my brain scanning back through the happy Christmas holidays, the rainy autumn half-term spent inside, Daisy's first day of P6. It was before that, I think with a pang of guilt. I hadn't seen Audrey since the end of August. She had driven down to see me. We'd gone shopping one Saturday and had lunch in a busy pub. I remember thinking it was such an ordinary place for such an interesting woman, kept worrying someone might spill beer on her expensive jacket.

Charlotte had been invited but she hadn't answered either of our calls.

'I'm not sure how I feel,' I say to Steve finally. 'Thank you for the coffee.'

I turn to give him a smile and he returns it, looking relieved. The kitchen is tidy. Tidier than we left it last night when, once again, the pull of bed was too much and we left dirty plates and crumbs over the worn wooden table and left the recycling in a little pile by the back door. Steve has done the dishes, taken out the rubbish, and I think I can smell Zoflora, so he's mopped the floor too.

'Aren't you freezing?'

I look back at my husband in confusion. I have my dressing gown tightly belted around my waist.

Steve nods down at my feet and I realise I haven't put my slippers on. The floor is freezing and I can't feel my toes.

'Oh. Yeah, a bit. I'll go and get ready now, I'll just have this.'

He comes to stand next to me at the window and we watch the robins. One of them has left the fatball and is now trying to tear pieces from the hardened slice of bread that Steve must have set out this morning. The bird gets a small piece of crust, flies off quickly, and returns a moment later. Though the window is closed, the kitchen is so quiet we can hear the chirps they make to each other. I shiver at the sound, try to keep myself rooted to this moment. Focus on the hum of the fridge freezer and nobody but my husband beside me. Not the birds.

'I'm sorry I never got to meet her properly,' Steve says after a moment.

'Mm.'

'She sounded really... unique. She was a great actress.'

'Yes,' I agree automatically, because that is what people say when they're talking about her and I am not going to disagree out loud. 'Yes, she was.'

'At least you can always stick her on DisneyPlus when you miss her.'

Steve is trying for joking, trying to gauge where I'm at. Which Cara am I today? Which Mummy? He'd probably know better than me where I'm at; I have no idea.

The robin has flown to the other side of the slice of bread and is determinedly picking at the corner. We watch as a huge crow soars down and grabs the whole slice in its beak, then jumps away and disappears from sight, the smaller birds scattering in all directions in a flurry of feathers and piercing cries.

I'm in the en-suite, splashing cold water over my cold face with my already cold hands when Steve pokes his head around the door.

'I've just called Frankie; told him I won't be logging on until Thursday.'

Steve 'works in IT'. It's what I say when people ask, and I give a half-shrug and smile when explaining, as if I'm not really sure what it all means, but that's not true. I know everything about his job, could explain his career from the very start to present day, know the names of the projects he's working on and what pisses him off about his day-to-day, and he could do the same with me. We are just one of those couples, one of the rare ones that actually speaks to each other about more than shopping lists and box sets. We care about where the other one is and what they are doing when we aren't together.

'There was no need for that,' I say quickly. 'Honestly, I can go on my own. I'll be fine.'

'Well.' Steve says it as an argument, a statement and a comfort all at once. As is his way. Of course I wouldn't be fine driving all the way to Anniskillen by myself and going to a funeral and coming all the way back. Of course I wouldn't, and he knows that. But he would never make me ask him to accompany me, and he would never acknowledge that it might just be out of my grasp. I wonder how many meetings he will miss, how many bad decisions his team will make without him there. I will worry about it all week even though I know Steve won't.

I pat my face with the clean towel he must have put in the bathroom when I got out of bed.

'Take Daisy with us,' Steve says, both a question and statement, this time.

'Mm,' I say, pumping Dramatically Different onto my fingertips. 'She has rehearsals after school on Wednesday. She won't want to miss the first one of term.'

'One missed rehearsal won't hurt. She'll be back in time for Thursday's.'

I glance at him as I gently massage the moisturiser into my skin, careful to slide my hands upwards, never downwards. One thing Mum taught me that I still remember from watching her do the same thing over twenty years ago.

'Discourages a wrinkly neck,' she'd say with a wink, and I'd smile back, unable to imagine my own plump skin with any wrinkles and unable to see any on hers either.

I spent so long among people who would have considered a missed rehearsal tantamount to arson that I always forget my nine-year-old's school play probably isn't the be all and end all of our lives, no matter how into it she is becoming.

I puff out my cheeks at my reflection now, tilting my head from side to side, checking out the lines around my eyes, determinedly avoiding the thin scar on my cheekbone.

'What?' Steve asks. 'What are you thinking?'

'I'm thinking I look bloody old.'

'You do not. Are you looking at your laughter lines?'

'They're called crow's feet, I think, Steve.'

'Not on you. It's a privilege to get older, anyway.'

I give him a tired smile and push past him. I open drawers at random, not sure what I'm after, closing them noisily, getting frustrated by how untidy they are. It's been on my list for weeks, months, to sort them, but the thought of starting it fills me with actual fear.

When I turn back to Steve, empty-handed, he is holding out a pair of black leggings and a sports bra. 'These ones?' he asks tentatively, though he knows he is right. He knows exactly what I would wear for a Sunday afternoon in the park. We are just one of those couples.

It is as I'm lacing my trainers that my dream comes back to me. Clear, perfectly technicolour like it's playing on a cinema screen. It had been a memory, I realise. I let myself remember.

Boiling hot summer. Not enough breath in the air, the sun on our faces, the smell of the suncream Auntie Audrey had watched us apply that morning. We were in the hammock Uncle Tony had put up, both of us, even though we were pretty sure it was supposed to be a one-at-a-time thing. There was a bee somewhere, and it was doing Charlotte's head in. She kept sighing and taking off her sunglasses, trying to find it so she could swat it away. I stayed on my back, with my arms stretched under my head and my eyes closed like I'd seen the women do in films.

'Bloody bee,' she murmured.

'Leave the wee thing alone,' I said. 'It's not doing you any harm.'

'It bloody is.' Bloody must have been her word of the month.

I opened my eyes just in time to see her demeanour change entirely. She sat up straighter, waved in the direction of the house, and smiled one of those Charlotte smiles. The ones I craved, that I used to get ten times a day but hadn't had for a while. Her whole face was alight with it, and she looked like a painting, with the hot sun behind her head and her dark curls everywhere.

'We're in the hammock!' she exclaimed, pointlessly.

I took off my sunglasses and squinted back at the house to see Lawrence coming towards us across the perfect green lawn, shirtsleeves rolled up past his elbows, his white linen trousers – like his huge tanned face – somehow totally uncreased. He was carrying two full glasses of pale green liquid with little umbrellas in them, and ice and even slices of lemon, and he handed us one each as soon as he got close enough.

'Are these cocktails?' I asked, immediately suspicious and a bit afraid.

Charlotte rolled her eyes. 'Ignore her,' she said. 'Thank you, Laurie.' To me she added, 'It's clearly lemonade, dummy. Say thank you.'

'Thank you,' I said, but I set my glass down on the grass without taking a sip.

'How are my two favourite girls?' Lawrence asked, voice booming across the garden for no good reason. 'Enjoying the sun? And the new hammock?'

'It's perfect!' Charlotte exclaimed. She took a huge gulp from her glass and smacked her lips together. 'Thank you for this. You make the best lemonade in the world.'

Lawrence guffawed – he actually guffawed, he was a guffawer – and waved her words away.

'I'm just popping down to say goodbye.'

'Oh.' Charlotte's smile vanished and she pouted like a child, even though she was eleven by then. 'When will you be back?'

'I'm not sure.' Lawrence was wearing black sunglasses that contrasted with huge white teeth that he showed us when he added, 'I'll miss you, though.'

'I'll miss you too!' Charlotte said, even though clearly Lawrence had meant both of us.

I was trying not to roll my eyes at Charlotte, as much as I wanted to. Becoming so frequently frustrated with my older, previously much cooler, smarter sister had come as as much of a surprise to me that summer as if she'd woken up one day and showed me an extra leg. I wondered what Mum would think if she saw me hiding an eye-roll at Charlotte, and I felt ashamed.

Lawrence and Charlotte continued to chat, and as usual it was all very boring stuff about the set and the filming dates and the promotional tour Lawrence would be going on. He was filming in Dubai, and I had no idea where that was and didn't care to ask.

I let my eyes idle back towards the house and started when I saw we were being watched. Uncle Tony's eyes met mine through the patio doors and he immediately busied himself with something in the kitchen. I wondered how long he had been standing there, watching us.

'...anyway. I best be off. Dad's waiting on me, he's going to drop me off at the airport and carry on into the city.' Lawrence pretended to heave a huge sad sigh. 'Hugs before I go?'

Charlotte went first, kneeling up on the hammock and wrapping both her arms around his neck. The hammock swayed dangerously, and I gritted my teeth and clenched the white fabric tightly even though it hurt my hands.

'Will you write?' she asked, a little breathlessly, and I thought maybe she was imagining she was in a film as well.

'I'll try.' Lawrence squeezed her and let her go, then turned to me, beaming. 'Come on, Cara. Will you miss me too?'

'Yeah,' I said automatically. 'Yeah. Write to me too.' I knelt, but less steadily than Charlotte had, my weight giving me less balance than her, and I fell into his chest. He and Charlotte both laughed and Lawrence righted me and pulled me in close.

'See you soon,' he said, squeezing me.

Uncle Tony was at the window again. I couldn't tell if he was watching the hug or looking at Charlotte, but I remember him watching.

I hated it when he watched.

'Will you give us a push before you go?' Charlotte asked as Lawrence finally let go of me. She batted her eyelids at him and he pretended to think for a moment. Then he used both hands to grab the hammock and pull it towards him. Charlotte shrieked and clutched at my leg, but I could tell she was delighted. Lawrence pulled the hammock back as far as he could, his face straining with the effort, but his sunglasses unmoving, his smile never leaving his face. Like he was made of wax or like he thought there was a camera on him.

'Are you ready?' he said.

Before Charlotte could respond, he let go, and the hammock whooshed back in the direction we had come from, faster than I'd thought it would. Charlotte screamed in delight, her laughs hurting my ear and her fingers digging into my shin. I held onto the corded sides and closed my eyes as we swung back to Lawrence, where I felt him push us with both hands, and back, and forth, and back, feeling sick. I could see the sun through my closed eyes, then I couldn't as we passed under the shade of the tree, then I could again when we came out the other side. Orange light. Black. Orange light. Sick.

'STOP!' Charlotte shouted, but she was giggling maniacally. 'Laurie, stop it!'

Orange. Black. Orange. Sick.

Hot sun.

'Laurie, *stop*!'

Charlotte's laughter right in my ear, the push of Lawrence's hands against us, and the image burned behind my eyelids when they went black of Uncle Tony standing at the window, always watching us.

Daisy likes to pretend she's too old for the swings, but she rushes over to them the second there's a free one.

Steve takes a seat on the bench, his hands in his pockets, and watches her. He is smiling like he always is when he watches Daisy, and even his garish orange T-shirt says SMILE LIKE YOU MEAN IT. Steve loves bright T-shirts with slogans or lyrics on them. Since it's the only imperfect thing about him, I let it slide and am even happy to iron them.

'So,' he says when I join him on the bench. 'Back to Anniskillen, then?'

'Back to Anniskillen,' I agree, feeling nothing at the words.

'How do you feel?' he asks again.

Steve is still watching the swings, where Daisy is now laughing with another girl. Daisy speaks to everyone, reaches out to everyone, wants to befriend everyone she meets. It is the thing I love most and like least about her, the fact that she has no fear. I keep telling myself it is time to have The Talk with her, the Don't Speak to Strangers, Don't Trust the People You Meet, Assume Everyone Wants to Hurt You talk, but every time I think I might, I don't. *Let her just be a kid*, I stop myself. Let her think people are good and kind and only want the best, like she does. Let her think that and we will just have to try to protect her.

'Right now,' I say after a moment. 'I honestly don't really feel anything.'

'That's normal,' Steve says. Steve has never had to grieve anyone, so he is speaking out of kindness more than experience, but I appreciate his efforts all the same. Steve comes from quiet comfort and modest money, and he has two living parents who are *compos mentis*, and he is both their son and their sun. He is and always has been a countryside boy with an interest in computers, and the worst thing that has ever happened to him is that he once tore the tendons in one of his legs and couldn't play five-a-side football with his friends any more and gained a bit of weight because of it. I have never begrudged him his happy and lucky existence; he's my sun too. 'It'll take you a while to get your head around it,' Steve continues. 'Are you going to phone CJ and tell him you're taking a few days?'

I let a little puff of air out of the side of my mouth. 'I suppose I should. I probably won't get much work done. I can work tomorrow, though, no problem.'

'Cara,' he says. 'Take a wee bit of time off. The world won't end.'

Time off to do what? I want to say, but I don't. If I'm not at work tomorrow, if I don't have my routine and my rules and my timings, what will I do? Where will my head go? I am absolutely not indispensable. I design logos for small companies and new businesses and do drawings and graphics for their online advertisements. It sounds fancy and exciting when I tell new people, but I work nine to five at it for a Belfast-based corporate, so it really just involves a lot of meetings, a lot of emails, and some drawing. It is just a job. I am good at it, but not amazing. I work hard, but I don't push myself. I need it because I can do it from home, but I wouldn't say it's my life's ambition or that I'm happily moving up a career ladder I've dreamt about.

The fact is I've done it for ten years, but we have an eighteen-year-old on an apprenticeship with us at the minute, and she could probably do it just as well as I do.

Daisy and her new friend, a much smaller girl with flaming red hair, race each other to the slide, still laughing. A red-haired woman at the other side of the park calls something to them and waves, and they both wave back. I look around her, to see if she is with her husband, but she seems to be alone and is attentively watching her daughter. I am stupidly grateful and I allow myself to relax a little, knowing another mum is keeping an eye.

Mumsnet and Instagram and the various parenting forums I frequented when Daisy was a baby – and still take a look at from time to time now, I'll admit – all talk about the worry that arrives the minute your child is born and never goes away. The worry that settles itself into your womb after it is empty and sits there and waits and waits. Only mine grows like another baby. Grows and grows and has been growing, thinking – obsessing, maybe – over Daisy turning eight, then nine, then ten. Always ten. She will be ten in April, one of the youngest in her class. And it feels like a deadline, it always has, and I can't help it.

Steve is talking to me again.

'Do you know, will it be a religious thing?'

'Hm? Oh. Yeah, probably. Auntie Audrey was a Christian. Supposedly.'

'And Charlotte, will she go?'

Charlotte.

I haven't spoken to Charlotte yet. I've called her phone – or at least the last number she texted me from – but no answer. I didn't leave a voicemail because I don't think I've ever done that in my life and it made me feel ridiculously nervous, and the WhatsApp message I sent hasn't been received yet. I dread to think where Charlotte might be. It is a thread of worry I don't have the emotional capacity to pull on just yet.

'She would definitely want to go,' I say. 'It's just finding her to tell her.'

'Should we... Should we go and try to find her?' Steve asks uncertainly.

Steve has a very complicated opinion of Charlotte, and I understand why. In some ways, he wants to take her into our home and feed her up and mop her forehead but, in the same way I can imagine this, I can also see him denying to his work colleagues that she is related to me. He loves her by association because I so clearly do, but any time Charlotte is around Daisy, I can feel his discomfort as if he is wearing it on his sloganed T-shirt.

'How?' I ask. 'Just walk the streets of Belfast until we see her?'

'Well.' He looks away from me and back to Daisy, though I can tell he isn't really seeing her.

'I'll just keep trying her,' I say. 'If she comes, she comes. If she doesn't, she doesn't.'

'When we get home, I'll have a look online and get us somewhere to stay in Anniskillen.'

'Oh, don't worry,' I say, feeling my gut twist at what I'm about to say. 'Tony has insisted we stay there. At Chaplin House.' I could hardly start arguing seriously with an old man whose wife had just died.

'Oh?' I can tell Steve is far more intrigued than he is letting on, but he has the good sense not to push it or ask any more questions. For the very first time in our eight-year marriage, our eleven-year relationship, Steve is going to see where I spent almost a year as a child. Not a lot of time, really. Not in the grand scheme of a whole existence. But a year that changed every aspect of my life all the same.

Chapter 2 | June 2000 | Chaplin House, Anniskillen

The car dunked into another pothole and Louise, the social worker, actually swore. Charlotte giggled awkwardly because she hated and loved swearing at the same time.

'Sorry,' Louise said. 'The car will be wrecked. These country roads.'

I thought of country roads taking me home, remembering a song Mum always used to turn up when it came on the radio. I let myself think about Mum for a few minutes, staring out the window from the back seat, the bright green hedges blurring in my eyes.

'It's not your car, though,' I reminded Louise after a moment, trying to be helpful. I had asked her when we'd set off and she'd told me as much. It was her work car; not her own. She ignored me. Or maybe I'd waited too long to say it.

'AT THE CROSSROADS. TURN. LEFT.'

All our eyes looked to the sat-nav that Charlotte had christened Sally. We'd never been in a car with a sat-nav before, and even though I was genuinely upset and Charlotte was trying to remember that she was too, we were both enthralled by the lady in the little computer.

'Why do I feel like we've just been turning left since we left Oldry?' Louise muttered. I watched her eyes flick between the little computer and the road, but I wasn't worried like I normally was in cars. We hadn't met any other drivers for at least half an hour. Nobody ever came out here, I thought. And maybe they had a good reason: I had counted fifty cows before I got bored of my game, and there were so many sheep I couldn't count them all before the wee blue car sped past. But there were no shops, and no hairdressers, and no Chinese takeaways, and no people out here, so even though it was getting greener and greener with every mile, I felt bluer and bluer. (Julie, our therapist, liked to use the word 'blue' when she suggested how we might be feeling. I had liked Julie a lot, but Charlotte had decided that we both hated her, so now I hated her.)

'Can I put the radio on?' Charlotte asked, but she was pressing buttons before she'd even got the words out. S Club 7's 'Reach' came on and all three of us groaned. Charlotte quickly turned the radio off again and sat back in her seat, folding her arms. She was pretending to be very relaxed, and very cool, and very sad about everything, but because I was her little sister (her little sister with only fifty weeks of difference, thank you) I knew she was nervous and anxious and worried (three more of Julie's words). Her knee was jiggling up and down; I could see it from my seat behind Louise.

'THE DESTINATION. IS ON YOUR RIGHT.'

Louise braked the car so hard that my head flew forward and slammed off her seat. Nobody noticed so I didn't say anything either.

'This can't be right,' Louise said, squinting out of the car window. 'There's no gate or anything. There's no number.'

She opened her door and stepped out, walking across the road to examine the hedges that lined it as if they might be hiding the house. Charlotte undid her seatbelt and jumped out too, her skirt swishing confidently away. She was in Charlotte Mode now, and would be until we'd met our new family. No, not our new family, I reminded myself. Mum was always our family, these people would just be our... temporary guardians. I think that was what Louise had called them.

Charlotte went and stood next to Louise. She only came up to

Louise's shoulder, because Louise was really tall, but she held her head up and looked into the trees as if we were waiting for the house to magically appear.

I got out too and went and stood beside them because I didn't want to be in the car on my own.

'There's a sign,' I said at last, pointing but not moving. There was a black metal sign sticking out at an angle from a wooden post that had been dug into the ground between hedges. If you tilted your head you could just make out the shape of a sheep and the words *Chaplin House*. If I hadn't already known what the house was called, I would have thought it just said *Cheese House*.

'Oh! Good spot, Cara!' Louise beamed and looked at where I was pointing. 'Chaplin House! This must be it!'

Louise was back to her normal self again too. Really happy and bubbly and just generally delighted about everything. We liked her but she was 'a bit much'. (That one was Charlotte.)

'Where's the driveway?' Charlotte asked.

'Over here!'

We all jumped at the call. A big old man had appeared from between the hedges and was striding towards us, his big face beaming and his big teeth catching the sun. He was waving, even though we weren't far away and could see him perfectly. He came to a stop in front of us and put his hands on his hips and did a big, exaggerated sigh. Everything about him was just big.

'Well!' was all he said.

'Hello!' Louise said, hurriedly reaching out her hands for a formal shake that really didn't suit her. (Louise was an adult, but she was very much 'on our level' and was quite cool and fun. She didn't look like a handshaker. But then maybe we'd just never really seen her around other adults.)

'Tony Wolfe,' the man said, enthusiastically shaking Louise's hand. 'You can call me Tony.'

'Louise,' Louise said, but she sounded like she was out of breath which was weird because she'd just been driving. 'You can call me… I'm just Louise. It's so amazing to meet you.' After a second she added, 'Tony.'

The old man chuckled and turned to Charlotte. 'You must be my lovely niece, Charlotte.'

'I think I'm your grand-niece,' Charlotte mumbled, all traces of her cool and calm act gone with the old man's arrival.

'Great-niece,' Louise corrected, giving a little giggle we hadn't heard before. 'Your Auntie Audrey – remember I told you? – she is your Mum's auntie, so she's your great auntie. Mr Wolfe is her husband, so that makes him your great-uncle. Isn't that so cool? Families are so interesting and diverse. And Mr Wolfe is an actor.'

'Tony!' laughed Tony. His voice was very boomy, like it was echoing, even though we were in the middle of the countryside and there were only birds and cows and nothing for it to echo off. 'You can call me Uncle Tony, if you'd like. It might be easier to forget all the greatness!'

Louise laughed again and Charlotte nodded and swallowed. She stepped back a bit so she was next to me and reached her fingers out to hold my arm. 'This is my wee sister, Cara,' she said. 'She's only nine.'

'I'm ten in August,' I corrected her, but I couldn't make my voice very loud and I didn't think anyone had heard me.

'It is so lovely to meet you both and we are so delighted to have you here with us. I'm really sorry about your mum, but I hope we can help you feel a little bit better while you're here with us. How long have you been staying with… what was it you said? Mrs Patterson?'

'Miss Prince,' Louise said. 'They've been with Miss Prince for four months now – since the accident. She's been a lovely foster carer for them, hasn't she, girls?'

Charlotte nodded for both of us and I thought of my little bedroom in Miss Prince's house and felt a bit sad. She had two cats and I loved them, and she said I could visit any time I wanted, but that was all the way back in Oldry and I didn't think I'd ever want to sit in the car for that long again.

'Well, that's great news,' said Mr Uncle Tony, and he managed to look both pleased and serious at the same time. I wondered if that was what it meant to be an actor, and decided maybe I wanted to be an actor too. He was wearing a navy jumper even though it was quite warm, and it had a shirt underneath it which was something I hadn't seen in real life before. He had trousers on that looked like a chess board, which I also hadn't ever seen, and shiny brown shoes. He had a white moustache and red cheeks and his face was really nice and kind and even though he was old with lots of wrinkles, his eyes looked shiny. He had quite a lot of white hair on his head. If we were in a film, he'd be the nice uncle. I so hoped it was like that.

'Shall we...?' Louise hesitated, one arm gesturing towards the gap in the hedges where Mr Uncle Tony had come from, and Mr Uncle Tony made a big fuss of slapping his forehead and apologising for his manners, and Charlotte and I looked at each other for the first time and I felt better being able to see my own worry on her similar though much prettier, slimmer face.

'We've let the dang thing get overgrown the last few months, I'm afraid!' boomed the actor. 'But we've recently re-hired Ronnie from the village. He's an all-rounder, bit of a handyman. Has saved us a lot of bother over the years, can turn his hand to anything. He'll be our gardener for the summer. He's out with his great hacking kit, fixing up the garden as we speak. By this time tomorrow, Chaplin House will be restored to its former glory!'

'Oh, you didn't have to go to any trouble for the girls,' insisted Louise.

'Nonsense! My son, Lawrence, is home from filming this evening, so it's really a very special day all round. Haven't seen him for, God, three months! We have a group of cleaners in making the place sparkling as well. For you too, girls,' he added to us, and I was grateful that Charlotte mumbled a thank you because

I wouldn't have thought to. It didn't seem like it was for us at all.

We got back into Louise's car and she drove slowly, slowly, through the gap in the hedges. Now that it had been pointed out, we could tell there was a gravel path under us, and Mr Uncle Tony led the way, pretending to walk into outstretched branches and making a whole show of clutching his eye as if in pain.

Louise giggled and so did Charlotte, so I did too.

'He seems nice, doesn't he, girls?' Louise whispered, though the windows were up so he couldn't have heard us.

'Yeah,' Charlotte said. 'Yeah, he seems nice.'

'He seems nice,' I echoed. And I supposed he did, even if he was really very big and a bit dramatic.

'You have no idea how lucky you are,' Louise continued. The driveway started to incline and the car didn't sound happy about it. It was the biggest longest driveway in the world, and the trees were heavy with green leaves, so the branches hung quite low on either side of the car. 'Mr Wolfe is a very highly regarded actor. He was in four films last year. Four! I saw three of them in the cinema and got one of them out on video twice. He is excellent. He's so convincing. He's the best ever to come from the island of Ireland. I think it's that voice.'

'Mr Uncle Tony,' I corrected.

'Uncle Tony.' Charlotte turned in her seat to glare at me. 'He said to call him Uncle Tony, you doughnut.'

'Girls!' Louise said, though she was too busy staring at Uncle Tony and trying to keep the car straight as it bumped over rocks and into potholes on the steep incline, so I didn't think she cared.

The thick trees either side of us thinned out until finally Uncle Tony bounced in front of the car with a flourish and held out both his hands. He actually gave a bow as we looked at Chaplin House for the first time, and even though I heard Charlotte give a little tut at that, I felt it was very understandable.

Now we really were in a film.

Little Darlings

Chaplin House was like the house in *Home Alone*. We watched that one twice last Christmas, and I liked it the most even though Mum had said she preferred the second one, and Charlotte had agreed with Mum but I knew she just did it to annoy me, so her and Mum could be on the same side. Our own house had had three windows at the front, one downstairs that was the living room and two upstairs (one for my bedroom and one for Mum's, so we were on the same side there, so I won), but fifty people must be living in Chaplin House because I had counted ten windows before I felt a bit dizzy with the sheer size of it and had to stop my game. The door was right in the middle of the house, which was something you only saw in houses where very rich people lived, and there was ivy hanging down the middle, from the roof to the top of the front door. The house was symmetrical, like the *Home Alone* house. We'd done symmetry last term, so I knew what it was. I hadn't realised they were rich and wasn't sure how I felt about that. Charlotte always said rich people were 'up themselves', but I didn't know how that worked, and it definitely seemed to be a bad thing so I was sure it didn't apply to nice Uncle Tony.

He was beaming at us when we stepped out of the car.

'What do you think?' he asked. He was looking at Charlotte when he said this, but it was Louise who answered him. She sounded like she couldn't catch her breath.

'It's wonderful!' she said. 'Truly wonderful. And you're so kind to share it with the girls. They're very grateful. Aren't you, girls?'

'Yes,' Charlotte and I said at the same time. We grinned at each other as we always did when we spoke in unionson. Was that the word?

'Well, don't just stand there!' Uncle Tony said. He slapped his hand on his leg and gave a little jig. 'Let's go inside! Welcome to Chaplin House!'

I felt like we were on a tour and he was our guide. It was very weird. He rushed towards the house like *he* was the child. He had so much energy for an old man, and I made a mental note to say that to Charlotte as soon as we were alone.

'I noticed the spelling of the name of the house,' Louise said, hurrying to keep up with Uncle Tony. 'It's like the actor?' She seemed to have forgotten that we had a suitcase and a backpack each to haul out of the car, and she showed no sign of helping us with them.

'Ah!' Uncle Tony looked delighted. 'I'm glad you noticed that. You're right – it's Chaplin House as in Charlie, not as in any of that religious stuff. He stayed here with my parents several times when he visited Northern Ireland in the sixties. He was something of a close friend of theirs, actually. The reason my father was able to get into acting himself.'

I thought Uncle Tony looked taller when I looked back at him, but that couldn't be right.

'He never summer-holidayed on the island without a quick visit up to see the Wolfes before he left. He was something of a mentor to me, actually, when I was a young man, so when I inherited the house, I decided to give it a name and named it after him. I remember a time…'

Louise and Uncle Tony marched on in front, laughing at something, leaving Charlotte and me struggling to wheel our old suitcases across the gravel. Charlotte's wheels got stuck between some stones and I had to let my own case drop to free it.

'Who are they talking about?' I whispered. 'Who is Harley Chapping?'

'Harley *Chaplin*,' Charlotte corrected. She rolled her eyes. 'How can you not know who that is? The house is literally named after him.'

I suspected Harley was someone very famous, so famous that Charlotte felt she didn't even need to tell me who he was.

The sun was really hot, so we paused to get our breaths back at the bottom of the huge steep stone steps that led up to Uncle Tony's – our – front door. Charlotte leant against a shiny dark blue car that was long and boxy and didn't look comfortable.

'I wonder what Audrey will be like,' I said, feeling I was voicing something that we were both thinking but that Charlotte would never say.

'Mm,' she murmured. 'Maybe she's an actress, too.'

'Actors are weird,' I whispered, and I was happy when Charlotte smiled at me.

Auntie Audrey was an actress. And she was weird.

But where Uncle Tony looked a bit strange but was really very nice, Auntie Audrey looked really, really strange but was also probably the most beautiful woman I had ever seen. Mum was beautiful, but Audrey was…

'Striking,' Charlotte would say later, with a serious nod. 'Auntie Audrey is striking.'

Her face didn't move when she came towards us and pulled us both into the same crushing hug, like her eyes and mouth and nose and forehead were all stuck in a permanently surprised pose. Her skin was white and smooth, and even though it was just a Tuesday afternoon, she was wearing a full face of thick, pale makeup, including bright red lipstick that left a mark on my cheek when she kissed it. I was itching to rub it off but a look from Charlotte told me I should wait. Like Uncle Tony, she was fully and properly dressed too, in a pale blue shirt and white floaty trousers and sparkly sandals, and her hair had a huge cream clip in it that I would have loved for myself but that would have looked better on Charlotte. Mum usually stayed in her dressing gown on her day off.

'The little darlings have arrived,' she announced to nobody in particular. She pulled back from the hug and leant down to look at us both in the eyes. 'I am so sorry about your mum,' she said, very seriously. 'Kathy was my absolute favourite person in the world at one point, and I'm devastated we've lost touch the last few years. And now it's too late.'

'She's not dead,' I said, helpfully, and I felt all of the adults and even Charlotte giving me a look that I hated. Louise coughed a bit awkwardly from where she stood with Tony at another door behind Audrey, so I took this as a warning and shut up.

The hall we were in was shiny and I could tell that it was supposed to be nice, but it was a bit chilly and it didn't make me feel cosy the way a house should. There were big shiny oak sideboards everywhere and they had loads of expensive-looking shiny ornaments on them and everything sparkled. Uncle Tony's cleaners had obviously finished in here. There were no rugs, and I always liked a rug because it felt nice in the morning coming downstairs for breakfast and being able to be barefoot and know there would be something soft and warm you could put your cold toes on. I'd have to wear slippers while we were here; it looked like the floor was made of bathroom tiles.

'We are going to get to know each other and love each other,' Audrey said, and I wondered if it sounded like a threat to anyone else. 'I just know it. Please, treat our home as your home while you're here and let me know if there is anything, anything, *anything* we can do for you.'

She reminded me of the lady who owned the B&B in Portdawdle that we'd stayed in with Mum the summer before, who offered us maps of the area and asked us what time we'd like to eat at.

'What time would you like to eat at?' Audrey asked. She rolled up her sleeve, careful not to crease it, to examine a silver wristwatch. 'Have you had lunch? I was thinking dinner at seven, so we can dine with Lawrence.' She clapped her hands together excitedly, which made me jump. Her serious and sad tone was gone and even though her face still looked surprised, I could tell she was suddenly very happy and excited. 'I can't wait for you to meet Lawrence. You'll just love him, everyone does. His flight should be touching down in another few hours. Tony? Tony! Is there enough petrol in the Audi? Did you get it valeted like I asked? I won't have him getting into a dirty car after he's been on an aeroplane all day. Now, do you want to go and choose your rooms while the adults talk?'

It took me a moment to realise Audrey was suddenly speaking to us again, for she had talked and talked so much in exactly the same way that I was starting to feel sleepy and confused.

'Oh,' Charlotte said. 'Sure. Thank you, Auntie Audrey.'

Charlotte slid her foot over to stand on mine, so I echoed, 'Thank you.'

Louise and Uncle Tony had been laughing and chatting by the door, but Louise had moved to stand behind us and was doing that thing where she put her hands on our shoulders.

'Yes, girls, do as your aunt says,' Louise said. 'I have a few bits of paperwork I need to go over with Mr and Mrs Wolfe—'

'Tony, please!' boomed Tony, and Louise blushed. I noticed that Audrey didn't say anything or correct her.

'You can have any of the spare bedrooms,' Audrey told us. 'Ours and Lawrence's rooms have been locked, so any bedroom you can get into is yours if you want it. Run along, now.'

Running along up the huge shiny staircase could not be done with a suitcase and a backpack each, so I let Charlotte lead the way and we both went up the stairs luggage-less and onto the huge landing.

We heard the adults go further into the house and then a door closed and we were left alone in the silence.

'Mum's not dead,' I said again. 'Why did you give me that look?'

'What look?'

'You gave me a look when I said Mum wasn't dead.'

'I didn't.'

'You did!'

'Cara!' Charlotte snapped. She softened and let her shoulders sag. 'Sorry. You just don't have to bring it up all the time. Haven't you worked out yet that everyone gets uncomfortable and doesn't know what to say?'

'So?' I asked, but already I felt less seriously about it than I had a minute ago.

'Let's pick rooms,' Charlotte said. 'In a house this big they're gonna be amazing. I shotgun the biggest one.'

'You can't shotgun a room,' I said. 'Can you?'

But she was gone, running this time, down the corridor, and it made me happy to see her running so I just followed.

The first room we came to was locked.

'Lawrence's,' Charlotte said wisely, even though she couldn't know that. The next door we tried opened up into a huge bedroom with the biggest bed I'd ever seen, and pure white bedclothes and cushions and pillows that had been plumped and washed and smelled good even from the doorway. When we pushed the third door open, a tiny woman popped her head up from where she had been scrubbing the bath and I screamed and ran away, and Charlotte came after me laughing her head off. We met one more cleaner, examined two more bedrooms, and then Charlotte dashed back into the hall and looked around.

'I think I'm going to have the first one,' she announced, and I was annoyed because I had wanted that one, but I was unsurprised because I knew Charlotte would want it too.

'Wait,' I said, suddenly hopeful. I pointed. 'You didn't see that room, maybe you'll like that one better.'

I led the way – going for confident – back across the huge hall to the final door on the landing. We'd run past it twice without noticing it, and Charlotte darted past me to get there first and came to a stop so sudden that I almost ran into the back of her.

'This room looks tiny,' she said. She was right: the door was narrower than any of the others. 'Bound to be a hot press. You can have it if it is, you'll be nice and warm.'

'Shut up, I'm not sleeping in a hot press,' I said, immediately a bit worried.

She turned the handle and pulled the door towards us. It gave the loudest, highest creak we'd ever heard and I actually clamped my hands to my ears.

'It sounds like a girl screaming,' Charlotte said, her eyes wide.

Little Darlings

'I bet it's the spirit of the little girl who used to live in Chaplin House a hundred years ago.'

'Stop it, come on,' I said, trying to seem like I was just keen to explore the room, not getting scared.

'She was tortured in here,' Charlotte said quietly, moving her face towards mine, but I could see a ghost of a smile on her face and I knew she was only trying to scare me.

'You hadn't been in this house until ten minutes ago,' I said, very proud of how reasonable I was being. 'How would you know?'

Charlotte considered this. 'Louise tells me everything. Things she can't trust you with until you're a bit older.'

'No she doesn't,' I said, but I wasn't sure.

I opened the door further and let the spirit of the girl shriek at us.

'Oh,' I said. 'It's not a room, it's just some stairs.'

'The stairs to the room where she was murdered,' Charlotte said.

'Stop it!'

'Honestly.'

'Stop it, Charlotte. I'm not going up.'

'Baby.'

I decided I would rather be called a baby than risk going up to the murdered girl's room, so I stood with my arms folded and turned my back to her.

'Come on, let's see what's up there.'

'I'm not going.'

'Yes, you are.'

'I'm not.'

'Cara, wise up. Come with me, I want to see.'

'No.'

'There is no murdered girl, I made it up.' She gave one of her huge exaggerated, loud sighs, where she breathed dramatically against the back of my neck. 'Sorry. Come on, now.'

The stairs creaked too, and I heard her slowly climbing up one, two, three...

I stood on the unfamiliar landing, glancing between the various opened and closed doors, trying to remember which room was which and what the second-best bedroom would be. One of the doors swung forward and I jumped, but it was just a cleaner leaving the bathroom with her mop and bucket and she completely ignored me and went downstairs. I heard a door open and close downstairs, and the landing was silent again. I suddenly decided that behind one of the doors there would be a bad man who wanted to hurt me, so I turned and quickly followed Charlotte.

The wooden stairs were really steep and every single one of them creaked and sounded like bedsprings. I'd gone up ten of them when Charlotte, a few above me, stopped and gasped. I went up to join her.

We were on a landing shaped like a big rectangle that had been decorated with only a thin cream-coloured rug – but it was somehow the nicest place I'd ever stood. And I was happy there was a rug. In front of us, instead of the wallpapered wall I had been expecting, there was a huge window, the entire size of the landing in every direction. Charlotte took a step forward and I automatically reached for her arm.

'Be careful,' I said. 'We're really high up.'

She rolled her eyes. 'Don't be a dummy.'

She seemed to move more carefully all the same. She put one palm and then the other against the glass and pressed her nose forward to look out over the back of the house. I was scared she was going to fall through the window and die, obviously, but I also didn't want to miss out. Slowly, slowly, I lifted my hands and put them out in front of me, testing the strength of the window. Nothing happened, so I pulled my body forward and rested my forehead on the glass, and even though it felt like there was no floor under us any more, I couldn't look away.

Little Darlings

The back of Chaplin House extended for what looked like miles. There was so much colour everywhere, and my eyes didn't feel big enough or old enough to take them all in in one go. There was a huge, raised patio directly beneath us, with those big wicker chairs you see in garden centres. (Rattan, we learned later from Auntie Audrey, who said it with an affectionate pat on an armrest.) An archway with roses tangled all around it led to some steps which then led down to the grass, which was so green it was like one of our drawings. There was a sprinkler on in the middle, and I felt an urge to run down to it and dance about in my bare feet. We'd had a bit of grass out the back in our old house, but there were always stones and worms so I was too scared to play in it. This garden didn't look scary at all.

The edges of the garden were surrounded with flower beds, some small and neat with new-looking soil, and some of them huge and wild, with no soil to be seen among the hundreds of petals, waving slowly to us. Surrounding the beds were some of the tallest trees and bushes I had ever seen. One or two of them seemed to be taller than the house, and there were two different stepping-stone trails that led off into them and disappeared out of sight.

We didn't say anything for ages. I began to fidget long before Charlotte did, but I didn't want to speak and make her annoyed at me.

'There's a pond,' I said finally, pointing.

'There's... everything,' Charlotte replied. 'Isn't it just amazing? It's bloody gorgeous.'

'Bloody gorgeous,' I echoed, thinking of how Mum always said that any time we wore a new dress or went to the hairdressers. Mum would have loved the garden at Chaplin House. She was forever taking us to castles and estates and garden centres on the bus, and while we usually got bored after an hour, it was worth pretending for her, to see her grinning and skipping about the place like she was really young herself.

'Their new gardener has clearly started down there,' Charlotte said. 'It's perfect. I'd forget about the driveway too if this was my house.'

'This is our house,' I said. 'Isn't it?'

'For now. I think we're going to be okay here,' Charlotte whispered, and there was nothing fake about her now. The role she'd been playing for Louise for months, and the role she'd been so keen to play in front of Tony and Audrey, was gone.

She reached out and squeezed my hand once, and I squeezed hers back.

It was just us for that minute, standing on the landing with the beautiful garden below and the horrible thing that had happened somewhere between us, but if what she was saying was true – and it always was, Charlotte was so clever and knew everything – then everything was fine and we'd be okay.

Chapter 3 | January 2023 | Dromary, County Down

We set off on Tuesday afternoon, straight from picking up Daisy from school.

'What if they don't want me to be Emilia because I've missed the first rehearsal?' she asks as soon as she has her seatbelt on.

'Yes, we're fine, thanks,' Steve says, pulling away from the kerb with a wave to the mum who has let him out. 'Our day was grand, thank you for asking.'

Daisy giggles, but it comes out in a nervous bark. She doesn't like any change to her routine (as I can understand) and likes it even less when anything interferes with the after-school drama club. This year is *The Comedy of Errors* ('For ten-year-olds?' Steve had exclaimed, taking the letter from her in surprise), and Daisy is delighted by her lines and has had them memorised since the Christmas break. Steve and I could probably have a go at reciting the whole play ourselves, the number of times we've had to practise with her. It's a kid-friendly version that the drama teacher has written herself.

'How was school?' I ask, glancing in at her from the passenger seat.

Her plaits are coming undone and her face is red, but her pinafore looks as though she hasn't spilt anything down it, which I'll take as a win. She only has the one and there won't be time to wash it before Thursday.

'Okay,' she says, nodding, a little breathless from her run across the playground. 'Had Art last thing. Making gargoyles.'

'Did you use Daddy as your muse?' Steve asks, glancing into his rear-view mirror for her reaction. She gives it to him obligingly, delighted as always to share her dad's jokes and keen to show him the same.

'How far is it again?' she asks.

'About two hours,' I say. 'Maybe a bit longer given the time of day.'

'I can't believe I'll get to see where you grew up, Mummy. It sounds so beautiful.'

'Yeah.'

'I've never been to Farm-anna, have I?'

'Fermanagh. No, pet.'

'Is it really lovely there?'

'Yes, pet. It's nice.'

'How come you left?'

'I met your dad,' I say, which isn't the reason. 'And aren't you glad I did?'

'Yes,' Daisy says seriously, and I smile at the solemn nod I can imagine her giving me from the back seat.

Steve pulls onto the motorway ten minutes later and the three of us lapse into a comfortable silence. I take a packet of wine gums from the glove box, even though I know I shouldn't, even though I've been quite good on my New Year's diet this year, this time, even though I'm carrying about three stone more than I'd like to, and I offer them around. We all take one. Then I take another few.

I send another WhatsApp message to Charlotte.

Where are you? Have you heard about Audrey?

I don't put a kiss at the end. My worry over her radio silence is just starting to turn to annoyance. If something had really happened to her, I'd know by now. Wouldn't I? She's always been unreliable with her phone. It must just be that.

'What are funerals like?' Daisy asks tentatively. We're sitting at fifty-six miles per hour because Steve read somewhere that it's the most economical speed. His hands rest somehow both

Little Darlings

casually and carefully on the steering wheel. He is a wonderful driver, Steve. He is pretty much wonderful at everything: he can do DIY, he can play a few tunes on the piano, he is a good listener, he is a wonderful dad, he buys good and thoughtful presents, he can cook an amazing lasagne, and his on-hold doodles look like professional artists' portraits. It used to make me feel sad and inadequate, but now I just find it useful and enjoy all the wonderful things he can do.

'Funerals are sad,' I say. 'Especially if it's someone young who has died.'

'Was Great-Great Auntie Audrey very young?'

Daisy was delighted when I explained that, technically, Audrey would be her great-great-aunt, and she's told all of her friends in school about it and keeps using the full title at any chance she gets.

'No,' I say, smiling. 'Not any more.'

'Early seventies is considered fairly young now,' Steve says. 'They reckon our generation will make it to 100, no bother. Daisy might get to 110.'

'Mm,' I say, imagining Steve in his nineties, then imagining myself. In some ways I can't think of anything worse. A fat old woman with tatty grey hair. I push the wine gums back into the glove box.

'Will everyone be wearing black, like in the films?'

'I should think so, pet. It's respectful.'

'Yes, respectful,' Daisy murmurs, going for mature.

'We've another hour yet before our first scheduled Penelope Pitstop,' Steve says. 'Shall we play the number plate game?'

'Yes! Yes! Yes!' Daisy shouts, clapping her hands together, all thoughts of maturity gone.

We have our own version of the number plate game. Everyone has to spell out their own name using letters found on the cars that are in front of us, but you can only pick one letter from each car.

'Mummy you have to go last because your name is the shortest,' Daisy states.

'Mummy has the same number of letters as Daisy,' I joke.

'Noooo! *Cara*!' Daisy always says my name with a particular tone, as if her mother having an actual human adult name is a bit silly and embarrassing. As if it's rude to have an identity that doesn't centre around her. 'Oh, I have a D already!' She points to the black Punto up ahead of us where a D starts the number plate. 'Okay, Daddy, you go.'

I let them play the game between themselves, letting Daisy find my letters for me, and I look out of the window at the already darkening fields and hills surrounding us. We are so unimportant, I think, not for the first time. Even this tiny country is really massive, and we are such a tiny part of that. We don't matter at all. The entire car could flip over and kill us and it wouldn't matter, not in the grand scheme of life and the universe and—

Just as I am thinking this, Steve swerves to the left, tyres crunching unpleasantly as they bump across the hard shoulder. I feel my gasp deep in my throat and look around to see what the problem is.

'Fucking idiot!' Steve shouts as a huge white BMW overtakes him far too closely, going far too fast. Probably over eighty miles an hour, if I had to guess. If Steve hadn't swerved, the car would definitely have clipped us. 'Everyone okay?'

'Yeah,' Daisy says weakly from the back seat. It only lasted a split second, Steve's careful thinking saving us as I have always known it would do some day.

'Cara?'

I don't say anything.

The BMW had an A on the number plate, I want to say. I want to join in, be normal, play the game. There's my last letter. I've won. But it wasn't just an A. For the three, four seconds the car was in my line of vision, I stared at the number plate. LAW 0LF3. Could be anything. Could belong to anyone. But what are the chances that the huge, expensive car with that number plate, travelling in the direction of Anniskillen the day before Audrey's funeral, belongs to anyone other than Lawrence Wolfe?

My heart pounds and I feel dizzy with the sheer number of feelings. Everything. Everything mixed in.

Nostalgia for something that doesn't exist.

'Cara?' Steve asks again. 'Are you okay? I'm sorry. He didn't touch the car. Prick.'

Prick, I think.

I think of Uncle Tony, always watching. I think of Auntie Audrey, never watching. I think of Charlotte, of my latest message to her that is hanging somewhere in the ether, undelivered. I think of Audrey, of Tony, of my Charlotte, of Lawrence and his white teeth and the white car that nearly caused an accident. Then I think of the navy Audi from back then, and that hammock, and the smell of bergamot and of petrol and the sound of birds outside the window and the metallic clink of an opening paint set and—

'Cara?'

'Mummy?'

I haven't felt any of the tears but my face is soaking with them.

Chapter 4 | June 2000 | Chaplin House, Anniskillen

There was another small flight of steps leading up from The Big Window, as we decided to call it, which led to a second floor only a quarter of the size of the first. Up there were two bedrooms and a bathroom. All of those were quite small and seemed to have been forgotten in a way the bigger, grander bedrooms on the first floor hadn't, but we liked The Big Window so much that we decided to take a bedroom each on that very top floor and, in Charlotte's words, 'just leave it at that'.

Charlotte got the bigger room, of course, and hers had two windows, one looking over the driveway at the side of the house and the other looking onto the beautiful garden. The bathroom was right in the middle, and you could access it from both bedrooms. 'Isn't this so cool!' I cried, running through the bathroom from one bedroom to the other. Charlotte shrugged and rolled her eyes, but I knew she thought it was cool. Then there was my little bedroom, which was quite small and dark, but I did still love it. I had a little square window, and if I stood on my tiptoes, I could see into the garden too.

We raced back downstairs to get our suitcases, but Charlotte suddenly stopped on the bottom step and held my arm so I would stop too. I waited, listening, thinking she might tell me she could hear the spirit of the murdered girl screaming again, but then I realised she was trying to listen to what Louise was saying, somewhere in the depths of the house.

We crept towards a closed door and both put one ear against it.

I thought the adults must be in a big room, because their voices came from such different places. I was proud of this realisation, and opened my mouth to tell Charlotte, but she shushed me with a look and I fell silent and tuned back into what Louise was saying.

'…every Thursday evening. Charlotte goes first, at six o'clock, and Cara goes in after, at seven. They just wait on each other outside, so if you make sure they remember to bring a wee book or something to do. Julie is great, I've used her before with loads of kids and the progress they make is incredible. Of course, if a Thursday night doesn't suit, she is pretty flexible. That's her card there.'

'Tony can take them,' Audrey piped up. 'He'd love to, wouldn't you, dear?'

'It would be my pleasure!' boomed Tony, and we both pulled our ears away from the door, wincing. 'Never had much faith in this sort of new-age nonsense before, but you're the expert, Louise, eh! You know what you're on about.'

Louise giggled and Charlotte pursed her lips, but I wasn't sure why.

'The only other thing is visiting their mum…' Louise trailed off, and even though we couldn't see her, I could imagine her cheeks going pink in that way they had when she talked about anything she was unhappy talking about.

'Yes?' Audrey demanded. 'What about it?'

'Well, the girls are visiting her every other week or so, but it's…'

I thought for a moment that Louise was suddenly speaking so quietly we couldn't hear her, but then I realised she was doing that thing adults do sometimes where they wait for ages to find the right words. Even when she spoke again, though, she hadn't thought of the right ones.

'It's upsetting for them.'

'No, it's not,' I hissed at Charlotte, panicked.

'Shh!' Charlotte's glare was enough to make me flinch.

'Is there much point, then?' Audrey asked. 'Is there much they get from it?'

'I'm not sure.'

I wanted so badly to throw open the door and scream at them all that they were wrong, we got a lot from it, she was our mum and we wanted to see her, but the fact that Charlotte wasn't doing just that made me worried.

'We'll ask the girls what they want, sure!' boomed Tony. 'They're big enough to decide for themselves, aren't they?'

'Well. Yes. I suppose, yes. They are.'

'Excellent! Well, that's settled then. Should we sign for them now?'

The adults laughed and I wasn't sure why they were doing that either.

'Have you much of a drive back, Lillian?' asked Audrey.

'Louise,' said Louise. 'And it's a long enough trek, I suppose, yes!'

'Well, you'll want to be getting back. Miss the rush hour.'

'Do you have rush hour in the countryside?' I whispered to Charlotte, but she ignored me.

'Nonsense!' boomed Tony. He liked that word. And he liked to boom. 'Louise will stay and have dinner with us. She's driven the girls all this way, plus she's looked after them so well since this whole thing started!'

'Darling,' Audrey said, and there was something different in her tone. 'You have to leave soon to pick up Lawrence from the airport, and you can't be late. We have a lot to do before then.'

'Oh. Right you are, as usual, darling. Right you are! Louise, I'd forget my own head if it wasn't screwed on.'

Luckily, the adults chuckled and chortled as they came towards the door, which gave us plenty of time to dash back into the hall and pretend we'd just come down the stairs.

'Ah, girls!' said Tony, clapping his hands together in delight when he saw us. 'You've chosen your rooms, then?'

'Yes,' we said together. 'Thank you,' Charlotte added.

'I'm away, girls.' Louise came over to us and knelt down. She looked a bit teary, like she really would miss us, and that made me happy because I thought I might miss her too. 'You be good for the Wolfes, okay?'

Be good for the Wolfes.

'We will,' Charlotte said. 'Thank you very much for all your help, Louise.'

Charlotte leaned in for a hug first, and it didn't look like there was any room for me so I just waited until she was done and then gave Louise a hug of my own. 'Thank you,' I mumbled, not wanting her to leave.

'See you in a few weeks,' she said, straightening up. 'You can always give me a call at the office if you need anything or have any questions, okay?'

'I have a question,' I said, unable to keep it to myself any longer. I was aware of Audrey and Tony standing watching from behind Louise, both of them smiling like they were posing for a photograph. I lowered my voice so only Louise could hear, 'How long do we have to stay here?'

Louise tucked a piece of hair behind my ear, which she always did and which I hated, and said, 'I'm not sure, lovely. But you'll have a great time here. Be good for the Wolfes, okay?'

We all stood on the steps to wave goodbye to Louise like we were a family in a film. Then Uncle Tony had to go down the steps and help her turn her wee car around because she got flustered, but once she was righted, we all kept waving until she went down the long driveway and was swallowed up into the trees.

Uncle Tony turned back to us and rubbed his hands together. I wondered if maybe he was just always cold, he was never done rubbing his hands.

'Right, now, girls. What would you most like to do in the world right now?'

I knew it wasn't my place to answer and Charlotte would be

cross with me if I did, but I wanted to say something like, 'Thank you very much, your house is really nice and I've enjoyed visiting, but please can I go back to *my* house to where all of my cuddly toys are and can I please see my mum?'

But Charlotte didn't say anything either, and that made me wonder if she was thinking exactly the same thing as me. She seemed to have deflated a bit since Louise announced she was going. She'd been acting like an adult for months, but maybe Louise brought that out of her, and she was back to my Charlotte now, the way she was at The Big Window.

'I bet I know,' Audrey said, in the same tone I'd heard adults speak to babies. 'I bet you two would love to go and play in the garden, wouldn't you?'

We looked at her. On some level, I recognised, yes, I would love to go and play in the garden. But was that the thing we wanted to do the most in the world? Absolutely not.

When Charlotte still didn't answer, I stepped forward and tried to be brave for me and my sister, because I had always thought it was easier to agree with adults when they tried to hint that you should do something.

'Yes,' I said, keen to make these nice people see that we were nice girls and we were grateful that they were letting us stay in their great big house. 'We'd love to. Thank you.'

It was just easier.

We ended up getting sunburnt. I'd never been sunburnt before and hadn't realised that it hurt. I also hadn't realised you could get it at home, I thought it was just something that happened when people went on a foreign holiday and it always made me glad that we had never been on a holiday, foreign or otherwise, because people with white shoulders and bright red faces looked so silly. Charlotte's nose and ears got it the worst, and I got it a little bit on the back of my neck and the top of my back where my sundress didn't cover me. Auntie Audrey was delighted to tell us all about her fancy Hello Vera cream, and she talked about it so much that she actually forgot to get it for us, and Charlotte had to ask her again. She sent Charlotte up to get it from her bedroom and even gave her the key, and I was jealous because I didn't get to look inside.

We were sent upstairs to our rooms after that, under strict instructions to have baths and apply the fancy cream – 'But not too much! Don't waste it, it's expensive!' – and get changed, 'Before Our Lawrence gets back'.

'I'm a bit nervous now,' I said to Charlotte as we reached The Big Window. 'Why is it such a big deal that Laurens is coming home?'

'Lawr-*ence*, not Laurens. Because he's their only son, dummy, and they love him.'

Charlotte strutted up the stairs in front of me.

'Where has he been?' I asked. 'On holiday?'

'I think he works abroad,' Charlotte said. It was a phrase a lot of girls in our school had used to describe their dads, and I knew Charlotte didn't really know what it meant. 'He probably just visits on special occasions.'

'Are we the special occasion?' I asked, my concern deepening. I didn't want to be a special occasion, something to be looked at and questioned and thought about. I wanted to be the opposite of a special occasion, maybe a slightly sad occasion or an awkward occasion that everyone would want to look away from and avoid.

'Yes, of course!' Charlotte said. She went and turned the bath on and started fishing in her suitcase for something to wear. 'I'm going first because I'm older.'

'I know,' I said, annoyed. 'You always do.'

She settled on wearing the dress I knew she would settle on wearing, because it was the only one she had. Mum had got it for her two years before in a charity shop – 'A thrift store!' Charlotte insisted – and apparently it was some big-name brand. It was red and had strappy sleeves and made her look much older than she was when she wore her hair down. That was all I knew.

'You'll have to wear your baby-pink dress,' she said. 'I know you hate it, but it's the only thing good enough.'

'Why are we getting dressed up if we're just staying in the house?' I asked as Charlotte climbed into the bath a few minutes later. 'It's not like we're going out for somebody's birthday, we're just going to be downstairs. And we live here now, so what's the point? Do I have to get dressed to go downstairs for my Sugar Puffs?'

'I don't think the Wolves will have Sugar Puffs,' Charlotte said, rolling her eyes dramatically like I was being ridiculous.

'The Wolfes,' I corrected. Then, uncertainly, 'Isn't it?'

'The plural of Wolfe is Wolve,' Charlotte said. 'Louise is wrong. Turn around, stop watching me.'

I turned around and sat with my back to Charlotte, facing the cupboard under the sink that looked as if it needed a good clean.

'What do you think they'll eat for breakfast if they don't have Sugar Puffs?' I asked.

'I don't know, Cara. Smoked salmon, probably.'

'FISH!?' I demanded, more shrilly than I'd intended.

'Shh!' Charlotte hissed. 'I don't know, okay? Can you please try not to show me up at dinner tonight? I don't want Lawrence to think we're children.'

'We are children,' I said.

'Yes, and he's a movie star.'

'What *movies* have you seen him in?' I asked in an American accent.

'Well – nothing you'd have heard of. But he's a big star. I heard Louise talking about it.'

'And Audrey and Tony, are they movie stars too?' I asked, pulling my legs up to my chest. I wasn't sure how I felt about people being famous. It wasn't a real job for adults, surely? It was just something you said you wanted to be when you grew up.

'Yes, I think so. Again, nothing you would have seen. Probably foreign films in different languages. Yes, that's it. They do quite serious films for adults.'

'So, you've not seen them either, then.'

'Shut up, Cara.'

We got washed and dressed and Charlotte spent ages brushing her hair and trying to make it straight, but the curls kept bouncing back up every time, and eventually she threw her hairbrush across her room where it whacked off the wall and made a big noise. I asked her if she would do something with my hair, but she was in such a bad mood by then that she said no, and I wanted to cry but I didn't, because that was just Charlotte being Charlotte and I thought she was brilliant anyway.

We went down the stairs to our landing. It took just three steps forward for us to reach The Big Window, and I was glad when Charlotte stopped just to look out. I looked out too and I felt very small compared to everything else. Compared to the huge garden, compared to the size of the house, compared to how much I missed Mum and the size of the lump in my throat that physically hurt sometimes when I thought about her. Even compared to Charlotte, I thought, I was small. There was less than a year between us, but she was way taller and a bit... fuller than I was. And while she was starting to look like a lady, I definitely wasn't, and I thought I'd probably just look like a baby forever, so she could get away with calling me her baby sister until we were really old, like maybe thirty.

'I hope he's nice,' I whispered to The Big Window. It was easier sometimes to say things to people if you weren't looking at them. I had realised this from my sessions with Julie.

'Me too,' Charlotte whispered back. She squeezed my hand and I felt better, briefly, until she said, 'Race you downstairs? Last one down is getting haunted by the screaming girl!' She shrieked with laughter and sprinted down the wooden stairs, not holding onto the rail or anything. I felt a thrill of fear and hurried after her, but my shoes were too big for me still, even though I'd had them for ages, and I couldn't go as fast as her without tripping.

Charlotte had stopped outside the kitchen door and I ran straight into her back. She tutted at me, but quickly began fussing with her curly hair and pulling at her dress.

'I think he's here,' she whispered. I wondered how much time we were going to spend in Chaplin House whispering outside the kitchen door. It was a bit boring; I didn't want to do it any more.

Sure enough, now that we were two floors down, we could hear laughter from inside the huge kitchen, and now there were two deep, booming voices joining in with Auntie Audrey's strange, exaggerated accent, like beautiful bright paint colours that, when you mixed them, made a gross brown you wouldn't even want to use for a tree.

Charlotte pushed the door open carefully and I followed her inside.

The kitchen of Chaplin House was my favourite room so far, apart from our landing with the window, and not including the garden. The kitchen had one massive window facing the garden too, or so I had thought, but I realised it was actually a long glass door. It had been folded into one side so that the garden was coming into the house. The dining table had been moved so it was half inside and half on the patio, and it had been laid for five people who apparently didn't like each other, because everyone was so far away from everyone else.

'There they are!' boomed a dramatic voice. I couldn't see the speaker because he was standing on the patio with a wine glass in his hand, and the sun was behind his head like a halo and it hurt my eyes. I could only see the wine glass and the shape of a man. 'The two little darlings. How are you both, girls?'

I was very confused now. These people were a family but they all sounded completely diffcrent. Me and Charlotte sounded the same and I knew that because sometimes when Charlotte answered the phone in our house, she'd roll her eyes and stop one of my friends from talking and say, 'I'll get Cara for you now. No, it's Charlotte, I'll get her now,' and she'd thrust the phone at me. But Uncle Tony sounded like a policeman from Belfast (I had never met one but I knew what they sounded like), Audrey sounded like maybe she was from America, but she kept forgetting and slipping back into something more recognisable as Northern Irish, and Lawrence was somehow English. He sounded like people in films. Maybe he had to speak like that or they wouldn't let him do his job, I thought, thinking I was very wise. So, while I was confused, I didn't ask any questions. I was starting to realise that actors were unusual and you just had to go with it.

'We're fine,' Charlotte said. She gave a cough and repeated, 'We're fine,' in a stronger way, but she was definitely nervous again and so I gave a big smile and a nod to show she was right.

'I'm Lawrence,' said the voice, and the man came striding over to us like he was in a power-walking race. He swapped his wine glass to the other hand and shook Charlotte's very formally. This was a family of handshakers and I was annoyed by it. 'But you can call me Laurie.'

I thought maybe I saw Charlotte fall in love with Laurie then. I wasn't sure because it had never happened before, but she looked at him the way you might look at someone you were falling in love with, like you felt dizzy and you might fall over. They did that in films sometimes, they *swooned*. She held his hand for a second or two once they'd finished shaking, and she looked like she'd just been punched in the stomach and was a bit hunched over and looked shocked. Yes, I'd definitely seen girls in films do that when they'd fallen in love, so then I wondered if Charlotte was just acting or if she really had just fallen in love with Lawrence.

He turned to me, grinning like he'd just been given his all-time favourite present on Christmas morning, and shook my hand too, and his fingers were warm and dry and his hand was really big clasped around mine.

Lawrence was dressed in a beige suit that didn't have any buttons on the jacket and that looked too thick for the warm evening that had joined us in the kitchen. He had a white shirt on under that which was all tucked in, and I thought glumly that clearly we *were* the special occasion because nobody would dress like that to have dinner in their own house unless it was a very important day.

'You must forgive the state of me, girls,' he said, ruffling his sticky-up hair. He said 'girls' like he was from here, like *gurr-uls*, but the rest was just film-star English. I made a mental note to ask Charlotte about that later. 'I've been on a plane all day, so I'm a bit creased and worse for wear.'

I didn't know what the second bit meant, but he definitely wasn't creased. It made me think that maybe we were creased, our good dresses having been in our suitcases for a few days. Actually, I wasn't even sure when they'd last been ironed. It would have been Mum who'd ironed them, and I felt sad again just thinking about something as boring and normal and lovely as Mum ironing.

'But I just raced home when I heard you were coming. I simply couldn't wait to meet you both, I'm so excited that you're finally here.'

The pressure was too much for me and I felt sick. Why had this man got on a plane just for us? Everyone would want us to be funny and sweet and – what was the word Charlotte used? Charming. I didn't feel like being any of those things. I just wanted to eat chips for dinner and go back to my room and draw or go to sleep.

'How are you finding Chaplin House?' Lawrence asked us. 'Have Mum and Dad been kind to you? I'm sure they have. Have you met Ronnie yet? He's a funny old thing. He's the gardener now, apparently. Although…' Lawrence turned back to his parents, who were standing on the patio with their arms around one another, watching us the same way I'd seen mums at the park watching their children make friends in the sandpit. 'He really needs to figure out what to do with that ridiculously overgrown driveway. Surely that should have been his first port of call.' Lawrence sounded like he was telling them off, but as they were his parents I thought maybe I was just misunderstanding it.

Little Darlings

'He's working on it, darling, he's down there now!' Audrey insisted. 'Never mind that. Look at last year's asters, Lawrence. Can you see them? Just beyond the archway. I've never seen a purple like that. I was thinking of having someone out to make me a dress in that precise colour.'

I didn't know what asters were, but purple was my least favourite colour and my own dress was starting to itch at the armpits, so I didn't ask.

Lawrence didn't look where Audrey was pointing but, still smiling he said, 'The path up to the house is dangerous. What if one of these two little darlings had tripped over a fallen branch? We couldn't have that.'

'We haven't had much need for taking the car out since you left,' Tony said. He took his arm away from Audrey and jogged to the kitchen island for no reason I could work out. Why was he always in such a hurry? I'd ask Charlotte that too. Tony added to us, 'Taking a bit of a career break, the two of us.'

'Only temporary!' Audrey cried, as if we'd gasped. She followed her husband into the kitchen. She'd changed into a long floaty dress that was trailing on the floor and was going to get dirty. 'Just a brief break to get some time to ourselves before the busy season starts again. I had an audition yesterday and I have high hopes that I'll get the part, so I expect from September I'll be away a lot for work. Tony too, won't you, Tony?'

'Hm?' Tony had produced a bottle of wine from somewhere and was pouring a glass for himself. 'Yes, yes. We'll be busy. I'm at the Opera House from September until Christmas. Give me your glass, Aud, I'll get you another.'

The adults drank their wine for half an hour until they remembered we were also humans, not a zoo exhibit, and then Lawrence made a fuss of putting flavoured sparkling water into two of those thin champagne glasses for us, and it made Charlotte giggle, but the bubbles just hurt my nose and I was afraid of smashing the glass.

We sat down at the table to eat soon after. Uncle Tony had made something in a huge big dish that he set in the very centre of the table so that it was far away from everybody. Tony sat at the head of the table, with Lawrence opposite him, at the other head, I supposed, or maybe the tail, and me and Charlotte sat opposite each other, and Audrey sat next to Charlotte. It meant that Lawrence and Audrey were technically outside and the rest of us were inside, and it was very weird. I felt lonely on my side of the table and drew pictures with my finger on the tablecloth until Charlotte hissed at me not to. I realised she'd been trying to kick me under the table, but we were so far apart she couldn't reach.

Uncle Tony served a large square of brown-looking mush onto my plate with a flourish, and Audrey added a big scoop of green and purple salad with some tongs that she kept clicking for no reason.

'Eat up!' she commanded when everyone had some food, clapping her hands together like the excitement was too much to bear.

'It's beef pot pie!' Tony announced. 'My speciality and Lawrence's favourite. Isn't it, my boy?'

'Nobody makes it like you do,' Lawrence said, raising his glass to his dad across the table. He caught my eye and winked, and I thought maybe that meant he didn't really like it, and that made me feel a bit better because there was something orange coming out of my slice and I knew I couldn't touch it.

'Lawrence, tell the girls about your film,' Audrey said. She slid her hand across the table as if she was going to grasp his hand, but he was too far away. 'Girls, you're going to love it. It's so clever. The script was written by an old friend of ours, wasn't it, Tony? Oh, he's just the most talented man with a pen. And Lawrence is the leading man. It's Laurie's first film, isn't it, Laurie? But absolutely not his last. Well, go on, dear, tell them about it. What are you waiting for? Lawrence?'

Little Darlings

Lawrence was laughing and shaking his head at his plate. I felt confused and tired again because Audrey kept talking so much and I wished she'd stop. And she had so much perfume on that it was giving me a headache even though she was half a mile away from me.

'I've missed you, Mother,' Lawrence said. He took a piece of beef on his fork, examined it, then tasted it on his tongue. His teeth were so white I worried they'd get stained. Lawrence chewed carefully, thinking, and I realised we were all watching him like he was putting on a performance. He swallowed, then grinned up at all of us. 'Delicious, Dad. Thank you so much.'

Then it was like everyone else thought they had permission to eat, and we all lifted our forks and some of us, but not me, tucked in.

'Your film!' Audrey said again. 'Tell them, Laurie!'

Lawrence took a deep breath, then started to tell us the plot of the film he had been acting in. He looked at me, his face moving so much that it was like he'd taken all of Audrey's face muscles for himself. She didn't move at all and he moved far too much. Then he looked at Charlotte, who smiled and nodded and seemed to be considering every single one of his words. Then he looked back at me and I realised I hadn't heard a word he'd said.

'...and then at the end,' Lawrence said. He was looking at Charlotte again. 'We fall in love and get married. And that's it.'

Audrey started clapping, and Charlotte joined in immediately, letting her fork fall with a clatter to her plate. If I'd done that she would have shouted at me.

'Bravo, my boy,' Tony said. He was raising his glass again but nobody was clinking with him because nobody had Stretch Armstrong arms. 'I just know you were fabulous. Ray called to tell me you were the most convincing enthusiastic young heir to a fortune he'd ever seen. It's like the part was made for you. Isn't that something, girls?'

I just nodded like I knew what was going on, thinking that

these people were far too strange and confusing for me to ever relax around them.

'What's wrong, dear?' Audrey barked at me suddenly.

I gasped and turned to her, my hands clasped under the table. Had I said something out loud?

'You're not eating anything,' she said. 'What's wrong? Aren't you well? It's beef pot pie, it's delicious.'

I looked at Charlotte for help. She looked annoyed at me, but said, to my astonishment, 'Oh, Cara's worried about her weight.'

I expected Audrey to flick this comment away from her like a bad smell, like most adults (Mum and Louise) had any time I'd hinted to them that I thought I was fat. I was, a bit, but I didn't mind too much at all because it didn't matter, usually. Audrey didn't flick the comment away, though. She looked at me instead. She looked at my arms and my face, thinking.

'Hm,' she said. 'It's never too early to think about your future figure.'

'Oh, yes,' Charlotte said, suddenly very earnest and not looking at me any more. 'Yes, we're both thinking about our future figures. I'd love to look like you when I'm older, Auntie Audrey.'

I felt like I was allowed to look at Audrey too, seeing as how she'd looked at me. She was really very thin, I realised. I could see two bones sticking out of the top of her dress, and the tops of her arms were almost the same width as her wrists. Charlotte would be much prettier than that, I thought. I hoped Charlotte didn't look like her at all when she was older.

'Well, I can understand that,' Audrey said, to me and to Charlotte, and she was smiling again and then they all went back to talking and seemed to forget I existed for the rest of the meal, which was fine with me because it meant nobody made me eat the weird pie and nobody asked me any questions. I noticed Charlotte didn't eat any more of her food either, but that she told stories and listened to the adults like she was just a short adult herself.

Little Darlings

I didn't understand much of what was being said, so I went back to drawing pictures on the tablecloth with my finger, thinking about the squishy sofa in our own house where we sat either side of Mum, with trays on our knees and bottles of red sauce on the wee coffee table that we could squeeze as much as we liked.

Tony and Audrey cleared the dishes and told us that we must be tired, which I was and Charlotte wasn't, but she thanked them for dinner and hugged them both and then shyly hugged Lawrence when he put his arms out.

'Goodnight, Cara,' Lawrence said, and he pulled me into a hug too. I didn't know what the smell of him was called, but he smelled the same as the men's section in Debenhams (you had to go through it to get to the toilets in our closest one).

'Night,' I said, feeling hungry and fed up and tired.

'Mum said you'd picked a room on the top floor?'

I pulled away from the hug and looked up at him, panicked. 'Why?' I asked, sure he was about to tell me that it was indeed haunted and I needed to be careful.

'Just checking.'

I followed Charlotte up the first flight of stairs.

'Aren't they wonderful?' she whispered when we got to the top. 'They're so…' She shook her head for a moment as if there were no words for them, even though I could think of loads.

'Weird?' I suggested.

'Exotic,' Charlotte said, sounding stern. 'They've really lived. They've been everywhere, they know everyone. They've been to America twelve times. *Twelve* times, Cara. Even Maisie in my class has only been twice. And oh my God, I soooo want to be an actress when I'm older. Or now, even. I suppose they have teenage actors.'

'You're ten,' I reminded her.

'But I look like a teenager. You heard what Audrey said, I could pass for fourteen. She's going to show me how to do my makeup as well. Isn't she gorgeous?'

'She's okay,' I said, not wanting to fight. 'Why did you say that about my weight? Do you think I'm fat?'

Charlotte sighed and stopped with her hand on the door to our secret stairs.

'No,' she said firmly. 'I don't. But you weren't eating and that was rude. I didn't want them to think you were rude.'

'I'm not rude.'

'I know that, but they don't.'

I accepted this and thought Charlotte was very clever. The door creaked and screamed open and she led the way up the stairs. Charlotte went on up to our rooms, but I stopped at The Big Window and looked out into the dark garden below. There were fairy lights around the little rose arch, I noticed now, and they were switched on and lit the patio in a yellow light. The trees further beyond looked black, but it was peaceful to stand there with my forehead pressed against the glass, looking into the unknown. We'd enjoyed our afternoon exploring all the paths and hidden corners of the Wolfes'/Wolves' garden, and I knew there was nothing scary down there.

The door to our secret staircase made the horrible screaming sound and I jumped and spun around. A footstep. Another. Another. Another.

It's the tortured girl coming to kill me, I thought. I was rooted to the spot, torn between wanting to close my eyes tight shut and hope that she passed by me and went to Charlotte, and wanting to scream as loudly as I could so someone would come running.

Another footstep.

Another.

'There you are!'

It was Lawrence. I let out my held breath so loudly that he laughed.

'I'm sorry, did I scare you?'

He wasn't booming his voice out any more, and his accent was just normal now, like dinner had been a play and this was the after-

Little Darlings

party bit where everyone hung out and accepted compliments.

'A bit,' I said, embarrassed.

'Sorry, little darling. Here, I just wanted to bring you this.'

He held out a small white plate and I went towards him. He was standing two steps below the landing, so when I stood in front of him we were the same height. The plate had a small slice of chocolate cake on it, and a tiny spoon, and a scoop of vanilla ice cream.

'Beef pot pie isn't my favourite,' Lawrence admitted. 'I kind of hate it too, but it's the only thing Dad can make so I just pretend. I didn't want you to be hungry.'

I blinked and smiled at him. 'Thank you. It was a bit slimy.'

He laughed softly. His soft laugh was much nicer than his fake one, and it made me feel so much better about everything, and I felt lighter all of a sudden.

'That door can surely creak, can't it?' he asked, jerking his head back downstairs.

'It sounds a bit like a woman screaming,' I said, feeling bold and confident and enjoying the fact we were the same height.

'It does, you're absolutely right. That must be annoying. Tell you what, tomorrow I'll get some WD40 from Ronnie and I'll sort that out for you. Sound good?'

I wasn't sure what his code meant, but I nodded. 'Yes. Sounds good.'

'Great. Well, enjoy your cake. And maybe just don't mention it to Mum and Dad, yeah? Don't want to hurt their feelings. You get it. Goodnight, Cara. I hope you sleep well.'

I didn't reply, but I nodded and smiled some more. Lawrence padded back downstairs in his shiny shoes, the door screamed, and then I was by myself by The Big Window with some quickly melting ice cream and a feeling like a bubble in my chest. The landing still smelled like him. Like Debenhams.

'What were you doing?' Charlotte demanded when I came into her room. She had already changed into her pyjamas and stood with her toothbrush in her hand.

'Lawrence brought me some food,' I said. 'Look. Cake and ice cream.'

Charlotte inspected the plate as if it might be fake, then looked at me suspiciously. 'Lawrence brought you this?'

'You can share it with me,' I said quickly. 'I'm sure he meant it for both of us.'

'Hm. No, thanks.' She gave a little sniff and pushed me aside so she could get into the bathroom. 'Now that really is the kind of food that will make you fat.'

Chapter 5 | January 2023 | Somewhere on the M1

We pull into the next Applegreen, half an hour earlier than our first planned 'Penelope Pitstop', and Daisy is delighted to be given free rein to explore. Free rein with the caveat that she has to be within my line of sight at all times, but it's something when you're nine. Steve deposits me at one of the rickety plastic tables outside Subway and goes to get drinks, smiling all the while like it's every day his wife has a near breakdown in the car. I watch as Daisy examines a car-racing arcade game near the door and try to steady my breathing. The Applegreen is loud, with different tinny music coming from speakers above the Burger King, above the petrol kiosk, above the toilets. And it is busy for a Tuesday afternoon, with parents and young kids running around and shouting to each other. Two boys race to the arcade area and all but push Daisy out of the way to get into the plastic cars. She steps back, nonplussed, and watches them. Their dad catches my eye and looks away again, not wanting to make conversation with the woman with bright red, freshly cried eyes.

Steve – today adorned in a green T-shirt that says YOUR DESIGN HERE – delivers our drinks to the table. He has ordered me a coffee and got a Coke for himself. He takes a seat next to me. The chair isn't big enough for him but he says nothing, only holds his plastic cup and watches Daisy, waiting. I can tell he has most of his weight on his feet; he has a fear of breaking chairs.

'Stop,' he says softly. I glance at him, unsure what he's talking about, but he's still watching Daisy. 'Your nails,' he adds.

Hannah King

I look down. My fingernails, bitten and weak and jagged as they are, are my most hated body part, and there are a lot of parts to choose from. I realise I am using my thumbnails to pick at my cuticles, and I make myself stop. The nails have never grown past the tips of my fingers. I never let them; I'm fussing with them and pulling at them and biting them as soon as there is any growth.

'Sorry,' I say, hoping the word covers the car and the nails.

'It's fine,' Steve says immediately. 'It was really scary. I only just caught him out of the corner of my eye; he came up so fast.'

Steve is talking about Lawrence Wolfe, and my stomach is liquid because of it. He doesn't know it, and he doesn't say his name, but it feels completely wrong for this man to be speaking about that man. They are night and day, my past and my future, black and white, chalk and cheese, rain and sunshine. A deep breath of air and a choke. Why haven't I realised before now that allowing Steve and Daisy to come with me would inevitably mean a collision of these two worlds? How have I been so stupid?

Steve is adjusting his T-shirt, pulling the neck away from his skin as if he might be too warm, but I know he isn't. It's just what he does. It was the first thing I noticed about him when I first saw him.

We were both in the McClay Library at Queen's, which had opened the year before. I couldn't get my computer to print out my final essay for my visual communication module, and the deadline was fifteen minutes away. I felt like my head was going to explode with panic, as it was a good five-minute sprint to the wee kiosk where I had to hand it in and sign the form. I'd been there all night putting the finishing touches on my essay, and had watched the library gradually empty out as students stood and stretched and logged off and walked out into the warming sunshine, some of their degrees totally finished, some of them done until September. There was one other student left in my eyeline: a tall, dark-haired guy with a beard, at the opposite desk who was objectively good looking, but whom I normally wouldn't have batted an eye at. He had long white-wired earphones in his ears, connected to one of the new iPod Nanos, and his music was so loud I could hear it from my own desk. He had a pen in his left hand and was writing quickly, but his right hand kept pulling at the legs of his skinny jeans as if he was trying to pluck some invisible fluff from them.

'Excuse me?' I whispered, leaning forwards. My heart was pounding with nerves.

He didn't hear me, obviously.

'Excuse me!' I called more loudly. Still he wrote and plucked.

Desperate, noticing the seconds ticking closer to nine o'clock, I stood and hurried over to his desk. He looked up and immediately pulled his earphones from his ears and stood up.

'Hello?' he said.

The tinny sound coming from his earphones was unmistakeable: last year's *X Factor* winner singing the Miley Cyrus cover. Despite my desperation, I gave a single, unsure chuckle. He grinned and shrugged.

'It's a tune,' he said.

He was happy to help me print my essay – and he made it look easy – and when he discovered I only had eight minutes to hand it in, he offered to take it for me. We hurried down the steps of the McClay together and the woman behind the reception shouted at us, but we kept running. He was much faster than me, as we had both known he would be, and I was left to puff on behind him as he sprinted towards my tutor's building.

He made it with two minutes to spare and saved my place in the queue of harried students, their feet tapping on the floor with impatience. When I finally made it, red in the face and sweating, he pulled me towards him and ushered me to the front of the queue. He was out of breath too, but was trying to pretend he wasn't. My essay was signed in at nine o'clock on the dot.

We stepped back outside into the sunshine and it felt like a different day. It was getting warm, and everything looked different on this side of the deadline. I looked up at the boy beside me and thought, yes, I think he's quite handsome.

I hadn't ever really thought that about anyone before.

'Thank you so much,' I said. 'Honestly. You've saved my life.'

'You're very welcome.' He grinned at me. 'It's Steve, by the way, Cara Chilver.'

'How did you— Oh.' Of course, he'd seen my cover sheet. 'Well, thank you, Steve.' He nodded and kept smiling, and I felt awkward all of a sudden, like I was supposed to have a line and I'd forgotten it, or like someone else had missed their cue and was supposed to hop in and save us. Something made me say, completely unexpectedly, 'Do you want to go and get some breakfast?'

Steve nodded again. 'I'd love to.' We took a few steps before he suddenly gasped. 'I've left all my stuff in the library. Will you come back with me?'

I did.

In the fifteen minutes we'd been gone, someone had stolen Steve's iPod Nano from his desk in the library and we never got it back or found out who it was. He'd spent his student loan on it and had spent hours of his life adding every song he'd ever loved, and it was gone in a blink. Bizarrely, when we discovered the theft and had searched all along the third floor of the library, we laughed.

'Breakfast better be your treat,' he said. 'And you better get a first for that essay.'

I don't consciously remember thinking, *Lawrence Wolfe would never admit to listening to that song*, or even *Lawrence Wolfe wouldn't have gotten himself so sweaty trying to help a stranger*, but I think some part of my brain must have thought this. Because Steve was safe from the moment he first looked at me in the library, in a way nobody else had ever been safe before.

'You did so well to avoid an accident,' I say finally, my mind back in the crowded service station. I let my coffee burn my tongue because it gives me something to do. 'You really did. Well done.'

'Over now,' he says, and pats me on the hand. 'These things repeat on you, don't they? You just keep thinking about what would have happened if you hadn't been paying attention. Honestly, people like that will get themselves killed.'

Yes, I think. But not Lawrence Wolfe. He is and always has been untouchable.

Daisy and I go into the bathrooms together and we both pee and I try to fix my face, but with my makeup packed in the car there isn't a whole lot I can do. Daisy watches me anxiously in the mirror and I try to make a silly face at her, but she doesn't always give me what I want the way she does for her dad.

'Why were you crying so much?' she asks. 'Is it because you're sad about Great-Great Auntie Audrey?'

'Maybe,' I say, turning to face her. 'Grief can pop up on you when you least expect it.'

'Really?' she asks, looking confused. 'Like even when you're just playing Mario Kart?'

'Even then.'

'I'm sorry for your loss,' she says eventually, and she says it with such sincerity and with such a serious expression that I let out a little bark of a laugh that makes her jump. 'What?' she asks. 'Is that not right? Mrs MacIntyre said it to me when I gave her your note about me not being in school tomorrow.'

'No, it is right,' I say. 'Sorry for laughing. You're just very mature and wise beyond your years.'

'Yes, I know,' Daisy says in total agreement, and this makes me laugh too.

She reminds me so much of Charlotte when she was wee. They have met each other maybe only ten times, and Daisy is a bit obsessed with her, but they have no idea how alike they are, how much of my sister I see in my daughter. It's one of those things that only I know, that I have for myself. One of the few things that fall into this category that I actually like. I'll see it in an expression or hear it in a tone of voice. Daisy sleeps splayed on her back with one arm and the opposite leg extended like she's dancing to 'Night Fever' in her dreams and Charlotte did exactly the same. I wonder if she still does.

We go back into the food hall and fetch Steve – who has, to my delight and dismay, bought some more wine gums. He asks me how I am feeling and I say, pointing to the sweets, that I'm on cloud wine. They both laugh far more heartily than the silly joke deserves because they are so grateful to see *this* Mummy, *this* Cara. They deserve this one. Not the other one. So I slip my hand into my pocket as we go back towards the car, not letting them see the torn skin around my thumbnail and the blood seeping from it.

We are off the motorway after another half hour, traffic lessening and fields becoming greener and greener as we make our way through tiny townland after tiny townland. I'm sure there was a faster route we could have taken, but Steve seems to have decided against the main roads after the almost-incident. Daisy looks out of the window, admiring window boxes and pointing to the impressive wildflower front gardens we pass. We can never get our flowers to last out the winter, so I admire them too. There are real red postboxes, some phone boxes that haven't been removed yet. I notice the signal on my phone comes and goes, and I haven't had 4G since we were at the service station. I've never come this way to or from Anniskillen before and don't recognise it. Or maybe I've just never paid attention before.

Steve pulls up to a give way, puts the handbrake on and lets the car idle. 'The house itself doesn't come up on Apple Maps,' he admits. 'You can type in the address and it just kind of leaves you in the middle of a field. You'll have to direct from here. Or do you want to drive?' He adds this but it's not a real question. It's just polite. Technically, I can drive. I even have my own car. I pick Daisy up from school a few times a week, and once, when Steve was in London for a conference, we even drove to the cinema a few towns over. But I hated every moment of it, and I knew Daisy did too because she had been completely silent all along the motorway, and if ever there is a sign that Our Daisy is unhappy or uncomfortable, it is her silence. We stuck to the school run after that.

'It's left, I think,' I say. 'I know the house is only ten minutes from the harbour, so we must be close.' Sure enough, when I put the window down a few minutes later to get some air, we can hear seagulls laughing overhead, or maybe screaming. Freezing January air fills the car and I take deep breaths without being too obvious.

'Mummy, it's Baltic,' Daisy says, and I put the window up again.

'Right, this is the road,' I say. Steve obediently turns into a narrow, winding lane. A white sign with a black stripe through it tells us that technically we could drive at sixty miles per hour here, but only an idiot would ever do that. The road is only wide enough for one car, and there is a line of grass in the middle of the lane that we can feel under us as Steve drives, carefully, leaning forward a little as if to see better. It is only half past five now, but it's so dark already. The headlights bump across trees and Steve jolts into a few potholes that are hiding under last night's rainfall puddles.

We are used to life in the countryside, to stopping for tractors to go past, to finding lone lost sheep in the middle of the road, but the lane to Chaplin House is like a lane that time forgot, and we meet no one else and see no signs of life but the vague outlines of barns behind the fields at either side of us, the odd light in the distance. If I ignore the sound of Daisy's iPad game in the backseat, I could be heading up to Chaplin House for the first time, twenty-three years ago.

We incline up a slight hill, and at the top I hear Steve make an appreciative, 'Wow'. The mountains in the distance are even blacker than the darkness. I'm struck again by how small we are, how much none of this matters.

I direct Steve into the driveway, the trees surrounding which are mostly bare and skeletal, allowing us to see the roof of Chaplin

House further up. I think of the first time we came, how the hedges and trees were so in bloom, so delightfully, wonderfully green and lush that we couldn't even see the driveway. How they hung down low, how they covered everything. It's so easy to forget that summer is temporary when you're living in it, and so difficult to imagine being warm and feeling the sun on your face when winter is pinching every inch of exposed skin. Temperamental. Fleeting. Transient, is that the right word? I can never tell if it's a good or a bad thing.

The house itself is tired. There is one light on in a downstairs window, and the rest are deathly black. Steve parks up next to the same navy Audi that has always lived here, and my stomach flips just seeing it. It still has an old tax disc in the windscreen, and there are bird droppings covering the roof, so I know nobody drives it now. I wonder why it is still here. Why nobody ever thought to get rid of it if it was just going to sit there.

'That might be worth a quare few bob,' Steve decides, looking at the car. He knows nothing about cars, and I know he is just saying it to break the tension in our own. He turns the engine off and pulls at his T-shirt, nervous. 'How you feeling, Dais?'

'Bit tired,' Daisy admits. She unclips her seatbelt and leans forward to put her head in between us. 'It's a big house.'

It's a big house, I think. Just that. Nothing more. She doesn't say anything else, but I can tell she is disappointed. Any time I've mentioned, 'The time Mummy lived with famous actors,' the beauty of the house and the stunning gardens were what I focused on, and Daisy always had so many questions, imagining it was something out of a fairytale. Chaplin House in 2023 is no such place. The ivy that once hung decoratively across the front of the house has crept out in all directions, so you can't see the brickwork underneath any more. I can tell that the windows are dirty even in the dark, and at least three of the roof tiles have fallen off. One such tile lies smashed just next to the front steps, moss covering it. Already it's starting to be claimed by nature.

Little Darlings

A security light comes on at the front door as we go up the steps together, a little nervously. That's a new feature, I think. Certainly no security lights when I lived here. I wonder what, if any, difference a few of those would have made to what happened. A shadow appears inside the front door, a lock clicks, and then Uncle Tony is in front of us, his arms outstretched.

I go to him more quickly and with a lot more emotion than I expected from myself. My uncle is slightly stooped now, so he's not much taller than me, and though there is a clear whiff of pipe smoke around him, what I notice most of all is that his cardigan smells like it hasn't dried properly, and I feel suddenly as though I might burst into tears.

'Thank you so much for coming, darling.' Uncle Tony's voice is hoarse, as though a lifetime of booming out lines on a stage has finally taken its toll and his vocal cords are protesting. 'I'm so glad to see you.'

I give him a squeeze and stand back. Blue chinos, a deep blue cardigan, brown slippers. There is no hair left on his head, but a little white moustache clings to his upper lip. His cheeks are only a little more hollow, and his eyes still sparkle. The only signs of grief are his pained-looking mouth and the sad smell of an old man doing his own washing for the very first time.

'Uncle Tony, this is my husband, Stephen.' I make a funny flick with my two hands as if instructing them to embrace. They shake hands and nod to each other and both say things like, 'Fantastic to finally meet you, I've heard so much about you, it's a pleasure, I'm sorry we have to meet like this,' and then Steve says, 'It's Steve. Cara always introduces me as Stephen, but if you call me that I'll not know you mean me,' and they both laugh to be kind and because I know they both feel awkward.

'And this is Our Daisy,' I say. I'm usually so proud and happy to introduce her to new people. She's polite and talkative and normally I'd be beaming by now, but I feel dizzy. Charlotte and I walked up these steps, once. We saw Uncle Tony for the first time, we shook hands for what was probably the first time ever, we took in Chaplin House for the first time... and then my life was ruined. Was it stupid to bring Daisy here? I've spent her whole life keeping her far away from this kind of place, from these kinds of people. I'm not thinking straight this week.

'Hello, Daisy,' Uncle Tony says. He shakes her hand, like I knew he would, and Daisy is shy all of a sudden, smiling but ducking her chin. She looks like Charlotte, with her curly fringe and her school pinafore.

'Well, come in, come in, all of you!' Uncle Tony says. He's trying to muster some of his former bravado, but he sounds like the old man he is now. 'Welcome, welcome. Sorry about the state of the place. I'm afraid we've rather let it go, you know. Getting too old to do much myself and I can't be bothered with finding people. Do you know, if you Google a window cleaner there are hundreds of thousands of options? How are you supposed to find anyone when there are so many?'

Steve laughs and takes up both his own and my cabin suitcases. He swings them as he follows Uncle Tony, as if they weigh nothing at all. Daisy adjusts the straps of her school bag and watches after them, uncertainly.

'Are you coming in?' I hear myself whispering. I feel like she needs to go first, or we need to go together. It's stupid. She's not Charlotte.

'How old is he?' Daisy whispers back.

'A hundred and ten.'

'REALLY?'

I giggle and shush her, and she giggles back. 'No, not really. He'll be eighty-eight in October. Do you think he looks very old?'

'No,' Daisy says. 'He just sounds very old.'

I lead her into the house. He really does. It was always the voice the women wanted, with Uncle Tony. If it was a film, they would want a scene with him making an impressive speech as the climax. The way all of his sentences ended with an inflection was never annoying, not with him. Not when every word was so clear, like you could hear every syllable being formed in his mouth. I got it, I really did. I understood the appeal. The few times I've seen him on stage, all before Daisy was born, it was like there was no breath in the room if he was monologuing, he needed it all for himself. And we all just let him have it.

And that's been replaced with a weak wheeze.

I hope it's just the grief that's done this. That he'll get it back with time.

'Is he a celebrity, would you say?' Daisy asks, gripping my hand and gazing around the foyer with a solemn curiosity.

'He used to be,' I whisper. 'He hasn't done any acting for years, but yes, when I was wee, he was a celebrity. He was everywhere.'

Chapter 6 | July 2000 | Chaplin House, Anniskillen

Charlotte was different from, as Louise would have said, 'the word go'. Normally she was happy to play games with me, sit and draw with me, pretend to be detectives with me, and laughed at my jokes, but as soon as we moved to Chaplin House she became a different person, and I didn't like the new person as much as I liked the old person, and I missed Mum and Charlotte in different ways, but just the same.

She stopped laughing when I made jokes, rolled her eyes at me a lot, and tutted and made over-the-top hair-flick gestures when I suggested games for us to play. Eventually I just stopped suggesting things and wandered off into the garden to play by myself, but she'd find me eventually and ask me what I was doing and half-heartedly join in, and I knew that must have meant that Audrey had become bored of her and sent her away. Charlotte was obsessed with Audrey. And with Tony. And with Lawrence.

We got into a routine, which is exactly what Louise had told us she wanted us to do, and I couldn't wait to see her again so I could tell her all about it. I always woke up first and, since Charlotte had told me not to come into her room, I just had to lie there in my little rickety bed with my unfamiliar sheets that smelled like fresh laundry, but not my mum's fresh laundry, and I would gaze at the square window opposite my bed. I couldn't see the garden from my bed, but a thick tree branch with gorgeous green leaves hung in such a way that I could watch it dance up and down when it was breezy outside. I watched it most mornings and thought about

Mum and about what I would draw that day. Maybe the window with the tree branch in it.

I got used to hearing the birds outside my window, and I wanted to ask Louise if we had had birds back at our old house, because I couldn't remember ever hearing them sing so loudly before. It was like they were talking to each other, planning their days, different tweets and songs that I couldn't tell apart, but I made up stories for them and pretended I knew what they were saying to each other, and that made me feel better.

Eventually Charlotte would come in, her curls brushed, and call, 'Are you awake yet?' and I would whisper back a yes, because even though we were on the top floor, I was afraid of waking everyone up. Charlotte made us get dressed before we went downstairs, which I hated, but I did it because I was always so hungry. It turned out the Wolfes did have Sugar Puffs, and I poured myself a huge bowl every morning and added milk until it was overflowing and I had to suck some off the edge of the bowl. Charlotte would tell me off, but I ignored her.

I liked Chaplin House the best when everyone except me and Charlotte was asleep. I wouldn't have told Charlotte this directly, but I made a point of trying extra hard not to be annoying so she would think the same. I imagined us living there together, just me and Charlotte and Mum, and I pretended we were waiting for Mum to come downstairs every morning. Until the Wolfes started coming down and my daydream was shattered.

Tony got up first. He greeted us with his big loud voice that made my ears hurt, and he was always so happy to see us and was always rubbing his hands together and asking us what our plans were. Charlotte would answer him and I would smile and nod, and then he would take a banana from a big bowl of bananas that sat on the kitchen counter and always seemed to be full, and smile at us and wave at us using the banana as he left. We would hear him opening the front door to collect the newspapers (they had about ten delivered to the house every morning, I couldn't believe it) and then he would go into his study next to the front door and we would hear him on the phone or talking to himself. (He talked so loudly on the phone that we heard his side of every single conversation. Charlotte always listened but I tried not to.) We had never been in his study. He hadn't told us not to go in, it just felt like we shouldn't. I had seen a big wooden desk in there that made me feel it was all very official and worky, and I didn't want to know anything more about it.

Audrey would come down after that. She was still in her dressing gown, I would point out to Charlotte with a look every morning, but Charlotte shushed me. To be fair, it wasn't like a normal dressing gown. It was a thin white robe with a small hood, and you could see silky-looking pyjamas underneath it and she had clean white slippers on her feet too. My slippers never stayed clean for long, so I thought she must just have an endless supply of new ones. She would say hello and wave to us as if she was still dreaming and would float around the kitchen. She would open a cupboard that was full of small glass bottles, and she would take one tiny pill from each of them and swallow them all down in one gulp with a huge glass of water. Sometimes she would make a smoothie and sometimes she wouldn't. Then she would leave us be with another wave and would go and get ready for her personal trainer/yoga instructor/vocal coach/singing instructor/beautician, depending on what day it was. I'd heard of all of these things before, but I didn't know why they all came to the house and why Audrey didn't go to them. Actors were very strange.

By then I would be finished my Sugar Puffs and ready to get started on our Barbie Trace & Colour (Charlotte would still play with this because 'Really, it's just fashion design, when you think about it,'), but Charlotte would make us stay in the kitchen until Lawrence finally came downstairs. He would greet us both with the same enthusiasm that his dad did, but it felt… real. Tony was acting and Lawrence wasn't, I thought. I said as much to Charlotte but she wasn't listening. He would grin at us, pour himself a cup of tea and sit down at the table beside us to listen to whatever it was we – usually Charlotte – wanted to say that day.

One such morning, he told us he had a new job offer and would start filming for a TV show (it was a 'period drama', which meant it was set in the past but didn't mean it was in black and white) late in August.

'You'll be here for our birthdays, then!' Charlotte informed him. She pushed her curls back off her shoulders and sat up a bit straighter. 'I'll be eleven.'

'I'll be ten,' I said, keen not to be left out. Double digits was a big deal. Mum had made such a fuss of Charlotte last year when she turned ten.

'You're like twins!' Lawrence said, his eyes popping. 'That's amazing. It must be so lovely to have a sister so close in age.'

'Yeah,' I said, at the same time Charlotte said, 'Oh, it's the best. I'm fifty weeks older, though. Cara was supposed to be born in October, but she was bored of waiting.'

I smiled at the story Mum had told us so often, and Lawrence laughed and gave Charlotte's hand a squeeze. 'You make me laugh,' he said. 'Both of you.'

The patio door opened and we all turned towards it. It was Ronnie, the kind gardener who always nodded to us and waved when we passed him in the garden. He stood with the door open, but he stayed outside because his boots were covered in damp grass, and I thought that was a good idea. Audrey didn't like dirt or mess.

'Morning, girls,' Ronnie said. 'Morning, Mr Wolfe.'

'What is it?' Lawrence asked, not looking at him.

'Just wondered if I could get a glass of water.'

Ronnie was about the same age as Lawrence, I thought, but I didn't know what age that was. Maybe forty? (When I said this to Charlotte she gasped and scolded me, telling me he was twenty-five and would I wise up, please?) He was really tanned too, but while Lawrence looked tanned in an 'I've been on a fancy holiday' way, Ronnie was tanned in an 'I've made a mistake' way. His arms were brown from his hands right up until just above his elbow, and then he was white as a sheet. His T-shirt that day showed a bit of his neckline, where he wore a strange necklace that kind of looked like it belonged on a lady and kind of looked like it belonged on a show dog. His collarbone was really white too, in contrast to his brown neck and super-tanned and slightly wrinkly face. I imagined the colours I'd need to use to paint him later, and thought maybe I would draw him beside Lawrence because the two of them were so similar and so different at the same time. I wondered, did anyone feel that way about me and Charlotte?

'Is the hose not working?' Lawrence asked, seriously.

Ronnie just looked at him, a bit confused. 'The hose? The outside tap? It's fine. Why?'

'Well,' Lawrence said, and he turned back to his cup of tea without saying anything else. I looked between him and Ronnie, wondering what on earth they were talking about. I noticed Charlotte looked confused too. Ronnie stared at Lawrence for a moment, then shook his head and closed the patio door again.

'Don't you like him?' Charlotte asked, folding her arms and leaning across the table towards Lawrence, like she always did when she was very interested in something.

'Not overly,' Lawrence said. He smiled at her. 'We were at school together and didn't get along. Why Mother hired him is beyond me.' He patted Charlotte on the hand. 'Nothing for you to worry about at all, little darling. It's just that he's not my biggest fan.'

'Who is Lawrence's biggest fan?' I asked Charlotte later, jumping up onto one of the huge velvety sofas in the living room. It had started raining, lashing down, and we'd been forced to run back inside, our bare legs getting soaked. It wasn't like summertime at all.

'It's a turn of phrase,' Charlotte explained. 'He just meant the gardener doesn't like him very much.'

'Why?' I asked.

'Well, I don't know.'

'Why?'

'Why what?'

'Why don't you know? You know everything else.'

I smiled because it was so rare I could tease Charlotte that it made me giddy with happiness any time I could.

'Shut up,' she said, but she was laughing.

'I like Ronnie,' I said, wondering if I was right to.

'You only like his Walkman.'

I felt a bit guilty then, because Charlotte was probably right. Ronnie had one of the new CD Walkmans – Walkmen? – that you could clip to your clothes, so he walked around the garden with his big wired headphones over his ears and he could listen to anything at all, and he let me listen too sometimes. He had a CD that had songs by all different people on it, which I hadn't heard of before, but it was something called Brit Awards, and there was a song I liked about having a girlfriend and it had been stuck in my head since the moment I first heard it.

Charlotte perched on the sofa next to me and looked glumly out of the window. 'I hate it when we can't go into the garden.'

'Me too,' I said. 'Do you want to play detectives?'

'No,' she said. 'What do you talk about with Julie?'

I furrowed my brow. Uncle Tony had taken us in the car the evening before to see Julie, our therapist. It took over an hour to get there and I felt car sick and ended up just talking about that the whole time.

'Nothing much,' I said, feeling the car sickness story might make Charlotte annoyed. 'What do you talk to her about?'

'Everything. Mum. This house. Audrey and Tony and Lawrence.'

'And me?'

She let out a little laugh and glanced at me. 'Yes. Sometimes. Do you talk about me?'

The honest answer was no. I never thought to talk about Charlotte, though sometimes Julie asked me and I answered her as best I could. I didn't need to talk to anyone about Charlotte because she was always there and I liked talking *to* her, not *about* her.

'Last night she asked me how I was feeling and I said "sick",' I admitted. 'And she asked why and I said, "Well, we live so far away now. It takes an hour to get here. I'm car sick".'

Charlotte gave her proper loud HA laugh that always took me by surprise and sometimes even took her by surprise.

'That's not what she meant by "how are you feeling?",' she said, but she was still giggling. 'You silly moo.'

'You're a silly moo,' I said, but I was glad she was laughing.

The phone rang in the study next door and we looked towards the noise. We heard a soft sigh from Uncle Tony as if he was in the room with us, and then we heard him shuffle to his telephone and say, in a big loud voice, 'Hello? Yes. Yes, I heard. It's in the paper, how else? Yes, I know. Not yet, she's gone into town to have her hair done ahead of the big party tomorrow.'

'There's going to be a party?' I asked Charlotte delightedly.

'Mm,' Charlotte said. 'They're going out to it, it's not here.' She was looking at the wall that separated us from the study. 'Tony sounds upset about something, doesn't he?'

'Does he?' I was bored of listening now. 'Do you want to play secret agents?'

'I said no.'

'You said no to detectives,' I pointed out. 'I asked did you want to play secret agents.'

'How is it different?'

I thought about this and couldn't come up with an answer. 'Do you want to play spies?'

'Shut up, Cara.'

We knew Audrey was home because the front door swung open so hard it crashed off the wall and the whole house shook. We had decided to watch TV, and Charlotte had made a big show of letting me choose *SpongeBob SquarePants*, but I noticed she was laughing even harder than I was sometimes. She really loved Patrick. We looked at each other when the house shook.

'ANTHONY!' Audrey yelled from the hall. 'WHERE ARE YOU?'

The door to the study opened and Tony called, 'Hello, darling. How was your hair appointment? It looks lovely. You'll be glad you missed that downpour.'

Charlotte got up from the sofa and went to the living room door. She missed one of my favourite jokes of the episode and I tried to tell her, but she had already opened the door and stuck her head out.

'My hair?' Audrey demanded. I followed Charlotte and leaned against her. Audrey sounded angry. Anger was red, Julie said, and it was normal to feel like that sometimes. I hadn't heard Audrey sounding angry before though and I didn't like it and wished she'd pretend not to be. She could act. Angry Auntie Audrey I thought to myself. I said it over and over in my head.

'Don't ask me about my *fucking* hair!'

I gasped and gripped Charlotte's arm and she didn't push me away. I felt her hold her breath and I did the same in case it helped.

'Is it true?' Audrey demanded.

Both our heads were sticking out of the doorway, so if Audrey turned towards us she'd see us, but I had a feeling she wouldn't care just at that moment. I peered in the other direction to see Uncle Tony was standing in his doorway too, just his head poking out, and I thought we would make a funny scene in a film, just a load of heads and one angry woman.

'Darling, why don't you come in here and we can—'

'IS IT TRUE?' Audrey shouted.

SpongeBob laughed on the TV.

Her hair did look nice. It was all bouncy and clean looking and maybe a bit shorter, and I wondered for a minute if telling her this might make her feel calmer or a bit happier, but I decided against it because I couldn't actually find my voice anywhere in my mouth.

'Audrey,' Uncle Tony's voice was louder now. He wasn't speaking to her like he always spoke to us, now. He was serious. He sounded a bit strict. 'Come inside, now. Not in front of the girls.'

She whipped her head around to face us and her bouncy clean hair followed. Audrey's beautiful plastic-looking face almost showed some *real* surprise then, and even SpongeBob gave a big gasp, like he was watching us.

'Sorry for eavesdropping,' Charlotte said immediately.

'Can you go up to your rooms, girls?' I thought Audrey was trying to be very calm even though I could tell she was still Angry Auntie Audrey. 'Or outside? There's the good girls, go on.'

She sounded like Mum when she said that. 'There's the good girls' was always what Mum said when she was trying to usher us off to sleep or to go and do our homework. Telling us we were good before we'd even done it, so we wanted to do it more, so we deserved the praise.

It had stopped raining, so Charlotte led me through the hall, across the kitchen and to the patio doors. We slid one open just enough to get out, and closed it again. We both let out a breath.

'What's happening?' I asked Charlotte. 'Why is everyone angry?'

Charlotte bit her lip. 'I'm not sure.'

'Her hair looked lovely.'

'I know it did.'

'Do you think we should get a haircut? Mum always takes us for one before we go back to school. Should we tell Auntie Audrey?'

'Probably not today.'

'No, probably not.'

We walked slowly across the patio, down the big stone steps, and into the garden. Ronnie had cut the grass the day before, which had made me sneeze a bit, but I seemed fine now.

'Maybe he said something mean about her,' I suggested, after Charlotte hadn't said anything for a while.

'Mm,' she said, which meant she wasn't really listening. We followed the few stepping stones that took us to one of the ponds, and I flopped down onto the damp grass and Charlotte did too.

'Maybe he broke one of her nice vases from the kitchen.'

'Maybe,' Charlotte said. 'It sounded a bit more serious than that.'

We sat by the pond for what felt like hours and hours, but it wasn't really, because Ronnie came to collect us for lunch soon after and the Wolves/Wolfes always ate lunch at one o'clock so it really couldn't have been that long.

'I'm reliably informed that it's just sandwiches today,' Ronnie said as we made our way back towards the house. He had his furry earbuds around his shoulders and they jumped about as he walked and they looked like spiders. 'But they look good. Mr Wolfe made them.'

'Lawrence?' Charlotte asked hopefully. 'Is he home from his meeting?'

'No,' Ronnie said, and his smile vanished. 'Not Lawrence.'

'Has everyone made up?' I asked, and Charlotte turned to glare at me.

'What?' Ronnie asked. 'Who fell out?'

'Nobody,' I said. 'Sorry.'

Ronnie stopped walking and looked at us. 'Were Mr and Mrs Wolfe fighting earlier?'

Charlotte seemed to decide that we had no choice but to tell the truth, and she launched into the entire story, exaggerating the argument a little bit, which I thought was unfair considering I had brought it up. I should have been the one to tell the story.

'And they sent us outside and told us never to come back,' she finished, sounding out of breath.

'Well,' I said. 'That's not true.'

'Oh, I know what that'll be about.' Ronnie tapped his nose and seemed to be smiling again, which made me feel hopeful that maybe it would all be fine and it was just a big joke.

'What is it?' Charlotte asked. 'What happened?'

'Oh, I couldn't say.' Ronnie glanced around the garden, then added, 'I think Mr Wolfe has been playing away.'

We looked at him.

'Away where?' I asked.

Ronnie laughed. 'I mean, he's been… unfaithful. To Mrs Wolfe. To his marriage.'

Faithful had something to do with religion, I thought, so unfaithful must mean the opposite of that. So he'd been unreligious to his wife.

'How do you know?' Charlotte asked. 'Who told you?'

'Nobody told me,' Ronnie said, starting to walk back towards the house. 'Nobody tells me anything. I'm just the gardener. A servant, really. It was in the paper this morning. The girl has written an exposé of sorts, all about her brief liaison with none other than The Great Anthony Wolfe, OBE.'

He'd said about ten words I didn't understand, so I walked ahead of Ronnie and Charlotte and went to the kitchen to have my sandwiches.

Charlotte found the newspaper. After lunch – which we ate alone at the big table, sitting two miles away from each other – Charlotte watched through the window as Uncle Tony opened the big green bin at the edge of the patio and pushed a thick newspaper into it. She made me keep watch in the kitchen (something that made me feel sick with nerves) while she went outside and reached into the bin, standing on her tiptoes and nearly pulling the bin down on top of herself with her efforts. Eventually she produced the newspaper and held it up to me, excitedly. She put it under her T-shirt and I tried not to think about what else might have been in the bin with it (my main concerns were spiders and snakes, which I'd decided were my two biggest fears), and we ran up the stairs

Little Darlings

as fast as we could. If anyone heard us they didn't stop us. The tortured girl shrieked as we opened the door to our floor, and we sprinted up those stairs too, though a little more carefully as we weren't as sure of the creaky wooden treads.

Charlotte spread the newspaper open on the floor of her bedroom and started to flick through the pages. I had expected the story to be on the front page, and I knew Charlotte must have too, since she quickly got impatient and flicked through so fast I was sure she would miss it. Since we didn't really know what we were looking for, we had to read – or at least scan – all of the headlines, and after twenty pages I was bored and a bit tired and fed up, so I lay on my back on the bare floorboards and walked my feet up the wall in front of me.

'You'll get your shoe prints on my walls,' Charlotte said, but she wasn't really telling me off because she wasn't looking at me. I took my shoes off and walked my socked feet up instead.

'It's not in here,' she said, throwing the paper across the room.

'Maybe that's not the right paper,' I suggested, putting my hands on my hips so I could walk my feet further up.

'This is the one he threw in the bin!' Charlotte snapped. 'Of course it's the right one, dummy.'

'Well, why haven't you found it, then?'

'You find it if you're so clever.'

I let myself fall back onto the floor and dragged myself over to the newspaper, then propped myself up on my elbows to flick through from the start.

I gave a triumphant hoot. 'There. Page five. You missed it. That's a picture of Uncle Tony, there. Look.'

I shoved the paper back to her and she lifted it up to read it more closely.

'Is it true?' I demanded.

'Shh!'

I waited impatiently for her to finish reading, even daring to give her a tut, which she ignored.

'It doesn't say much,' Charlotte said finally. 'It's just this wee box at the bottom. I'm not sure I understand it.'

Charlotte set the paper down in front of me and looked at her fingers. They were grey with ink.

I hated the tiny writing and the smell of the paper, but there didn't seem to be any snakes or spiders hiding among the pages.

THE CAT'S OUT OF THE BAG screamed the headline. Were we getting a cat?

'Cat Molloy, 17 and winner of this year's NIFTA Rising Star Award, has revealed the identity of her secret beau. When this paper spoke to the young actress back in January, she hinted that she was in the early days of a new romance, but wouldn't reveal any more… 'We're still getting to know one another,' Cat insisted all those months ago. 'We talk on the phone a lot and we get on so well when we're together. I don't want to jinx it by saying anything else so early!'

Well, Cat has changed her mind and has revealed to us, exclusively, that her fancy man is none other than Tony Wolfe, OBE, 64 (pictured, left). It seems the two have been photographed leaving the Spinach Theatre in Holywood together, and Miss Molloy wants to set the story straight…

'Tony and I have been seeing one another casually for a few months,' she tells us. 'I'm aware there is an age difference, but I don't think things like that matter when you connect on the level that Tony and I do.'

When asked how she responded to claims that she is using the older actor to 'get a leg up' in her career, so to speak, Cat said the following:

'I understand that might be what people will think, but the truth is we really enjoy each other's company. I can learn from Tony, of course. He's a wonderful actor. But my career is doing just fine on its own, thank you very much!'

Indeed, Miss Molloy will soon be starring as a young Penelope Wasp in the BBC adaptation of Wasps by Hadley Keenley, which is set to hit our screens this autumn.

Meanwhile, her older lover, Mr Wolfe, will be returning to The

Grand Opera House in September to reprise his role of Hamlet. *Tickets can be purchased over the phone or directly from the venue. Eagle-eyed readers will recognise this photograph of Mr Wolfe from the premiere of last year's major motion picture,* A War of Two Halves, *where he played Father Thomas, a priest who must flee his hometown and take with him his terrible secret. It seems Mr Wolfe's character isn't the only one with something to hide…*

Mrs Audrey Wolfe, Tony's wife (who has had small roles in Channel 5's Troubles *and RTE's* The Doctor) *has yet to comment on the matter.*

I looked at Charlotte expectantly. She looked back at me, just as expectantly.

'Audrey will be sad if he's in love with Cat,' I said after a moment. 'That's really nasty.'

'If it's true,' Charlotte said. 'There's no proof.'

I looked down at the paper, then let my eyes travel to the square black-and-white photograph of Uncle Tony. In it, he was wearing a suit and looking back over his shoulder at whoever was taking the picture. He wasn't smiling but his eyes were all twinkly as they usually were.

'He looks sad about it,' I observed.

'That was obviously taken a while ago,' Charlotte said. 'Before the story. At that premiere thing.'

'Oh, yeah.'

We didn't say anything for a while. 'Will they get a divorce?' I asked eventually.

'I should think so. That's what usually happens.'

It was true. Our own parents had divorced when I was a baby and we hadn't seen our dad since. Nobody could find him, which I thought meant he had moved somewhere very far away, like maybe England, and had forgotten to leave his new address. Charlotte sometimes talked about him with her school friends, and she would hang her head and try and look like she was crying, but I knew for a fact she couldn't remember him any more than

I could, and I said this to her any time I caught her at it. She'd shoved me in the playground for doing that once, and Mum shouted at her when she found out.

'What happens to us if they get divorced?' I asked.

'Not everything is about us, Cara.'

I knew that was true, but I thought it would be nice if just some things were about us.

We ate dinner with Lawrence and Uncle Tony that night. Uncle Tony muttered something about Auntie Audrey having a headache, and even I knew he was lying. Lawrence kept his eyes on his food most of the time, but would look up at his dad every now and then and shake his head. It wasn't like him not to make conversation or ask us questions, but nobody said anything the entire time and nobody noticed that, because it was just spaghetti we were having, I ate my entire plate. I usually wasn't good at Wolfe family dinners. There was often too much carrot and too many unknowns. We hadn't had chips the entire time we'd been there, and it had been a whole month. We went upstairs to bed after that, glad to be away from the silence, but as we approached the shrieking door, we heard Auntie Audrey crying from her bedroom. It was soft. Not like the wailing you do when you fall in the playground, and not like the silent tears I'd found on my face like a wet surprise recently when I thought about how much I missed Mum. These were little sobs. Desperate. Kind of like a baby.

Charlotte and I looked at each other.

'Should we go and see her?' I asked, not sure what answer I was hoping for.

Charlotte hesitated, one hand on our shrieking door.

'I don't think so,' she whispered. 'I don't think she'd want us to.'

The tortured girl shrieked open, then shrieked closed, shutting out the sound of Auntie Audrey's sobs.

We climbed the stairs to bed and my heart felt heavy.

Chapter 7 | January 2023 | Anniskillen

Uncle Tony asks if we want to sleep on the top floor of the house, and before Daisy can get excited by the idea, I shut it down totally and say my back is a bit sore and I can't be doing with any more stairs than are necessary. We set ourselves up in one of the spare rooms looking out over the front garden, and I can't help but notice that, from up here, the old Audi, once shiny and imposing, looks tiny and frail in comparison to our Qashqai.

There is a bizarre sense of excitement in the room as Steve and I make up the bed with some sheets we found in the hot press. Daisy has taken out her script for the school play and is reciting her lines while holding the script away from her, and Steve keeps interrupting with his own made-up lines in a silly, posh voice, and all three of us keep laughing and it feels inappropriate. There is a rattle outside the door and then a knock. Daisy bounds across the floor to let Uncle Tony in.

'I've brought some tea things!' he announces, clutching a metal tray with a teapot. I wonder how he knocked on the door. 'It's too cold in the kitchen to invite you all down there, it's such a big room to try and heat, so I thought you might be cosier up here.'

'That's brilliant, Tony. Thanks so much.' Steve takes the tray from him, all silliness gone, and I know Steve and I are both remembering we're here for a funeral and that our host is grieving. I am suddenly sober and sad.

'Brought some biscuits for the little one too,' Uncle Tony says, happily. 'Do you like custard creams, wee woman?'

Daisy nods politely and says, 'Thank you very much.'

'Which room are you staying in? I'm sorry I didn't think to make any of them up. Audrey would usually have sorted that sort of thing.'

'Daisy is just staying in here with us,' I tell him, going to pour tea into three thin and weak-looking China cups. I know these can't be the tea things Audrey would have chosen; they look more like ornaments. 'The three of us will curl up together, we'll be grand.'

'What!' Uncle Tony gives a little laugh as if I've made a funny joke. 'There are five bedrooms in this house! Seven if you count the top floor. No need for anyone to share, we've plenty of sheets in the—'

'She's staying with us,' I say again, my tone perfectly friendly. Even so, Steve looks at me, as usual able to read something in me that I can't identify myself.

'Okay,' Tony says. 'Well, look. One of the neighbours brought a frozen lasagne on Sunday when she heard, so I thought we could heat that up and eat in the living room? Everyone happy enough?'

We all nod and smile and make noises of agreement and we arrange to meet downstairs in an hour.

Daisy goes back to her script, mumbling to herself and making notes on it with a pencil.

'You okay?' Steve asks lightly. He has swung his case up onto the freshly made bed and I think about all the germs on the wheels, on the outside cover of it that I've never thought to clean, and I know I won't be able to sleep tonight because I'll be thinking of viruses and bacteria all over the bedsheets. I don't say anything because he doesn't deserve to be a part of this part of me. He unzips the case and lifts out his pyjamas, and then mine, and puts them on the pillows.

'Yeah,' I say, watching him. His pyjama bottoms have become unfurled, and he carefully folds them back into a perfect rectangle. 'Just want her in with us. Don't want her to be alone in this house.'

Little Darlings

Steve's eyebrows try to touch each other. 'Why?'

'I just don't. Not here.' I swallow. 'I should have insisted we get a hotel.'

'Tony would have been crushed,' Steve says. 'I can tell. He seems to really care about you. Who wouldn't?'

He smiles but his eyes are still searching mine, reaching desperately to find whatever it is that I keep from him. The thing that he knows exists somewhere inside me, that he's been looking for for twelve years and has never been able to find. Something he's come close to two-dozen times – usually without even realising it – but that always, at the last moment, shrinks away into the shadows like a frightened child. The thing he won't ask for directly, because he loves and respects me, but also because he comes from a home where there are no secrets and there never have been. The Harrises are of the unsaid opinion that if someone is keeping a secret well into adulthood, then it must be a secret worth keeping, and it must be terrible and horrible and awful, and while Steve wants to help and I know he is so curious he can sometimes hardly sleep with it, he wants our life to be perfect more than he wants to know. And I let him live in ignorance, both because he deserves it and because I deserve to be Cara Harris when I'm with him, and not Cara Chilver.

I have fobbed him off for twelve years with something along the lines of, 'It wasn't a very happy time.' In some ways it is a lie – there were happy times at Chaplin House, at the beginning, of course there were – but it is also a massive understatement. He has never directly asked why it was so unhappy… so I have always found reasons never to directly tell him why.

And isn't that a huge part of why you love him? Because he is clean and safe and kind and because in some ways, he doesn't want to know.

I shake my head at myself.

Cara Harris sips her tea with her husband and they listen to their daughter reciting lines of botched Shakespeare and they think she is wonderful and they are in awe of her.

Hannah King

Cara Chilver is somewhere above us on the top floor. The tortured girl in the attic.

The black dress I wore to my graduation when I was twenty-one still fits, and it makes a perfect funeral outfit. I wore it to Steve's nanny's funeral, and again to his granda's, so it has a certain feel to it now and I don't think I'll ever be able to wear it to a restaurant again. Three funerals makes a funeral dress. Steve's suit jacket, on the other hand, won't close, but we decide that doesn't matter and maybe it shrank in the wash. He looks handsome and lovely and I wouldn't want him to be any different. When he reaches his hand into his jacket pocket, he pulls out the order of service from his granda's funeral, last May, and then the one from his nanny's, six years ago. We say nothing about the fact it obviously hasn't shrunk in the wash, then. Daisy is delighted to get to wear her black and silver dress. So delighted, in fact, that Steve has to remind her where we're going, and she obediently adopts a sombre and serious expression for a whole five minutes before she excitedly asks me to plait her hair.

The church is loud, considering it's a church and there's about to be a funeral. The room is packed with people, and if it weren't for the sea of black clothing, you could be forgiven for thinking this was a surprise party. People lean across friends to speak to one another or tap shoulders and exclaim in delight at seeing old faces.

We find seats near the front that have been reserved for us, and Tony moves away to talk to the minister. I notice a few people glancing at Steve with a slight confusion in their eyes. The front row is reserved for family, they are thinking, but that huge man is not *the* Lawrence Wolfe, and Audrey only had one son.

Daisy sits quietly, gazing up at the impressive roof or glancing behind her as more people enter and try to find a seat. The church is already full, so the latecomers find spaces to stand against the back wall. Tony leaves with the minister, murmuring something to us about how he'll be back, and he has to push through the huge crowd to get outside again. People clap him on the back or speak condolences to him, and he nods gratefully.

'Auntie Audrey had loads of friends,' Daisy observes.

I think about this. I wonder how many of the people around us were her friends and how many are fans of Tony and Lawrence, keen to glimpse the male Wolfes in the flesh.

'Was she very famous?' Daisy asks.

I try to think of a way to answer and can't. The truth is that no, she wasn't famous as an actress at all. She did act, she was on TV, but she wasn't... *known* as an actress. It's a complicated thing. Corrie superfans might have recognised her from a part she played for six months around the year Daisy was born, but Audrey Wolfe was known, first and foremost, as Tony Wolfe's wife and Lawrence Wolfe's mother. I've never considered how sad it is before. That she existed, to most people, as an extension of the men around her.

'She had lots of friends,' I decide to answer, and Daisy nods like she is satisfied with this.

There are four women in the pew behind us whispering to one another, and I try to glance at them surreptitiously to figure out who they might be. Their accents and their tones do not seem to match those around us. They all look to be in their early seventies or so, but while the rest of the women in the church smell like they have emptied bottles of floral perfume all over themselves and look as though they've just that morning been to the Boots Estée Lauder counter, these women are dressed plainly in black trousers and jumpers, their four unmatching coats all balled up together between them.

'The 90s, I think,' one of them is whispering. 'Maybe Barbara Hynes' funeral. Jesus, Mary and Joseph, that's so sad.'

'We should have made more of an effort,' another answers.

'We were not the problem.' This from the third, accompanied

by a little 'Hmph!' of agreement from the fourth. 'From the day and hour she married yer man she had no interest whatsoever in being associated—'

'Stop it!' the second woman hisses. 'Remember where you are now, gurls.'

Daisy has noticed me eavesdropping and turns dramatically in her seat to face the women.

'Were you friends with my Great-Great Auntie Audrey?' she demands.

I put my hand on her hand and try to laugh it off.

'Sorry,' I murmur.

The four woman sit straighter and all of them try to smile.

'Oh, yes,' the first one says. 'Yes, we were the very best of friends with Audrey, back when we were younger. Inseparable the five of us. We grew up on the same wee row of terraces in Seabank Parade. Walked to school together every day of our lives, went to our first wee discos at the Seaview Church Hall. Real bosom chums.'

'I'm very sorry for your loss,' Daisy says.

The four women really smile at that, and they nod solemnly.

'Thank you, lovely,' says the second woman. 'It's such a shame, we were just saying we hadn't seen her for years.'

'You lose touch as you get older,' the first says, nodding.

'Me and Ellen are going to be best friends forever,' Daisy says simply. 'We won't lose touch. We're going to live together in a big house with our husbands.'

'Are you now?' the third woman chuckles. 'That sounds good, apart from the husbands.'

They all laugh, and their minor disagreement seems to be forgotten. I smile at them and turn Daisy back to face the front.

So those were Audrey's school friends. Try as I might, I can't seem to remember ever seeing a photograph of Audrey as a child or a pre-teen. Even as a young woman. I can't visualise her at all before she met Tony. These four women might well be the only people who knew Audrey before she was a Wolfe.

I become aware that the murmuring congregation has gone quiet for a moment, like time standing still after an explosion. I glance behind me once more and my heart leaps from my chest into my throat. There isn't enough air in the church, and I am very aware of my blood pounding through my body because I can hear it in my ears. Mine is not the only head that has turned, and I hear one or two badly concealed gasps.

Lawrence Wolfe has arrived, clad in a smart slim-fitting black suit and tie. His mouth is closed in solemnity, but I feel like I can see his huge teeth through his cheeks, somehow. Nearly fifty, Lawrence Wolfe looks ten years younger than that. His eyes sweep the faces in the church and he knows everyone is looking at him. He doesn't see me, or if he does he doesn't react. He nods to a few people, careful not to smile, then spots someone he wants to speak to, and makes his way along a pew, excusing himself.

'Cara,' Steve murmurs, squeezing my knee. I turn to him with a heightened sense of awareness that Steve, my Steve, is in the same room as Lawrence. He is breathing the same air as him. That is wrong. That is so wrong. 'There's Charlotte.'

My head snaps back around. Indeed, Charlotte has come into the church behind Lawrence and is looking around for somewhere to sit. Her eyes fly past me, then back, and I see her recognition written on every inch of her. I am so happy to see it is relief and delight that cross her face. I stand and go to her, barely aware of the black-clad bodies moving and shuffling all around me, feeling like I'm probably moving too quickly and with much too much excitement for the occasion, and not caring, and not giving a shit what anyone thinks. She's okay. She's standing there, whole, and it doesn't matter where she's been because she's here now. My sister's arms find me before I find her, and then we are hugging and we grip each other and cling on like we're both afraid the other might fall.

'You didn't answer my calls,' I murmur in her ear.

'I'm sorry,' Charlotte says. 'I'll give you my new number.'

We break apart and look up and down at one another. She is probably a size six now, and we're both in small black kitten heels, so she is just a little bit taller than me, but she looks tinier in every other way. Her face is different than it used to be. Where she was once open and wore her every thought on her face, her features seem thinner and weaker now, like her smile is rarely used and is out of practice. I'm glad to see her curls are still untameable, like mine, and she seems to have embraced it and not bothered with straighteners just as I have. I try to detect a hint of – what, exactly? What am I looking for? Some powder stuck to her nose? Dilated pupils? No, even Charlotte has too much respect for our late aunt to do that. She looks tired and just a little bit gaunt, but completely sober, I decide, feeling guilty that I've checked.

What does she see when she looks at me?

'Is there a seat up there for me?' Charlotte asks. 'I'd love to see that niece of mine.'

'Of course,' I say. 'We'll make room.' We go back towards the front and I am pleased when Charlotte grips my hand in hers. I squeeze her back and it feels right, like no time has passed and I'm just a child holding her older sister's hand and expecting her to navigate the world first so it's not as scary when I get there.

I stop dead and an older man walks into my back and exclaims his hushed apologies and taps me on the shoulder, like he's checking I'm not broken.

'What?' Charlotte asks. 'What's wrong?'

In the front row now, Lawrence Wolfe is leaning down and speaking to Steve. My husband's broad back takes up half of our row, and for one bizarre moment I think Lawrence must be asking him to move and sit somewhere else. I am torn between needing to be there immediately and wanting to turn around and run from the church and never look back. I watch as Steve's head nods slowly – understandingly, I think, even though I can only see him from the back – and Lawrence nods too, and then Steve is standing and looking around for me, and he smiles a bit when he sees me. I can feel Lawrence looking at me and I keep my eyes on my husband.

We meet halfway up the aisle and I wait for him to speak, convinced that my life might be ending.

'I'm going to help carry the coffin,' Steve explains. 'Mr Wolfe was just asking if I'd mind stepping in to be the sixth man. Being so big comes in useful sometimes, I suppose!' He is being a bit too cheery about it. 'I'm a bit starstruck, meeting a celeb! Hello, Charlotte. Lovely to see you.' He kisses Charlotte on the cheek and she hugs him. She is fond of Steve in the kind of unconditional way you're fond of the family guinea pig. She sees him as harmless and cute, but not someone to be taken seriously, something I've never found fair.

'I'll see you in a bit,' he says. He squeezes my arm and makes his way out of the church, pushing his bulk between a group of old ladies and saying sorry to them, as if apologising for how irritating his size is in such a small and busy church.

He is joking about being starstruck. Steve cares nothing for celebrity, and while he often has the TV on with some film or show or another, he's usually not paying attention, preferring to read or look up the news on his phone. Maybe it is another of the many little things that attracted me to him: the fact that, until meeting me, he had never heard of the Wolfes.

Lawrence has waited for us at the front and is standing tall again, all six foot one of him looking so at home even in the dusty old room. He could always make himself fit, no matter where he was. It was what made him such a good actor. He acted like every room was his own, like he had a right to everywhere and to everything and to everyone, and you believed it.

'Hello, Cara.' He has the good sense not to hug me, but he looks at me warmly and leans forward to grip my free hand. 'It's so very good to see you. Although, the circumstances could be better.' He smiles sadly and I find myself nodding because that's what he wants me to do.

'I'm so sorry for your loss,' I hear someone say, and then I realise it's me. I wait for him to acknowledge Charlotte, but he doesn't. He just nods and smiles sadly, looks at Daisy, and walks away.

We take our seats and Charlotte and Daisy have a brief hug and a whispered, excitable conversation. Then Daisy leans across her aunt and says, 'Mummy, who was that man?'

I don't answer, afraid that if I do, I'll throw up all over the pew.

'That's our cousin, Lawrence,' Charlotte explains. 'He's Uncle Tony's son, and he was Auntie Audrey's son.'

'Auntie Audrey was my great-great-aunt,' Daisy informs her proudly, speaking so loudly that Charlotte gives her a gentle 'Shh'.

'I know,' Charlotte whispers. 'She was my great-aunt. And I'm your aunt. And Fanny's your aunt and Bob's your uncle.'

Daisy giggles and puts her hand over her mouth, and the two of them lean their heads together to whisper some more.

A hush seems to have fallen over the room, everyone waiting for the service to begin. I try to focus on the paintings on the wall opposite, but everything blurs together. If I can just get through the service, I think. If I can just get through the service, say goodbye to Tony, we can get into the car and we can leave. And I never have to come back here, and I never have to see any of these people again.

The back of my neck prickles and I glance around. Nobody is looking at me. People are reading through the order of service or shuffling awkwardly in their seats, a mass of black clothes and makeup like a sinister fairytale. I look to the door and see Steve standing in a semi-circle with a few other men around the minister, nodding intently and listening. His serious face. His face of duty. The face he makes when someone pushes into a queue in front of us and he tells them politely but firmly of their mistake. My eyes flick to the man next to him, and I was wrong, Lawrence is watching me. My whole body burns, not just my face. We look at one another until my eyes blur and I turn around and look at the paintings again.

Jesus stares back at me from one of them, blood pooling at his feet, his face screwed up in silent agony.

Chapter 8 | July 2000 | Chaplin House, Anniskillen

We decided – or rather, Charlotte did – that the story in the newspaper about the lady called Cat must have been completely false. We heard not another word about it after that day, and Audrey had come down for her smoothie and her tablets every morning since with her usual plastic-looking smile, and I was relieved that nothing was changing and that we could forget all about it. It was exhausting having to think of adults' feelings and it was definitely easier if they didn't get divorced.

The summer decided to be hot every single day after that, and we didn't see rain for weeks. We played outside from morning until night, and the sun seemed to have put Charlotte in a good mood because she played along with everything I suggested until one of the Wolfes appeared (and then she would once again pretend to tut at me like she was too old for my games now). Then she would follow Audrey around like a puppy, doing little chores for her, talking to her, listening to her, like she was one of the little moths in *A Bug's Life* and she couldn't drag herself away from Audrey's light.

Lawrence found us by the pond one day and wandered over, waving excitedly like we hadn't seen him at breakfast.

'Hello, little darlings! How are you?' he called. His hand was over his eyes because he wasn't wearing his sunglasses, and he was holding something in his other, waving hand. He came to a stop next us and gave a huge sigh. 'It's hot today. How are you not roasting to death out here?'

Little Darlings

'I love the sun,' Charlotte declared.

'You were just saying you're sick of it,' I reminded her. Lawrence chuckled, but Charlotte ignored me.

'Well, I'm not stopping. I'm off out to meet a friend for a catch up. But I thought I'd give you these, in case they're of any interest.' He held out two books, face up. 'I'm not sure which one will suit who, but you can decide among yourselves!'

Charlotte reached out and took them both and grinned. 'Thank you so much. I've missed reading!'

I wondered if maybe the sun was making Charlotte ill, because she had always hated reading and told me I was a nerd if I did it.

'Cara, say thank you,' Charlotte instructed.

'Thank you.'

Lawrence beamed and reached down to pat my hair. I tried not to flinch because I didn't want to hurt his feelings, and I gave him a big smile.

He was wearing his loose white trousers and a pale stripy shirt, and it looked too warm, and I felt too warm just looking at him. Nobody dressed for the weather in Chaplin House and I found it annoying.

'Enid Blyton is one of a kind, so I know you'll both love that collection, and I just adored *The Railway Children* when I was a boy,' he said, nodding at the book. 'I used to be obsessed with trains, and now, I admit, I'm a bit obsessed with cars.'

We had learned that the big shiny car out the front of the house actually belonged to Lawrence *and* Tony, and it was called an Oddy. It was a type of very fast expensive car that everyone was really happy about and that seemed to be impressive. Auntie Audrey and Uncle Tony had gone out in the car with Lawrence a few times 'for a spin' to a restaurant or the shops, and the wheels had skidded on the stones of the driveway as he sped off with them, leaving us home alone for almost three hours at a time.

We just sat in the living room and waited for them to get back, too nervous to go anywhere else or do anything. I had convinced myself that there were masked burglars watching the house and just waiting for the adults to leave, so I hated it when this happened. Lawrence had asked if we wanted to go for one of these 'spins', but I had said no every time, telling him I didn't feel well or I was very busy, which had made Charlotte annoyed with me for full days. I didn't like being so ungrateful when he was being so lovely, but the thought of being in the fast car with him made me sick. It was bad enough going in the car with Uncle Tony to see Julie once a week. (I thought Julie was getting annoyed with me because every week in our sessions she would ask how I was feeling and I would talk about being car sick and she would explain that she wanted to talk about how I was *really* feeling, and would remind me about all of the words we'd talked about in our early sessions, but the only thing I ever really felt was car sick so I just pretended to be feeling other things. I think she knew I was lying but she was always very nice about it. I had thought of a joke about how I wasn't car sick, I was *Cara* sick and I'd made a note to tell it to Julie next time I saw her.)

'You have such good taste in cars,' Charlotte said. 'When can we come out with you?'

I bit my lip.

'Maybe next week?' Lawrence suggested. 'We could go and get ice creams, if you're both up for it?'

'Yes, definitely!' Charlotte beamed. 'We'd love to.'

'Brilliant!' Lawrence seemed to be really happy and I felt bad for not wanting to get into the fast car because he was really very nice and kind. 'Well, I'll see you both later. Enjoy your books!'

Lawrence gave a wave and turned back towards the house, but he stopped in his tracks and turned around again. 'I think Mum was going to put a film on tonight, if you'd like to watch with us? You probably haven't been in the cinema room yet.'

'Definitely!' Charlotte said. 'See you then!' She gave a little wave and flicked her curls over one shoulder and leant down to examine the books in her lap.

I waited until I heard the click of the patio doors close before I demanded, 'Where is the cinema room? It can't be in the house; we've seen it all. Is it in town? Will we have to go in the car?'

'No, dummy,' Charlotte said. 'It's in the house. I knew about it because Auntie Audrey told me.' She tutted and thrust a green hardback book at me. 'This one looks like it's for kids, so you can have that. I'm going to make a start on Lawrence's favourite.'

'Lawrence's favourite,' I mouthed to myself, too afraid to mock my sister out loud. I was jealous that she was reading his favourite book first and would be able to talk about it with him before I could, but I didn't say anything.

That night after dinner, Uncle Tony said he had some calls to make and he went to his study and closed the door after him. There was a moment when I felt Lawrence and Auntie Audrey looking at each other, but I didn't know what it meant. Charlotte looked serious, like she understood something.

'Let's go and put that film on,' Lawrence declared. He stood up and made a gesture with his hands so that we all followed him. 'The dishes can wait. I'll lead the way.'

He put his arm around Audrey's shoulders and she leant into him, and they went across the kitchen and through the utility room and down the little hall. I had thought there was only a toilet down there, and I avoided it because I'd used it once and seen a daddy-longlegs in it. I shivered at the memory. We followed the Wolfes and I was surprised when Lawrence opened a door next to the washing machine that I hadn't ever noticed before. There was a staircase inside it. I looked at Charlotte and was happy to see she was as surprised and excited as me.

We went carefully down the stairs, holding on to the rail. It got darker as we went down, and I tried not to reach for Charlotte and was proud of myself when I got to the bottom all on my own.

'Welcome to the cinema room!' Lawrence announced. He let go of Audrey to raise his hands in the air as if he was showing off something he'd created himself. From the look on Audrey's face — she was beaming at him, her eyes shining — I thought maybe he had.

We were in a small cinema, somehow. There were three rows of deep red leather sofas facing a huge TV screen. A hole in the wall opposite the screen had a light flickering in it, and I watched some dust floating.

'What do you think?' Lawrence asked. 'This is Mum's pride and joy. After me, of course.'

Audrey laughed and pushed him, but she wasn't being serious.

'It's amazing,' Charlotte said. 'This is so cool. How do you get the films?'

'We have a collection,' Audrey explained. 'Mostly older classics that you girls might not have heard of, but we're very proud of it. There's nothing better than sitting down to watch the masters on the big screen. There's really nothing better.'

I could think of loads of things that were better. For a start, the cinema room was freezing cold, and second, it was so dark I could only see the outlines of everyone's heads in the light from the projector. And I'd seen *The Wizard of Oz* four times, so I didn't think it was very fair for Audrey to say we hadn't heard of any old films.

'I thought we'd start with Hitchcock tonight,' Lawrence said. 'Can't go wrong. What do you think the little darlings would like, Mother?'

'*Rope*,' Audrey said decisively, and I guessed that must be a film, because Lawrence bounded up the few stairs, past the sofas, and opened a little door.

'Cara!' he called after a moment. 'Come and help me find it!'

I looked at Charlotte, panicked, but she had already skipped across the room to sit on the sofa at the front, the furthest from me she could get. Audrey followed her and was chatting excitedly like Charlotte had never seen a film before.

I went up the stairs slowly, hoping Lawrence would find the film before I got up there. I didn't want to help. I never could

Little Darlings

think of anything to say to him, and we'd not been alone for long before.

I got to the top of the stairs and poked my head inside the tiny room. The big projector took up most of it, black and whirring with two big wheels going round and round at the top. There was a stool behind it, and two walls filled with more little wheels, these ones with labels on the side that someone had written on in scratchy handwriting. I waited, watching the back of Lawrence's shirt as he knelt down to examine some of the titles.

He turned. 'Come along,' he said. 'I won't bite.'

I shuffled into the room and looked around.

'It's really impressive, isn't it?'

I nodded.

'Big movie buffs, Mum and Dad,' said Lawrence. 'They've been adding to their collection for... God, must be over twenty years now. They had this room built around the time I came to live with them.'

I thought it was a weird way to talk about being born, and my confusion must have shown, because Lawrence gave a little laugh and said, 'I'm adopted.'

'Oh!' I hadn't meant it to sound so surprised or sad, but it was too late to cover my exclamation, and Lawrence laughed again.

'When I was five,' he added. 'So, a long time ago. I feel like they're my parents, and they've been so good to me. That's what matters.'

I thought of Harry Potter. We'd got through the first two books with Mum, and nobody had ever mentioned reading the third one so I hadn't brought it up.

'Are you an orphan?' I asked. 'Like Harry Potter?'

Lawrence laughed. 'No, I'm not. As far as I'm concerned, Tony and Audrey are my parents, but I do have biological parents... somewhere.'

I thought this was very strange, not knowing where *either* of your parents were, but it felt rude to ask any more.

'What was your mum like?' Lawrence asked. He had turned back to search for whatever it was he was searching for, so he didn't see the angry face that I accidentally made. I waited for a second before I answered.

'She isn't dead,' I said quietly, feeling my heart beat faster. I was glad Charlotte wasn't there to tell me off for saying it. I looked back at the door just in case she'd crept up the stairs.

'Oh, I know, I know!' Lawrence said. 'Sorry. I just meant, what was she like... before?'

I thought about that, not really sure what he wanted me to say. Did he want me to describe what she looked like?

'Funny,' I decided to say.

'Well that makes sense.'

'And really nice. And friendly. And she worked really hard at her job in Tesco, and if she hadn't cared about working so hard it probably would never have happened.' After a moment I added, 'Do you know what happened?'

I could never be sure what adults shared between themselves and what they didn't. Sometimes I would tell people things and they would act shocked and say things like, 'Oh, really?' even though I knew they already knew. They were hard to figure out.

'I think so.' Lawrence turned back to face me. He had a look on his face that was kind of like Julie's, and his head tilted to one side the way Julie's did. I knew what the head tilt meant, it meant, 'Tell me things'.

'She was on her way to work and she fell,' I said, and it was strange because it was obviously the worst thing that had ever happened to us but I was so delighted to have a chance to talk about Mum to someone who wasn't shushing me or looking embarrassed and who also wasn't *being paid a big fat fee*, as Charlotte called it. 'It was that really bad snow in February. Mum checked the Teletext and all the schools were closed so we had to stay with our neighbour because Mum had a shift at ten. She slipped on ice in the carpark and hit her head on the ground. Really hard. Her brain is injured.'

Little Darlings

I kept my eyes on Lawrence's, feeling strangely brave all of a sudden. I was waiting for him to turn away and be embarrassed like everyone else, but instead he reached out and took my hand. Our fingers gripped each other for a second, swinging in the air between us and then he let go.

'I'm really sorry that happened to you.'

'So am I. She's not in hospital; it's called a home.'

'Yes.'

'Everyone there is really friendly.'

'I'm sure they are.'

'So we're only here for temporary, you see. Because we'll go back home with her as soon as she's better.'

Lawrence nodded looking very serious, and then he turned back to look at the rows of labels. Normally when I said that to adults, they tried to explain things to me that I didn't want to hear, and I was glad that Lawrence hadn't and I decided he was my friend.

'Ah!' He straightened and held up one of the little wheels to me. 'Found it. This is a real classic. It was made in 1948!'

I gawped. 'Wow,' I said. 'It's so old.'

Lawrence chuckled. 'Don't let Tony hear you saying that. Do you want to have a go at putting the reel in?'

I wasn't sure what this meant, but I knew from the look in his eyes that he wanted me to say yes, and he'd been so kind to me, so I nodded and I let him show me how to stop the projector from moving, how to open the wheel, take out the film, and put it inside the projector.

'Now you press play,' he said, and he pointed. I reached out and put my hand on the button, and he put his hand on top of mine and we both pressed it. The projector whirred and made a low buzzing sound, and I thought for a minute we'd broken it, but then the cinema screen flashed white, then black, then sound came out of the speakers on the walls that I hadn't seen. I gave a gasp. In the next room, I heard Audrey and Charlotte clapping and cheering, and I craned my neck to see out of the hole in the wall.

'Here,' Lawrence said. He put a hand under each of my armpits and lifted me up. Audrey was beaming up at us from her seat, and she waved. Charlotte waved too, a little less enthusiastically, and I waved back. The film had started already, and I was happy and surprised to see that it was in colour. I didn't know they'd had colour back then.

'Nice job,' Lawrence commented. He set me back down. 'You're a natural. Shall we go and watch the film?'

I nodded, feeling happier now that I'd done something right. Something Charlotte hadn't done. That thought made me just a little bit uneasy. It was nice that I'd done something myself, but it seemed unfair that Charlotte hadn't done it first. I wondered why Lawrence had picked me. Lawrence closed the door after us and I hesitated. The flickering light from the start of the film wasn't quite enough for me to easily find my seat in the darkness. Lawrence took my hand and led me down the first few steps, pulling me into the row behind Charlotte and Audrey. He took his seat and I took mine, and Charlotte glanced back at us. I smiled at her, but she turned back to the screen.

I tried to watch the film, but my eyes kept moving to Charlotte, the side of her face lit up by some of the scenes and in shadow for others. I wished we were sitting beside each other so she could explain the film to me. She seemed like she was barely blinking, her attention on the film, but I couldn't do the same. I kept shuffling and yawning and wringing my hands for something to do, feeling tired and bored and wanting it to be over so we could go to bed.

'You're so fidgety,' Lawrence murmured, leaning towards me. I thought he was telling me off, so I immediately apologised and tried to put my hands under my legs to stop myself, but I saw he was trying not to laugh. 'You're like a little ferret or something.'

I giggled and put my hand over my mouth. I saw Charlotte glance at me, then she turned back to the screen.

Little Darlings

'Only ten minutes left,' Lawrence whispered. 'You've done well. It'll be over soon.'

And then he took my hand in his and held my palm against the top of his leg. It made my arm stretch just a bit too much to be comfortable, but I didn't say anything because I didn't want to fidget. And then I found I wasn't focusing on Charlotte any more, I was focusing on myself and on my hand and on the weight of Lawrence's own hand on top of mine, and the way he was holding my hand on his leg. It was the only thing I could think about. I wanted my hand back so badly I could feel my muscles jerking.

I chanced a glance at him when the music got loud, but he was looking at the screen, smiling ever so slightly, and even though he didn't look back at me, he gave my hand a squeeze.

Chapter 9 | January 2023 | Anniskillen

The funeral reception is to be held in the upstairs conference room of the Macklin Hotel. Tony tells us he will go in the car with an old actor colleague whom he is delighted to see again, and the two of them amble off into the carpark behind the church. It is decided that Charlotte will come with us, and she sits in the back with Daisy.

'Where are you living now, Char?' Steve asks, glancing at her in the rearview mirror as we sit in a line of cars waiting to get out of the church carpark.

'The Opal Building,' Charlotte tells him.

'Opal?' Daisy asks, sounding impressed. 'That sounds beautiful, can I come and visit?'

We all laugh. The Opal Building is simply a block of flats in the city centre, but they are admittedly known for being well furnished and bright and airy, and expensive.

'How are you affording that?' I ask. The question is out of my mouth before I can stop it.

I can't see Charlotte, but I can feel her bristling.

'I'm doing fine,' she says. 'And a friend is helping me out.'

'Oh.'

Keen to change the subject and aware of the tension in the car, Steve clears his throat and says, 'How did you get here today? Them trains are so unreliable, aren't they?'

Charlotte doesn't drive either, but whereas I can happily drive to the school or even the closest shop if I want to, she has never learned. Unless she has recently and this is just another thing she hasn't told me about, like her miraculous move to an impressive apartment block.

'Oh, I got a lift,' Charlotte says. She seems to hesitate, then makes a noise, then hesitates again. Then she says, as if she never trailed off, 'With Lawrence.'

'Ah, that was handy!' Steve says.

I keep my eyes on the ancient Fiat Punto in front of us, not daring to breathe in case she says something else and I miss it. She doesn't say anything more though, and as soon as we are out of the carpark, Daisy insists we all play the number-plate game, and my chance to ask questions is gone.

Steve goes to the bar and comes back with a half pint of beer for himself and three sparkling waters for me, Charlotte and Daisy.

'You're not drinking,' I observe as we move from the bar and into the big, windowed conference room, which has been lined with tables of buffet food. The sun has come out and the day through the window looks almost summery. A *Simpsons* sky.

'No flies on you, Cara Boo,' Charlotte says, nudging me with her hip. 'You're not drinking either. Still not arsed about it?'

'No,' I say.

The conference room looks like a crossword: black blazers are now mingling with white shirts, some of the men having taken off their jackets in the warmer room. The phrase comes back to me, *You'll not feel the good of your jacket outside if you don't take it off now.* I had always thought it was our mum's phrase, but as I got older I realised everyone said it.

We take a seat at a huge circular table and I feel uneasy about setting my drink down without a coaster, but nobody else seems to notice and there is no other option. Steve takes Daisy by the hand and they go and take plates so they can get some food. Charlotte and I look after them, and when I tear my eyes away I see Charlotte is lost in thought.

'What's up?' I say.

She gives a little start and smiles. 'Nothing. Just admiring your lovely family.'

It is such a raw thing to say that I have no response, and my questions about Lawrence threaten to die in my throat again.

'You did well,' she adds. She bites her lip.

'I know,' I say. 'I'm very lucky.'

'Mm. Luck is only part of it. You're a good person; you deserved a good man.'

'Where's this come from?'

'Oh. Death makes you broody, I suppose. Makes you wonder who will be at your own funeral.'

'Awful morbid of you. What on earth put that in your head?'

We both give little snorts and Charlotte looks at me finally. 'Seriously. You and Steve. Are you happy?'

'Yes,' I say immediately. When was the last time I gave such a definite and truthful answer to anything? Probably never.

'Really?'

'Yes,' I say again. As easy and honest as breathing. 'He's my best friend.'

She looks at me and I think it is surprise on her face. She is still so beautiful, her features pulling through in spite of the abuse she's put her body through the last few years. Charlotte started her reckless, party-girl phase early, and while other teenagers always grew out of it or were forced out of it by responsibilities and work and real life, that just never happened to her. Her party-girl phase continued into our twenties, and now into our thirties. Drink, mostly. But drugs too, I know, even though we've never talked about it.

'That's really nice,' she says, and I've forgotten what I said.

The room has filled up and is now packed, the funeral guests looking like swarms of black flies hovering around the tables. I can see Uncle Tony in the far corner of the room, his bald head still standing taller than almost everyone, his stoop seemingly gone. He seems to be telling a funny story, and even over the hum of the guests I can hear his distinct, thick accent. He is louder here in this room than he was in Chaplin House last night and this morning. His audience was smaller then, I suppose.

'So, you came with Lawrence.' I try to make it sound casual, like I'm making conversation and I've plucked that out of thin air. Charlotte shoots a glance at me, and I know she's seen right through me.

'He offered,' she says. 'I wasn't going to turn down the lift.'

'Has he helped you with your flat?' I ask, my fingers gripping my glass. I can't see Lawrence anywhere, but I'm aware of his presence in the big room nonetheless. I am struck with a horrible feeling that he might be behind me, and I turn around to check, but he isn't there.

'Well. Yes. He offered that too. He's been very good to me.' Charlotte sips her fizzy water and clears her throat. 'I know you don't like him, Cara, but—'

'It's a bit more than that,' I say, surprised at how measured and calm I sound. 'I didn't realise you were in touch with him. You're not even in touch with me.'

'That's not fair,' Charlotte says. 'I just forgot to give you my new number.'

'You could have been dead for all I knew.'

'Cara!' Charlotte forces her shocked mouth shut and shakes her head.

'You nearly killed us yesterday.' I say, on a roll now.

'What? What are you talking about?'

'On the motorway. We were driving along and a big show-off BMW overtook us and nearly took us out. I'm assuming that was you and Lawrence?'

Charlotte blinks. 'I don't know.'

'He drives too bloody fast. He could have killed us all. Where are you staying?'

'Here. In the hotel.' Charlotte sets her glass down. 'I'm going to get some food.'

I stare after her, annoyed at myself for sniping, annoyed at Charlotte, annoyed at everyone, and feeling the familiar surge of panic that creeps up on me far too often, no matter how I try to combat it. I take a deep breath, counting, hold it, let it out. Nobody deserves to have to take care of me today. I can't lose it. Today is not about me. *Be the Mummy and the Cara and the grieving niece that everyone needs me to be.*

A small woman barrels towards me and sits down on Charlotte's vacated seat. Caught off guard, I smile uncertainly and try to breathe. The woman takes my arm and pulls me in towards her, and there is that complete disregard for personal space that Northern Irish women of this age seem to have. I promise myself I will never be like this, that I will never touch anyone I don't have to. That I won't make anyone feel uncomfortable because of me. I breathe. *Be Audrey's niece here. That's all I have to do.*

'Hello,' she barks. 'Terrible, all together. Isn't it just terrible?'

'Yes, it's terrible,' I say quickly. Like so many of the others in the church, her perfume is overpowering, like she's bathed herself in it. Her black blazer looks expensive and so do her teeth. She looks about Audrey's age, maybe a little older, but her makeup is so expertly applied that you could be forgiven for thinking she was a much younger woman.

'Mad that she's gone before her husband, isn't it?' she says, nodding.

'It is, yeah. Mad.'

'Bit of a shock.'

'Yeah, massive shock.'

'Not a very good actress, all the same. But a lovely woman, don't get me wrong.'

'Yeah.'

'Which one are you?'

I blink, dizzy from the stream of chatter. 'I'm Cara.'

'Aye, but which one *are* you?' she demands again. She is speaking harshly, and her tone is serious and accusatory, like there is a right answer and I must give it, but I know she is just making conversation and showing interest. She's still holding my arm and it's starting to hurt a bit.

'I'm Cara,' I say again, pulling my arm from her and, bizarrely, feeling rude for doing so. I give her an apologetic smile and then hate that I've done that.

'Yes, yes, yes. You said that. But are you the older one?'

'Oh. No,' I say. It's been a long time since I identified myself in relation to Charlotte, and it feels strange to add, 'I'm the younger one.'

'Ah, yes. Do you know, you haven't changed a bit. You're the one who…'

She trails off and motions towards my right cheekbone. I feel myself flush with a mixture of anger and embarrassment, annoyed that she would point out my scar when I have clearly tried hard to cover it with makeup.

I shake my head a little and decide to let it go, though my cheek is tingling. 'I'm sorry, I don't think I remember you. Were you a friend of Audrey's? Did we meet at Chaplin House?'

'Oh!' The woman gives a little chuckle and pats her bobbed hair as if embarrassed. She straightens her blazer before she adds. 'Goodness. I was never invited there. No, no, but I used to work with our dear late Audrey on *The Doctor* for a few years, and I remember the photograph of you all in the paper. The article that was done when she adopted you. Or fostered you. Whatever it was. It reminded people she existed, you know. You were a big part of the reason her career survived, I think.'

Chapter 10 | August 2000 | Anniskillen

On my tenth birthday, we had loads of plans, but these were scuppered (a word I learned from Uncle Tony) by the death of Sir Ally Kinnis, who I thought must be one of Tony and Audrey's friends, but it turned out he was a big-deal actor and the whole of Chaplin House had to go into mourning. Auntie Audrey wailed all morning and cancelled on her yoga instructor, who was already halfway to the house, and went upstairs to have a lie down. Uncle Tony was on the phone all morning, speaking seriously to various different people about, we presumed, funeral arrangements and the like, so Charlotte and I determined that even if he was a big-deal actor, Ally Kinnis must have also been a very close friend to the Wolfes for them to be behaving so dramatically.

Charlotte had made me a birthday card, which she did every year, but on this one she'd drawn a picture of Chaplin House and the two of us standing on the steps of it, hand in hand. It was a really good drawing and I gave her a big hug.

'Turn it over,' Charlotte said excitedly.

I did as she said and saw that she'd drawn the back of the house on the back of the card, and had spent ages colouring in the green ivy that hung below our huge window. Below the house stood three figures. I knew who they were because of their clothes; there was nobody who dressed like the Wolfes. Audrey had been painted in some kind of jumpsuit, and I wondered how Charlotte had managed to get the hot pink colour that Audrey always wore with just our colouring pencils. Uncle Tony had a very clear moustache and an old-man hat, and Lawrence was in a black jacket that looked leather even though it was just a drawing on a page. I looked at the figures for a long time, thinking of my ninth birthday, when Charlotte had drawn me and her and Mum at a fairground that we'd never been to. It didn't seem fair she hadn't put Mum in the picture, but I didn't say anything.

Auntie Audrey had promised to take us to Belfast after her yoga session, but I watched the hands on the clock moving round and round until it was four o'clock, and I thought everywhere probably shut at five and it took nearly two hours to get there so that probably meant we weren't going shopping for a new set of paints and we wouldn't be having any mocktails either.

Charlotte and I played in the garden for a while, using the Swingball set that Uncle Tony had found in the shed, but we kept finding spider webs on our bats and eventually we threw them to the ground and wandered off down the garden doing cartwheels instead.

'Do you think Audrey will take me to see Mum if I ask her?' I asked Charlotte. 'Not today, obviously. It's too late now. But tomorrow, maybe.'

'It's Sunday tomorrow,' Charlotte said. 'She'll sleep until the afternoon. You'd need to have asked her before now, probably.'

I thought Charlotte was right but I didn't say so.

We sat beside the pond for a while, using a stick to try and touch the fish, but it seemed like it was too warm for them and they couldn't be bothered coming near the top to get some air. I imagined them at the bottom of the pond in the cool darkness, maybe in little fish beds with little glasses of fish lemonade. I tried to explain this to Charlotte but I could tell she wasn't listening. She was in a world of her own and I wondered if maybe she was in mourning for Ally Kinnis too without even realising it.

Charlotte went inside to go to the toilet, and she met Lawrence leaving the house. They spoke for a moment, nodded together, and then Charlotte continued to skip inside. I realised Lawrence was coming down the garden towards me, and I wondered if it was too late for me to slip into the trees and hide from him. I had five seconds to decide, torn so equally between not wanting to see him, and wanting nothing else.

We had become very close, talking more and more frequently as time went on, sometimes even without Charlotte around. He wasn't hard to talk to any more. He never rolled his eyes at me or tutted, and he didn't think any of my games were stupid and seemed genuinely interested in asking about them.

But sometimes I didn't want to be near him, and I couldn't really explain why and so I hadn't tried to tell Charlotte.

I decided suddenly that I did want to see him, because I could tell him about my fish bed idea and I knew he would laugh and I loved making him laugh.

'Happy birthday, little darling!' Lawrence called across the garden. He waved and I waved back, feeling guilty that I had checked his hands to see if he was carrying a present (he wasn't).

'Thank you,' I said. 'We were supposed to go to Belfast, but I think Auntie Audrey is sad about her friend.'

'Oh, Alec,' Lawrence plopped down on the grass beside me and let out a sigh. 'Yes. They were big fans of his. He was a terrific actor. One of Dad's inspirations.'

'Inspirations,' I repeated, nodding.

'Did your sister make you this?' Lawrence picked up the card Charlotte had made and examined it. 'She's very good at art, but I thought you were the arty one?'

'I am,' I said. 'Well. We both are, I suppose. I love drawing.'

'I know you do. I'm sorry about Belfast.'

I wanted to look as though I was both very upset and very mature, but I couldn't figure out what to do with my face, so I'm not sure what I did with it.

'I have a present for you,' Lawrence said. 'I hope that might make it up to you.'

'A present?' I asked, as if I'd forgotten it was my birthday. 'Thank you very much.'

'I'll give it to you later, though.'

We heard the patio doors sliding open, then closed, and we looked over to watch Charlotte running back to us.

'I don't want Charlotte to see the present and get jealous and think I'm favouring you,' Lawrence said quietly. 'So, I'll give it to you tonight. Okay?'

'Tonight?' I asked, but then Charlotte was there, breathless, and she lay on the ground next to Lawrence.

'What are you talking about?' she asked.

'Nothing at all,' Lawrence said, smiling.

'I wish we had a sun lounger,' Charlotte said. 'The grass keeps staining all my nice white tops.'

'I'll see what I can do,' Lawrence said, and he gave her a wink. 'See you later, girls. I think in homage to Mr Guinness, we might have to stick a film on tonight. Can I expect you both to attend?'

I had no idea who Mr Guinness was, or homage, but Charlotte seemed to and she nodded excitedly.

'See you later,' she said. 'Bye, Laurie.'

He grinned at us both and left.

'What were you talking about?' Charlotte demanded as soon as he was out of earshot. 'You had your heads really close together.'

'Nothing!' I said.

'Do you swear on Mum's life? It didn't look like nothing.'

Of course I wasn't going to swear on Mum's life, but I also couldn't tell her that Lawrence had bought me something so expensive and special and cool that Charlotte couldn't even know about it. How would I play with it if Charlotte couldn't see it? Where would it go? And when was he going to give me it when she wouldn't be there?

'What were you talking about?' Charlotte insisted.

'He just said he was sorry about Belfast,' I said. 'That was it.' She would know I was lying. Mum always said lies could be seen, even though they were words. Mum had always known if we were fibbing about having done our homework, and she knew for absolutely certain that a bird hadn't flown into our living room and bashed against the TV and broke it that time. She knew that had been us fighting over the channels and accidentally tipping it forward and onto the floor.

'Oh,' Charlotte said, and I was surprised when she lay back on the grass and closed her eyes and left it. Maybe you couldn't see lies, I thought. Or maybe Charlotte couldn't, anyway.

Tony and Audrey were able to pull themselves together enough to come and have dinner with us, and by the time we had all finished and the plates had been cleared away I would almost have said they'd forgotten all about their dead friend, except they kept raising their wine glasses and toasting to him, and making us raise our cups of juice to do the same. I thought they were quite drunk, Tony and Audrey and Lawrence, and everyone was quite giggly, even Charlotte. I tried to have fun too, but it didn't feel right to be having a birthday dinner with a family that didn't have Mum in it.

Lawrence produced a huge white cake with ten candles on it, and he carried it towards the table, everyone beaming and singing to me, and I felt myself blushing but it was in a nice way for once, and I liked that everyone was looking at me because I knew what to do when a cake was coming towards me. I just smiled and nodded and said, 'Thank you,' like I'd done for all my birthdays before.

'Make a wish,' Lawrence said when the singing was over. He had come to a halt next to me and I could smell what I had stopped thinking of as Debenhams and what I had started to think of as just Laurie. It was fresh and maybe slightly woody, not like Uncle Tony's fake perfumey smell. Lawrence was like something you would find outside, but not in a bad way. Like maybe a fruit from a tree that hadn't been discovered yet, still covered in some rainy soil, mixed with mint from the chewing gum he constantly kept in his mouth. I'd seen it moving around sometimes when he talked, and I always imagined it was a tiny person inside the mouth of a giant, trying to escape but being pushed around from tooth to tooth to tongue.

I glanced around the table. Charlotte was smiling at me, like she always was in front of the Wolfes. Auntie Audrey was smiling at Lawrence, like she always was, just always. Uncle Tony was beaming, but swirling his red wine around his glass, his teeth a little black. All of them had black teeth, I realised. Even Charlotte's mouth was a little dark from our blackcurrant juice. I looked up at Lawrence and he raised his eyebrows excitedly at me, encouraging me.

I felt sick all of a sudden, like I might throw up all over the cake, but everyone was looking at me so I swallowed it down and took a deep breath, and instead of wishing to be back with Mum, which was what I really wanted, I found myself blowing out my ten candles and wishing with my fingers crossed that the projector would be broken and we wouldn't have to go into the cinema room that night.

We had been to the cinema room every other night after dinner since the first time when we'd watched – or the others had watched – *Rope*. Sometimes Tony came with us, sometimes he didn't. Audrey was always there, and so was Lawrence. He would make me choose a film with him in the projector room, which meant Audrey always sat next to Charlotte in the front row, which meant I always had to sit behind them with Lawrence. I had started to dread these evenings, and it felt very unfair that we had to have one on my birthday. I had tried to tell Charlotte that I hated going in there, but she shushed me and told me I should be grateful that the Wolfes had taken us in and were so keen to spend time with us, and she was so tutty about it that I never tried again.

That evening, we watched *Oliver Twist*, and I started to relax and be happy because I had heard of it before and kind of knew the story and one of the scenes, so it felt okay to be watching it, and I was even able to concentrate. I was glad Tony was there, because he sat next to me and would lean in to explain some parts of the story (even though I was pretty sure I understood what was happening) his breath smelling like wine but not in a bad way. Lawrence, on my other side, seemed to be smooshed up into his corner of the sofa, one of his long cricket legs crossed over the other, keeping his eyes on the film. He didn't look at me once, which was weird because normally he always made a point of catching my eye and smiling, or holding my hand, or putting my hand on his leg. I thought it was Tony being there that was making him annoyed.

After a while, one of the characters was shot and kind of accidentally hanged himself and I hated it and couldn't stop thinking about it. What if I accidentally fell and hanged myself? I doubted Mum would have made me watch such a horrible film. There was a quiet scene a few minutes later and I felt all the Wolfes perk up a bit as if they wanted to hear the film better. I could hear Lawrence breathing.

Then the phone upstairs trilled, the harsh beep carrying all the way down to the cinema room and making us jump. We all looked at each other.

'Late for a social call,' Audrey said, craning her neck back to look at Tony.

'Ah, I know what this is!' Uncle Tony bounced up with even more energy than I had seen from him, ever, and he gave me his wine glass to hold. 'Won't be a tic. Don't stop it for me, I know it by heart.'

My own heart sank as he bounded up the stairs, and we heard him answering the phone a few moments later. The others went back to the film and I tried not to be too obvious as I shuffled across the sofa and into Tony's seat. Lawrence didn't appear to notice, and I felt relieved and concentrated on not spilling any of Uncle Tony's wine.

I needn't have worried. Uncle Tony bounded down the steps

Little Darlings

again a few minutes later and sat in between me and Lawrence, not seeming to notice we'd switched places.

'Who was that?' Audrey asked, her neck craned around again.

'I'll tell you after!'

He took his glass from me with a wink and settled himself back to watch the end of the film.

The credits rolled and Uncle Tony bounded over to switch the lights on. We all blinked, and Audrey stretched her back like a cat in the sun. Charlotte copied her. Lawrence gave a yawn.

'That was *Stage Weekly*!' Tony announced. 'They've agreed to run the story. They're going to come tomorrow afternoon.'

Audrey gave a gasp and put her hands on her chest as if she was having a heart attack. 'Photos too?' she asked in a whisper.

'Photos too. Three of them. In colour.'

Audrey gasped again and stood up to hug Tony. The two of them held each other for a moment, rocking and giggling, and Charlotte and I looked at one another, completely baffled.

'You'll get a name for yourself, Mother,' Lawrence said in his pretend telling-off voice, but he was smiling too. 'They'll think you only do it for the press coverage.'

'Awk, away with you!' Audrey said, sounding very Northern Irish, and batting her hands at Lawrence. 'That's nonsense. It's just nice to be recognised, that's all.'

Finally, she turned to look at Charlotte. 'There is a journalist coming here tomorrow,' she said. She glanced at me, and I understood that I was part of whatever this was too. 'They're going to interview me and ask me lots of questions about how you've come to live with us. And they'll want to get some photographs, so you'll need to dress nicely and look like the adorable girls you are. Is that okay?'

'Why?' I asked. 'Why do they want photographs of us?'

'To go with the article,' Audrey said. 'Obviously.'

'We'll be in the paper?' Charlotte asked, clapping her hands together.

'Yes! Well, it's a weekly magazine, but it's very popular and it's a very serious publication. For actors. And budding actors.'

'We're not actors,' I said weakly, feeling my stomach churning at the thought of having my photograph taken. It was like the end of every school year, when Charlotte knocked on the door of my classroom to pick me up for the sibling photo. She would beam at the camera, tilting her head any way the photographer told her to, and I would sit next to her feeling like I was made of wood and wanting to be back in class and learning about the Egyptians. Mum always said she loved the photo, and she got a new frame for each one every year. We hadn't got one this year. Even Charlotte hadn't felt like beaming.

'No, but we are and you live here.' Audrey sounded like she was getting a bit cross with me so I bit my lip and didn't say anything else.

'It's going to be a human-interest piece,' Tony said. 'Audrey will talk to the nice journalist and explain the circumstances of your being here, why she wanted to help, what it's been like for you both, and then they'll just ask you a few questions and snap a photo and leave. Nothing to worry about. You'll do that for your Auntie Audrey, won't you, little darling?'

Tony was smiling at me, nodding like I'd already agreed. So I did.

I changed into my pyjamas and got into bed and looked out the little window at the branch. There was no breeze tonight, so it didn't move. I stared at it until it blurred, thinking about how I was ten now, practically an adult, and that I would soon be expected to do adult things like pose for photographs for magazines and talk to journalists. That was just the price we had to pay for living amongst famous actors, according to Charlotte. I wasn't sure that was very fair, and didn't think it was worth it, but everyone else seemed buzzing with excitement about the next day, so I would have to pretend I was excited too.

I fell into a light doze and dreamt I was in the garden of

Chaplin House, chasing after Mum and trying to show her the card Charlotte had made me, and trying to apologise because she hadn't drawn Mum, but she kept running and she was too fast for me and I couldn't catch her. In my dream, a bird tapped its beak on a tree and it sounded like a soft knock. The bird tapped again, then again. Then I was awake and it wasn't a bird, it was a knock on the wooden door of my bedroom, and I sat up in bed, staring at the door and straining my ears.

The knock came again. Two soft taps. It wouldn't be Charlotte. Charlotte would come through the bathroom and into my room. I thought of poor Mr Sikes with the rope around his neck and felt sweaty and sick all of a sudden, imagining it was his dead body that had climbed the stairs and wanted to kill me.

'Cara? Are you awake? It's me!'

Lawrence's whisper was such a relief I let out a little sigh and immediately sprung out of bed and went to the door before I really thought about it.

I opened the door, the wood giving a little creak that made me wince.

Lawrence was there in his pyjamas. I had never seen his pyjamas before, and it was weird. They were purple and long sleeved and long legged, even though it was so warm. I thought they were made of silk, because they seemed to glint in the moonlight from my window.

'Hello,' he whispered, grinning. His teeth lit up the dark. 'Did you have a lovely birthday?'

'Yes,' I lied. 'Thank you.' I tried not to look at the package and card in his hand, and I acted surprised when he thrust them toward me.

'Happy birthday,' he said. 'Even though it's technically two hours late.'

I blinked. It was two o'clock in the morning? The middle of the night? What was he doing here? This present must be amazing, if it was a middle-of-the-night secret.

'Thank you,' I said. I took the package from him and awkwardly used my shoulder to hold the door open. Lawrence gave a little laugh and gently pushed me back inside. He followed and shut the door after him.

'I didn't hear the lady shriek,' I said. I went to my bed and sat down on it, putting the present on my lap.

'Ah. That's because it worked! I oiled it myself, just now. Finally got around to it.' He held up a little blue bottle but it was too dark to read the label. 'Should do this one too!' He threw his head back in the direction of my bedroom door.

'Yeah,' I said, trying to smile. I didn't want to start ripping the paper off my present in front of him, but I wasn't sure what else I was supposed to do while he was in my bedroom in the middle of the night. I glanced around, suddenly embarrassed by the toys and games scattered all over my bedroom floor. My Baby Born doll sat in the corner, unplayed-with since Mum's accident, but suddenly so obvious and childish-looking. I wanted to tell Lawrence I hadn't played with her for months, but it would seem like a lie just mentioning it, and there was still a chance he wouldn't see it.

The clothes I'd worn to dinner were in a heap in the middle of the floor, and I reached my foot forward and used a toe to skite the skirt and top under the bed. The mess, the untidiness, was one thing – the main thing – that Charlotte gave off to me for, but with Lawrence standing there in his fancy pyjamas, the room felt small and babyish, like a child's room. And I wasn't a child any more, I was ten.

Lawrence glanced around, spotted my huge bright-green inflatable chair and took a squeaky seat. I'd had to squeeze the air out of it at home, pack it in my suitcase and blow it up again once we'd got here, and I'd done it all myself and was strangely proud of it. I told Lawrence that and he beamed.

'Clever girl. It's really cool, I never had anything like this. It wouldn't be to Mum and Dad's taste, I don't think.'

I blushed and looked away.

'But I love it,' Lawrence said quickly. 'I wish I'd shown my personality a bit more in my room growing up. I really admire that you have.'

I smiled. I wasn't sure if he really meant it or if he was just being kind, but I appreciated it all the same.

'Now, hurry up and open your present or you'll be eleven and we'll be starting all over again.'

I giggled and he shushed me. I carefully peeled the Sellotape away from the pink sparkly paper and pulled out a cardboard box, blue with huge writing.

'Sea Monkeys,' I read. I looked up at Lawrence. 'What is it?'

'They're little pets!' he said. He bounded up from the blow-up chair as quickly as it was possible to and came to sit next to me on the bed.

'You grow them from the little packet,' he explained, pointing at a picture on the box. 'And there is a tank for you to grow them in. You always said you'd wanted a pet, and this was the only thing I could think of that Audrey and Tony might let you keep.'

My face ached from grinning. 'Sea monkeys,' I said again. 'That's amazing. Thank you.'

There was more I wanted to say, more that was hanging in the air. My chest felt lighter than it had for a long time, because someone had given me a kind present that was made for me. Someone had seen me for me, and not as a tag-along to Charlotte, the shadow to her sun.

'You're very welcome,' Lawrence said. He tapped the top of my head and slid himself off the bed. 'I hope you enjoy them. You can set them up tomorrow.'

'What is this thing about tomorrow?' I found myself asking. I wanted to know, but more than that, I found I didn't want Lawrence to leave.

'Oh, that.' He rolled his eyes and put his hands in the pockets of his pyjamas. 'I'm afraid lovely Audrey is going to parade you like animals in a zoo.'

I blinked, having no idea what he meant.

'The article is so she can get her name out there again. She hasn't had any roles for a while, and she doesn't want people to forget about her.'

'What's that got to do with us?'

'Well. Nothing really. But when they adopted me they did almost exactly the same thing. There was a huge eight-page spread about the adoption. They came here and took photos of the house, and we went to a studio and had photographs taken of how happy we all were, and they interviewed Mum and Dad and they jabbered on about how selfless it was to adopt. Tony was cast in his first Shakespeare after that, and Audrey became a regular on an RTE show.'

I was still frowning and Lawrence gave a little chuckle. 'Nothing for you to concern your pretty head with, little darling. It's a very selfish thing; adults using children to get what they want. They try to tug on heartstrings, they pose for a few photos, and then suddenly everyone remembers them. They're a hot topic. They're relevant. Big news.'

'Right,' I said. 'And it'll just be a photo and a few questions?'

'Yes. Nothing to worry about. I promise.' He held his hand out and I thought he was going to shake my hand again, but then I realised he was holding his pinky finger towards me, making a promise. I reached out and we entwined our little fingers, and he laughed again. 'Tony had to pull a few strings with the magazine. They weren't too bothered about it, but he called in a favour and now they're pretending to be keen. Don't mention that to Audrey though, will you? That's our little secret.'

The door creaked open, then closed, and then I heard the soft pat of Lawrence's slippers on the treads. I held my breath, listening for the shriek of the door downstairs, worrying the oil had only worked for a while, but no sound came.

Lawrence had silenced the girl in the attic.

Chapter 11 | January 2023 | Anniskillen

'Oh, that,' I say to the woman in the blazer. I purse my lips, annoyed by the directness and lack of tact that is supposed to be ignored when someone is elderly. 'Yes, I remember. She didn't adopt us, we just stayed with them for a while when... when we were younger.'

I think back to the article in *Stage Weekly*. I haven't thought of it for years. The two of us in identical orange dresses that arrived at the house early in the morning, smiling for the camera, perfectly smooth, unscarred cheeks, one on either side of Audrey as she put her arms around us and squeezed tight. I can remember the dress pinching me under the arms and feeling too hot and wanting to get out. I can remember Lawrence watching us from the doorway of the living room, laughing and giving us all stage directions that the photographer said was great for 'easing the tension'. The photographer had wanted Lawrence to join in with the photos, but Audrey immediately insisted Lawrence had better things to be doing and should be getting off, and he left with a wave to us, and I could hear the engine of his car rumbling down the drive soon after.

That day is the first memory I have of Uncle Tony watching Lawrence watching us. As Lawrence stood in the doorway, grinning, Tony stood in the corner of the room, his arms folded, smiling good-naturedly... but he kept looking at Lawrence.

I make a mental note to look up the article again when I get home; I can't remember anything that was said in it.

'Yes. Another of Audrey Wolfe's charitable schemes! I still remember the Rags to Riches story they ran about her when they adopted Laurie!' The woman chuckles and it turns into a cough, so I look away to give her a chance to stop.

My eyes find Charlotte, who is putting a vol-au-vent onto her plate and chatting with Steve. I frown, eyes searching the crowd for my daughter. A young couple move towards the door and I see Daisy in the space they have just left. Her plaits are starting to fall out, and her face is red with the heat in the room. A woman with a child passes in front of my vision again, blocking Daisy from sight for a moment, and then she comes back into view and I stand up and nearly knock the table over.

The blazered woman has started to say something else, but she stops.

'Excuse me,' I mutter, gripping my handbag and elbowing my way over to Daisy.

'...and after that it was *Richard III*. Have you seen that one? I don't suppose you have. People have a habit of saying they've *read* a play, which I find most irksome. Plays are not something to be read, they're something to be—'

'Daisy!' I say, coming to her side and cutting Uncle Tony off mid-sentence. 'Come on. We have to go.'

'You're going?' Uncle Tony cries. 'Surely not. So soon?'

'Yes. Am I okay to get a key off you? We'll leave it under the mat.'

'Cara, there's no need to rush off,' says Lawrence, opening his arms wide, his wine glass swooping over our heads. 'We're here to celebrate Audrey. And your Daisy was just telling us she has a part in a play at school. It must run in the family, this acting business, eh!'

I refuse to look at Lawrence. I can't. But I am so aware of him. He is within reaching distance of me, of Daisy, and the panic is in my chest and making it hard to breathe.

'The key?' I ask again, staring at Tony. He blinks at me, glances at Lawrence, then switches his own wine glass to his other hand so he can fumble in his pocket. 'Here you go, love,' he says softly. 'You just leave it out for me somewhere. You're sure you won't stay?'

'No, sorry.' I can't think of anything else to say, so I just say again, 'Sorry.'

I reach for Daisy's hand and steer her to the door. She stumbles a little, and says, 'Mummy, what's wrong?' but she moves with me, sensing that I'm serious and not to be argued with.

At the door, I glance back, looking for Steve, but he has already seen me and is striding towards us.

'What's up?'

'Can we go?' I ask. 'I need to leave. Now.'

Steve nods, and he comes with us and doesn't look back.

We pull up to Chaplin House and Steve parks next to the old Audi. I don't look at it. Nobody says anything for a moment, then Steve turns into the back seat.

'Why don't you do the honours, madame?' he asks Daisy. 'Go and pack up your school bag. We'll be in in a sec.' He prises the key from my hand and passes it to Daisy, and she hops out of the car obediently and goes to the front door. She glances back and smiles at me and I smile back. Or try to.

'What was that about?' Steve asks. 'Are you okay now?'

I'm not sure how to answer. Yes, here in this car, with Steve beside me, Daisy in sight, nobody else around, I'm fine. I am okay. Inside my head I'm not so sure.

'I'm sorry,' I say. It's all I can find to say.

'Don't be sorry,' Steve says softly. 'Just explain.'

Did I really think I would get away with it forever? That I could keep a huge part of myself from my own husband, from my favourite person in the world?

Yes, I suppose I did. But I have always felt like I will have to tell him someday, like something will happen and it will all come spilling out and it will be a relief. Is this that something? Does he, somewhere inside, suspect the truth?

Daisy opens the door and goes inside. I exhale.

'I was just sitting at our table and when I looked up, Daisy was on her own, talking to Tony and… Lawrence.'

Both things can't be true at once. I'm aware of that. She can't be both alone and talking to them. But Steve knows what I mean. He looks down and shakes his head.

'I'm sorry. That's on me. I could see her, but yes, I left her.' He waits a minute before adding. 'It was only your uncle.'

'And Lawrence,' I add. 'I don't want her talking to him.'

'To Lawrence?'

'Yes. I don't want her to be around him. Not ever. I should have told you that before, but I'm telling you now. Do you understand?'

I make him look at me and he does. His eyes search mine, his irises the same bright blue as the Smartie, the one that everyone in school always said had more E-numbers than its other coloured friends. He has wrinkles around his eyes too. Why do I love it on him and hate it on myself?

'No,' he says. 'I don't understand. What's up with Lawrence?'

'I don't trust him to be around Daisy,' I say. I feel tired, on edge. Annoyed at Steve for no reason other than he is here to be annoyed at and Lawrence isn't. I want to give one-word answers, I want to make my anger clear. But then he reaches across and puts his big hand on top of mine and doesn't make me say anything. And that's why I decide that I will tell him. Because he won't make me, because he would never make me. Because he loves me in a way that nobody else ever has or ever will again, apart from Mum. Because I looked, didn't I, for years for a safe place? And then I found my safe place in the form of a man with thighs as thick as tree trunks and feet like flippers and I owe him the truth.

'It's a long story,' I say after a moment. I debate telling him when we're home, asking if we can schedule in a big important talk and wait for it and count down to it. But that's ridiculous. We're not in a film. And I don't want our house, our real lives, to become infected by what I have to tell him. I will tell him here, and we'll infect the already poisonous Chaplin House, and then we'll never come back. It'll go back into the box and the box will stay untouched.

I look at Steve, then let my eyes slide across to the window behind him, to the Audi parked next to us, and I shiver with a new memory, because a lot of bad things happened at Chaplin House, but they didn't all happen to me.

Chapter 12 | Late August 2000 | Chaplin House

Since the success of the article in *Stage Weekly*, Audrey had been on three auditions. She hadn't been cast in anything, but she blamed various things for this.

'They're looking for someone older,' she said of a toothpaste advert.

'The director was jealous of my nice jacket,' she complained of a non-speaking role in a horror film.

'They've gone with Pippa Thornton,' she tutted of an adaptation of a very popular romance novel. 'They're so unoriginal. She's the next big thing for *now*, but she won't last. Looks only get you so far.'

She hadn't mentioned any of her auditions since, and seemed to spend less and less time downstairs with everyone else and more and more time in her room. I didn't know what she did in there, and when I asked Charlotte, she didn't either.

I had set up my Sea Monkeys on my windowsill, and I fed them from the little paper packet once a week. They had grown and there were five of them. I didn't know who was a girl and who was a boy, but I loved watching their little skeleton tails as they swam around in the tank. I named them after characters from my Jacqueline Wilson books, but after Ruby and Garnet and Star and Dolphin I couldn't remember any more, so I called the fifth one Jacqueline, which made them all girls. Charlotte had demanded to know where I'd got the Sea Monkeys, and when I admitted they were a present from Lawrence, she seemed happier, and I knew she was expecting something similar when her birthday came around.

He didn't get her anything, but he gave her a hug and wished her a happy birthday, and while she thanked him and beamed, I noticed she was in a bad mood for the rest of the day, having not got a present. When I went to feed my Sea Monkeys the next morning after breakfast, I found the tank empty of water and empty of Sea Monkeys.

Charlotte denied touching them, but I wasn't so sure.

There was only one week left of summer until we started at our new school. We were still in the same school as each other, thankfully, but for the first time our classrooms and playgrounds would be totally separate. We'd been on a tour of it with Uncle Tony and the P7s had their own private mobile classroom and study rooms for their eleven-plus test, while us in P6 were with the younger ones, so I was dreading it more than I was letting on. Charlotte had gone for a uniform fitting the week before and she looked like an adult, strutting about with her cool blazer that had loads of pockets, another thing that was reserved for the oldest ones in the school. I was glad that I was still allowed to wear tracksuit bottoms and polo shirts, because as cool as the blazer was, I wasn't sure about how comfy it would be to wear all day, and how would you paint or run about in the playground wearing it? Charlotte was going to be so uncomfortable and I told her as much, but she was very quick to tell me that she wouldn't be doing any of that *childish nonsense* any more, because she was going to take up studying really hard for her exams and she was basically an adult now. I thought that was funny, considering she'd read four pages of *The Railway Children* and thrown the book to me and said, 'Reading is bloody boring.'

'Who fancies a trip to the beach?' Lawrence asked over breakfast that morning.

Charlotte gasped and nearly choked on her cereal, but she flung her hand in the air and said, 'Yes, please!'

I stared into my bowl and hoped that everyone would forget I existed.

'Cara?' Lawrence asked.

We hadn't been alone since the night he'd brought my present to my room, and though we had watched three films since then, he hadn't tried to hold my hand or anything. I was half relieved and half worried that I'd offended him in some way, but I couldn't figure out what I'd done.

'I don't like being in the car,' I said after a moment. I could feel Charlotte glaring at me.

'Oh, never worry about that!' Lawrence chuckled. 'I'm a very good driver. I'll go nice and slowly. But you two have barely left the house all summer, so I think you deserve a day out. I'm only here another few days myself and then I'll not see you until Halloween!'

Lawrence was off to film something in a desert somewhere. Everyone, including Charlotte, put on an American accent any time they talked about it, and it was really annoying.

'I get car sick,' I said. 'I don't want to get sick in the nice Oddy.'

'Owe-dee,' Charlotte said, over-pronouncing it and rolling her eyes. 'Don't be such a baby, Cara. Just come.'

'It's only a car,' Lawrence said. 'You're far more important. Now go and get your summer clothes on, girls. I'll go and find Mum and see if she wants to come.'

The drive wasn't too bad. Lawrence did drive slowly, more slowly than I had ever seen him drive, to the point where Audrey told him to 'step on it' and he laughed and said, 'No, I don't want to make Cara sick,' and Audrey and Charlotte rolled their eyes at each other and I felt like I was annoying everyone just by existing. We got to a place called Vetobridge after what felt like sixty years. I got out with my legs feeling shaky and weak and pulled my T-shirt away from my clammy skin. I thought of a joke about clams on the beach and clammy skin, and made a note to myself to tell Charlotte later. Lawrence had parked the car across two spaces and a man walking past with his kid in one hand and an ice cream in the other called, 'Quare bit of parking there, mate!' I crossed my fingers that nobody would start fighting and was relieved when Lawrence just laughed, showing all of his perfect teeth.

'What's first?' he asked us, practically jumping from foot to foot in his excitement. 'Ice cream? Swim?'

'It's too cold for a swim,' I said, at the exact same moment Charlotte said, 'Oh, yes! A swim!'

'I didn't bring my costume,' I muttered to Charlotte, and she rolled her eyes as if I was being ridiculous. She skipped on towards the promenade. Audrey, dressed in her floaty white trousers and a tight T-shirt and huge sunglasses, went after her, smiling all around her as if expecting to be caught on camera at any minute.

It was busy on the promenade and busier on the beach. Clearly everyone had had the same idea as Lawrence. We had to walk along the beach for fifteen minutes until we found a quiet enough spot, which was fine for everyone else who was wearing sandals or, in Lawrence's case, going barefoot, but I was in my best guddies and they were covered in wet sand and my feet felt gritty inside. I tried to ignore it and ran to catch up with Charlotte so she couldn't tell me off for being miserable.

Lawrence laid out a huge beach towel and plonked himself down on it, and I was happy to sit next to him. Charlotte and Audrey went towards the sea, Audrey telling Charlotte about the importance of daily SPF, which sounded dangerous. I assumed it was one of her pills.

'How are you feeling about going back to school?' Lawrence asked me. He had pulled his sunglasses onto his forehead and was squinting at me, which seemed silly.

'Okay,' I said. 'I like school. Or I did. If this one is the same then I'll like it fine.'

'Good,' he said.

'Did you go to Holy Trinity?'

'Yes! Then I went to high school in Belfast.'

'In *Belfast*?' I repeated. 'From Chaplin House? You must have been knackered.'

'I wasn't, actually! But I know what you mean. Seems ridiculous now.'

'Did you have to get the bus?'

'No, Tony drove me.'

'Every day?'

'Yes! Except when he was working.'

'Did you give Ronnie a lift?'

From my conversations with Ronnie, I had established that he and Lawrence had gone to the same primary school and the same secondary school, but from the things he'd said I was sure they hadn't been friends.

Lawrence closed his mouth for a moment.

'No. He got the bus from the village. I think his grandmother wanted him to… do something. You know? That's why she made him go to such a good school. Didn't really work out the way she planned, did it? Anyway, he only stayed for the first few years and then he went to tech.'

I watched as Charlotte dipped her toes in the water, shrieked and ran out. Audrey was laughing and seemed to be genuinely having a nice time, but it was hard to tell with her plastic face. Seagulls flew in a circle over the top of them, calling happily to each other. It was sunny but not too warm. I was determined to have a nice time too, so I tried not to think too hard about whether or not Lawrence was being mean about Ronnie.

'I loved school when I was your age,' Lawrence said. 'I was in all the school plays.'

'What plays did you do?'

'Joseph and his Dreamcoat, that was the main one. I was Joseph, of course. Was Joseph in the Nativity every year as well, come to think of it. I must look like a Joseph. Then *Blood Brothers* was my leavers' play. Oh, and *Grease*. I was Danny in *Grease* when I was in fifth year of high school.'

'What's *Grease*?'

Lawrence gave a huge gasp that made me jump, thinking he had seen a crab. 'You haven't seen the greatest musical film of all time?'

I wondered if we had changed the subject but then I understood. 'I'm not really into those kinds of films,' I said. 'Or any films, really. Except Disney.' It felt strange and bold and a bit dangerous to admit that to one of the Wolfes. Lawrence just laughed.

'Yeah, I never see you paying much attention. Tell you what, tonight when we get back, we'll watch *Grease*. I guarantee you'll love it. It won't be in the cinema room, though, probably just in the living room. It's a video.'

'Okay.'

Charlotte had waded in so far that the tide was lapping at her shorts. She seemed to have gotten over the shock of the cold, and was dancing, skimming the surface of the water with her fingertips. Audrey was looking up at the sun and smiling, and she looked like an actual person and I realised she hadn't ever looked like an actual person before, just an actress.

'I like going to the beach,' I said to Lawrence, my voice sounding odd because it was rehearsed. 'But when it's too warm, it makes me *clammy*.' I put a lot of emphasis on the last word, hoping he would understand me, and he did. He laughed instantly, loudly, and slapped his hand on his thigh.

Audrey and Charlotte turned to look at us, and looked away again.

'You're a geg, Our Cara,' he said. 'Did you make that up?'

'Yep,' I said proudly. 'I love making up jokes.'

'You should be on stage.'

'Doing what?'

'Telling your jokes!'

'Oh.' I tried desperately to come up with something else,

anything else. I looked around me for inspiration, but nothing came.

'What about the books I gave you? Have you been enjoying them?'

'Yes!' I said, my face flushing. It was true, I had loved the Enid Blyton, but here on the beach in the sun, weeks later, I couldn't really remember anything about any of the stories. They didn't stick the same way Jacqueline Wilson did. 'Thank you.'

'No problem. There are a load of books in Dad's study. You can have a look and take any that you want.'

'I don't want to go in there. It's very... official.'

He chuckled.

Charlotte was quite far out now, and a part of me wanted to call to her to be careful, but I was the younger sister, and nobody ever listened to me and they didn't have to care if I was worried.

'Did you do things like this with your mum?' Lawrence asked.

I was so surprised I didn't say anything for a minute. Then I said, 'Not really. Sometimes.'

'Do you miss your mum?'

'Yes. Do you?'

'Do I miss your mum?'

'No, do you miss *your* mum?'

'I was joking, I knew what you meant. I told you, Audrey is my mum.'

She wasn't though, and I knew she wasn't.

'We'll do things like this when she's better,' I said, watching as Audrey tried to follow Charlotte into the sea. The two of them were laughing and talking all the while. They looked like they could be mother and daughter, and I didn't like that suddenly. 'And she will get better.'

'Oh?' Lawrence asked. 'Did the doctors tell you that? That she'd get better?'

'No,' I said. 'But I think she will.'

'Then I think she will too.'

Little Darlings

I looked at him to check if he was taking the mickey out of me. He didn't seem to be. He was resting back on his elbows and looking up the beach, back towards the carpark.

'Our blissful haven didn't last long,' he said. He was watching a huge family coming towards us, colourful plastic buckets and inflatables blocking their faces. They seemed to be shouting to one another instead of talking. 'I could talk to you, just the two of us, for hours.'

He turned to grin at me and I grinned back, happy that he had liked my joke, happy that he thought Mum would get better, happy that he liked speaking to me when it was so obvious that nobody else did. I decided I liked Lawrence a lot more than I liked Charlotte.

Then I felt guilty and took it back.

Chapter 13 | January 2023 | Dromary, County Down

It is dark when we get home later that day. Nobody said much on the drive home, a mixture of tiredness and unease making us all fed up. I expect Daisy to ask why we left in such a rush, to pester about when we can visit her lovely Uncle Tony again, but even she seems to sense something strange is going on, and she doesn't mention it. Instead, we eat dinner early and she obediently goes to have a shower without her usual grumbles.

The bathroom door clicks closed and Steve and I look at each other.

'I'm so sorry,' he says, as if moments have passed since we were alone in the car outside Chaplin House, and not hours. 'I'm so sorry you went through all that. I can't believe I shook his hand.'

I'm not sure how to respond to that, so I stack our plates and put them next to the sink. I fill the kettle and click it on.

'I can do that,' Steve says. For once I hate the softness in his voice, hate that he's acting as if it's ridiculous for me to do dishes in light of what he now knows. 'Leave it for me.'

'No, it's fine. I'll do it.'

He doesn't argue, but I hear his chair squeak on the floor and I know he's turned it so he can look at me. I imagine him fixing the leg of his pyjamas.

'Does Tony know?' he asks.

I look out of the window, past my reflection at the bird feeder. It has been emptied of peanuts in the time we've been away, and there are no birds to be seen in the garden. Our watering can has been on its side in the middle of the patio since about September, and it's covered in droppings. None of us has bothered to lift it, and it's right in the middle. You stop seeing things if they're always there, sometimes. You stop recognising that you have to do something about them.

'Yeah,' I say eventually.

'Did Audrey know?'

'Definitely not.'

The kettle clicks and I busy myself with filling the sink, starting on the dishes. Steve takes a tea towel from the radiator and comes to stand next to me. He looks out of the window too.

'What about Charlotte?'

I pause, one hand clutching a sponge and the other deep in the hot water. It's too hot, burning my hand, but I let it. I swill a little circle and then say, 'No. She didn't know.'

Steve exhales loudly and starts to dry a plate. 'You could have told me about it. I hope you know that.'

'What would the point have been?' I ask. 'What could you have done? Too late to change anything.'

'I know, but you might have been…' He opens the cupboard at his eyeline and puts the clean plate inside. 'Better. In yourself.'

'I'm fine,' I say. I have cleaned the glass in my hand so thoroughly that it is squeaking. I rinse it, and when I pass it to Steve his eyes are on me and for the first time, possibly ever, I can't tell what he is thinking.

'You're fine?' he repeats.

'Yeah?' I am genuinely surprised by this and don't know what else to say. He gives me the look for a few seconds, then takes the glass from me and puts it away.

'What do you want to do about it?' he asks when we have been working in silence for a few minutes.

I like that he has asked me this question and not told me what I *should* do. I like that I know he is angry, but that he isn't letting that take over. I knew that if ever I felt the need to tell him, he wouldn't let me down. Charlotte, yes. She would let me down. Tony, yes, and Audrey, sure, even if she didn't really know what she was doing. But not Steve. Never Steve.

I don't answer for so long that the dishes are done and dried and put away and I still haven't said anything. I give the sink a quick clean, squeeze my sponge, leave it to the side.

'I'm going to go and lift that bloody watering can,' Steve says. 'It's doing my head in sitting there. I must have walked past it twenty times.'

I smile and he goes out the back and moves it, and pretends to slip and teeter to make me laugh, as if I'm ten, and I do laugh but then it turns into a little sob and I have to put my hand over my mouth. He has gone to the shed to put the watering can back and he doesn't notice.

'I'll phone you at lunch time,' Steve promises the next morning, clad in his most professional T-shirt, that says I MAY BE WRONG, BUT IT'S HIGHLY UNLIKELY, and I know he will because he always does.

'Bye, Mummy!' Daisy calls, and she rockets out the door, schoolbag over her shoulder. Steve closes the door and I hear their chatter down the drive until the two car doors slam shut.

I have the house to myself, am alone for the first time in what feels like years. I brush my teeth, wash my face, poke at my eye bags, frown, and go back downstairs.

My home office is a built-in desk in the tiny corridor that connects the house to the sunroom. With both doors closed, I can spread my fingertips out and touch all four corners if I try, but it's comfortable enough, and the door to the sunroom has a pane of glass in it so I can look out across the blank-canvas fields when I take breaks.

I log on to work. Eighty-seven emails. I let myself groan and feel for a moment like I'm just a normal person. Like I'm a person whose greatest gripe is that she has a lot of emails after a few days off. I want to be that person. I want that to be the worst thing about my day.

Hey!

A Slack notification pops up. Then another. An email comes in.

I ignore everyone and go to make coffee. Steve has refilled the bird feeder, and a lonely robin picks at the fatball. He is looking around furtively, and moves like a trained dancer. When he has his beak full, he flies off into the trees.

I have another email when I get back to my desk. I take a deep breath and try to think logically. The logo for the new online bakery is the most urgent; they open on 1 February and I still haven't made a proper start. I open my email chain with the founder and re-read it, making notes of what I can remember from our meeting. It was before Christmas and that feels like a lifetime ago.

Another email. Another Slack message, this time from CJ, my boss.

Hi Cara. Hope everything went okay at the funeral. Can we have a catch-up call at midday?

Another email. *Paula's retirement party!* it screams.

I slam the lid of my laptop down.

Lawrence Wolfe shook my husband's hand. He spoke to my daughter. He looked at her. I feel vindicated, almost. Life was too lovely and everything was too perfect and there was no way I could get away from him for good. This was always going to happen and I knew it.

I pull the lid of my laptop up again and, remembering the conversation Daisy had with the women in the church, type in *Seabank Parade, Belfast.* I scroll through a few property listings, then go onto Google maps and plonk myself down virtually on the street. Orange-brick terraced houses stare back at me, each of them neat and tidy and small. I try to imagine a young Audrey coming out of this front door, meeting one of those women, walking to school. It is too normal, too working-class. It doesn't suit her at all.

I type in *Audrey Wolfe* and find, with a little stab of pity, that she doesn't have a Wikipedia page. Instead I find a short blog about her four or five roles, all of which seem to gloss over *her* and focus on who she was. *Tony Wolfe's wife's latest character… Lawrence's Wolfe's adoptive mother played…*

I type *Tony Wolfe* into the search bar, and immediately there are hundreds more results.

I click onto his Wikipedia page, which is long and full of details and links to further reading. On the right-hand side, under the bold heading 'Spouse', the page reads 'Audrey Wolfe (m. 1968; died 2023)'. The page has been updated already and we only buried her yesterday. There is something uncomfortable about it. Then I glance at the date again. Audrey had married him when she was only eighteen. And he would have been… My brain grapples with dates and ages for a moment and then I shake my head and give up.

I go back to the search bar one last time and type in what I was always going to type in. What was inevitable.

Lawrence Wolfe.

Immediately there are hundreds of thousands of results. Every newspaper article, every magazine story, every photoshoot. I click onto his Wikipedia for the first time in years.

Lawrence James Stewart Wolfe (b. 1974) is a Northern Irish actor, philanthropist, writer and model. After studying at The Royal Drama College, Dublin, he made his television debut as a young Terrence Barber in Troubled (1997), for which he received several award nominations. He is best known for his roles as Paul 'Macky' Mackay in the 2002 film <u>Desert Sons</u> and as Lord Lindsay Melling in the BBC period drama <u>Hardacre Abbey</u> (2010-2015). He is the only son of world-renowned Shakespearean actor <u>Tony Wolfe</u>.

Little Darlings

I glance up from the screen, though I know I am alone. I feel guilty for being on the page, and I know I'll be deleting my search history as soon as I'm finished. It feels dirty to even read his name. I scroll. I get to 'Personal life', my chest feeling tight, and I click on it.

Lawrence Wolfe was adopted at the age of 5 by Tony Wolfe and his wife.

Wolfe has described himself as an atheist and humanist. In 2020, during the COVID-19 pandemic, he volunteered at The Patterdown Hospital in Belfast and donated over £100,000 to an NHS fundraiser. Wolfe was married for two years 'as a much younger man', he revealed in an interview with Stage Weekly in 2016, but he claimed he 'hasn't found the right person to settle down with yet'. He was in a relationship with Rumour Mill actress Brooklyn Farrow from 2004 to 2009, but the couple broke up due to differences in their hectic schedules.

Wolfe divides his time between his houses in London and Nice and his parents' family home in the foothills of the Greeve Mountains, Northern Ireland.

I sit back in my chair, fingers poised on my mouse. He had been married? What did 'a much younger man' mean? How did I not know that? I click onto his filmography and scroll through dozens and dozens of TV and film appearances, then onto his awards section and the huge block dedicated to *Hardacre Abbey*, awash with green 'WON' boxes. Lawrence's whole life since around the year 2000 seems to be reported on the page, so this marriage must have happened even before I knew him. It is a strange thought. When I lived in Chaplin House, I had never had any need to consider the Wolfes' lives before. I had always thought of the Lawrence I knew as someone whose life had barely started when I met him. Ridiculous.

I think of Daisy, affronted by any mention of life before she was born. It is natural, I suppose, for children to assume they are the centre of the adult world.

He'd had a wife before I moved into Chaplin House. Why had nobody ever mentioned her?

Slack pings with a message and I ignore it. Instead, I go back to my Google search and scroll further through the results for *Lawrence Wolfe*.

Steve calls at lunch time like he said he would.

'How's work?' we ask at the same time, and we both laugh.

'Fine,' I say. 'Yours?'

'Busy enough. Been in meetings all morning. Having a salad, though.'

'Just to make your day even worse?'

'My jeans are loose on me already. Daisy's finishing at half four today.'

'I know,' I say, my brow furrowed. She always finishes at half four on a Thursday, after drama club. Why is he telling me this?

'Yes, of course you know. I'm just blethering. Are you okay?'

'Yeah, grand.'

'Okay. Well, hope this afternoon goes well. See you tonight.'

'See you tonight.'

'Love you.'

'Love you.'

I have wandered into the kitchen. I hang up the phone and put it down on the counter. The birds are loud, so I shut the kitchen window. I open the fridge, then realise. I didn't make any lunches this morning. While Steve gets up and gets himself and Daisy ready to leave, I always make lunches. I didn't do anything this morning except lift the butter out of the fridge and leave it on the side. What was I doing when I should have been making lunches? Staring into space, I think. Watching the birds. I've sent Steve to work with an empty lunch bag and sent Daisy to school with her unicorn lunch box, her water bottle empty and Tuesday's sandwich crusts still inside. My stomach churns. Mrs MacIntyre won't let her starve, she'll get lunch in

Little Darlings

the canteen and I'll pay for it tomorrow. That isn't the point though, is it?

I decide my punishment is that I won't have any lunch either, and I go back to my laptop with just a third cup of coffee.

I'm in the archives of a teen gossip magazine from 1997. Lawrence was something of a heartthrob even then, it seems: he has appeared four times already in this year and I'm only on September. Full-page technicolour photos of him with dashed lines on the side so teenagers could cut out his face and stick it on their bedroom wall. I shiver at the thought. He was modelling for a well-known clothing brand by that time, and many of the photographs I've come across show him posing with unbuttoned jackets or his thumbs hooked in the pockets of expensive jeans. He'd just had his first TV role, and there is a glint in his eyes like he knows the whole world is just waiting for him.

What was I doing in 1997? Walking to school hand-in-hand with Mum, I thought. Getting the bus into town on a Saturday morning. Having sleepovers with friends. Sleeping soundly. Thinking that dark scene in *Pinocchio* was the scariest thing imaginable. Falling in the playground and thinking my skinned knees were agony. Being nervous without being anxious. What a lovely privilege that was and I didn't even know it.

My cheekbone is tingling like a ghost has stroked my face.

I keep scrolling. Finally, in December, Lawrence is featured in a short article that somehow takes up the entire page. He is pictured next to the article looking a little blurry, walking with a blonde woman in what looks like Botanic Gardens in Belfast. He is glancing behind him at the camera with a slightly embarrassed smile that doesn't suit him.

Are we all too late?!

The ever-gorgeous Lawrence Wolfe (the real star of this year's A-MAZE-ING show TROUBLED, sorry John Hurt!) was spotted in Belfast over the weekend, all loved up with his mysterious new lady friend. Eagle-eyed readers will spot not only that Lawrence is looking as fine as ever... but that he is sporting a huge gold WEDDING RING. He has yet to comment on his marriage, but sources have claimed that his new wife is a teacher from Belfast named Bridget Spears. We assume she is now Mrs Bridget Wolfe! He's been snapped up, girls, we're too late!

Bridget Spears, I think. I let myself sit back for a moment, looking at the photograph, lost in thought. He was married, and then there was no mention of it. At least, not in front of us. Why would Audrey and Tony keep that a secret? Why wouldn't Lawrence bring it up? Then I jump forward, pushing my face close to the screen. A third person has been cut off from the photo, just their arm in view. A pink, dotty raincoat. A small palm, small fingers. A little girl, clutching Lawrence's hand.

Chapter 14 | Late August 2000 | Anniskillen

Three days after we all went to the beach, Uncle Tony surprised us by hanging a huge hammock between two trees in the garden.

'It was Lawrence's idea at the start of the summer,' he admitted, walking us down the path towards it. 'I must admit, he bought it over a month ago and I only just yesterday asked Ronnie to put it up. I'm sorry, but you should be able to enjoy it into September. It will still be warm for a while.'

'It's wonderful,' Charlotte said, and she was grinning. 'Thank you very much, Uncle Tony. Will you come and push us in it?'

He looked at his watch and clicked his tongue. 'I can't. I have to pack my bag and have some lunch before getting up the road to rehearsals. I'm sorry, little darling. Maybe Audrey will push you.'

Even I knew Audrey wouldn't be pushing us on the hammock. I had never seen her even walk on the grass in her own garden, and I didn't think she had any shoes that would be suitable.

Charlotte got in first, and I didn't want to but she gave me a look so I carefully climbed in and lay at the other side. It was warm, and the birds were calling to each other.

'Bliss,' Charlotte said with a nod. 'The girls in my class are going to be so jealous.'

'And in mine,' I said. I got the tight feeling in my stomach when I thought about going to school the following week, but I didn't want to talk about it with Charlotte again, because she kept telling me to grow up and wise up.

'Uncle Tony is so kind, isn't he?'

I agreed. I liked Uncle Tony the best out of everyone in the house because he was the most normal and even though the other two weren't necessarily mean or rude to me, I couldn't be comfortable around them. We all got on well, but I couldn't be myself any more. Even, it seemed, in front of Charlotte. But Tony was kind and bought us things and was always smiley, so I tried to be grateful for that. Lawrence was kind and generous and smiley too, but it felt different from him, like there was a price to be paid for his kindness, but I couldn't explain it because I had never paid him anything.

'I'll miss him,' Charlotte added. 'It'll be quiet without them.'

Uncle Tony was starting rehearsals for his latest play in Belfast that week. They'd been rehearsing on and off all summer, but the real play was opening up in a few Fridays and then they would be performing until Christmas, so it was time to 'knuckle down'. We had tickets for the opening night, and Charlotte and Audrey seemed excited. I had never been to a play before, and I hoped it was better than all the films they kept making us watch (though I had now seen *Grease,* which was a real film with good music and a story I understood, and it was my new favourite film ever).

Lawrence too was travelling for work, but I kept forgetting the name of the place he was going to and had to be told twice a day. He said (and everyone seemed to agree with him) that it was going to be the number one tourist destination in a few years, and apparently it was very rich and hot and sunny and desert-y. I'd thought the Wolfes were very rich, and that summer had been hot and sunny enough, so I didn't understand all the fuss. He was excited though, and as much as I agreed it would be quiet without the men, I didn't think I would miss Lawrence. It was an American film and he would be doing an American accent, but the place they were filming wasn't even in America, and that made my head hurt when I thought about it so I tried not to.

Little Darlings

A few nights before, watching *Grease* on the sofa, he had put his arm around me in front of everyone. I sat completely still and tried to focus on the film, and the songs were so good I ended up relaxing into him and we sat like that for the last hour of it. Nobody had said anything and I wasn't sure why, but I thought it would be nice to watch films and not be worried about being touched. They were a touchy family. I didn't like it.

'Mm,' I said to Charlotte.

'Will you get me my sunglasses? They're just in the kitchen.'

'Why can't you get them?'

'Awk please, Cara. I do stuff for you all the time.'

'Do you?' I asked, genuinely confused.

'What are you two bickering about now?'

It was Ronnie, emerging from the depths of the garden with a wee shovel in one hand and his plastic headphones in the other. Sweat was making his face shiny and he had some mud on his wrists, but he looked happy, and I could hear someone singing through the headphones, sounding like they were far away.

'Nothing,' Charlotte said, and she turned her body to face away from him. Lawrence's dislike of Ronnie was one of the things that she had adopted as her own, but I knew for a fact Ronnie had never done anything bad to her. It meant I made a special effort to be kind to him, because I didn't want him to think I was nasty like she was.

'How are the pak chois?' I asked, hoping I sounded intelligent. I'd learned from Ronnie all of the different vegetables that grew in their various locations across the property, and saying 'pak choi' was one of my favourite things.

'Doing rightly!' he said. He held up a little basket that he was carrying. 'I imagine there'll be a stir-fry for you all tonight.'

'Not us all,' Charlotte said. 'Laurie and Uncle Tony are leaving today.'

'Tony will be back late tonight,' I reminded her, but she sighed and flopped onto her back. 'Will you give us a push on the hammock?' I added to Ronnie, because I knew it would cheer Charlotte up. He grinned and set down his basket and came towards us.

Just then, the door of the house flew open and Auntie Audrey came running towards us. My first thought was that Uncle Tony had had a heart attack and my second was that Lawrence had fallen down the stairs, but in the few seconds it took for her to cross the patio and rush down the steps, I had decided that really she could have just dropped her favourite face cream and her reaction would be the same, so there was no point in panicking just yet.

'Girls! GIRLS? GIRLS! You'll never guess what!'

Charlotte sat up straight, squinting at her. 'Auntie Audrey, what's happened?'

'I got it!' she screamed.

Charlotte seemed to know what this meant, but I didn't, and Ronnie clearly didn't either, because while Charlotte struggled to get herself out of the hammock, Ronnie and I looked at each other like we were trying to do the numbers round on *Countdown*.

Charlotte eventually got out of the hammock and ran to Audrey, and the two of them hugged so tightly and with so much feeling that I felt sad again, like I had at the beach when I knew everyone thought they must be mum and daughter.

'How?' Charlotte said, her eyes round in delight and wonder. 'How on earth? I thought you said they went with Pippa—'

'Little darling, it's the most remarkable thing!' Audrey's run across the grass had worn her out, she sounded breathless. I wondered if she'd ever set foot out here before, and I knew she'd be annoyed later when she walked grass all through the living room. 'It's fate, it's meant to be! I knew it, I knew this would happen. I'm so happy I could burst, and I just had to come and tell you first. I'm just off the phone with my agent, I start on MONDAY!'

'On MONDAY!' Charlotte gasped, both hands over her face like she was afraid her nose was going to fall off. 'This is amazing! But what happened?'

Little Darlings

'She broke her leg!' Audrey's eyes were popping, but her face was the same as it always was. I wondered if I'd heard her wrong, because breaking a leg was a bad thing, but then she added, 'Fell off a horse or something, I don't know. But they want ME! Isn't it wonderful?'

Charlotte seemed not to know what to say, but it didn't matter because Audrey had turned on her heel and was jogging back to the house screaming, 'Tony! Tony! Laurie!'

We heard the door open and close and then the sounds of her screaming for the others became more distant.

Finally, Ronnie said, 'Well. That was something. I better go in and nab Tony before he goes, in that case, girls. Need my cheque. This is my last shift!'

'What?' I asked. 'Why? Where are you going?'

Ronnie shrugged and picked up his basket again. 'They only got me in for the summer, so I've said I'll go and help a mate with his pallet business.'

I didn't know what this was, but I tried to look intelligent by nodding.

'So… we won't see you again?' Charlotte asked.

'Until next summer. Hopefully!'

'Oh.' She sniffed and shrugged. 'Well, bye.'

'Bye,' I said, feeling blue.

'Good luck with the Wolfes,' he said, and he looked at me meaningfully. 'Don't take any of their…' he trailed off, then said, 'Nonsense.'

I wasn't sure how we could avoid taking their nonsense.

Nonsense was all they seemed to give.

As it turned out, we needn't have said goodbye to Ronnie. As he was getting his last wages, Tony realised that with Lawrence in the desert, him in Belfast six nights a week, and Audrey filming for her new romantic film Monday to Friday down South, there would be nobody to look after us. So the adults came up with some sort of deal, and instead of leaving to help out his pallet friend, Ronnie was tasked with bringing us to and from school, cooking dinner for us, and just generally taking care of us until somebody else got home.

'Like a nanny!' Auntie Audrey assured us. 'It's quite retro, really. We had a nanny when Laurie was a boy and it just makes good sense. And Ronnie's a harmless old thing.'

I couldn't help but wonder what Lawrence would have to say about it all when he got back at Halloween, but that was two whole months away and I would worry about it then.

We fell into a new routine that smelled like black patent shoes and slurry from the fields that surrounded Chaplin House. Tony organised for a wee car for Ronnie, so every morning at half eight we would hear him beeping outside and we'd grab our school bags and run out the door. Sometimes Tony would call a hello and goodbye from his bedroom, but usually he was still asleep as he didn't get back from the Grand Opera House until long after we'd gone to bed.

Charlotte insisted she had to get out of the car around the corner before we got to the school, and even though he sighed and rolled his eyes, Ronnie stopped so she could get out and jog along ahead of us. I thought she was embarrassed by the old and whiny car, and then I thought maybe she was embarrassed by Ronnie, and didn't want people to think he was our dad, and then I realised with a feeling like being punched in the stomach that she was probably embarrassed by me. I knew that Ronnie must know it too, because he was extra nice to me on our last three or four minutes to school and even let me pick what CD we put in, and he always told me to have a good day, and he was always on time to pick us up afterwards.

I was waiting in the car with Ronnie after school one Friday at the end of September, both of us peering out through the heavy rain for any sign of Charlotte.

'You're sure she didn't have an extra-curricular?' Ronnie asked me for the third time. I still didn't know what an extra-curricular was but I shook my head for a third time.

'Unless the new drama club started today,' I added. 'That might be it.'

Ronnie groaned. 'Yes, okay. She did tell us that, didn't she?'

'She didn't tell me,' I said, hurt that Ronnie knew something about my sister that I didn't.

'Aye, I think that's today. Flip sake, I blanked. We may just wait on her. Did you not fancy it?'

'Didn't fancy it,' I said, shrugging like I didn't care.

It was true that I hadn't wanted to join any clubs, but if I'd known Charlotte was going I might have given it a go. The girls at Holy Trinity Primary were nice enough to me. In fact, they'd been lovely for the first week, elbowing each other out of the way to sit beside me at lunchtime and asking what Laurie Wolfe was like in real life because he was *boyfriend material* and they could all look into his eyes *for hours*. I had mostly just let them talk, nodding in agreement and saying, 'Yeah, he's really nice,' when I had to, but apparently I wasn't giving them quite enough, because they left me alone eventually and went into the P7 playground to talk to Charlotte at break and lunchtimes instead. She was much better at telling stories about Laurie, and even though she would roll her eyes at her new friends in P7, I knew she was delighted to swing her blazer over her arm and strut around the playground with a line of younger girls following her, hanging off her every word.

With Laurie in a different country, I could finally relax and not feel so tense all the time, but at the same time I missed him and I felt a bit ashamed for missing him. It was very complicated and mature and I wanted Julie to ask me about him so I could say that, but she never did. We'd started to see her once a fortnight by then, because Louise had agreed that was enough and the drive was a bit much.

We had started doing practice papers for the eleven-plus test, and even had to take some home with us, so I pulled one out and put it on my lap and stared at it, hoping I could just absorb the knowledge with my eyes.

'I passed mine,' Ronnie said, looking over at it. 'Probably wouldn't pass it now if I tried, though.'

'I won't pass it,' I said. 'I'm a bit thick.'

Ronnie laughed. 'Who told you that? You're definitely not thick, I can tell.'

I didn't say anything, but continued staring at the page in front of me.

'The famous *Laurie* didn't pass his.'

I looked up at him and he laughed again.

'We were at Holy Trinity together,' Ronnie said. 'I think they wanted him to have as normal a childhood as he could.'

'And he didn't pass?' I said.

'Nope. He got a D. I got a B2. You'll not, though. You'll get an A. That's my prediction for next year. Oh, and!' He leaned across me and opened the glove compartment and took out a cassette tape in a hard plastic case. 'I found this in a wee charity shop in town. A couple of scratches on the case but it should sound fine. I think you'll like it.'

There was a picture of a girl with short pigtails on the front, looking right at me.

'What is it?' I asked.

'It's that singer you like with the "Girlfriend" song. There's a few tunes on there. Here, we'll listen.'

Ronnie took the cassette back, fiddled with taking one out of the car tape player and putting the pigtailed girl in. Then the car filled with music and he turned it up, starting to dance with his head. I giggled and joined in. It was the kind of music you'd want to dance to, upbeat and happy with the girl singing the way I used to sing in the bath sometimes. It sounded like she was with her friends and I wondered what it would be like to have a big group of friends.

We sat listening to the cassette for a few minutes, Ronnie drumming his fingers on the steering wheel and nodding in time to the music. There were leaves trapped under the wipers of the car and I occupied myself with both dancing along with the music and memorising their colours so I could paint them later.

'What was he like at school?' I asked as the third song ended.

'Laurie?'

'Mm.'

Ronnie turned the knob and the volume went way down. 'Do you want the honest answer or do you want me to tell you what you want to hear?'

I frowned, considering that. What did I want to hear? I had no idea. How could Ronnie know? Luckily, he didn't make me answer.

'The honest answer, Cara, is he was a dickhead. I'm sorry to swear in front of you, but that's the truth. He was horrible. A bully.'

'How come you work for him now then?'

'I don't,' Ronnie said. 'I work for Tony. Tony's okay. I'd never work for Wolfe Junior. Not in a million years.'

I tried to imagine the two of them as boys in my class, wearing their tracksuit bottoms and yellow polo shirts, but I couldn't. Laurie had always been an adult to me, and though I had of course seen dozens of photos of him as a child all over Chaplin House, I could never animate them. Child Laurie lived in pictures, but to me he wasn't real. Ronnie too, with his long nose and big tanned hands and the popped bubble-wrap marks on his jaw, he was never a child to me either.

'How was Laurie a bully?' I asked. I turned in the passenger seat so I was lying on my side, facing Ronnie, and I drew my legs up to my chest. He never shouted at me for getting my feet on the seats. He never told me off for anything.

'He thought he was better than everyone else,' Ronnie said. 'Well. I suppose he was. He had more money. He had the big house. But he wasn't nicer or smarter or funnier. He'd pick on the really poor country kids, laugh at their hand-me-down uniforms and all. Poke fun if someone had Tesco Value pens instead of good ones. Stupid stuff, but it sticks.'

'Was he good at drama?'

'Yes. He's always been good at pretending.'

We sat for a while longer, Ronnie looking out the window and me looking at Ronnie and thinking about this. The singer was still carrying on, but it didn't sound as good with the volume so low.

'I'm sorry for slagging him off,' he said finally, and he turned to grin at me. He shook his head. 'He brings out the worst in me. I'm not normally a slabber.'

'What's a slabber?' I wrinkled my nose.

'Someone that… slabbers. Slags people off. Talks about other people. It's not a nice trait, I'm sorry. I know you like him and I can see why.'

I thought about this too.

Yes, I did like Laurie. Laurie listened to me and he was my friend. And I was very lucky that such a handsome, famous, nice person wanted to even glance at me. Lots of people would love to switch places with me. But I thought sometimes maybe I would like to switch places with them.

'I don't always like him,' I said, and I felt my heart beat faster because it was thrilling to tell the truth and it felt a bit dangerous and I both wanted the conversation to be over and I wanted Ronnie to ask me why.

'Why?' Ronnie asked.

I opened my mouth to respond just as the door to the gym opened and a hoard of students came flying out. Charlotte and three other girls came out, all arm-in-arm, laughing and chatting in their new drama club T-shirts.

I sighed and opened the passenger-side door.

'Where are you going?' Ronnie asked.

'In the back,' I said.

'You sit in the front for once, she doesn't have to get everything.'

Little Darlings

I didn't reply, but went around and got into the back seat, knowing it was hardly worth falling out with Charlotte over a seat, and feeling strange that, in reality, she didn't get everything. She hadn't got Lawrence, I thought, as I strapped myself in. I wasn't sure if I wished she had or not.

Chapter 15 | January 2023 | Dromary, County Down

I am outside the school at half four on the dot, waiting patiently for Daisy. I achieved absolutely nothing today, work-wise, but did eventually speak to CJ and ask for a bit more time off. I told him I was taking Audrey's death really hard, and it felt sick to use her like that, but I reassured myself with the idea that she definitely wouldn't mind. It was like something she would have done herself. CJ agreed, and I'm taking another week off. I think I need it.

The fire exit door of the PE hall opens and a tiny blur of a girl, all dressed in black, rushes towards her mum's waiting car. I hoke out my phone, knowing for a fact Daisy will talk and talk and talk to her friends and be the very last one out, as usual.

I open the message Charlotte sent me this morning.

It's me, save this. How come you rushed off yesterday?? Xxx

I type a reply. *Just had to get back. Did you know LW was married??*

I hit send before I can think about it too much, and put my phone deep in the pocket of my big coat, vowing not to look at it until I'm home, even if it vibrates with her response. I am always making deals and bets with myself. If I don't have anything to eat between lunch and dinner, I can have dessert tonight. If I stick some cardio on YouTube on Saturday morning, we can add a sharing bar of Galaxy to the Sainsbury's shop. Once, years ago, it was, if I don't Google Lawrence Wolfe for a whole week, we can go to The Funky Duck for our anniversary and share a bottle of champagne. And I did it. And then I did another week. And then another.

Little Darlings

The only deal I know never to make with myself is in regard to thinking about Lawrence. With the best will in the world I couldn't ever stop, and I know that. I want to stop more than I want anything else, but it's impossible. It's been especially hard the last few days.

I glance at the door to the PE hall. Two boys race each other out of the gate of the playground and towards the main road and I wince, wondering where their parents are. Around me, cars pull out into the darkening evening, and I imagine the happy chatter from inside them, the 'What's for tea?s' and the 'How was school?s'. I watch as a boy from Daisy's class opens the door of the car in front of me and swings his school bag in. He sees me watching and grins, showing me the gaps where his two canine teeth have come out, and I laugh and wave. When I look back, there is a small, squat man standing at the door to the PE hall, his hands in his pockets, talking to a girl with plaits—

I fling my door open without looking and hear someone driving past braking hard and slamming on the horn. I ignore them and fly out of the car, into the playground and towards the door. By the time I reach Daisy, the man has gone inside.

'Who was that?' I demand.

Daisy's mouth falls open in surprise. 'He—I don't know—'

'Daisy, I've *told* you a million times—' I am hissing, my blood pumping in my ears, throbbing at my temples, and I force my mouth shut. I grip her arm and steer her towards the car.

'Mum, that *hurts*!' she exclaims. One or two parents look towards us, and normally I would care, but I don't. 'It bloody hurts!'

I let go and look at her. Charlotte's word and Charlotte's exact tone of voice and Charlotte's expression on her face, the former brand new, a gift from their chat at the funeral. But she's not Charlotte. She's nothing like her and this is nothing like that.

'Sorry,' I say on an out breath. 'Come to the car. Good girl. I'm sorry.'

She gets into the passenger seat, even though she's not really supposed to, even though Steve usually insists on the 'pre-teen car seat' as he has christened it. In our day, I remember telling him once, we barely bothered with seat belts. 'It's the law, Cara,' he'd said, holding his hands out, 'doesn't matter if we don't agree with it.'

It's the law.

I get in and switch the car back on and turn the heating on, but I don't drive.

'Sorry for snapping,' I say after a moment.

'That's okay,' she says immediately, and my heart fills because she's just so good. How did she get to be so good? I must have done something right. Or maybe she's just Steve all over.

She's wary though, and I can feel her looking at the side of my face.

'You're... stressed?' she asks after a moment. 'Anxious?'

I didn't know the word anxious when I was nine. They teach them all sorts at school these days. They have people come in to talk about mental health struggles, they do a bake sale every year to raise money for a charity on World Mental Health Day. A man in Steve's work has a son who suffers with depression, and the kid is twelve.

'How can they be depressed when they're twelve?' Steve had asked me, genuinely baffled. 'How does he know the word? What does he have to be depressed about?'

Steve wasn't being unkind; he was just confused. Despite his gentle nature, his polite demeanour, he always stiffens a little if Daisy ever talks too much about big feelings. Luckily for us, hers are only ever positive. She was *elated* by her birthday present, she was *delighted* it was such a bright day, she was *perfectly content, thank you* with beans on toast for dinner. But sometimes she will tell us that Mrs MacIntyre *seemed to be struggling today*, and she will nod wisely and say *perhaps she's having a bad mental health day* and Steve will look at me, wanting me to roll my eyes with him, wanting me to agree that our nine-year-old shouldn't be talking about bad mental health days. She shouldn't be aware they exist. She should think that adults have it all together and can fix anything and are unbreakable.

'It puts ideas in their heads,' Steve said to me once. 'It makes them think they're depressed when they're just a bit sad and need to go outside for half an hour. Bad mental health days just weren't a thing when we were kids. Especially not *for* kids.'

I can nod along with most of what he says usually, choosing not to feel strongly about it either way, but there is something reassuring in knowing that someone is teaching Daisy about things I don't feel I can talk about, and things that Steve doesn't really have the vocabulary to talk to her about.

And then she goes psychologist on me and analyses me like this and I wonder if she has ever said to her friends in the canteen, 'My mum is having a bad mental health day,' and I feel ashamed because maybe Steve is right, maybe she should think I'm unbreakable.

But maybe not.

'I just didn't know who he was,' I say to Daisy now. 'That man. So, I panicked.'

'He was looking for Dean,' she says. 'That must be his granda or his dad.'

Nothing more sinister than that, I think. Just a man looking for his son. Asking a child who has just come out of rehearsals if she has seen his son. He probably recognised Daisy from his son's class. That is it.

'Why did it make you panic?' she asks.

The cars around us have all gone. We're the only ones left. I should smile and shrug and put the car into gear and ask her how she got on today, and if she has much homework. I should let myself fall into the warmth of innocence.

And yet.

I think of the photograph of Lawrence, taken nearly thirty years ago now. The girl in the pink raincoat in the picture, whoever she was, who would be a little older than me now, maybe. I have been assuming she must be the daughter of Lawrence's wife. She couldn't be *his* daughter, there was no way Audrey and Tony would ever keep that a secret. Where is she now? I have wondered all day, and what happened to her when she reached out and took the hand of a handsome, smiling actor, because nobody had ever told her to be cautious?

'Because I don't like you talking to strangers,' I say to Daisy finally. 'It makes me worried.'

'I know,' Daisy says.

'Especially men,' I add.

She frowns at this. 'Why?'

'Because...' I look out at the empty carpark. Rain has started to fall, fat droplets tinkling on the windscreen. I watch one drop until it slides down towards the wipers and out of sight. 'Because they can be very dangerous.'

'Men?' Daisy asks, and her confusion is genuine. How lovely to know and trust a man so completely wonderful as your dad that the idea of their sex being dangerous is a cause for confusion.

'Yes.' I think for a moment about saying that women can be dangerous too, and that she shouldn't trust any stranger, but that feels like a lot to get through, and too vague, and there's only one thing I really want her to know.

'You just need to be on your guard,' I say. 'You don't have to be polite to every man who speaks to you.'

'What?' Daisy is again baffled. Politeness is something that has been drilled into her since she could talk. Maybe she is too young, maybe it is too hard to explain.

'You don't owe them anything,' I say. I shake my head, because it's not quite what I want to tell her, it's only scratching the surface. 'It's hard to explain, but I just want you to know that you don't have to do anything that anyone asks you to.'

'What about Mrs MacIntyre?'

'Daisy—' I almost snap but I stop myself. I look at her, her two plaits almost totally undone, pink hair ties slipped down and curls escaping any way they can. Her pink cheeks and the freckles on her nose and the blue eyes and the long lashes that all belong to a baby, to my baby, but there is concern in her face and her mouth is serious. I know she is trying to understand. And she does need to understand. How much do I wish someone had had this conversation with me?

'When I was younger,' I say slowly, my voice wavering. 'A man hurt me very badly. A man that I trusted and… loved. And I let him do it because I didn't know any better and I was all on my own and I…' The words catch in my throat and I realise that not only have I never said them out loud before, but I've never even thought them. I'm on a roll so I keep going. 'And I wanted him to like me. I wanted him to love me. I would have done anything, anything at all for him. But I was wrong. I didn't have anyone to tell me what I'm telling you. That not everyone is like your dad. Some men are…' I trail off, not quite wanting to use the word 'monsters', but unable to think of anything better.

'Bad?' Daisy asks.

'Yes.'

She waits for a second, processing what I've said, and my heart pounds with a feeling like guilt. Is it selfish to want your daughter to be afraid, or is it sensible?

'Who was it?' she asks finally. 'Who was the bad man?'

I take a deep breath. 'It was the man you met at the funeral. Lawrence.'

'Great-Great Uncle Tony's son?'

'Yes.'

Daisy frowns. 'Auntie Charlotte's friend?'

I feel my fists trying to clench and I stop in case she sees me. 'Yes.'

'But why would she be his friend then, Mummy?'

'She didn't know,' I say, and the guilty feeling in my stomach intensifies, because I've tried to be honest with Daisy, but this part

I'm just not sure of. I think and I hope and I want so desperately to believe that it is true, that she didn't know… But I just can't swear to it.

They did exist when we were kids, I imagine myself saying to Steve as we drive away from the school. Bad mental health days did exist, we just didn't have the words for them. Just because you don't understand something, just because you can't name it, that doesn't mean it isn't real. My hands grip the steering wheel hard and it's ridiculous, because he's not even here, because he hasn't said a word, but I am so angry with Steve. Or maybe it's just with what he represents, and that's not fair either. They did exist, I imagine myself saying, and it's scary when the adult world sweeps you up and holds you tight and you have to live in it and you don't even know the words for what is happening.

Chapter 16 | October 2000 | Chaplin House Halloween Party

The Wolfes threw a Halloween party and invited all their friends, and there was a rule that everyone – absolutely everyone, even Old Mrs Miller who owned The Wee Shop where we sometimes got sweets – had to dress up. Charlotte was delighted by this, obviously, and she decided she was going to be a cat, and Audrey took her shopping in Belfast to get a costume and I stayed behind and pretended to have a headache because they were so excited and I missed feeling excited and happy about things and Charlotte barely spoke to me any more and I knew I would be bored. Apart from my chats with Ronnie before and after school, it felt like I never saw or talked to anyone at all, and that made me miss Laurie more than ever and I was counting down the days until he was back home.

Uncle Tony had gone into the village to meet his friend for lunch, so for the whole morning that Audrey and Charlotte were in Belfast I felt as if I was the only person in the world and Chaplin House was *my* house. I made breakfast and even put my bowl and spoon in the dishwasher, which made me feel very adult. Then I stood on the patio for an hour looking out into the garden and shivering, sort of because Auntie Audrey had drilled into us that getting sunlight in the mornings was important, even when it was cold, and sort of because it felt like a very adult thing to do, and I was lonely and wanted to hear the birds.

I thought about Mum and about how different life had been the year before. How she'd taken us to Only a Pound and we'd both chosen to be witches and we were delighted with our matching outfits, and Mum took a photo with her orange Kodak camera and said we looked like twins. Where were those photos now? I didn't remember ever seeing them. That was the same camera that had the Christmas pictures too. Maybe Louise would know, I thought. Maybe I could phone her. Maybe I could also tell her that our new therapist was nowhere near as nice as Julie.

Uncle Tony had found a man in the village who spoke to us every other week about our feelings, so there was no need to go and see Julie any more. Although I was happy that it only took ten minutes in the car and not seventy, I was annoyed that Uncle Tony had only booked one session, so Charlotte and I had to go in together and sit side by side on the fat leather sofa that stuck to my legs and squeaked if I moved. I couldn't really talk or be honest with Bernie (that was his name – I had laughed and thought it was a joke in the first session because I'd thought that was a woman's name but apparently it isn't) with Charlotte sitting right there beside me, so I mostly just let her speak and I nodded and said, 'Yeah'. Bernie and his office smelled like chips which made me hungry some weeks and feel sick the next.

During our sessions with him I usually pretended I was speaking to Julie about my *real* feelings, and sometimes Bernie would say, 'Cara, did you have something to add?' and I would realise I had been mouthing words to myself and I'd have to shake my head. I didn't like him, but he wasn't unkind so I didn't say anything as I didn't want to hurt his feelings.

I went back inside and walked slowly through the house, wondering if I would grow up and get married and have a house like Chaplin House. I wasn't sure I would want one; it was a bit too big. Even if I had a husband and a child, there was so much empty space. What was the point in having a big room full of nothing? My footsteps echoed into the hall and I stood and listened for a moment. Birds outside. That was the only sound. No wind, nobody talking on the phone, no film on a projector screen. Just me and the silence and the birds. I liked to hear them, but it made me feel like I was the only person alive.

I went back up to my room feeling strange, like I was in a film myself and the camera was following me. I wondered what Film Cara would do. I closed the door after myself even though I normally wouldn't, and I sat down on my bed and gave a big sigh, because they did that a lot in films too. Film Cara looked around at the clothes and books and toys everywhere and Normal Cara decided that her room wouldn't look so good on the screen. So one of us gave another sigh and made a start on hanging up jumpers in the wardrobe, putting socks and pants in the washing basket, and stacking up her books in a neat pile.

I crouched to pick up my Baby Born, still unplayed-with since we'd moved – *it's for babies, Cara, just throw it in the bin* – and thought hard. I certainly couldn't throw her away. But I did feel a little bit older now, and I couldn't imagine a time when I'd want to play with her again, so I crawled to the wardrobe and went to put her inside. Then I noticed a little door behind the wardrobe. I frowned and slid myself across the floor to inspect it further. It was built into the wall and had been painted the same colour, but there was definitely the outline of a tiny door with a little knob on the front. Bigger than it would need to be for Borrowers, but not quite big enough for Hobbits, I decided.

The wardrobe was old and made of a heavy dark wood that made it really hard to shift by myself, but once I took some more of my clothes out, I was able to push my feet against it and move it just far enough that I could open the little wall door.

Film Cara was expecting there to be something magical inside. Maybe not quite Narnia, but a map to a treasure buried in Chaplin House would have been good enough for me.

Normal Cara was disappointed by the empty, dead space inside. It seemed like it had been a built-in cupboard at one point, but had been forgotten about. I stuck my head in and looked left, then right. The storage ran all the way along the room, and I waited to see if a monster would jump out at me – that would have been okay, actually, because then at least I'd have found something worth putting in a film – but it didn't. I looked at Baby Born and then mumbled, 'Sorry,' and shoved her into the space. Then I closed the door and moved the wardrobe back as best I could.

My room looked slightly less terrible when I finished, but it did still look like it belonged to someone who was just staying for a few days, and not like it belonged to someone who had lived there for four months. Everything that didn't fit in the wardrobe was just sitting on the floor in piles like it was waiting to be packed again. Maybe that was a good thing, I thought. Maybe it meant that the second Mum was better, we wouldn't waste any time and could be out the door in ten minutes and on our way back to her. I felt better with this thought and picked up the little pile of clothes I'd decided to give to Charlotte. A peace offering was what Ronnie always called it when he was trying to make us stop bickering and be nice to each other. Or rather, when he was trying to make Charlotte stop bickering with me and be nice to me.

I'd chosen my black-and-white stripy jumper, a pair of pyjamas, a scarf and a hat to give to her, the former because it didn't fit me any more and the others because I knew she liked them. I liked them too but I liked my sister more and I would rather have her. Nothing had happened between us, nothing specific that I could point to, but we were very different now and I missed her.

I went through the bathroom and into Charlotte's room and set the pile down on her bed. I looked around. Her room looked lived-in in a way mine didn't. She had tacked up a poster of the man from *Titanic* opposite her bed, and there was a framed black-and-white picture behind her headboard that said ALFRED HITCHCOCK under it and showed a weird old man. The name was familiar but I didn't know who he was, and I felt sure that this was something Audrey had given her. It made me feel sad, but I wasn't surprised. Audrey liked Charlotte heaps more than she liked me. Charlotte was more fun and they liked all the same things, and she treated Charlotte like they were friends and me like I was a child. Charlotte's *Edward Scissorhands* poster was the only thing I recognised from home, and that reassured me.

I was just about to leave when I noticed a clear plastic folder poking out from under Charlotte's bed. I used my foot to push it back in, imagining Charlotte coming in with hundreds of bags of clothes from Belfast and slipping on it and banging her head on the wall, but then I hesitated. I listened to the house for a moment – still just silence and birds – and then lifted the folder and opened it.

It wasn't schoolwork, like I'd thought. They were pages cut from magazines. Glossy and clean, some of them articles with far too many words in them, and some of them photographs. I looked at the photographs. Most of them were of Lawrence, posed close-up pictures that you were supposed to cut out and use as posters, and some of them were of TV and film casts, but they all had Lawrence in them. I wondered why she hadn't put those up on her wall. Audrey wouldn't care about Blu Tack when it came to pictures of Lawrence. She'd probably let Charlotte draw with permanent marker over all the walls as long as it was a picture of Lawrence she was drawing.

The door downstairs opened and I quickly stuffed the pictures back inside and slid the folder back under the bed again. I rushed back into my room and closed my door, then listened again.

'Helloooooo?' came a call from downstairs. 'Anyone here?'

My breath caught and I sprang towards the door. Ignoring The Big Window, I raced down both flights of stairs and skidded in my socks across the hallway downstairs, my heart racing but full.

'Laurie!' I shouted, and the man himself came running from the kitchen, his arms wide open and his smile taking up his entire face. We hugged and he spun us around and around until I was crying with laughter and relief and something else. He smelled like mint.

'I'll make us both sick,' he said, and he set me down and leaned back as if to see me better. There was a piece of chewing gum on his tongue when he grinned at me. 'What a lovely way to be welcomed home. How have you been, Cara? Have you missed me?'

'Yes,' I said. 'So much. Charlotte's barely talking to me and I don't know why, and the girls in my class don't like me and they think I'm weird and they only want to know about you but I don't know what to tell them and Audrey has been so busy at work and Tony is always tired and—'

Lawrence laughed and put his arm around my shoulders and led us into the kitchen. I was still talking, but I could barely understand myself. He was here and he was real, and he was delighted to see me. That was all that mattered.

'Wow, wow, wow. Slow down, little darling. There will be plenty of time for a proper catch up. I'm going to make a cup of tea, would you like one? Or maybe you'd prefer a hot chocolate?'

I nodded, not caring what I was agreeing to.

'How was the desert?' I asked.

'Dubai? Hot. It got up to fifty degrees on set most days.'

'Fifty?!'

'Fifty. Talk about sweaty weather. Where is everyone?'

I leant against the counter while he busied himself with mugs and the kettle. He was wearing a tight jumper and dark jeans and posh shiny shoes, and his face looked more tanned than before, but I was reassured by his big smile and the way he kept looking over at me while he made our drinks.

'Uncle Tony has gone to meet a friend for lunch,' I said. 'And Charlotte and Auntie Audrey have gone to Belfast to pick out—'

'Costumes for the Halloween party?' Lawrence asked. He sighed. 'Yes. I've heard all about it. They do this every year, it's a terrible bore, honestly. Didn't you want to go with them?'

'Didn't feel well,' I said, remembering at the last second my lie. 'Didn't fancy it.'

Little Darlings

'I don't blame you. Belfast over half term is no joke. Here you go, little darling.'

He passed me a mug and we walked carefully to the living room and sat down side by side.

He stretched out his long legs and kicked off the posh shoes, showing his bright purple socks underneath. I giggled and showed him my feet.

'We match,' I said, wiggling my purple-socked toes.

'So we do!' He reached over with his free hand and squeezed my big toe. 'Meant to be. God, it's good to be home, and to see you. I'm so glad to be finished filming for a while. It's very full-on.'

'So, you're home for a good while?' I asked, wanting to be clear.

'Until at least Christmas,' he said, and he grinned at me. 'Then I'll be away in January, and then all yours again from February. How does that sound?'

It sounded perfect and I told him so. I blew on my hot chocolate, then took a sip. Lawrence did the same with his tea.

'It's so quiet,' he commented, looking around the living room. 'Bit eerie.'

'I know,' I said. 'It was just me and the birds earlier.'

'The birds?'

'Yeah. Singing. It was lovely, they sound so sweet.'

Lawrence chuckled. 'They do sound sweet, don't they? Do you know what's funny, though?'

'What?'

'We hear beautiful songs, but in reality they're probably screaming at one another to clear off.'

'Really?'

'Yeah! They *sound* lovely, but the meaning behind their squawks is quite different. They're saying, "No, this is my tree, bugger off and build your nest elsewhere, you big stupid bird!" Either that or they're trying to mate, ha!'

I laughed obediently, and he seemed pleased.

We chatted for an hour about his trip to the desert. Or rather, Laurie talked about his trip to the desert, and told me stories that were either funny or quite serious, about the experience of *a budding actor in a foreign country, competing with some big names,* and I laughed when I was supposed to and nodded seriously when I was supposed to do that. It was easy, and I fell back into the flow we had had before he left.

'What about you? Have you done much painting?' he asked.

'Some,' I said, which was only partly true. I'd done a few paintings and then thrown them in the bin because they were terrible. 'I've basically ruined my paints, though. The colours are all squashed together.'

'That's a shame,' Laurie said, and I felt a bit guilty that I'd been hoping he would offer to buy me some new ones.

He stretched himself out in his seat and put his arms behind his head. 'It's so nice to be here with just you, you know.'

The guilt disappeared and was replaced with a bubble of happiness. 'I know,' I said. 'Welcome home.'

'It will always be like this, just you and me, when we get married.'

The bubble was still there, and it remained there as he quickly launched into another story about losing his character's glasses on set and having to tear his dressing room apart trying to find them, only to glance in the mirror and see they were on his head. It was there, but it shrunk just a little bit to make room for another bubble, this one less uplifting and more sickening, in the pit of my stomach. Small, unsure. Hesitating.

Maybe I had misheard him, I thought. Married? Had he definitely said that?

I wondered if I should ask him.

I didn't. I let myself relax into the sofa and listen to Laurie talk. My friend was back and I was happy.

I didn't want to spoil it.

*

Little Darlings

Audrey screamed so loudly when she saw Lawrence that I actually thought my ear drum might have burst. She threw herself at him and kissed his face, and he laughed and let her do it, and then he hugged Charlotte, who was blushing but seemed delighted that he was home. There was a lot of guffawing (Lawrence), breathless agreement (Audrey), and polite nodding (me and Charlotte) before it was agreed we would all meet downstairs in two hours to put the Halloween decorations up before the guests arrived.

I took half of the bags that Charlotte pointed to and we went up the stairs, trying not to fall with the weight of the bags.

'Did you have a nice time?' I asked. 'You got a lot of clothes.'

'Audrey is soooo kind!' Charlotte bounced on ahead of me towards the attic. 'She bought me pretty much anything I liked. And we went and had mocktails in this amazing little bar overlooking City Hall. It was, like, dreamy.'

'Like, dreamy,' I echoed under my breath. We went into Charlotte's room and I happily dumped the bags on her bed.

'Got you a kiddie costume,' she said. She threw her hand towards one of the bags. 'In there, somewhere. I think it's a witch or a zombie or a ghost or something.'

'Thank you,' I said automatically. I thought of what Lawrence had said and added, 'Their Halloween parties are a terrible bore.'

'You've never been to one,' Charlotte said. 'How would you know?'

She had a fair point, so I let it go. 'I left you some of my clothes,' I said. 'They're on your pillow. The pink scarf you like.'

'Oh, thanks, but I got a new scarf today. It's from Miss Selfridge. It was expensive.'

'Right.'

I thought of the folder of photographs hidden under Charlotte's bed and wanted to ask about them, but I didn't want to admit that I'd been snooping. I was considering dropping something on the floor so I could pretend to find the folder for the first time, but then Charlotte said, 'I'm not being rude, but can you go away, please? I want to get ready for the party and I don't want you watching me.'

It turned out that the costume Charlotte and Audrey had bought for me was a pumpkin, complete with black tights and a small orange hat, with a huge orange ball that sat around my middle. Charlotte laughed her head off but stopped when she saw I looked upset, and she told me I was cute and adorable and everyone would love it, and I forgave her for everything and was happy she was being nice to me again.

She was a cat, but I'd never seen any cat like her. She was wearing a pair of those shiny black trousers like Sandy at the end of *Grease*, and a tight black top and a pair of black ears, and she'd used eyeliner to draw whiskers on herself and she'd put in some fake white sharp teeth so when she smiled she looked like a tiger. That wasn't the most shocking part though. Somewhere along the line, Charlotte had grown some boobs. They weren't huge, but they were definitely there, under her tight top for everyone to see. She obviously knew it too, because she was suddenly walking down the stairs to the party with her chest pushed out in front of her, and it was very embarrassing and I wished that she would hide them. I imagined Mum taking our photo on her little orange Kodak this year. We wouldn't look like twins any more. We'd barely look like sisters. We'd look like a teenage girl who happened to run into a toddler at a party and thought she was cute so she made someone take a photo. Charlotte looked like a woman and I looked like a beach ball.

Lawrence had dressed up in a green mask and was calling himself Frankenstein, and Tony was shouting loudly that he was actually Frankenstein's Monster, and I thought Tony hadn't dressed up at all, until he put some tiny circular glasses on and produced a foldy-up chair and everyone laughed and he called himself Steven Speelburger. I pretended to get it.

Charlotte and Audrey made a start on lining silver trays with

Little Darlings

finger food for the party, and I got excited thinking it meant sandwiches and sausage rolls, but I didn't recognise any of the blobs on the trays and left them to it. Tony (who had come back from his pub lunch quite tipsy and full of even more life than he usually was) sent Laurie out to the shed to get the Halloween banners and the light-up ghost, and he asked him in an American accent and shouted, 'ACTION!' before letting him go, and everyone laughed again.

'Cara!' Laurie called from the patio. 'Will you come and hold the torch for me? It's pitch black out here!'

I skipped towards him and took the torch he was holding out, a beach ball following a monster into the dark night.

The shed was halfway down the garden, near the pond, and the grass was soaking wet so my feet squelched all the way down. Laurie laughed, so I laughed too, and we both exaggerated taking huge big steps as if we were jumping into puddles, until I slipped and had to grab onto his arm to stop myself from falling down.

'Does the garden scare you?' he asked. He opened the door to the shed and I shone the torch inside. 'It used to scare me when I was wee.'

'Sort of,' I admitted. 'But I do love it. I like the fish and the birds and the rabbit I saw once.' I remembered a quote from a film we'd watched in the summer and added, 'Been chasing that high ever since.'

Lawrence laughed loudly and went into the shed, shaking his head. 'You crack me up. Right, come inside. I think the ghost is in one of these boxes.'

With anyone else, I would have been terrified to have been in a dark shed in a dark garden with only a torch on Halloween night, but with Lawrence the dark wasn't scary at all. He had flipped his monster mask up over his head so the face was hanging down the back. It made him look like he had a huge growth out the back of his head, and I told him and we giggled about that. His hair was sticking up where the mask had sat, and he looked messier and realer than I had ever seen him. It was like seeing him properly for the first time. Like maybe I'd seen him through a foggy bathroom window until now, but now I was right up close. He was just a real person, and it was strange to think that.

Laurie wrenched open a cardboard box, then tossed it aside. He opened another, made a satisfied, 'Aha!' and lifted out a huge, white ghost. I could see wires coming out the bottom of it so I wasn't scared. He set it to the side and put his hand deeper into the box. 'Right, here we go. We're flying. They do this party every year and I'm pretty sure these are the same decorations they've had since I was in primary school.' He lifted out a handful of slippery banners and rolled his eyes. 'Very 80s.'

I giggled politely, then said, 'You went to school with Ronnie.'

'Yes! I told you that, didn't I?'

'Yeah. He was telling me about it too.'

'Oh yes? What did he say?'

'Nothing,' I said, and I must have said it too quickly, because Laurie looked at me and frowned.

'Mm,' he said. 'Dad told me he's been babysitting. What's he like? Do you like him?'

I wanted to argue about the word babysitting, as I was hardly a baby and Charlotte definitely wasn't, but I decided to let it go and be the bigger person.

'Yeah,' I said. 'I like him, he's really nice.'

Laurie straightened up and continued to frown at me, and I felt nervous like suddenly maybe I had to pee.

'Well. Just keep an eye on him. I don't trust him,' he said at last.

He threw the Halloween things back into the cardboard box and went to pick it up, but then he suddenly reached inside again.

'Sparklers!' he announced, and he showed me a purple plastic packet with a big flourish of his hand, like he was a magician at a birthday party. 'Have you done sparklers before?'

Little Darlings

'No, I don't think so,' I said. 'I know what they are, though.'

'We have these every year as a bit of a joke. For kids, really, but we've always done them. We can't have fireworks out here, you see. It would scare all the livestock in the neighbouring farms, so there's a signed agreement between all the village residents.'

'No fireworks?'

'Nah, not tonight. We can do this though, come outside! I'll use the barbecue lighter.'

He lifted it and took my hand and we went outside onto the wet grass again.

He opened the packet and handed me a skinny piece of wood with pink on the end, then took a sparkler for himself that was green.

'I'll do mine first and then I'll light yours with it,' he said. He clicked the barbecue lighter and lit the green end of his sparkler. Instantly a bright white light appeared and there was a crackling sound. I jumped back, my eyes wide.

'It's perfectly safe,' he said, smiling. 'Come here.'

I went to him, holding my sparkler out in front of me, and he lit the end of it. My first thought was to drop it onto the grass in case it burnt too quickly and hurt my hand, but I kept my arm steady, looking at Laurie for guidance instead of at the bright lights.

'You can write with them and everything, look.' He swished his sparkler in front of him and made his initials, LW. 'You try it.'

I reached my arm out and made a small CC in the air. It hung for less than a second, but I felt like I could still see it even after it was gone. I gave a little laugh, keen to show I was enjoying myself even though I was nervous.

'Good girl,' he said. 'The light will follow you.'

He turned and moved away from me, holding the sparkler out to the side. The light trailed after him, and he went further and further until all I could see was the little ball of crackly fire and the already disappearing trail it left. And I went to him and did the same, my heart beating fast with a mixture of the bubbles again. Happy, so happy, but just a little uneasy. But choosing to be happy and follow the light.

I caught up to him and we drew each other's initials in the dark. Then, so quickly I nearly missed it, I watched as he wrote LW L O V E S CC.

I giggled and pretended I hadn't seen it and turned away.

'Shall we go and bring the decorations up?' I asked. 'Everyone will be waiting.'

'Yes, of course.'

I was pleased when I heard him following me back to the shed, and I gave him my sparkler so he could put it out. The torch was where I had set it on the steps to the shed, and I picked it up. Laurie went into the shed, and I thought he was going to pick up the box, but instead he turned around, leant down, and kissed me on the lips.

'Enjoy the party tonight,' he said, as if it hadn't happened. 'I might not get to see you very much, I'll have to schmooze. I'm sure you'll have a ball, though.'

He picked up his box and came out of the shed, closing the door after him. I couldn't think of anything to say, so I pointed to my pumpkin outfit and said, 'I *am* a ball today.'

He laughed, and the bubbles swirled around a little bit, not sure which one was right. We went up the garden and nearly ran straight into Tony, who had been standing in the shadows on the patio.

'What were you doing?' he asked. He was looking at Lawrence, not at me, so I was happy not to answer.

'Getting the decorations.' Lawrence shook the box as if to prove it. 'Like you directed me to, Steven.' He laughed and I waited for Uncle Tony to laugh, but he didn't. He had a tumbler in his hand that had the horrible-smelling liquid inside, so I dodged around him to go back inside, but he said—

'Cara?'

Little Darlings

I turned to face him. Uncle Tony blinked at me a few times, then looked at Lawrence, then staggered on his feet just a little.

'Nothing, little darling. Nothing. Ignore me. I've had a few too many drinks. Have a lovely party.'

I smiled and went inside and thought of another joke about how the trays of food had silver linings, and I wondered how I could get the joke in.

That night at the Halloween party, while I stood by myself sipping a fruity cocktail and looking at all the guests in their costumes, was the first time I chose not to think about something. There would be plenty of time to think about what it had meant, but I didn't have room for it while Audrey and Tony's friends were coming up to me and telling me how cute I was, how lucky to have such a generous aunt and uncle. So I put the kiss in a little box and told myself I would think about it a different day, or maybe in a different life.

Chapter 17 | February 2023 | Dromary, County Down, Online

Without agreeing it out loud, Daisy and I decide to keep our conversation in the school carpark private. I feel lighter, a little unburdened, and I hope that doesn't mean I've just unloaded all of my worries onto her. She seems fine, though she does give me a tight hug before we get out of the car, and I wonder what is going on in her head.

Charlotte has replied, and I open her text with shaking fingers.

Yeah he got married when he was really young. Why??

Who was she, do you know?

Idk Cara, why are you asking?

I don't reply to this.

Steve gets in a few minutes after we do, and there is the usual chatter and laughter from him and Daisy as they tell each other stories about their day while simultaneously getting changed and unpacking their things.

'When was Daisy's staff training day again?' Steve asks, coming into the kitchen where I am setting out placemats.

'Oh, did Daisy get a job?'

He laughs and kisses my head. 'You should take it on the road. Is it next month? I was going to book it off and maybe take her somewhere.'

'That would be lovely,' I say. 'Did you enjoy your shop-bought salad today? I'm sorry I forgot.'

'No problem,' he says. He pats his stomach. 'Was good for me, actually. Do you want to feel my six pack?'

Little Darlings

'Is it in the car?' I ask, and I poke him affectionately. 'I am sorry, though. Completely blanked. Sent Daisy in with an empty lunch box too. She says Ellen gave her an apple and half her sandwich, though.'

'No harm done,' Steve shrugs. 'You must have been distracted.'

He lets that hang in the air, waiting for me to speak, but I just smile at him. 'Tea in ten,' I say.

'Lovely. Would you mind checking what date the training is, please? It'll be on the mums' Facebook thing, I'd say.'

I stop, one hand stretched out to put a coaster at Daisy's place.

'What?' Steve asks.

'Nothing,' I say quickly. 'Yeah, I'll check for you later, sure.'

Facebook.

It takes all my will power to get through dinner and TV and a shower. My mind is far away from sausages and chips and *Gavin & Stacey* and Herbal Essences. When Daisy's bedroom door is shut, Steve tells me he is going to go up and read and I tell him I want to check one thing at work and will be up with him soon. I haven't got around to telling him that I've taken the next week off on compassionate leave. I'll tell him later.

I hear his big feet on the stairs, then our bedroom door closes. Downstairs is silent and cold.

I open my laptop and log into the Facebook account I made when Daisy started school. Steve's right, the best way to find out anything is on the *Cherry Hill Primary School Mums* page. 'Bit sexist,' Steve said the first time we looked at it. I write down the date of the staff training day in February, then let the mouse hover over the search bar.

Because I only use it to check our bin day and anything school-related, I have less than 100 Facebook friends, which is not a lot for a millennial, I have come to realise. I had a group of friends at university, of course. They were all girls, most of them studying English or History or Fine Art, and we went to the Queen's Film

Theatre and out for coffees while we all lived in Belfast, and proudly stuck to our monthly meet-ups for a good six months after we graduated, but each of them has messaged less and less frequently as the years have gone on, and it is with a jolt now, looking at my Facebook homepage, that I realise one of them has just given birth to her third child. I type in a few more names to discover that half of them have deleted their Facebook profiles, and most of the other half haven't updated their statuses for five or six years. They could be anything, be anywhere.

It's a strange thing to admit, but it feels like relief. Nobody is missing me or thinking about me. I don't have to keep up with anyone – it was so exhausting. I have never liked the ease of social media, have stayed away from it as much as I can. I am glad to be forgotten.

I go back to my home page and type in the search bar:

Bridget Spears

I scroll through a lot of Americans before I think to filter the results. I select Belfast as the city and cross my fingers that she hasn't moved away. It takes twenty minutes for me to click and scroll through the rest of the results, my heart sinking further with every clearly wrong woman. I let my shoulders drop. It was a long shot anyway. I rub my eyes and look back at the screen. I decide to click on 'posts' instead of 'people' and scroll half-heartedly through the results for this. More Americans. A newborn called Bridget Britney Spears. Then—

I click on a photograph of a smiling woman with short grey hair – dyed grey and shiny and straight. A fashion statement. There is a birthday cake in front of her with candles announcing to Facebook that she has turned fifty. It was posted four weeks ago by someone called Donal Spears. I click on the caption of the photo.

50 years of this absolute legend – my lovely big sister! You make every day better just by being you and we all love you so much. Three cheers for Bridget Spears!

Little Darlings

Donal has put a line of champagne emojis on the post. I click on the comments.

Bridge, you're looking awful well!

Happy birthday Bridget, hope you got spoilt xxx

Don't look a day over 49 ha ha only joking hbd Bridget you're some pup

My heart is beating faster. Is this her? Lawrence's wife? She'd be the same age as Lawrence.

The final comment has been written by someone called Aoife Marie Spears, and reads

The best mummy a girl could ask for! with a line of heart emojis and kissing faces.

I click onto Aoife's profile. It's private, so I can't see any of her information, but I can scroll through her profile pictures.

The current one shows a pretty woman with a blonde bob – Aoife, I assume – beaming with her arm around a handsome boyfriend or husband at a party somewhere. The next one is a much older picture, and shows Aoife in a university hall holding up a plastic cup to cheers with the camera. The one after that is the same woman, a lot younger now, in a sixth form blazer with braces, sticking her tongue out. The next one makes me freeze. It is a photograph that has been taken on an iPhone of another printed photograph, clearly one stuck in the filmed folds of a photo album. It is blurry and there is light reflecting awkwardly off the printed photo. The caption says,

LOL bit of a throwback Thursday

And Aoife has added a line of tongue-sticking-out emojis to this, old school. It is a photo of her as a child, maybe eight or nine, sticking both thumbs up to the camera, and even though the quality of the photo is terrible, I can tell that in it she is wearing a pink, dotty raincoat.

Chapter 18 | Christmas 2000 | Chaplin House

The Wolfes were kind to us in their own Wolfe-y way on Christmas day. Audrey bought mostly clothes for Charlotte, and hair products and face products and makeup, and Charlotte seemed genuinely over the moon about all of it and hugged everybody in delight, including me, even though she hated me now in this new life. I got new clothes too, and I was polite and thanked everyone, but I could tell from the labels that most of them wouldn't fit me. The only thing I'd actually asked for was new paints because my yellow one had a big splodge of brown in it and wasn't bright enough any more, so I hadn't been able to paint the sun for ages. I looked hopefully under the tree after we'd finished opening presents, sniffing because my nose kept running, hoping maybe my paints were wrapped up in the back, hidden from view by all the fancy silver decorations, but I couldn't see anything and was sad.

'Take that bloody look off your face,' Charlotte hissed at me while the adults were pouring something fizzy into their morning orange juice.

'I don't have a bloody look,' I snapped.

'Shh!' Charlotte glared at me. 'You do, you look miserable. Are you crying?'

'No, I'm just sick.'

'You're not, you're being a cry-baby.'

'I'm not!'

'Cara, I'm not going to fight with you on Christmas day. Can you please at least pretend to be happy? They've been very generous.'

'To you, maybe,' I muttered. She shoved me on the shoulder and I wasn't expecting it so I fell backwards into the kitchen island and scraped my arm and everybody fussed over me and I had to pretend I'd just tripped.

Uncle Tony cooked a bird that wasn't a turkey, and the crackers didn't have hats in them, they just had fancy presents inside, so instead of a pink paper hat I found the pockets of my pinafore dress filled with a tiny jar of honey, a leather bookmark, a fountain pen and a packet of luxury sweets that tasted like alcohol.

It was the worst Christmas Day that had ever happened, and when I tried to ask when we could go and see Mum, Charlotte pinched me on my sore arm. I told everyone I didn't feel well after dinner, which they believed because I had sneezed and sniffed about six hundred times during the meal, and I went up to the attic and lay on my bed and cried.

I must have fallen asleep, because I dreamt I was in our little terraced house with Mum, and she was ironing my pinafore, but I asked her to stop because I'd forgotten to take my Baby Born out of one of the pockets, and she stopped when I asked her to, but then she forgot and kept going. The house was cold but the iron was warm, and it was making my face sting. And then when I looked up, Mum was starting to melt. First her head and then her neck and then suddenly there was no body inside her clothes, and the clothes stood upright for a minute and then they fell into a heap on the floor. I tried to lift them up, shouting for Mum to come back, but I hurt my arm on the iron and it was so hot, and it hurt, and—

I woke up covered in sweat and not alone.

Lawrence was sitting at the side of my bed, and was shaking me gently with one hand.

'Cara? Cara, I think you're not too well. Are you feeling bad?'

'Yeah,' I panted, half holding the iron in my dream and half in my bedroom. 'Is it still Christmas?'

'What? Yes, it's still Christmas. You're roasting. This room is freezing and you're burning up. I'll get you something for your forehead. Wait there a sec.'

My head was heavy and my eyes were heavy and I could only breathe if I opened my mouth. I was still wearing my pinafore dress with the pockets, and I must have rolled over in my sleep because I could tell through my foggy brain that the jar of honey had broken open and was now all over the bed.

Laurie came back from the shared bathroom either five minutes later or twenty minutes later or maybe twelve hours later, and this time he had a facecloth with him. He was still in his shirt and trousers from earlier.

'What time is it?' I asked. 'Is it still Christmas?'

'Of course it's still Christmas,' he said. He gave a little laugh. He put the facecloth on my forehead and it was so cold, and nothing had ever felt nicer. 'You didn't think Christmas would pass without me getting you a present, did you?'

I smiled at his words and at the feel of the facecloth on my head.

'Do you have the flu?' Laurie asked. He was sitting at the edge of my bed again, his beautiful face concerned, his smooth skin pulled awkwardly like he was in pain.

'Maybe,' I said. 'I don't know. My head hurts.'

He pressed his palm onto the facecloth, and the relief was instant. My whole head was numb. I put my hand on top of his and pressed down too.

'Thank you,' I mumbled.

'Of course. Here, take this as well.' He held two tiny pills to my mouth and I took them obediently. He passed me a glass of water and I took a small sip and swallowed it all down.

'I had a dream about my mum.'

'Tell me about it.'

'Really?'

'Yes, of course. I feel like it's always me boring the life out of you with my anecdotes. You tell me something interesting for a change.'

'It's not interesting,' I said, my voice quiet and far-away-sounding. 'She was just in our old house doing the ironing. Just the boring ironing. But it was so lovely, because she really did used to do the ironing.' I closed my eyes, feeling like I was on a boat that was rocking. 'But then she melted away. It was nice to see her. But then it was sad.'

'I bet. I'm sorry you didn't get to see her today.'

'I thought someone would take us,' I said. I coughed. My throat felt scratchy.

'Maybe I'll take you sometime. How… how much is she aware of? Would she know if I was there?'

I opened my eyes to look at him. There were two Lawrences, two faces swimming in my vision.

'She's not really… there. Her body is, but she's not. But I don't want to just never see her again. She had a fall, you see.' I shook my head. Lawrence already knew that. We'd discussed it before. Had we? Maybe this wasn't Lawrence, maybe this was someone else. Someone with two floating faces. Where was I? Why was it so cold? 'She fell and hit her head.'

'I know, little darling. It must have been horrible for you.'

'It was,' I said. I wanted to add something very mature and sensible about how it was worse for her, but the words wouldn't come. 'She doesn't know who I am any more.'

'I know. It's so sad.'

'It's so sad,' I echoed. 'She couldn't remember how to walk or talk.'

'Yes.'

'Her brain was damaged,' I said, but it sounded slurry when it came out, and then I wasn't sure if I'd really said it. My head didn't hurt any more, but I was still on the sea in a boat, and I wanted more than anything to sleep. The bubbles weren't in my chest any more. I wasn't even afraid of the girl in the attic or the big bad wolf.

'I know,' Lawrence said. 'I know.'

'Thank you,' I murmured, feeling hot and cold and relieved and in pain. 'You always look after me.'

'That's what I'm here for. This is what it'll be like when we're married.'

I wasn't sure if he said it or if I did, and the next thing I knew I was in a pit of deep, dark sleep.

When I woke up again, it was the daytime and I was hungry and I had to pee. I stumbled to the bathroom, knocking into the doorframe, and only when I was finished and came back into my bedroom did I notice the rectangular, wrapped parcel sitting neatly at the end of my bed. It was covered in the same bright red crinkly paper as all my other presents had been, but while those ones had looked as though they'd been wrapped by a professional, this one certainly didn't. There was too much paper bunched at one end, and the Sellotape was already coming off the other. I knew who it was from, and even though my brain still felt hazy and confused, I grinned and sat on my bed to open it.

Windsor & Newton read the metal tin. I opened it to see over fifty different colours of paints, and four brushes, all different sizes. I was still smiling when I noticed the label that had been clumsily stuck onto the wrapping paper.

To my little darling with love from Laurie x

I was sick for days, so I mostly stayed in my bedroom and re-read some of my Jacqueline Wilson books, and I tried to use my new paints but I couldn't think of anything to draw. Audrey and Tony seemed to accept this, and while they poked their heads in to say hello once or twice, they seemed distracted by that funny week between Christmas and New Year, and according to Laurie they were always heading out to meet friends for drinks, or having people over, or watching films in the cinema room.

Lawrence came up to see me every evening to bring me a tray

with some dinner on it. He'd usually stay for an hour or more as I picked through my food, and he'd ask how I was feeling and he'd tell me funny stories. There had been a shift in him. Where before he'd been nervous and quiet about coming to my room, now he was loud about it and let everyone know, and it meant he was more relaxed and comfortable when he came in, which was good.

We would sit next to one another on the bed to chat, and when I told him I couldn't think of anything to paint because I hadn't seen anything but my room for days, he told me I should try and paint the birds I could hear outside.

'It doesn't matter if you can't see them,' he said. 'You're an artist. You just have to listen to them and imagine what they might look like.'

On the afternoon of New Year's Eve, I listened to the birds outside my window for a while and imagined a robin with a red breast wishing his family a happy new year. I smiled at the image and went to try and paint it, when the bird outside chirped suddenly loudly, close to the window. I thought of what Laurie had said about the birds screaming at one another, and I didn't like it. Suddenly I was afraid of birds. They weren't what you thought.

Charlotte came into my room through the bathroom and stood with her arms folded.

'Are you getting up today?'

'Yeah, I think so,' I said. 'I feel better.'

'Good. You've wasted the whole week off school.'

I shrugged.

'I'm having champagne tonight.'

'Okay. So?'

'You're not allowed any.'

'So? Don't want any.'

Charlotte tutted and came over to sit on my bed. She was wearing a sparkly skirt and black tights and boots that had a heel that clip-clopped on the floor. She was wearing eye-liner and she looked about twenty.

'What are you drawing?'

I turned my page over to show her the outline of a robin.

'Mm,' she said, twisting her lip. 'Head's a bit small.'

'Yeah, I know. I've given up on this one anyway. Don't like birds any more.'

Her eyes fell on the bright red cover of my new paints and she snatched it up off the bed before I could stop her.

'Where did you get this?'

'It was a present,' I said, feeling panicked, my brain working hard to think of who might have given me it. But Lawrence hadn't told me to keep this one a secret, had he? I could hardly remember, my brain hadn't been working properly.

'Who from?' she demanded. She opened it up and her mouth fell open at the number of paints inside, each of them a perfect little square, mostly untouched. I couldn't help but feel a tiny squeeze of pride at the look on her face.

'From— Well, from Laurie.'

She looked at me, her eyes wide. 'What? When?'

I shrugged. I wanted to take the paints back from her, but I knew if I reached for them she'd just hold on tighter.

'Christmas present,' I said.

'You're lying.'

Charlotte stood up, the tin still in her hands, and pulled it to her chest protectively.

'Give it back,' I said, standing up to face her. She was only a little bit taller than me, but her boots doubled the difference.

'You're lying,' she said again. 'Laurie wouldn't give you this.'

'Well, he did. Give me them back, Charlotte. They were expensive.'

'Why would he give you a Christmas present?'

'I don't know.'

'He doesn't even like you.'

I laughed, thinking maybe she was joking, but her eyes were bright and wide and staring at me.

'He does,' I said. 'Look.'

I went to the little wastepaper basket in the corner of my room. I hadn't emptied it for days. I fished around some used tissues, trying not to touch them, and pulled out the label Laurie had signed.

'Look!' I held it out to her and she took it. The bubble in my chest was back. A strange… pride. Something I had over my older sister that now, with this evidence, she couldn't deny. She could ignore me at school and shake her head at me and tell everyone I was a baby… but I was Lawrence's favourite. And I knew that would hurt her.

She stared at the label for a moment, then threw it on the floor.

'Here.' She thrust the paints back at me and I felt sick with relief. 'Now that I think of it, I think I've seen those in the pound shop. They're no big deal.'

'When were you in the pound shop?'

'They're cheap, *okay*?'

'No, not *okay*,' I said, mocking the American accent she'd adopted. 'They're expensive and you know it. And Laurie bought them for me for Christmas because he loves me.'

Charlotte snorted and folded her arms, but there was a pink tinge in her cheeks that hadn't been there before.

'As if,' she said.

'He does. He loves me, and we're going to be married when I'm older.'

'You're… What?'

'You're just jealous because he loves me and not you. You can play dress-up like you're Audrey's toy doll all you want, but me and Laurie are together, and I'm his favourite. He kissed me on Halloween night.'

The toy doll comment had been something Laurie had said that week. I wasn't exactly sure if it was an insult, but Charlotte definitely thought it was, because she backed away from me and went towards her room. At the last moment she turned back and said, 'You're insane,' and left.

I felt bad about hurting her feelings, and immediately wished I could take it all back, but I called her and she didn't reply, and then I heard the door to the attic close a few minutes later and I knew she'd gone downstairs.

Something told me that I shouldn't have brought up the Halloween kiss. Laurie and I had never discussed it, and it hadn't happened since. I was starting to think maybe I'd imagined it, and felt sick at the idea that Charlotte might ask him about it, only for him to deny it ever happened. The week after Halloween, in school, I had been sure that everyone would be able to read on my face that I'd had my first kiss over half term, but nobody brought it up.

I didn't go down to join the rest of the Wolfes for New Year's Eve, afraid that Charlotte had told them all my secret and Laurie would be angry with me for telling her.

But it seemed she hadn't said a thing, because Lawrence snuck away from everyone else at midnight to wish me a happy new year and he gave me another kiss.

And then he came up to my bedroom every night.

Just for a chat.

And sometimes for a kiss.

Chapter 19 | February 2023 | Belfast

The following Monday, I do something I have never done before. I load an address into Apple Maps, get into my car, and drive to Belfast after Steve and Daisy have left for work and school. I put off telling Steve about my compassionate leave all weekend, and now I've decided not to bother. I feel guilty for lying, but not quite guilty enough. There are levels to every feeling; it's all a delicate balancing act.

I have just missed rush hour, so I am able to move steadily north at fifty-six miles per hour, my hands at ten-to-two, pretending I am as safe as Steve. My eyes bounce between the mirrors and the road, not relaxing for one second, and my neck and shoulders are aching with the tension. There is a parking spot exactly where the map guides me, and I breathe a sigh of relief when I put the hand brake on and can sit back for a moment. I have done it. This thing that has hung over me for years, the idea of driving to and in and around a city I know well. I did it. And it took less than an hour.

I get out and pay for four hours of parking, not caring how much it is, not knowing how long this will take. I put my little sticker on the windscreen and pull my coat tighter around myself. In the cold air, I can feel the scar on my cheek more acutely, and I imagine it raw and red and new as if it happened two days ago and not twenty-two years ago.

I know where I am from days and nights out during university. Steve and I have eaten at the fancy jazz bar just around the corner, and the cinema that Daisy likes isn't too far. I walk blearily towards

The Big Fish monument, happy to walk slowly behind a group of tourists, getting my head together. Seagulls scream at one another above Donegall Quay. They're the only honest birds; they sound angry when they are.

I find the building and sit on a bench opposite it, still hardly able to believe what I have done this morning. Something has changed. Cara is altered. There is a little fire. I drove to Belfast on my own. Maybe there are other things I would do. I want to tell Steve, like I always do when something good happens. Nothing feels real or worth anything until we've celebrated it together. For some people it is the thrill of an Instagram like, for some it's the first drop from a wine glass, and for me it's the grin of uncomplicated delight on my husband's face when I tell him a client liked my design or that I've managed to get two weeks off over Christmas. The same smile that appeared instantly when I showed him the positive pregnancy test after only a few months together, and that has barely wavered since.

I sit there for two hours, watching people come and go, picking at my cuticles until they bleed, peeling off a ragged nail, unable to stop myself. Harland & Wolff's distinctive yellow crane across the water makes my stomach lurch. *Wolfe*. I try not to look at it.

A woman with a blonde bob exits the building and my heart soars as I stand up – it isn't her, though, and I sit back down on my bench with a thud. The girls on the bench next to me share a look and giggle.

I wait another hour. Past one o'clock, past two o'clock. My parking is going to run out. At two-fifteen, I decide Aoife Marie Spears must bring her lunch from home and stay in the building on her break. I try to decide what to do. I could go back to my car and wait until finishing time, try to catch her as she runs for her train after work.

In theory, I could go and wait in my own office. It's only a fifteen-minute walk away from here. The thought of going inside, seeing CJ and the others in the flesh for the first time in nearly

Little Darlings

a year, turns my stomach. They'll have sympathetic hugs and compassionate nods for me, and subtle but probing questions about how the bakery logo is coming along. I can't do that.

I am just mustering the courage to go back to my car when another blonde head emerges from the automatic doors, buried in a huge shoulder bag. I tense, watching. She looks up – it's Aoife. She's wearing small navy heels and a gorgeous navy trouser suit I would never be able to pull off. Before I can take in anything else, she's darted around the corner of the office and out of sight, moving far more briskly in her heels than I can in my flats.

'Aoife!' I call when I get around the corner. She stops and turns, her smile ready and her face bright, expecting someone from her office or a kind stranger who has picked up her dropped wallet.

'Yes?' she asks, cautious but still happy.

'Hi,' I say, rushing up to her. 'Hi, do you have a minute to chat? Are you on your lunch break?'

Her eyes widen. 'I'm sorry?' She glances at my fake Converse and my wide-leg black trousers. I convince myself she has already noticed my awful broken nails, that she's copped the scar on my cheek immediately, despite my concealer. 'Do I know you?'

'Well, no. My name is Cara Harris. You don't know me but I feel like I know you. I just wanted to talk to you for a few minutes, if that's okay? It's about you and your mum and—' I hesitate. Once his name is between us, this turns into something else. 'And Lawrence Wolfe.'

'Oh.' Aoife takes one small but serious step backwards, clutching her shoulder bag into her like she's afraid I'm going to steal it. Her eyes are blue and match perfectly with her earrings – or the other way round, I suppose. They're round, and she's very pretty, and if I didn't know better I'd say she was at least eight years younger than me. Sometimes you can read people's lives on their faces, and when you can't that means something too.

'How did you know where I worked?' she asks. 'Why are you here?'

'LinkedIn,' I say, shrugging apologetically. 'I'm sorry. I just want to talk to you for a minute. I thought maybe you wouldn't want to talk on the phone.'

Of course what I mean is, *It would have been really easy for you to hang up on me, but it's harder to say no when I'm standing in front of you.*

She shakes her head, eyes widening even further. 'No, I wouldn't have.' She takes another step back. Then another. I think of the girls in the playground, my last term in Holy Trinity Primary, all keen to get as far away from me as possible. All giggling and pointing after what happened.

'Look,' Aoife says. 'I don't know anything about Lawrence Wolfe, honestly. I was so young then and I haven't seen him since. I assume you're a journalist and I understand it's your job to talk to people, but this is very, very weird. Please don't contact me again.'

Or what? I think. You'll call the police? Good, tell them I want to speak to them.

Aoife is still shaking her head as she turns around and begins to walk away from me, even faster than before. I haven't just driven all the way to the city by myself for her to walk away from me. Not when I am sure – *I am so sure* – that she will have the answer for me that I need. She maybe doesn't even know she has it. I can feel my breathing quicken, and my chest begins to hurt. Not now, I think, bitterly angry at my body and completely unable to do any of the techniques that I know would stem a panic attack.

'I need you to talk to me,' I say, as loudly as I can without shouting. A couple walking past arm in arm keep their heads down and pretend not to see me. I take a deep breath, and the next bit comes out as a panicked shout. 'About Lawrence Wolfe. I need you to talk to me because he sexually abused me when I was ten and I think he might have done the same to you.'

There are some things you can shout in the street that will see you ignored. Most things, in fact. What I shouted at Aoife was,

Little Darlings

evidently, not one of them. Ten minutes later sees me sitting on a hard wooden chair in Café Nero, facing the window. Aoife is behind me. I hear her order a latte and an Americano, even though she didn't ask me what I wanted. She asks for two caramel squares too.

When she joins me a few minutes later, I've calmed down somewhat. My breathing feels easier just knowing she is here and that she is willing, if not to talk to me, then to listen. Maybe something of my story will resonate with her.

She slides the small white plate towards me, then carefully moves everything off the tray and onto the table. She hesitates for a second, then sets the tray on the floor. When she has placed both hands around her tall glass, she finally looks me in the eye.

'Right. What did you say?'

I clear my throat. Look down at my plate, then at my coffee, and decide to start on the latter. It burns my tongue but it's good, because I can feel it.

'Sorry for stalking you,' I say finally, trying to crack a smile. I feel my eyes fill with tears and I will them away. I don't want this to be a pity party. I want this to be facts and not emotion. I've had my whole life for emotion and it's got me absolutely nowhere.

'It's a bit weird,' she says lightly. 'Eat that up. Get the sugar into you. You're awful pale.'

I take an obedient bite. The caramel square is good, but it's not as good as my mum's were. I don't think anything ever will be.

'How did you know my name to look me up?' she asks. 'I've never heard of you.'

'I got your mum's name,' I say. 'And then I saw a post about her fiftieth birthday—'

'Fucking Facebook,' Aoife says, and I give a nervous little laugh. She shakes her head, but she is smiling. 'I hate it. I'm addicted to it, but I hate it. This is the kind of thing they warn kids about in schools nowadays, isn't it? Don't put your personal details online, someone will catfish you or find out where you live—'

'I'm not really stalking you,' I say quickly, taking another bite of caramel square. I chew and swallow. 'I just got a bit… desperate for answers. Your Facebook was private, but LinkedIn said you were a paralegal at Davis and Cross, so.'

'So,' Aoife says nodding. 'Fair enough.' She sips her latte, then looks at me expectantly.

I cough and take a deep breath. 'So, how long was your mum in a relationship with him?' I ask, not wanting to say his name again.

'They were married,' Aoife says. 'But it wasn't that long. I think they were together maybe three years in total.'

'And what age were you?'

Aoife blows some air out of her mouth, thinking. 'I was in P3, I think, when they met. About seven. And they had separated before I was in secondary school so, fleeting enough. But it doesn't feel like that when you're wee, does it? Time moves differently.'

Yes, it does, I think, but I don't reply. It moves differently when you're wee. My cheekbone is so itchy it feels like it is on fire but I resist the urge to scratch it by taking another sip of coffee.

'How did they meet?'

'God, now you're asking. I honestly don't know, I can't remember. It's weird…' Aoife trails off, looking down at her shoulder bag on the floor as if thinking carefully. 'They were together for three years, married, even… but we never really talked about him much again after they separated. I brought it up a few times at the start, asked if I could see him, but Mum wasn't having any of it. And then I just stopped asking, and then she met Ted. They never got married but they've been happy ever since.' Aoife shrugs as if this is all there is to it, and I feel myself start to deflate. That was really it?

'What was he like?' I whisper, my eyes on the table, wishing she'll say this one thing and dreading just the same.

'He was…' She considers for a moment, seems torn between what she wants to say and, I can tell, unable to get from her mind what I shouted at her in the street. Eventually she says, 'He was lovely. It's so weird to see his face everywhere now, because I knew him so well when I was a child. We were really close.'

My heart beats faster. *Really close. Really close. Really close. Me and Laurie were really close too. Really close.*

'But he was so lovely. I'd never had a dad before, never had any kind of man around, really.'

Me neither. Me neither. Me neither.

'I was wary of him at first, this really good-looking, charming guy that just swooped in and quite literally swept Mum off her feet. She got so… dizzy when she talked about him. She was different around him. It's only now, looking back, that I realise… She was happy. I'd never really seen her happy before.'

I'd been happy, I think. Before Chaplin House, when life was small and simple and boring. I'd been so happy and I'd had everything I could ever have wanted and I didn't even realise it. I used to dream about living in a big house in the country, and then I got it, and then the world fell apart and I was the only one left trying to hold it up, but I was too small.

'They bought a house. Well, he did, I think. Actually not too far away from here, up Stranmillis direction.'

The bedroom with the blue wallpaper. I'm not there. I'm here. I'm not there.

'It was lovely. Huge. Or it seemed that way to me, back then.'

Rocket light rocket light rocket light

'It's weird, I used to think they were so… adult. Like they were really old and knew exactly what they were doing, but I suppose that's just how you look at adults when you're a child, isn't it? You don't differentiate much between people in their twenties and people in their forties. Mum was really young when she had me, just turned sixteen, so I think the pair of them must have been… Shit, about twenty-three.' Aoife laughs and gives a soft snort that I wasn't expecting. 'That seems so young now, doesn't it? So young to have a seven-year-old kid and a big house. I was mental when I was twenty-three, were you?'

'Yeah,' I say, and it's true, but we mean completely different things. 'I met my husband when I was twenty-one, though, and we had our wee girl the next year. On purpose,' I add quickly, but then I feel ridiculous. Daisy was a wonderful accident, but I don't have to explain myself to a stranger. Although, granted, she is explaining herself to me.

'You have a daughter?' Aoife asks, her face brightening so genuinely that she looks even younger. 'What's her name?'

'Daisy,' I say. And even though my skin is crawling with memories, my cheekbone aching, and even though I'm in a busy coffee shop and it's too loud and I'm surrounded by people, I feel my chest expand as it always does when I talk about her or say her name, and the other conversations in the coffee shop are drowned out and then muted, like she is a tonic. 'She's coming ten now in April. She's fab.'

It's such a simple thing, such a short word. It means what it means, but it's nearly too vague and too overused for what Daisy is. Little girls can do so much without even realising it. I think of Charlotte, who threw me to the wolves, and Daisy who saved my life.

'Aw,' Aoife says, in that way that people do.

I glance at her hand and spot no wedding ring, but I don't think that means anything. 'Do you have kids?'

'Not yet,' she says. 'Soon, I hope.'

She doesn't elaborate, doesn't tell me about a partner, and I don't ask. That's not what I'm here to ask about.

'So… You all got on well?' I ask, hoping she'll go back to her story.

Aoife nods slowly. 'Yeah. Honestly, we were really happy. He was a good role model. He made me laugh. He was… present. You know? We used to go to the cinema all the time, it was my favourite thing to do and his favourite as well. I went to see, like, action films and sci-fi and stuff with him. Didn't understand it half the time, but I loved it. And he took me to see all the kids' ones. Didn't mind at all. He was really present. A lot of men would have found out Mum had a kid and run a mile, but not him…' She trails off and seems to register something. Suddenly serious, she says, 'Sorry. I shouldn't be saying any of this, should I?' She looks around the café for a minute, but I don't think she's as uncomfortable as I would be if I was her. She lowers her voice, 'What was it that happened to you?'

'No, no,' I say. 'I want to know all of this. I want to get an idea of what he was like… before.'

Before I was alone. Before I felt like this. When I could hear birds singing and it made me think only of Cinderella. When I could go to the bathroom and wash my hands and look in the mirror and smile at my reflection and my cheeks were even. When I could watch films, when I could smell mint, when I could do all of the other things that people do every day. Before, when I was a person. I think of the look Steve gave me in the kitchen when I said, 'I'm fine.' Maybe I do know what that look meant.

'So he never…' I start. I think, wait a second, start again. 'So, he never did anything inappropriate with you? Never touched you or… or anything?'

Aoife's face has contorted, and she looks so sad – heartbroken, actually – that I am positive for a moment that she is going to burst into tears and tell me that he did. She is surprised and confused all at once, but most of all she looks devastated. Her head is tilted to the side in what I know is a subconscious gesture of compassion. She shakes her head at me so sadly, and it is the pity party that I didn't want, that doesn't help.

'No,' she says. 'No, he didn't. Honestly. I'm sorry if that's maybe not what you wanted to hear' – I open my mouth to assure her that isn't true, but she keeps speaking – 'and I'm so, so, sorry for whatever happened to you.'

I am aware in a corner of my mind of how lucky I am that we are having this conversation in 2023. That I haven't told her any specifics, but summed it up with a phrase, and she, this stranger who has never met me, believes me without question. That she knows, instinctively, that I am telling the truth. And I realise with a physical thud to my stomach that she is only the second person I have told who has ever believed me. And she doesn't even know it.

A strange place to be is with your legs swinging over a fence between relief and disappointment. But that's unfair to Aoife, and I can't in all seriousness be disappointed that nothing bad ever happened to her. I'm just surprised, genuinely.

'Thank you,' I hear myself saying to her. I don't know if I'm capable of saying much else. 'Thank you for talking to me and thank you for saying that.'

'You were ten?' she asks hesitantly. I wonder if she is curious enough to push me for details. If she is the kind of person who might happily take what I am saying to a journalist, who might choose money over morals. I don't know her, but I don't think she is.

'Yeah, nine and ten,' I say, thinking of the presents and the whispered conversations before the shed, of my bedroom on the third floor, of The Big Window, of the room with the blue wallpaper. My fingertip finds my cheek and Aoife notices.

'Did he do that to you?' she asks, nodding at it.

'No,' I say, then I add, 'Not directly.'

'Do you talk to anyone about it?' Aoife asks. 'A professional, I mean.'

'Not about that, no.'

She grabs her iPhone from where it has sat, face down on the table, and begins to scroll through it.

'I'm not telling you what to do,' she says, 'You're a grown woman, I know. But my therapist, honestly, she is amazing. She's the best there is. If you do call, tell her Aoife Spears recommended her. I think she could really help, you know.'

And it's thoughtful, and it's earnest, and I suppose on some level it's helpful. But it's absolutely not the help I wanted today. And I take the number, and I smile at Aoife, and she tries to make some inane small talk when she realises I am not going to divulge any details about what happened with Lawrence Wolfe, and I know she has a good heart, and I am happy that she has lived a life that didn't go the same way as mine.

But I am also exhausted, and I am glad when she leaves.

A few evenings later, lying on the sofa with my head on Steve's lap, my phone rings. Steve reaches to the windowsill and picks it up for me, passing it to me without looking at the screen. It's not that he doesn't care, and it's not that he isn't surprised that my phone is ringing on a Friday evening when I have almost no friends and barely any family to speak of, it's that he has always perfectly respected my privacy.

I don't recognise the number, so I sit up and stare at the screen.

'Everything okay?' Steve murmurs. He has paused the TV, expecting me to answer.

'I don't know who it is,' I say. 'What should I do?'

'Answer?' Steve suggests, but there is no hint of sarcasm.

I slide the screen and put the phone to my ear. 'Hello?'

'Hello, is this Cara Harris?'

'Speaking?'

'Hello, Mrs Harris. My name is Bridget Spears, but I used to be Bridget Wolfe.'

Steve looks questioningly at me, but I smile and cover the receiver.

'Just a work call, won't be a sec.'

I try not to race out of the room, but I can feel his eyes on me as I close the door. He always knows when I'm acting.

I climb all the way to the top of the rickety wooden stairs and push our bedroom door closed before I speak to Bridget again.

'Hi,' I say, hating that I'm out of breath from a trip up the stairs. 'Bridget – Mrs Spears—'

'Bridget, darling, is fine. I hope you don't mind me phoning you so late.' My bedside alarm clock says it's just past ten o'clock. Maybe that is late for people who sleep well. 'I found your profile on your graphic design website and the agency gave me your number,' Bridget continues. 'Well, that was on Wednesday. I wasn't sure if I should call or not. I hope it's okay that I have.'

'That's fine,' I say. 'Thank you for calling.'

She's phoned to tell me off for bothering Aoife, I think. And I deserve it. I hope she shouts at me and I hope I'm upset. What the hell was I thinking, tackling a perfect stranger in the middle of her work day to ask her if she had ever been sexually abused? What is wrong with me?

'I believe you wanted to know about Lawrence…' She trails off, and I don't blame her. I wouldn't want to say the words either.

'Yes,' I say. 'That's right. I'm sorry I bothered Aoife; I think I took her by surprise. Is she very annoyed with me?'

'No,' Bridget says. 'She's not annoyed.' She hesitates for a moment and I hear her shuffling, maybe on a leather sofa. 'She's a bit confused, is all. She hasn't seen Lawrence since he and I got divorced, and that was in… God, 1999 we started the ball rolling, I think. We were only married two years, only together for three. The divorce took longer to come through than the whole relationship lasted, really.' She gives a dull kind of chuckle, then clears her throat. 'Aoife says Lawrence was… inappropriate with you.' She waits for me to answer, but my voice is stuck somewhere in my throat. 'Sexually inappropriate. Is that right?'

I wish she was here so she could see me nodding. Instead, I whisper, 'Yes.'

Bridget doesn't so much as gasp as she does give a long, drawn-out sigh of something. 'Oh, I'm sorry, Mrs Harris. I'm very sorry that that happened to you.'

I still think she is phoning to tell me off, so I don't say anything.

'Have you spoken to the police about it?'

I'm not sure what the right answer is. Once, I want to say. I tried, once. But that was twenty years ago, so I don't think it counts.

'Not recently,' I say finally. 'I was a child when it happened and nobody believed me at the time.'

Little Darlings

'When was this?' Bridget asks.

I can give her the dates, if she wants. I can say it started on Halloween night, in the year 2000, and it ended six months later. I know she doesn't mean it like that, though, so I say, 'The early 2000s.'

This time it is a small gasp. 'I'm sorry,' she says again. 'I'm very sorry. Why were you asking Aoife about him, if I can ask that? Are you planning to go to the police?'

'Yes,' I say. It is the first time I have admitted my plan, even to myself. 'Yes, I think I am.'

'Good for you,' she says immediately. 'You should. He should be punished. I see his big smarmy face on the Netflix and it makes me sick.'

'Why?' I ask. My heart quickens. I am aware that if we were in a film, we would be talking in person. Bridget would have called, asked me to meet, and this would have been an important scene. We'd look at each other the way I looked at Aoife, and emotions would be running high and everyone would do their very best sad faces and so much would be said using our expressions.

I'm cross-legged on my bed, though. The sheets are fresh because Steve changes them on a Friday. The bedside lamps are on because we light them in the afternoons in winter and never switch on the big light. There is a perfectly circular hole in the sleeve of my jumper, in exactly the right place for me to stick my thumb through. Bridget can't see any of these things, and we're not in a film, and I can't visualise where she might be, but I can visualise the grey-haired woman I saw in the birthday photo.

Bridget hasn't responded.

'Why did you divorce him?' I ask, rephrasing and hoping this will be easier for her to answer. I am looking at the skirting board opposite me, where I have just noticed a tiny chip.

'He didn't touch Aoife,' Bridget says slowly. 'But I think the only reason he didn't was because he never got a chance.'

Chapter 20 | February 2001 | The House in Stranmillis

Lawrence was gone from the start of January until the start of February, and when he came home it was with stories of glamorous parties and dinners that Audrey and Tony listened to without blinking, laughing at all the right times and clapping him on the back when the hero of the stories – always Laurie himself – did something impressive. I tried to laugh too, even when I didn't fully understand what was going on, but I noticed that Charlotte seemed not to listen with as much attention, and wasn't quite so smitten with Laurie as she had been before Christmas.

Ronnie dropped us off after school one Friday and we went up the steps to Chaplin House chatting happily for the first time in what felt like ages. Charlotte was on a high because her drama club were going to be doing *Annie* for the end of year assembly, and she'd auditioned as Annie and was pretty sure she'd be cast. I was on a high because Charlotte was speaking to me, and I'd made a plan that I was going to spend all weekend painting and letting Charlotte use my nice new paints, and I'd try to make us best friends again because it would be nice to have a friend.

When we went into the kitchen and let our schoolbags fall onto the floor, we saw the three Wolfes gathered around the dining table with their heads together. They looked up when we came in, all of them beaming. They had a little white flyer between them, and Lawrence held it up in the air.

'I have a surprise for you!' he called in a sing-song voice.

'For us?' I asked.

'For you, Cara! There's an open audition in Belfast tomorrow for the lead role in *My Fair Belfast*!'

I blinked at him. 'Your what?'

He laughed. 'It's a new film!'

Laurie came towards me, thrusting the flyer in my direction. Audrey stood behind him, dressed in a bright purple blouse and lots of necklaces for no reason, clapping like a seal.

'A whole family of actors!' she cried. 'It's going to be wonderful. Tell her what you did, Tony, tell her!'

Uncle Tony's chest was puffier than usual and he was grinning. 'I called my good friend Neal, the director, and he's expecting you! I gave him your description and he says you sound just perfect for the role of Eliza Long. It's a comedy, but it'll be well handled. And it's just your first, so it's a good start.'

I looked between the Wolfes, confused and annoyed that everyone was looking at me and I didn't have a clue what was going on.

'You're going to audition for a film,' Charlotte said from beside me, her arms folded. Her teeth were gritted but she was smiling. It was weirdly scary. 'Uncle Tony has kindly called his friend to make sure you get the part.'

'Even though it's an open audition,' Lawrence added. 'And you didn't need to call anyone, Dad.' I thought maybe Lawrence sounded annoyed as well, but I didn't like to say anything.

Tony batted his words away as if they were a compliment and nodded at me. 'Well? How do you feel? They'll give you a little part of the script to read and you'll just do your best and then all being well you'll be cast in a *film*. Isn't that exciting, Cara?'

It wasn't exciting at all, I thought. It was horrendous. It was scary and awful and I didn't want to do it and I wouldn't do it.

Everyone was looking at me, waiting for me to answer.

'Why isn't Charlotte doing it?' I asked finally, in a small voice. Beside me, I heard her breathe in.

'Oh, I know it would have been lovely to audition together, but the part asks for an eight-year-old.'

'I'm ten. And a half.'

Uncle Tony chuckled. 'Yes, I know, but I think they would believe you were a little younger, whereas Charlotte…'

We all looked at Charlotte, whose eyeliner had smudged all over her eyes so she looked a bit like a panda. She had her hair up in a complicated bun that Audrey had shown her. There was no way she could ever be an eight-year-old.

'She can still come with you tomorrow to Belfast!' Tony said, clapping his hands together. 'It'll be a jolly fun day out. You both deserve it. Anyway, is young Ronald still around? I want him to take a look at something…'

Uncle Tony left the kitchen, muttering to himself.

'You'll have to leave here bright and early,' Audrey said. 'You'll have to queue up, I'm afraid. Don't want the other children thinking you're getting special treatment.'

'I'm going to drive you,' Lawrence said. 'Won't that be nice?'

'Not for you, Laurie,' Audrey said. She was fixing her many necklaces around her neck, and I noticed for the first time that her neck wasn't quite as smooth as the rest of her. It was sagging a little, with lots of lines running all down it. 'You'll just be waiting about on her all day.'

'Well, I've said I'd meet a friend for lunch.'

'Good for you, darling. Now, Cara, run along! Go and pick something nice to wear. Nothing too dark; we want them to remember you. And I'll do your hair in the morning. Maybe plaits, if I can tame those curls of yours! Off you go, there's a good girl.'

I picked up my backpack and ran along, because I was a good girl, my mind running through everything that had just been said. I let my backpack trail along the shiny floor and bump up the steps behind me.

'Lift it, would you?' Charlotte said. 'The noise is giving me a headache.'

Little Darlings

I hadn't realised she'd followed me and I turned around. 'Sorry.'

'What are you going to wear tomorrow?' she asked. We got to the door to the attic and I opened it and let her go in before me.

'I don't know,' I said miserably. 'I don't want to read out lines. I don't want to act. It's not fair.'

'It's nice of them to think of us,' Charlotte said. 'You should be grateful.'

'It's you who wants to be an actress,' I insisted as I clomped up the stairs as loudly as I could. 'I don't. I don't want to go. I'm not going.'

We got to The Big Window and Charlotte paused. I stamped my foot, but then looked down into the garden below. The trees had all lost their leaves, so we could see all the way to the end of the garden. The trees swayed and looked as if they were shivering without their leafy coats on. It would make a nice painting, I thought, but you would only be able to use a few colours, and I liked to use lots of colours.

'Will you come with me tomorrow?' I asked. I reached for Charlotte's hand but she pulled her own away.

'I don't want to hang about waiting for you all day,' she said. 'You'll have Laurie, just go with him.'

She turned and went up the second flight of stairs and into her bedroom.

I followed her, but waited in the doorway, not wanting to go inside.

'Please?' I asked. 'Will you please come with me?'

'No, Cara. You don't need me to. Laurie will be there.'

I hesitated. 'I don't want to go with him.'

'Why?' Charlotte dumped her school bag on her bed and came to stand in front of me, her arms folded. 'Thought you two were best friends. Loved each other. That's what you said.'

I blushed and looked down at the floor of her bedroom. 'I don't want to be on my own with him.'

I felt like I was standing on the edge of a cliff and I was about to jump off it into the sea. I was teetering. I wanted to jump and see what happened.

Charlotte tutted. 'Wise up,' she said.

'I'm scared of him.'

I had jumped off and was falling through the air, waiting to see if she would catch me. I had known for a while that it was true. I was scared of him, of Laurie. But I wasn't sure I could put into words exactly why.

He had never done anything bad.

It was the opposite. He listened to me. He talked to me. He wanted to know things about me, and he bought me presents, and he was nice to me. And he told me I was beautiful, and that he loved me. And I believed him. And I thought maybe I loved him too.

But I didn't like it when he came to my room at night.

Usually we just talked more, but sometimes he would kiss me. And when that happened I wanted him to leave, but I couldn't say that because I didn't want to hurt his feelings. So I would say I was tired or I had a headache, and he would stop, and say goodnight, and go. He always listened to me.

'No, you're not. Just go and do your stupid fucking kiddie audition. Leave me alone.' Charlotte sighed and closed the door in my face, and left me standing outside her door, my nose almost touching the wood of it.

Charlotte told Auntie Audrey the next morning that she didn't want to go with us because she didn't feel well, and so Audrey sent us off by telling me to break a leg – which Laurie had to explain to me – and then we were in the Oddy car, speeding towards Belfast.

Well, not speeding. Laurie drove slowly with me next to him, very aware of my fear of the car, and I was grateful.

It meant it took what felt like four hours to get to Belfast, and the warm air in the car made me feel sick. When Laurie finally parked up on a little narrow street, I threw open the car door and vomited onto the footpath below. A woman walking with her toddler pulled the child out of the way and looked at me in disgust, like I'd chosen to get sick. Laurie ran around to my side of the car and helped me out, lifting me over my puddle of sick.

'Is it nerves?' he asked, his face concerned. 'Maybe this was a bad idea.'

'Nerves and car,' I mumbled, wiping the back of my hand over my mouth. 'I'm so sorry. I didn't want to get sick in the car.'

'Don't worry about the car, little darling.' He smiled and put his hands on my shoulders and looked into my face. 'If you really don't want to do it, you don't have to.'

'Really?' I asked, hardly daring to believe it. 'But Uncle Tony, won't he be angry? He's asked his friend—'

'Don't worry about that. There are going to be hundreds of girls auditioning today. Neal won't notice if you don't show up.'

We had to move out of the way so a family could pass us. We both pressed ourselves against the front of a shop window.

'Do you promise?' I asked. 'Promise I won't get in trouble?'

'We can keep it as our secret,' Laurie said. 'I won't tell if you won't tell. I'm just sorry I suggested it in the first place. I thought I was doing something nice for you. I thought you'd be happy.'

'It's Charlotte who wants to act,' I said. 'I don't.'

He nodded and straightened.

He was wearing a long black coat that was soft to the touch, and it covered up his shirt and his trousers so you could only see his black shoes poking out the bottom. They were so big they looked like he was wearing skis.

'Shall we go for a walk?' I asked hopefully. 'Maybe we could get hot chocolates.'

'Mm...' He looked up and down the street. 'I don't want people to recognise me is the only thing.'

'Because you're famous?' I said, taking a moment to realise what that meant. 'Do people know who you are? Does everyone know your name?'

'Yes. Sometimes it's a bit of a pain…' He took a deep breath. 'Tell you what. I know a place we can go. We can have hot chocolates and watch a film. We'll wait a few hours, then head home and just… tell everyone you didn't get the part. Okay?'

'Okay,' I said, my heart lifting. Everything was going to be fine. I wouldn't have to read any stupid script, I could take my hair out of the stupid, tight plaits. The dress Audrey had insisted I wear was too short for me, and my tights itched, but I was delighted that my nightmare was over and I could spend the day with Laurie, out in front of other people, where I liked him the best.

As it turned out, I was not quite so lucky. My bubble of relief lasted as we got back into the car and drove again. Then Laurie parked up in a driveway in a quiet street and we got out. I looked around in confusion, wondering where we were going.

We were outside a semi-detached brick house with a white front door that had a window on one side so you could see right in if you were walking past.

'Where are we?' I asked, looking up and down the deserted street.

'My house,' Laurie said. He was searching among his keys, looking for something.

'I thought Chaplin House was your house,' I said, not understanding. I lifted my school bag from the floor by my seat. I had filled it with books that I'd thought I'd have time to read while I was waiting for my audition. I had tried to look for my paints, but I couldn't find them anywhere.

'This is my other house. I used to live here.'

'Oh.'

Laurie found the right key and put it into the front door. It opened with a squeak along the ground and I hesitated, standing with my backpack in my hand, feeling the bubble in my chest as if it was a real thing. My heart was beating too quickly, so I thought it might puncture it.

Little Darlings

'Come on.' Laurie was standing in the doorway, smiling at me, but looking left and right down the street as if hoping not to be seen. There was a sheen of sweat on his forehead that I'd never noticed before. He wasn't a sweaty person.

I felt, strangely, as though I wanted someone to see.

I wanted an old lady to come out of her house across the road and spot us and start chatting. A dog walker could come around the corner at any moment, I thought. That would be good. Maybe next door would have heard the car, and they'd come and ask Laurie for an autograph.

But it was a Saturday morning, and it seemed everyone who lived here was elsewhere.

I couldn't describe it, but I didn't want to go into the house.

'Cara, come on.' He was smiling, but he sounded a little bit impatient, and I hadn't heard Laurie sound impatient before. 'I thought you didn't want to go to your audition,' he said after a moment, giving a little sigh.

And I didn't want him to be annoyed with me.

I didn't want anyone to be annoyed with me.

So I went in.

And there was a kitchen that didn't have any hot chocolate in it. And the TV worked, but there were only a few channels.

And then there was a bedroom with blue wallpaper with a white design on it, and something happened.

And there was a rocket in the corner of the room, next to my backpack, so I looked at that.

After a while, when I had managed to remove myself completely from what was happening, I realised that it was a light fitting. It was supposed to be on the ceiling so that when you looked up, you would see a rocket in the sky. It was rusty, and a bit dirty and dusty like the rest of the house.

I just looked at the rocket and pretended I was somewhere else.

Chapter 21 | February 2023 | Dromary, County Down

'Go on,' I say to Bridget, hardly breathing. I hear a creak on a floorboard downstairs and will Steve not to come up. I have never not wanted to see his face, but if he opens the door and looks at me he'll break the spell and I won't be able to go through with this conversation.

'He hit it off with Aoife right away,' Bridget says. She sounds a little dreamy, as if she's back in the 90s already. 'I had her so young, I was still a child myself. Most men woulda run a mile if I said I'd a seven-year-old at home. A few did. Her own da didn't even stay with me long enough for her to know his face.' I hear her fumbling, and then the unmistakeable sound of a cigarette being lit. She takes a drag and I can almost smell it. 'But Lawrence was like nobody else I'd ever met. He didn't care. The opposite, actually. He seemed delighted by her. Asked about her all the time, seemed genuinely interested.' Bridget gives a little cough-laugh and takes another drag of her cigarette. I put my thumb through the hole in my jumper and wait.

'My friends couldn't believe how lucky I was. This was… start of '96, I think. Thereabouts. He'd just been in some BBC drama. He had about four lines, but back then, my God. He was famous to us. It got him a part in a play in the Lyric Theatre. God, what was the name of it? I can't mind, but we all went to see it and he was just wonderful. He was filming for that show when we met, *Troubled*, did you watch it? And he was going on auditions for big films and everything, and he was just so… captivating. Not just

Little Darlings

on the screen, not just on the stage. People hung off his every word. His own da probably showed him how to do that. Back then all the mams and the grans and the daughters were doolally over Tony Wolfe.' Another drag.

'I met him in the Europa, in the wee bar. He musta been just finishing up his work for the day and he was having a drink with some of the cast. I was out with a few girlfriends, ones I worked with up at the school. Had persuaded my ma to babysit for me. We got chatting and we just… clicked.

'We'd been out only twice when he suggested we plan something the three of us could do. I was so pleased to introduce Aoife to him. She was young for her age. Seven and a half, I think, when they met, but she was still playing with her dollies and she still sucked her thumb to sleep. She was happy and healthy so I didn't mind. There were no parent police about then, nothing went on the Facebook or anything so there was nobody to say, "Stop her doing that, she'll get buck teeth." It's all bollocks anyway, Aoife has lovely teeth and she sucked that thumb till she was near in high school.' Another chuckle, another drag.

'Anyway. We went to the cinema. I remember that because that was always what he suggested. A trip to the cinema was his idea of the perfect day out. He watched everything, you know. He wasn't… pretentious about his films. He'd watch action, romance, horror. But we went to a kids' film that time. We went to see the dalmatians, that time.'

It takes me a minute, and I've missed a bit of what Bridget is saying before I realise she is talking about *101 Dalmatians*.

'…and after that she was buck mad about dogs. Dalmatians everything. He took her to the Disney shop after the cinema, do you mind the one in Donegall Place? And he got her this big plush dalmatian teddy. She had it for years, even after we separated. She thought he was the bee's knees.' Bridget takes a drag of her cigarette, then another. 'We got married in 1997. We were so in love. We were a family. We were young, I know, but it felt right and it made us happy. We just got married at City Hall and went for a meal. It was just the three of us.'

'Tony and Audrey didn't go?' I ask, surprised. Their only son, their golden boy getting married, and they didn't make the trip to Belfast?

'No,' Bridget says. 'No, I never met them. He never introduced us.'

I frown. 'I don't understand. They were really close, why didn't you meet them?'

'I'm not sure,' Bridget says, but she sounds as if she's holding back. I don't push it.

'We bought a house in Stranmillis. Well, I say "we". He bought it, it was his name on the papers. Tony had given him a big chunk of money when he turned twenty-one, you see. He'd gone travelling for a while but still had a pot left, so he bought it outright. We moved in there. We were so happy… for about a year.'

The bedroom with the blue wallpaper. It was blue with dalmatians on it. I had forgotten that detail. The dalmatians.

I'm not there. I'm not there. I'm in my house in my room on my bed, my husband is only shouting-distance away. My child sleeps beneath me. I am safe here.

The light fitting shaped like a rocket.

I'm not there. I'm not there.

'We grew apart a little,' Bridget continues. 'He wasn't getting work. He went on auditions and he got bit parts. Is that what they call them? Little bits to do for TV, but that wasn't good enough for him. He thought he was better than all that, and he wanted to do something bigger and better. He turned things down if they weren't big enough. I tried to encourage him, but he sort of… started ignoring me. I know it sounds weird to say it out loud. But he ignored me. My own husband, in our own house. He stopped inviting me on their cinema trips; he went with Aoife alone.'

I stare at the chip in the skirting board but I can see the blue wallpaper. The rocket light. Aoife's bedroom.

Little Darlings

'She adored him. Came home fulla stories, funny things he'd said, things he'd bought her. The personal jokes they had. The way they were.' This last she says with a different tone. Suspicion. Disgust, maybe. 'They were very physical. Nothing alarming, just… Huggy. Kissy. Cuddly. It was good, I'd thought, at the start. He was her stepfather, after all. I wanted them to be close. But he was being close and affectionate with her, and not with me…' Bridget takes a deep breath. 'I started to feel like a third wheel with them, if I'm honest. It was like I was in the way of something. They would stop talking when I came into a room. And once or twice…'

She gives a sniff and I wonder if she's crying. 'Once or twice, if we were all sitting on the sofa, I got the impression he was kind of… stroking her arm or her leg. I'm probably wrong. I'm probably exaggerating it in my mind, now. But it was strange. He was strange with her. And he always watched her, Mrs Harris, that's the thing. When Aoife was in a room, to him it might otherwise have been empty. I know what an affectionate parent looks like, and this was just different. I'm sorry I can't describe it better.'

'You don't think you're exaggerating,' I say. 'Do you? Because you divorced him shortly after you married. So, you don't think you're exaggerating.' I wait to see if she will say something, but she sounds like she might be crying and I don't want to lose her. 'Did you think he was grooming her?'

Bridget makes a noise like I've stepped on her toes.

'It wasn't a word back then,' she says. She sniffs. 'Not one I'd heard of, anyway. But looking back on it now… I think, yes. He probably was. Right in front of my face.'

I let her cry quietly for a moment or two, glad that we aren't next to each other so there is no expectation that I will have to comfort her.

'When we left, I asked her about it,' Bridget says after a moment. 'I asked her if he ever touched her inappropriately, if he ever made her feel uncomfortable. She looked at me like I was crazy. She was angry with me for leaving him. For years, actually. But I believed her when she said he'd never hurt her. As far as she was concerned, he was perfect.'

'So you never told the police?'

'Told them what?' Bridget sounds defensive, and I wish I'd worded my question differently. 'Nothing happened. Aoife said herself, nothing happened. What would I have told them?'

'Yeah,' I say in a small voice. 'Yeah, okay.'

'Do you think if I had it would have made a difference to you?' I can't tell if she is asking me that seriously. Would it have made a difference?

'Yes,' I say finally. 'Yes, I think it probably would.'

I uncross my legs and tiptoe to the door and press my ear against it. I can just about hear the TV in the living room, then the unmistakeable sound of Steve clearing his throat from the same place. I tiptoe back.

'I'm going to go and speak to the police next week,' I say, my mind made up. 'I'm not sure how it will all work, seeing as it's so long ago, but if I give them your name, would you be happy to—'

'No!' Bridget bleats. 'No! I'm sorry. I can't. I don't want Aoife to know any of this. I only called because I… Well, I felt guilty. Aoife told me about your conversation and I couldn't get you out of my head, so I knew I had to speak to you. But I don't want Aoife to have all of this to go through. She's having a hard time at the minute and I don't want to add to that. Please, do what you have to do, but don't involve me.'

Frustration squeezes my eyes shut and I clench my phone tightly. 'Mrs Spears. Bridget. If I go to the police, if I tell them everything that happened… Surely they'll have to look into his relationship with you.' I refuse to say his name. She knows who I mean. 'They'll ask you questions anyway. I have to do this. I have to.'

Until she tried to snatch it away, I don't think I realised how ready I was, how strongly I felt. How sure I was that I was going to the police. I drove to Belfast. I can do this.

Little Darlings

'Do I have your word that you'll tell them the truth?' I ask. 'That you'll tell them what you just told me?'

Bridget sobs and I hear her shuffling, maybe mopping at her nose with a tissue.

'You don't understand,' she moans. 'My Aoife – she's been trying to get pregnant for five years. She's had three rounds of IVF, her third one just a week ago. I don't want this for her. Not now. You don't know how many times she's lost…' Bridget chokes back a sob. 'Do you have children?'

I wait, not wanting Daisy, the fact of her beautiful existence, to get in the way or distract me.

'Do you?' she repeats.

'Yes,' I say. 'A daughter.'

'Then you can't possibly understand how hard it's been. The last thing she needs is all of this being brought up. The stress of it. Being interviewed, asked questions by the police. What good would it do? She's so desperate for a baby. You don't understand.'

I imagine a girl in a police station, asked questions by the police. No, not an image, a memory. The officers raising their eyebrows, even the kind ones.

'Okay,' I say finally, and I hate that I am doing it again, that I am agreeing and nodding along and not standing up for myself. I tell her exactly what she wants to hear. 'Okay. I understand. Thank you.'

Chapter 22 | February 2001 | The Driveway of Chaplin House

Lawrence talked the whole drive home. I couldn't speak, so I just tried to listen, but it was so tiring that I had to give up. He was driving too quickly, much more quickly than before, and I wanted to ask him to slow down, but what was the point? He didn't listen to me any more. He didn't care what I had to say.

It was dark because it was always dark in February unless I was at school, even though it wasn't that late, and the headlights bumped down the road towards Chaplin House.

'The farmers have been spreading slurry,' Lawrence said, with that little twist to his nose that I had learned meant he was unhappy. 'It stinks, doesn't it?'

I looked out at the muddy road, thick piles of manure in wiggly lines, puddles of water from the rain. The headlights caught a gate, then the road sign that I had come to recognise as our road, with a name I still couldn't pronounce, then Lawrence braked suddenly to turn and I flew forward in my seat.

'Oh, I'm sorry, little darling!' He reached across and put a hand on my forehead like I had a temperature. 'I wasn't concentrating.'

He sped up the long driveway towards the house. Much too quickly. All the trees were dead, their branches sharp and long and thin and moving in the breeze, and they didn't look pretty any more, they just looked dead. I could smell the slurry, and my head was sore, and I wanted so badly to cry that it was hurting my throat not to, and I wanted to talk to Charlotte, and at the same time I never wanted to look at her again. I opened my mouth and thought I was going to be sick, but then I screamed—

'RONNIE!'

Lawrence braked hard again, and both of us flew forward. This time, my neck snapped back and hit the seat behind me with a thud.

'Shit,' Lawrence said. I could hear him breathing. I kept my eyes shut tight to the image of Ronnie walking towards us down the drive, his green backpack over his shoulders and the snaking wire of his bulky headphones connecting his pocket to his ears. We'd killed him. He was dead. We'd run him over. It was all my fault.

'Stop it,' Lawrence said. I heard him rolling down the window. 'Stop it, Cara. It's fine.'

I realised I had been whimpering *no no no no no,* and I stopped and opened my eyes.

'What the FUCK are you PLAYING AT?' Ronnie shouted. 'You could have killed me, dickhead!'

I gasped. We hadn't hit him after all. He had dodged aside, into the muddy bog at the side of the driveway, and was shaking his head at Lawrence, his eyes wide. He stepped back up onto the road, carefully, using his outstretched arms to balance. He pulled his headphones down from his ears and let them hang around his neck.

'You must have been doing fifty, you daft bastard!'

Lawrence tightened his fingers on the steering wheel, his breathing still hard like he'd just been running. After a moment, he let out a little laugh that sounded like a sigh.

'Ah, Ronnie!' Lawrence sounded surprised and I had no idea why. He also sounded cheery. 'Sorry, mate! Didn't see you there. A few solar lights either side of the driveway wouldn't go amiss – there's an idea for you over the winter. There's a good lad.'

Ronnie came closer to the window, and looked like he might punch Lawrence, but then he glanced at me in the passenger seat and stopped in his tracks.

'Cara? What are you doing?' Ronnie looked between us for a moment, then came to lean in Lawrence's window. 'Are you all right?'

I tried to make my head move in a nod, but I must not have been successful because his eyes widened.

'Where were you? Cara, you don't look well at all.'

'She's fine,' Lawrence said sharply. 'She thought we'd hit you, that's all. But no harm done. What are you doing here anyway? It's Saturday. Where's the wee car?'

'Where were you?' Ronnie repeated. He was completely ignoring Lawrence, his eyes fixed on me the same way Julie's had fixed on me when I was telling her something. Like he was concerned and he cared and he was listening to me.

That wasn't the same way Lawrence looked at me now. Had I been wrong about him the whole time?

'She had an audition in Belfast,' Lawrence said. 'For a new film. Didn't you, Cara? I was being a good uncle and drove her there. Not that it's any of your business.'

'Is that true, Cara?'

I had a strange feeling then, like there was one part of me in the too-hot car, breathing in Lawrence's aftershave with the funny long name, and there was another one of me looking in through the sunroof, and that one was watching the other one like it was a TV show. And I knew how she wanted the next scene to go.

I looked at Ronnie, then at Lawrence. Both men were looking at me, Ronnie's tanned face all round and soft and a bit scared looking, and Lawrence's all sharp lines and pointy nose and that sheen of sweat on his forehead that was back. The car engine thrummed and made me feel like I was vibrating.

I made a noise that was supposed to be a no, but it didn't sound like anything, really, and before I could try again, Lawrence revved the engine.

'Well, it's been lovely chatting, Ronnie. Sorry about the near-miss but have to get this one home. Can you get off the car, please, mate?'

Little Darlings

Ronnie looked at Lawrence, finally.

'I'm not your mate,' he said softly. I could barely hear him. He seemed to hesitate, then said, 'Actually, I think I've forgotten something in the house. I was up fixing the projector for your dad; think I left something in the cinema room. I'll come back up with you.'

Lawrence hit a button on the dashboard and I heard the doors lock.

'You can get it tomorrow,' Lawrence said.

'It'll only take a minute, and sure I'm here now. The car wouldn't start earlier so I walked all the way up. I'll just come up to the house. Go in and get it. Ask Tony if he knows anything about this audition.'

'He does,' Lawrence said. I could tell his teeth were gritted and he was trying not to show it. The Cara on the roof couldn't see how white his knuckles were on the steering wheel, but the Cara in the car could. 'But again, like I said, it's none of your business. Why don't you go home to Nanny, Ron?'

Ronnie gave a little laugh and stepped back from the car.

'As you wish, s*ir*.' He gave a bow that even I knew was just pretend, readjusted his straps on his shoulders and walked off in the direction we had just come from. Lawrence watched him in the rear-view mirror for a moment and then let out a breath.

'Nosey bastard,' he said. He gave a little laugh. 'I'm sorry if I scared you, little darling. Maybe I was going just a bit too fast.'

He put the car into gear and drove slowly, the driveway inclining and making the car struggle.

'If he brings it up again,' Lawrence said. 'Make sure you stick to the story. Okay? We were in Belfast. You did have an audition. You're not lying; you just didn't go. We had a lovely day together instead. Didn't we?'

'Yes,' one of the Caras said quietly. I didn't know which one.

'Oh, what the fuck is he doing now,' Lawrence said under his breath. I looked at him. He was staring into the rear-view mirror, his eyes huge and manic. 'Why is he following us?'

I turned in my seat to look out the back window. Indeed, Ronnie was following us. He was moving slowly, cautiously, walking on the very edge of the driveway, close to the bog. He stopped when he noticed that Lawrence had stopped, and he sunk back into the shadows.

'Silly boy,' Lawrence said. He was turned to look out the back window too, his chin touching the top of my head.

And then we were moving backwards. I waited a beat before I panicked, waiting for Lawrence to stop the car or put it in gear or out of gear or whatever it was that would make it stop. But it picked up speed instead, and a glance at Lawrence told me that we were moving on purpose. His mouth was a straight line, and he didn't seem to be breathing. His eyes were the only part of him that was alive, so white they shone in the darkness as he reversed the car back down the drive faster, and faster, and faster. He swerved to one side, and then—

A thump.

Lawrence braked and the car jolted forward just in time before we slid down into the bog.

I just sat there and didn't do anything, because that was what I was good at.

He turned the car off but kept the lights on, and it was suddenly so quiet I heard him swallow. Someone was whimpering and it was one of the Caras or both of them, and she was stupid and young and useless and she couldn't help anyone, not even herself, and there was no point in her being alive.

Lawrence opened his door and took off his seatbelt in one heartbeat. Got out and closed the door again with another. In three heartbeats, he had stepped around to the back of the car, looked at something, and got back inside.

He put his hands on the steering wheel but he didn't put the car on.

'Time to go inside, Cara,' he said quietly. I could tell he was concentrating on every word. Every syllable. 'Lift your wee rucksack and go back up to the house. Quietly. Go straight up to your room.'

'Aren't you coming with me?' I whispered. I hated that I needed him, but the thought of walking up the hill in the dark all by myself was the only thing worse than doing it with him. Something that I couldn't name told me that I was safe from Lawrence for tonight. He wasn't going to touch me again. Or make me touch him. Something else was happening.

He looked at me and his face softened.

'Of course. Sorry. I'll walk you up, little darling. Don't be scared.'

He got out of the car and I tried and failed to undo my seatbelt. My fingers kept missing. Lawrence opened my door, leant across me and clicked the seatbelt. Then he put his hand on my cheek and kissed my forehead and just waited there for a minute, breathing slowly like he was Auntie Audrey meditating on the patio. I waited for him to be finished, then got out of the car, taking my school bag in my hands and holding it tightly.

'Today was our secret,' he said again. 'We're the only people in the world that can know, okay?'

'Okay,' I said. I turned my head to the back of the car and Lawrence sucked in his breath.

'Don't,' he said. 'Don't look. If you love me, Cara, you won't look—'

He stopped and we both looked towards the house. Footsteps were coming across the gravel and around the corner, towards us. If there was supposed to be a plan, there wasn't time for it.

A beam of light came around the corner, followed by Uncle Tony who was wearing a beanie hat and holding a torch out in front of him.

'I thought it must be you two!' he said cheerily. He came down the steep driveway towards us, practically skipping. 'The lights came up the drive a few minutes ago but you never came inside, so I thought maybe you'd got a flat tyre or something. Ronnie seems to be having trouble with his motor too, maybe something in the water. How did the audition go, Cara? Do you think you got it?'

'No,' I said, glad to be able to answer with just the word.

'Oh, don't say that! I'm sure you were wonderful. What's up with the car, Laurie?'

Uncle Tony's face changed when he got a bit closer. 'Good God. What's happened to you pair? You look as if you've seen a ghost.'

'Dad,' Lawrence said. There was something in his voice I had never heard before, ever. He sounded like a child. He sounded like he was about to cry. 'I need your help. I need – I need—'

And then Lawrence was crying, and I was so surprised that my mouth actually fell open. And then he had fallen to the ground in a big ball, and Uncle Tony looked bewildered, but he leant down to hug him anyway, and he didn't even know what was wrong, and I thought it must be nice to be loved like that. The word came to me and I didn't know where from.

Unconditionally

Between sobs, Lawrence tried to explain, but he wasn't making enough sense for Tony to think to look behind the car, so I moved back slowly to have a look myself.

I stared at the dark mass on the ground – half underneath the car and half fallen into the ditch. I couldn't see his face and I was glad, because I didn't think I could look at him. I couldn't see any blood, it was too dark, but I knew there must be some. There was always blood when something bad happened.

I wondered if Mum had looked like this when she had her accident. I wondered who had been the first person to see her, who first realised something was wrong.

Ronnie's Walkman had become separated from the headphones. I reached down and picked it up, and was surprised by how warm it was. Then I realised it was warm blood and I felt sick.

'Cara?'

I snapped to attention and thrust my hands behind my back, sure I was looking guilty.

Uncle Tony was coming towards me.

'Come on now, sweetheart. You go inside. I'm sure Ronnie isn't too badly hurt. I'll get him to a hospital now. This is a horrible accident.'

'I think he might be dead,' I heard myself saying, and I hadn't realised it was true until I said it. He really might be. There was no way he was choosing to lie in that position, his arms and legs bent at those funny angles. There was no way his neck would be lolling back into the ditch if he was alive. It made me feel cold, and not just because of the cold night.

'No, no,' Uncle Tony said, his eyes moving to Ronnie and back to me. 'I'm sure he's fine. He's just hurt. You go on inside. And Cara, maybe don't say anything quite yet, okay? Not to Auntie Audrey or your sister.'

I started to move towards the house.

'There's a good girl,' Uncle Tony said, and I knew he wasn't really looking at me or paying attention because he didn't even notice I was still holding the Walkman. I put it in my backpack and didn't know why.

Lawrence was too upset to walk me back to the house, even though he had said he would, but I didn't say anything because I could tell something really quite serious had happened and I knew everyone would be angry with me if I hung around asking questions and being annoying. I sprinted up the drive as quickly as I could, my backpack swinging in my hand and banging off my knees. I didn't care. I went up the steps to Chaplin House and flung the door open and ran inside.

I didn't care what Uncle Tony had said. I was going to tell Charlotte. I had to. How could I keep it a secret? How could anyone? When Ronnie didn't come to pick us up on Monday, then they would all know something had happened and ask questions and be angry with me for not telling them.

Unless Uncle Tony was right, of course. That he was just hurt and not dead.

Yes, maybe he was just hurt.

If he was, he would be so upset to see that his Walkman was all smashed.

Either way, I would tell Charlotte. Ask for her advice. It didn't count if I told Charlotte because she was my sister. Maybe she would know what to do. Or even better, she could tell me I was being a stupid cry-baby for even worrying about it. Yes, that was it.

I opened the door to the third floor and barrelled up the stairs, not caring about the dangerous spaces in the treads, not even glancing out The Big Window. I threw myself into Charlotte's bedroom, and said breathlessly—

'Charlotte!'

I looked around, breathing heavily. She wasn't there. I checked in our bathroom, then poked my head into my room. No sign. I went back into her bedroom, just in case I'd somehow missed her and she had somehow missed me, and I realised something wasn't right.

Her things were gone.

Her Furby that always sat on the bed was gone. The wardrobe was open and there were no skirts or sparkly tops inside. The poster of *Edward Scissorhands* was missing, and the *Titanic* one, and the black-and-white one, a few tiny nubs of Blu Tack marking the corners where they had been.

'Charlotte?' I called, feeling afraid.

Had she run away?

She'd been so angry about the audition, I thought, and I let myself slide onto her bed feeling miserable and sore and tired and ashamed and everything else there was to feel. I wanted to talk to her more than I wanted to talk to Mum, more than I wanted to go back in time. I just wanted my sister because even though she sometimes hated me I knew she loved me and she would forgive me if I told her the truth. If I told her everything and just explained.

Footsteps came up the stairs past The Big Window and I jumped.

Charlotte came into her room and she jumped too when she saw me. She was wearing her long tartan pyjamas and she had her hair in rollers, the way Audrey had showed her. She barely looked like my sister. She quickly folded her arms and looked me up and down.

'You're back,' she said.

'Yeah.'

'Did you get it?'

'Get what?'

She tutted and sighed and moved past me. She opened her chest of drawers and lifted a handful of clothes in her arms.

'What are you doing?'

'Skateboarding,' she muttered, not looking at me. She was fussing with picking up a few socks that had fallen.

'Where's all your stuff?'

'In my room.'

'This is your room.'

'Not any more.'

'What do you mean?'

'I've moved downstairs.'

'What? Why?'

'Just fancied a change. I'm in the room opposite Audrey now.'

I stared at the back of her head.

'But why?' I asked again.

'Don't want to be in this shitty wee room any more.'

I blinked at her.

'It's not a shitty wee room,' I said quietly. 'You love this room.'

'No,' she said simply. She strutted to the door and I thought she was going to leave without saying anything else. Then she turned on her heel and looked at me.

'Did you get the part?' she demanded.

'Oh,' I said. I thought of the room with the rocket light and then I stopped thinking about the room with the rocket light because I was never going back there and it didn't matter. 'No.'

She seemed to relax a bit and she let her shoulders fall.

'Oh, well,' she said, and she gave me a bright smile. I was so surprised I couldn't even smile back.

She started down the stairs and I called, 'Charlotte, wait!' but either she didn't hear me or she didn't care. She just kept going, and I found I didn't have the energy left to chase her, or even to get up to go to my own room. There was no point.

I let myself fall sideways and put my face on Charlotte's pillow. It smelled like expensive shampoo and I hated it, and I hated all of them, and I hated Charlotte, and I hated Lawrence, and I hated myself the most for making all of this happen.

I didn't expect to sleep, but it came for me quickly. I dreamt I was trapped under a car and I was trying to scream but nothing was coming out, and people were walking past and ignoring me and turning their heads the other way while I cried and screamed and fought, and in the grey sky there was a motionless rocket.

Chapter 23 | March 2023 | Belfast

Knowing that I could drive to Belfast now made it easier when Charlotte WhatsApped me asking to meet for lunch a few weeks later. I told Steve I was going into the office and I don't know why. Because I still hadn't told him I was off on further-extended compassionate leave? Because it was the only way I could realistically not be there when he got home on a random Tuesday? He was surprised and pleased for me, and believed me completely without a second thought, even though I haven't been to my office for over a year.

I am to meet her outside the Opal Building at midday. I'm not surprised that I'm there before her, despite the fact that she lives inside and I've had an hour's drive. I zip up my puffy coat, shivering and looking up at the tall building. Young professionals enter and exit the tower like it's an office block, all sensible wool coats and black boots and laptop cases, takeaway coffees in hand. Aoife's office is only a ten-minute walk from here.

Maybe I could speak to her again, tell her what her mum told me, try to get her on my side.

'Hiya!'

I jump in shock as Charlotte comes up to my shoulder, feeling guilty – as I have so many times over the last few weeks – that I have been caught with Lawrence Wolfe in my head. I want to think about something else but him. I want to talk about something else and actually concentrate. I don't want him to be the backbone of my every day. He was for so long, but he hasn't been for years.

'What's wrong?' Charlotte asks.

'Nothing,' I say quickly. I peck her on the cheek. 'You surprised me.'

'Oh, good. I'd hate to be predictable.'

She links her arm through mine as we walk into the city centre, and that makes it hard for me to look at her properly, but I take as many glances as I can towards her as she leads the way. She has on a grey button-up parka, with a stripy pink scarf tied a few times around her neck, and jeans, and boots. Almost the same outfit as me, all high street brands.

I think of the Charlotte who lived with me in Chaplin House – the husk of me, towards the end, the shell of the child I once was – and how she wouldn't have been seen dead in anything from the high street. We weren't close enough in the years that followed for me to know when she changed back into Charlotte from the doll version of Audrey she'd been. I wonder how much of her I've missed.

Charlotte has chosen a restaurant with only seven rickety tables inside, but a glance at the menu prices tells me it's shabby chic and not shabby. I can never tell. The walls and high ceiling are painted to look like a beautiful blue sky, and there is an orange tree – fake? I think? – hanging down above our table, trying to push the glass chandelier away. I have to squint at the tiny print on the menu; the chandelier is merely decorative and provides no light whatsoever. There are two other couples in the restaurant, but they are far enough away that we can't hear their conversations.

'How are things?' Charlotte asks as the waiter takes our menus away. She tucks her fringe behind her ear. It is so strange to be so close to her. I have seen her maybe a dozen times over the years, but always *for* something, and always with other people. My wedding, where she was one of only four guests, the odd birthday, four or five Christmases. Two funerals, now. We haven't been alone for a long time.

'Yeah, fine,' I say automatically.

Little Darlings

'How's work?'

I feel myself blushing against my will and look down, pretending to examine the plastic tablecloth, which has been decorated with Italian postcards from different cities.

'Fine, fine,' I say. 'And before I forget, Daisy wanted me to invite you to her school play. It's at the end of June; shall I tell her to get you a ticket?'

'Yes, definitely. What is it?'

'*Comedy of Errors.*'

'Ah, yes. You look really well for having a twenty-year-old daughter, by the way.'

'Kid-friendly, apparently. Not sure what it'll be like, but she has lines and everything, so she'd love you to come.'

'I'll be there.'

'But how are things with you?' I ask. 'You do look really well.'

She smiles and she looks even better. Her teeth have always been pretty perfect, even when she's not been taking care of herself, and they're white and even and her cheekbones are high. She's still too slim – her face just a little too gaunt under her expertly applied makeup, but her eyes look clear and bright. Her curls have been pulled back into a ponytail today. She looks younger than she has in years.

'Thank you,' she says. 'Yeah, I'm trying to… I dunno. Be better.'

'Good for you.'

The waiter brings us two sparkling waters and we make an awkward little cheers with them. I sip mine and look at her.

'Why do I feel nervous like I'm on a first date,' I say finally, and we both giggle and smile at each other. 'Been over a decade since I've been on one of them.'

'I was on one a few months ago.'

'Oh?'

'Not going to happen. He had seven cats.'

'Seven? That's a lot. And you're allergic.'

'I am, well remembered. I just thought it wouldn't work out if I ever had to move in. Plus, not sure his mum would have liked that.'

'Oh, I see.'

'He'd never seen *Edward Scissorhands*, Cara.'

'Are you serious? Is that legal?'

'That's what I said! I told him to get a life. Well, no, I didn't. I was very nice about it but I did tell him we probably weren't right for each other.'

'Understatement.'

'Oh well. Plenty more fish.'

Something stirs in my mind that I want to say, but I have gone for nearly an hour without thinking about it, so maybe I shouldn't tarnish such a lovely day with the mention of such a name.

A beat.

I can't help myself.

'I always wonder if you're… with Lawrence.'

I hate that I've said it, but my eyes fall on hers and I don't blink, afraid I'll miss something. I don't want him here, in between us, but I do. I have to know.

With Steve and Daisy, I wake up every day and decide who I am going to be. For most of Daisy's life I have managed to be worthy of her, even on days when I don't feel worthy of getting out of bed. Like putting makeup over my scarred cheekbone, I can wear motherhood like a mask and make that my personality. Just a slightly anxious but funny mother, nothing more. Before Daisy the good stretches were shorter, but I made enough of an effort that the early days of mine and Steve's relationship were mostly giggly, mostly comfortable, almost always honest and unfailingly loving. The past was locked in a box, and with Steve I let my hold loosen enough to lose the key.

But I don't have to pretend with Charlotte. I don't owe her a mask, and I don't have to think about which Cara I should be in front of her.

'*With* him?' Charlotte asks, her eyes widening in alarm. 'Cara, he's our—'

The waiter brings our chicken Caesar salads and we thank him and he nods and leaves our table.

'He's not our cousin,' I say, picking up the thread, afraid it will unspool and be lost to us forever. 'Or our uncle or anything. Not really.'

'No, I know, but no.' She shakes her head. 'No, never. It's not like that.'

'What is it like? I've always wanted to know.'

When the question has hung in the air between us for ten seconds, I pick up my fork and spear some chicken onto it. I swallow without tasting.

'I've just always kept in touch,' Charlotte says finally. She looks down at her lunch but doesn't make a move to start. 'He's got me out of a fair few tricky situations, you know?'

'Drugs?' I ask.

'Well. Yes. I'd have been homeless three times over if it wasn't for him.'

It feels like a punch to my stomach. I'm more hurt than I have been in a long time.

'You'd never be *homeless*,' I say, turning the volume down on the word as if it's a curse. I put my fork down and lean towards her. 'You've always had me. You could have stayed with us any time.'

She lets a little laugh escape through her nose. 'You're kind to say so. But that's not true, is it? Having Daisy's alcoholic auntie sleeping on the sofa isn't part of the picture of the life you've painted yourself. Steve never would have—'

'Steve would do anything for me,' I say. 'Sorry for interrupting you.'

'You don't have to… anyway.' She takes a deep breath. 'Laurie makes a lot of money. He was around. I had to rely on him a lot more than I ever expected I'd need to.'

'But why him?' I insist. 'Why not Uncle Tony?'

Charlotte shrugs. 'Same thing. Or thereabouts. Laurie… cared about me. He cares. I don't like having to be so reliant on someone else but there's nothing else I can do. Or, there wasn't. Until now.' She sits up straighter, suddenly, and smiles again. 'I have some news.'

'Okay?'

'I'm going to be in a film.'

'You – Oh! Right. Okay. Wonderful. What's the film?'

'It's an adaptation of last year's Booker Prize—'

'*The Girl Who Moved the Mountains?*'

'You know it!'

'I read it, it was amazing.'

'It's the best book I've read in years. I went to an audition for it ages ago, and they called the other day. They want me. Cara, I'm going to be the lead.'

We spend the rest of the afternoon talking about Charlotte's new job while the restaurant fills up. It seems the role is the reason she has managed to keep herself so clean for so long; she knew she was meant for the part, and it seems she was right. It's a huge British production company, and they start filming over the summer. She is animated and bright, the Charlotte that I have always kept in my head. It is like going back in time and rocketing into the future. It could be Daisy in front of me or my sister aged eleven. It's the strangest thing.

When the bill comes I grab for it, but Charlotte beats me to it.

'This was my idea, and you've come all this way,' she says. 'What time is your bus back?'

'I drove,' I say, feeling ridiculously proud. 'I'm parked not far from you.'

'Good for you,' she says. 'How come you aren't working today?'

I blush and consider lying. She notices my hesitation and gives an exaggerated smirk. 'Are you playing hooky?'

'I'm on compassionate leave,' I say, wincing. 'I know it's horrible to use Audrey like that but I couldn't face work just yet. I'm going back on Monday though, so don't tell Steve.'

'It'll be hard to keep it from him. We do see each other, oh, once a year.'

'I'll tell him eventually.'

'He's not noticed the bank balance?'

'He never checks it.'

'Must be nice.' Charlotte gives a little sniff and looks down. She frowns at the bill.

'Have they added something extra?' I ask, trying to read it upside down.

'No, I just didn't realise the date.'

I blink.

'Would have been Mum's birthday today,' Charlotte says with a sad smile. She pushes the bill towards me as if I need proof of the date.

'Shit, yeah.'

Our mum had a seizure and died when Daisy was six months old. The cruellest thought I've ever had was that it was a tiny relief. For so many years she had been a presence. An idea, but not a person. Not our mum. Someone I used to know who didn't exist any more. Daisy stayed with Steve's mum while we went to the funeral. Tony and Audrey were in Australia when it happened. Travelling, for once. Not working. Audrey offered to come back but there really wasn't any point in a fuss.

I didn't cry because I'd already been grieving for nearly fourteen years by then.

'I'd have loved to tell her I was an actress,' Charlotte murmurs. 'I'd have loved for you to tell her about Daisy.'

'All of this would have been different, if she hadn't had her fall,' I say. 'The series of events would have been altered. I probably never would have met Steve; you wouldn't have got your part.'

'Might have got a bigger part,' Charlotte muses.

'Maybe. Or you might not have cared one bit about acting.

I think it's fair to say that was always the Wolfes' influence on you.'

'I'll give you that. They are a very influential bunch.'

'Especially Audrey. You adored her.'

'I did. I worshipped her. When I got the news about my part, the first person I wanted to tell was her.'

This hurts too, but I try not to show it. Steve is the person I want to share my good news with, so it's unfair for me to be sad that I wouldn't be Charlotte's first choice.

The bell above the door makes a tinkling sound. The waiter greets two men in suits and glances towards our table, and the two men nod and take menus and go to stand at the bar.

'I think we've overstayed our welcome,' I say to Charlotte. I nod and smile at the waiter and make a point of standing up and grabbing my coat from the back of my chair. 'They need this table.'

'I remember,' says Charlotte, when we are back out in the cold street. 'When you used to book a table and you were allowed to sit there for as long as you wanted. You only get ninety minutes now.'

'In these post-COVID times.'

'Yes. It's shit. What if I wanted to sit and talk to my baby sister all day in there?'

I smile and don't say anything. We walk in a contented silence back towards Charlotte's building. She stops and looks in the window of a few designer shops, pointing out brands I've never heard of, talking about jackets or shoes that she's had in that brand.

'I'm being sensible with my money recently,' she says as we walk away from a particularly garish pair of green stilettos. 'I've been working in a bar and giving art lessons on the side.'

'You're teaching?'

'Well. Not officially teaching, sure I've no certificates or anything, but I've built up a good enough wee portfolio over the years and I made a Facebook page to show them off and I have a couple of people who want to learn.'

Little Darlings

'I have no idea how I'd even start to teach other people to paint,' I say, baffled. We have reached the River Lagan and follow alongside it. With fewer buildings surrounding us on all sides, the wind pinches our cheeks and Charlotte's bare hands are pink with cold.

'I just make it up as I go along,' she admits. 'I think that's all any of us are doing, really.'

The Opal Building comes into view and panic flares in my chest. I had wanted to tell Charlotte one thing today, and that one thing has not yet been said, and here we are, almost back at her flat, and my opportunity is growing fainter and fainter with every step.

'Charlotte,' I say eventually, coming to a halt and putting one hand on the railings overlooking the river. There is a man standing on a fishing boat, curling a never-ending piece of rope around and around, his eyes watching the water as he moves his hands in a rhythm he knows by heart. 'I'm thinking of doing something and I thought I should tell you about it.'

'Okay.' Charlotte has stopped too, and she puts her cold hands on the railings close to mine. In between us is a square red box that should contain a lifebuoy.

It's empty.

'I think I'm going to go to the police,' I say. I don't think I've conveyed any emotion in my tone. If I have, I can't even work out what that emotion might be myself.

Charlotte's brow furrows as she looks at me. 'Why?'

'Well. You know why. Don't you?'

Her mouth falls open just a crack, and she continues to look at me. I find I can't look back at her pretty face without seeing a leaner, better version of my own. How is it fair that she is the one who has abused her own body with drugs and drink, and I still want to look just like her?

'Is it— is this about Laurie?' Charlotte says quietly.

'Yes.'

'Is this the thing with the police? When I was in P7?'
'Yes.'
'Oh. I thought – I always thought—'
'That I was lying?' I guess. 'That I wanted attention?'

Charlotte's blush is fierce and unkind on her pale face, and she tries to shake her head but we both know it's true.

'It's fine. It was pretty unbelievable. It must have come as a shock to you that I was saying he was less than perfect. If it had been the other way around I know I wouldn't have believed it for a second.'

Her eyes are on the water now, and I can tell she is thinking hard. 'The police asked me questions,' she says after a moment. 'I can't— I can't remember what I said.'

'He used to come into my room at night when he was at home.'

At this her eyes spring back to mine and I see that tears have formed in them. Shock, I think.

'Into your room…' she murmurs, and she sounds like her thoughts are far away. 'In the attic.'

'Yeah.'

'Oh my God.' Her head is shaking slightly, as if she isn't even aware of it. 'Into your room. Oh my God,' she says again.

'Did you know?'

Her head continues to shake, but I'm not entirely sure if she's still processing what I've said or if this is an answer. I wonder what she's seeing, what she's remembering. Her eyes have gone glassy.

'Did you know he was a paedophile, Charlotte?'

She gasps at the word and looks left and right. I'm not sure if she's just uncertain, or if she's making sure we aren't being overheard. Then I feel unkind. Audrey was her hero, but she is not Audrey.

'I didn't know,' she whispers. 'I didn't. I didn't know.' I wonder if I am imagining the emphasis on the last word. 'I thought you were making it up.' One tear falls, then another. She makes no attempt to wipe them away. 'I didn't know it was... that. I thought you just liked each other and *you* got carried away, I didn't know you— I didn't realise.' She takes a deep breath, trying to calm herself. 'What did he do?'

I look back at the fisherman, who is still winding the dirty rope and watching the surface of the river.

'There was only one *really* bad time,' I say. 'Only one really bad thing.'

Only one, I think. Why have I worded it like that? As if one is not enough. What if Daisy told me that had happened to her, but that it had happened *only* once?

Charlotte's hands are shaking and she brings one to her mouth as if she is scared she'll throw up.

'He's been in my flat,' she says after a moment. 'I've had dinners and drinks with him. He put down the deposit on my fucking flat.' Her voice breaks and her other hand comes up to her mouth too. She rests her elbows on the railings and looks into the water, but I don't think she is seeing it.

What if the fisherman fell in? I think. There's no lifebuoy. We'd just have to make a phone call or hope he could swim. We'd be able to watch but not to help.

'Cara, I'm so sorry. You tried to tell me; you tried to tell the police. I wish I could go back in time, I wish I'd—'

'You were a child,' I interrupt. 'You were eleven. I'm not angry with you. Not at all. What could you have done?'

The question hangs in the air. The fisherman hoists his rope over his shoulder, a complete, perfect circle, and goes into the covered helm where he disappears out of sight.

'But the police,' Charlotte says eventually. Her eyes are dry now, but her brow is still creased and I fear it may never unwrinkle. 'What are they going to do? They won't believe you.'

I look at her in shock.

'I believe you,' she says quickly, nodding. 'I do believe you, Cara, I swear. I just...' Charlotte looks away, trouble in her eyes, in her whole face. She looks different now than she did in the restaurant. Like she is a beautiful painting in a museum, and the longer you look at it you finally realise that actually the subject is crying. That she is devastated. She is biting the insides of her gaunt cheeks.

I remember with sudden clarity that her teeth are veneers that she got a few years ago; they're perfect but they aren't hers. Laurie maybe even paid for them.

'That was twenty years ago,' she says at last. 'And you spoke to the police at the time and they didn't believe you. There was no evidence then and,' she looks as if she is in pain as she adds, 'there's even less now. If there ever was any it's gone. What makes you think this time will be different?'

Chapter 24 | February 2001 | Chaplin House in the After

Nobody was there when I went down for breakfast the next morning.

Everything was different now in the After, where Lawrence was no longer my friend and instead he had done something that made me feel like I was a different person. He was a different person to me now too. But even though nothing was the same, I still had to eat. *Keep your strength up*, that was what Julie would say. *Look after yourself even when you don't feel like doing it.* What would Bernie say when I next saw him? I wouldn't be telling him anything about my audition, that was for sure.

Birds still flitted past the huge doors in the kitchen, looking for a way to get out of the rain. The wind still howled, and I realised that the whole garden looked different when it wasn't sunny. It wasn't beautiful in the rain; it was just grey and boring like everything else. I stared out at the rain for a while, then poured myself some cereal and orange juice, and I sat alone at the big table which felt even bigger when you were the only person sitting at it. I ate my cereal slowly, staring at a spot on the floor, thinking that being in the After all on my own was even worse than being in the Before all on my own. At least I felt safe in my own head then.

I had just finished when I heard footsteps on the stairs, and then Auntie Audrey came down, her silky white robe pulled around her. She looked tired.

'Morning,' she said. She went over to her cupboard and started pulling out her pill bottles. 'You on your own this morning?'

'Yes,' I said. 'Not sure where everyone is.'

'Oh, probably having a Sunday lie in. I think Tony and Laurie must have gone for a few pints in the village last night – Tony didn't come to bed until late.'

I didn't look at her.

'Oh!' Audrey suddenly clapped her hands and spun around. 'The audition! How did it go? Tell me I'm looking at Eliza Long! I am, aren't I?'

'No,' I said quickly. 'No, no. I didn't get it.'

'Oh,' Audrey sounded genuinely devastated. 'Well, are you sure? They didn't ask you to come for a second audition?'

'No,' I said. Then I added, 'Sorry.'

'Oh,' Audrey said again. 'Well. Never mind. Did you get up to anything nice in Belfast? You were gone all day. You didn't even say goodnight.'

I wasn't sure which of the questions she wanted me to answer, so I just said, 'Sorry. I was really tired,' which was true.

'I'm sure. Do you think you have the acting bug now? Did you enjoy it?'

I shook my head but she wasn't looking at me. She was taking a huge gulp of water and swallowing her pills.

'Did Laurie go and meet his friend while you were up? He said he might do that after he dropped you off.'

'I don't know.'

Audrey put her bottles back in the cupboard and then turned around to smile at me. 'I'm sure you did your best, darling. There's always the next one.'

'Auntie Audrey,' I said cautiously, aware that she was about to go back upstairs and leave me alone again. 'Can I ask you something?'

'Of course,' she said. She blinked at me, waiting. I thought she was probably very beautiful if you took away all the other stuff, like the false eyelashes and the hair extensions, and the strange wrinkly neck that Charlotte had told me had come from sunbed use. She had nice eyes, and they looked way better in the mornings before she put her blue eyeshadow on, but I knew I would never say any of that to her because how she looked was so important to her. Just as I would never tell Lawrence that his fake accent was stupid, and I would never tell Uncle Tony that actually I hated black-and-white films, and I would never tell Charlotte that I didn't want her to grow up, I wanted her to stay wee with me and play games with me and be my sister again, but I didn't want to hurt anyone so I would keep it all to myself and tell everyone what they wanted to hear because that was easier.

'Why did you adopt Lawrence?' I asked.

Audrey's surprised face tried to look more surprised, I thought, but it couldn't.

'Oh. I didn't realise he'd told you about that.'

'Sorry,' I said for the third time in five minutes. 'I didn't know it was a secret.'

'No, no, it's not. It's a fair question I suppose. Would you like the truthful answer or the answer I give in interviews?'

I wasn't sure if that was a real question. Why would anyone want anything but the truth?

She gave a little laugh and came to sit next to me at the table. I watched her.

'I tell people that we were desperate for a baby for a long time, and that we finally looked into adoption and met a little boy who just… swept us off our feet.' She smiled, caught up in some memory I didn't know about.

'But that's *not* true?' I asked.

'No, not really. We never tried. I never wanted to do the whole pregnancy and birth thing. Scary as hell. We had always wanted a son, I suppose. That bit was true. But I knew I wanted to adopt, and then we met Laurie when he was five and the rest is history.'

I thought the whole thing was history, really, because it had happened so long ago, but I didn't say that.

'Did he sweep you off your feet?' I asked.

She laughed again. 'No, actually. No. I would never admit this to anyone but… No. He was a terror.'

'Really?'

My heart started to beat faster. Maybe I could tell Audrey. Maybe she wasn't quite as under Lawrence's spell as everyone else was. Maybe she was my way out.

'He was… troubled. Let's put it like that. He'd been taken off his parents because they weren't very nice to him, and in turn he wasn't very nice to the world. He was difficult for a few years, I have to admit. I had to give up work to look after him. I was a regular on *The Doctor*, you know. I'd been nominated for awards.'

She was away in the past again and I was keen for her to stay in the present.

'Is he still troubled?' I asked. *Please say yes. Please say you understand what he's like. Please tell me you'll believe me when I tell you this horrible thing—*

Audrey blinked and shook her head. 'Goodness me, no. He's wonderful. After such a tough start, it's amazing the man he's grown into. I'm so proud of him. I couldn't love him any more. Even if I'm not biologically anything to him, I'm still his mother. You'll understand it when you're a mother yourself. He's intelligent, he's charming. He's a wonderful actor, a kind person. He can be wildly funny. He's a good boy. Anyway, why are you asking me about this?'

I looked at her, then looked back at my empty bowl, trying to think of what to say.

'Oh, I understand,' she said at last.

'You do?'

I let her take my hands and look into my eyes. I waited for her to say it so I could agree.

'I need you to know, I'd love to adopt you and Charlotte if I could,' she said seriously. 'It would be an honour to raise Kathy's two lovely girls, but the doctors still think there's a chance your

Little Darlings

mum can make a recovery. Adoption isn't an option at the minute, little darling.'

I shook my head and tried to speak, but she made a shushing noise.

'I know it's hard. But we'll love you like this for now. And I know it's not adoption, like with Lawrence, but it's enough. With any luck, your mum will be back to herself in a few months and then you'll feel silly that you ever wanted us to adopt you in the first place!'

She gave her little laugh again and stood up and tightened the belt on her robe.

'Looks like it's clearing up out there,' she said, looking into the garden.

I looked into the garden too, like I knew she wanted me to, and I made a noise of agreement, like I knew she was expecting. It had stopped raining but the sky was still grey and it looked freezing.

'Maybe put your wee coat on and go and play outside for a while? There's a good girl.'

I pushed my chair back and went to the hall to get my coat.

'Where's Charlotte?' Audrey asked as I forced my arms into the sleeves.

'Dunno,' I said. 'She doesn't sleep on the top floor any more. She doesn't want to be near me.'

'Yes, she asked could she move. I think she wanted the room with the bigger wardrobe, to be honest, darling. I don't think it's anything to do with you.'

The next day was Monday. Uncle Tony got up at the same time as us and had breakfast with us and made conversation. I hadn't seen him the day before, and nobody had seen Lawrence. I expected Charlotte to ask about him, but she didn't.

'Ronnie's late,' Charlotte said, craning her head at the front door. 'I like to be in for half-eight on a Monday so I can get changed. I have drama first.'

'You'll not be late, love,' Tony said. 'I'm taking you to the bus stop.'

I froze, one arm twisted behind me to get my school bag on my back.

'Why?' Charlotte asked.

'I have to nip into the village anyway,' he said. 'We can all go to the bus stop together; it's on my way.'

'Oh, okay. I'll do my teeth and we can go, then.' She hopped off her seat and went to the little bathroom behind the kitchen.

I waited until I heard the door close before I said, 'Where is Ronnie? Was he okay?'

'Shhh!' Uncle Tony's eyes were round and wild and serious. 'Cara, not a word. Yes, he was fine. He's just not feeling well.'

'But he's okay?' I asked breathlessly, hardly daring to believe it.

'Yes, of course. He's fine. I just don't want you mentioning what happened to anyone. Not Charlotte and definitely not Audrey. Do you understand?'

'Where is he?' I asked.

'Cara!'

'Yes, yes, I understand. Where is he?'

'He's with his grandmother, I'd expect. Recovering.'

'Will he be back soon?'

'No, I shouldn't think so.'

I opened my mouth, but then Charlotte came back in and Tony did the thing with his eyes again so I didn't say anything.

At least Ronnie was all right. That was all that mattered. My heart felt a little less sore and I felt like I could breathe a bit more. That was something. He was okay.

'What's Laurie been up to?' Charlotte asked as I closed the front door behind us and we went down the steps. The Oddy car had been reversed up the drive much more tidily than usual, and it looked clean and shiny in the weak sun, like someone had washed it. But there was a dent in the back that I had never noticed before.

Small, but deep. Charlotte went to open the door of the car, but Uncle Tony said, 'There's something up with it. It's not working. We're walking to the bus stop.'

I noticed he didn't look at the car as we walked down the driveway.

'Where is Laurie?' Charlotte asked again.

'He's gone away for a few days.' Uncle Tony wasn't looking at us. 'He had a few things to do before he goes to London on his latest job.'

'So, he's not coming back before he goes?' Charlotte demanded. She sounded whiny which was very unlike her, and I could see how it could be annoying so I made a note to stop being whiny if I could.

'No, he's gone,' Tony said. 'He'll not be back for a while.'

Charlotte made a huffing sound and sped up so she could walk ahead of us. She even folded her arms, and I worried she would trip and not be able to right herself.

Halfway down the driveway, I held my breath, looking for any sign of what had happened on Saturday night. Blood would be soaking the tarmac, I thought, or Ronnie's shoe would be lying abandoned in the middle. Uncle Tony seemed to slow down as we passed the bend where it had happened, and I saw his eyes move to the very place. All was as it should have been, though, and he quickly looked away and walked faster down the steep drive, leaving me behind.

I wondered for a brief moment if maybe I had imagined the whole thing or exaggerated what had really happened. I hadn't been in my right mind, after all. I had been someone else, on the roof of the car. But then I glanced up and Tony was looking at me, and as soon as I caught his eye, he looked away and put his hands in his pockets.

We turned left at the end of the driveway and made our way along the country lane, all of us jumping over the puddles and moving around the piles of mud so we didn't ruin our shoes. I fell into step next to Charlotte and was pleased when she didn't rush off or pull back.

'I feel like a pov,' she said to me, sounding huffy.

'What's that mean?' I asked.

'A pov. One of the poor kids. The bus will be stinking; it'll be full of povs.'

Mum had walked us to our old school, in the Before, but if it had been any further away, we would have been bus povs too. I wondered if Charlotte had always been annoyed by our lack of money, or if this was a new, Audrey-inspired thing. How much of my sister was still my sister and how much of her was Audrey?

How much of me was still me?

Charlotte was looking straight ahead, which gave me a chance to look at her face without her shouting at me. Her eyelashes were painted with mascara and some of it had fallen down her cheeks already and it was only eight o'clock. Her pale skin was clear, though, and she looked beautiful. Her curls weren't frizzy any more, thanks to whatever special cream Audrey had given her. They were smooth and big and bouncy, and even under her jumper and blazer I could see her boobs.

It made no sense why Lawrence had chosen me and not her. She was the obvious choice and even I knew it. I hated that he'd picked me. I wished he'd picked her and left me alone, even if it meant never having him laugh at my jokes or cheer me up or buy me presents. I'd give all of that up. I wished he'd picked her instead.

She must have known I was watching her because she turned to look at me.

'What?' she demanded.

'Nothing.'

'Stop staring at me, then.'

I looked away obediently and stared up ahead, the bus stop coming into view.

*

Little Darlings

There was a knock at the door while we were eating dinner that night. Well, Charlotte and Audrey were eating dinner. I had pushed my food around the plate to make it look like I'd eaten, and I noticed Uncle Tony had had two glasses of wine but hadn't eaten much of his plate either.

'Oh, that's probably my new exercise bike!' Audrey clapped her hands together excitedly and dashed off to answer the door.

'She's going to let me use it,' Charlotte informed Tony and me. 'I want to shift a few pounds before the Easter break. There's an open audition for a new film, you see. It's really gritty and serious. Auntie Audrey says I'm perfect for it. It's for thirteen-year-olds but she says I'll have no problem. But I want to shift my tum.'

I stared at her flat stomach and didn't say anything.

We heard Audrey talking to someone at the door. Audrey's loud voice went from surprised, to concerned, to consoling, and we all sat still and listened. Audrey's small heels clicked through the hall and back into the kitchen, and an older lady came and stood behind her. She had a beanie hat on that looked ridiculous over her head of huge grey curls, and her coat was one of the big puffy ones that Charlotte had told me were for losers.

'Tony!' Audrey's eyes were wide, and I knew she was trying to look concerned, but she actually looked excited and it was a strange mix. 'This is Rosa Hilditch, Ronnie's nana. She's looking for Ronnie: he didn't come home on Saturday night.'

'Oh?' Uncle Tony stood and went towards the two women. He really did look concerned. 'That's strange. You haven't heard from him?'

'He hasn't got a mobile phone,' Audrey said, and I got the feeling she was proud of knowing this little bit of information about her employee. 'He asked for this week off, didn't he?'

'Yes, yes,' Tony said. 'He asked for this week off and I said that was fine. We're both off this week so it works out well. Bit short notice but no big deal. I got the impression he was going somewhere…'

Tony ushered Audrey and the older lady back into the hall and closed the door.

'What's that about, I wonder?' Charlotte said.

'Why didn't Ronnie come home?' I murmured, looking at the door where the adults had left.

'That's what I just said. Maybe Laurie knows! We could ask to phone him.'

'I don't think that would help,' I said.

'How the bloody hell would you know?'

'It just wouldn't.'

'Shut up, Cara. You don't know what you're talking about.'

'*You* don't know what *you're* talking about.'

'Stop being such a baby. I've memorised Laurie's number in case of emergencies, so I could phone him now.'

'Don't.'

'You can't tell me what to do.'

'Just DON'T Charlotte!'

'DON'T SHOUT AT ME!'

'DO NOT PHONE HIM. IF YOU PHONE HIM I WILL NEVER SPEAK TO YOU AGAIN FOR THE REST OF MY—'

The door of the kitchen opened and we both closed our angry mouths and turned to face it.

'Girls!' Audrey hissed. She closed the door after her and tiptoed towards us as if she was afraid of making any noise. 'Mrs Hilditch is very upset. Tony has offered to walk her home. She's thinking of phoning the police about Ronnie, she's very worried.'

'Where do they live?' Charlotte asked.

'Oh. That's a good question. I've never thought to ask. In the village somewhere.'

'Why didn't he drive her?' I asked, feeling bold and brave and wanting to draw attention to it. I even folded my arms and stared at Auntie Audrey.

Audrey clicked her tongue. 'The car isn't starting. You know that. Plus she's upset. Tony said the walk would be good for her and I agree. It'll only take half an hour to get there.'

I thought of the tiny dent in the back of the Oddy, of the screech of brakes, of Ronnie lying motionless underneath it. Why hadn't he come home? If he was okay, like Uncle Tony said, where was he?

Unless, of course, Uncle Tony had lied.

'It'll be good for her,' Charlotte said, nodding as if she was wise. 'Good for the shock. I'm sure nothing has happened to him.'

'I'm sure you're right, sweetheart. I'm sure you're right.'

The next morning saw Uncle Tony walking us down the drive and along the country lane again until we got to the tiny bus stop with the single seat and the shelter with a roof that was half coming loose. The seat was soaking wet with the rain from the night before and there were empty cans on the ground, so neither of us sat down. Charlotte had insisted she had to go on the 'first bus' that morning, which wasn't a school bus at all, just a normal bus for adults that happened to stop half a mile away from the school, and I was surprised when Tony didn't argue with her. We'd even left the house twenty minutes earlier than usual so she could get on it.

The first bus drove past, and nearly did just drive past, only Tony flagged it down and stepped in to speak to the driver, who was a bit starstruck and seemed to know exactly who he was. Charlotte got onto the bus and didn't say bye to me or even look at me, but she let Uncle Tony kiss her cheek. As the bus roared away down the road, Uncle Tony turned to me.

'You haven't forgotten our agreement, have you, little darling?'

Little darling. Why could nobody in the Wolfe family call me by my name? Why did it always have to be little darling?

I didn't say anything, just looked at the cans and the wet seat and wished he would go away. I understood now why he hadn't argued with Charlotte – he wanted to speak to me on my own.

I wished nobody would speak to me on my own, it never meant anything good.

'Because you can't say anything to anyone, okay?'

'Where is Ronnie?' I asked, and I wanted to know but it came out like a dull, half-bothered question.

Tony looked like he was struggling with something. A yellow school bus appeared on the hill and he checked his watch.

'That won't be yours yet. It'll be ten minutes.'

'Where is Ronnie?' I asked again.

'I think he's gone away for a while,' Tony said. The yellow bus flew past, far too quickly for the country road. 'I don't think he'll be back. But I don't want anyone to know about the accident on Saturday night. That's very, very important, Cara. Okay? Can you look at me? It's our little secret.'

I was Cara when he wanted me to keep a secret, I thought, and I felt like folding my arms and stamping my feet. I didn't believe him, even though he was looking at me seriously and wasn't flinching. I didn't answer and I didn't say I would keep the secret. I was very careful about that. Uncle Tony seemed to think I'd agreed though, so he let it go and we stood in silence for ten minutes.

He flagged down my bus when it came and it braked so suddenly some puddlewater came flying up and soaked my tracksuit bottoms.

'Make sure you walk home from the bus stop with Charlotte after school. Okay? Tell her that's an order; she has to walk with you. Do you understand?'

I knew he didn't mean about the walk. I nodded because I didn't know what else I could do and adults just wanted you to agree to stuff no matter how you felt about it.

'Good girl. I'll be away when you get back later so I'll see you tomorrow. Have a lovely day at school, little darling.'

He leaned in and kissed my cheek.

'When will Laurie be back?' I heard myself asking.

Little Darlings

'Not long. He'll have a break over Easter, I think. He might come back. He might not. Then he's finished in May. You'll see him before you know it, don't you worry.'

'I don't want to see him.' I said quickly. 'I never want to see him again after Belfast.'

Then I dashed up the steps to the bus and sat down in the first row and didn't even look at the driver. A handful of countryside kids chattered behind me but I got the impression nobody noticed me. I was just there without really being.

The bus pulled away and I glanced back to the bus stop to see Uncle Tony standing with his hands in the pockets of his patchwork coat, his eyes on mine and a look on his face I didn't think I could copy if I tried. Like he'd just come to understand something he didn't want to understand.

My worry over Ronnie had kept everything else 'at bay'. That was what I imagined Julie saying to me if I ever told her about that weekend. That was something I did a lot. I ran things past Julie and imagined her answers to them. I'd stopped speaking to Bernie completely because his chippy office just made me feel sick now and his voice was stupid and boring and Charlotte spoke enough for both of us so he didn't even notice if I went an entire session being silent.

Sometimes the imaginary Julie was very helpful and sometimes she couldn't think of anything to say.

So my feelings had been at bay. I had thought Ronnie was dead, and no matter how I was feeling, that was more important and that worry was the one that needed my attention. I couldn't worry about everything all at once or I'd explode. One worry at a time. Ronnie had been my one worry... but Uncle Tony clearly wasn't going to tell me anything more, and I couldn't think of anything more to do to help Ronnie, wherever he was, so I felt myself starting to worry about me.

I was in a world of my own later that day when Mr O'Shea

suddenly said, 'Cara! Are you listening?' My head snapped up. 'I've asked you twice now, how would we solve question six? You weren't paying attention.'

'Sorry,' I mumbled. I pulled my handout towards me and looked for question six. The page looked fuzzy. I forgot what a six would look like.

Mr O'Shea sighed like I'd really disappointed him and I felt terrible. He was a nice teacher, even though he did always smell like egg sandwiches. 'There's no point in studying for your eleven-plus if you're just going to stare into space, Cara. Cathy, help her out?'

Cathy Hopkins immediately launched into an explanation of how to solve the problem at question six, and I let my mind wander again. I imagined I was in Julie's calm and cosy office, curled up on the big armchair, and I was telling her about the trip to Belfast. She would nod and take notes, never interrupting me unless she had to ask for more detail, and that was how I knew she was really listening to me. Lawrence used to listen to me. He used to care about my feelings and take me seriously and would stop when I told him to stop. Not any more. Then my Julie's-office fantasy was ruined because Lawrence was standing there in the middle of the room in between me and Julie, with his arms folded, and he took up so much space and he took up all the light in the room so there was none left for me.

I took out my box of fancy paints from my school bag (I'd found them under my bed, even though I had definitely checked there), thinking that maybe I could ask to stay inside at break and paint instead of going into the playground. I hadn't painted for weeks. But when I pulled them from my bag, I saw the red tin was dented in the middle. I opened it up.

Over half of the little squares of paint were completely missing, and the other ones had had lumps taken out of them with something sharp. I stared at my paints and felt nothing. Maybe a slight confusion. Had I done this myself? Had Lawrence done this as a warning? Had Uncle Tony?

Little Darlings

I was aware in the back of my mind that a month ago the thought of my paints being ruined might have broken my heart, but there was no heart left in me to break, so I didn't mind.

I walked in circles around the playground at break time. I didn't have the energy to ask to join in with the skipping games, and there was no way I was looking for a quiet corner to hide in for hide and seek. I watched my classmates standing in groups and whispering secrets, watched the boys from the other class kicking a football against the wall of the P5 classroom and being told off by Mrs Harkin.

I liked Amelia the best in my class, but there was no way I could ever imagine telling her what had happened to me. I didn't think I had the words, and if I did have them, I didn't want to say them, and even if I did say them, I didn't want her to hear them. So I watched her and a few others making up a dance routine and shouting at each other when they put a foot wrong, and I felt like I was different now. Like even just a few weeks ago I still could have joined in with their games, could have talked to them and shared their excitement and gossiped with them. I was just a girl with a secret boyfriend then. But I was something new now, and that something wasn't glamorous or mysterious. It was dark and dirty and awful, and I was back to being the other now, like being the new girl all over again. I was in a different world now called the After and I was the only person in it.

Chapter 25 | April 2023 | Dromary Police Station

I stand on the footpath opposite the police station for fifteen minutes. Twenty. I relive my conversation with Charlotte and feel like she's standing next to me.

What makes you think it's going to be any different this time? There's no evidence.

Twenty-five minutes.

I phoned her last night and explained to her my decision. What I have decided to do and my reasons – complicated and uncertain as they are. She was shocked, then supportive, and she has already texted me four times today, checking I'm okay.

I have a sister who texts me and checks I'm okay.

After twenty-seven minutes I'm ready, but I wait until I've been standing there for exactly half an hour before I walk across the road, because that seems better, more sensible, more round.

The building is surrounded by a stone wall, but there is a raised, windowed observation area, and I've watched as the lone man there opens and closes the automatic gate for, it seems, anyone who comes near it. I go to the gate and glance up at him, and he nods and must press a button, for the gate makes a buzzing sound and slowly opens ahead of me.

I walk through what looks like a huge loading bay, past a single police car, and towards the only door I can see, praying it's the right one. It must be, for it too swings open as I approach, and it closes after me once I'm inside.

I stand, unsure. It smells like Pot Noodles, and I can hear

Little Darlings

chatter down a corridor to my left. The floor is the same as the corridors were in Holy Trinity Primary, I think. Plastic. Easy to clean. There is an old, worn-out sign, most of its letters missing so it spells R—N instead of RECEPTION. I try to pretend it doesn't look like RUN.

I take a moment to myself and then go in the direction it is pointing.

I walk past a vending machine that only takes coins. It could have been there since I moved to Chaplin House, it is so old. There is a small machine that dispenses both water and soup, and I frown at it. There is some mould around the little nozzle where the liquids comes out. It's made me feel unsure and I can't work out why.

My cheekbone tingles as I approach the high reception desk. At first I can't see anyone, but as I get closer I can make out the top of a blond head. A man. I falter and stop walking towards him, considering how much of a scene it would make if I turned on my heel, went past the soup and water dispenser, down the corridor, out the door, through the carpark, past the man in the observation deck, across the road, up the street and back into my car. The only person who would be annoyed at me would be the man in the observation deck, but I would never have to see him again. I could be home in fifteen minutes. I'd even have time for a sandwich before I'm due back at work.

'You're very welcome,' the man behind the desk is saying. He gives a chuckle. I can't see anyone else so I think he is on the phone. 'I know. I know. The end of June next year, love. Plenty of time to get your outfit sorted. You're welcome. I know I am, but sure, you deserve it. All right. No problem, no worries. Bye. Bye, love. Bye.'

I hear the unmistakeable crunch of a landline being set back in its cradle. Landlines, coin-only vending machines, worn-off signs. My head is spinning. I don't know why it's made me so uneasy.

The blond head pops up and a shiny forehead and a pair of glasses follow it.

'Hello there. I'm sorry, I didn't see you. Have you been waiting long?'

'No,' I say as brightly as I can, keen to make sure he knows I'm a nice girl, terrified he'll think I'm awkward or unsure.

'Come on ahead,' he says. 'That was my daughter on the phone. I'm Dad of the Year with her now, I snagged a pair of Swiftie tickets for Dublin next year.'

'Wow, that's amazing,' I say, floating towards the desk as if I'm dreaming. 'You'll be popular. How old is she?'

'Fourteen going on forty!' He laughs to himself.

Now that I am right up at the desk, I can see down to the man and the chair and the chaos below. He is in the khaki green police uniform, his tie a perfect knot and his big black boots just visible. He stands up and smiles at me, and I have a feeling that without the boots, we might be around the same height. He is not yet fifty, and his eyes are dark and kind and the lines around his mouth make me think he's laughed a lot. I make no conscious effort to take him in, but I have a peculiar feeling like I will remember him for a long time. This stiflingly warm room, the smell of Pot Noodle, the way he put the phone down. His kind face, looking expectantly at me.

'What can I do for you?' he asks, and there is no expectation on his face. He hasn't tried to guess. He hasn't looked me up and down, tried to figure anything out on his own. Or if he has, he's done it so subtly that I've missed it.

My cat could be missing or I might have just stabbed someone.

He looks at me all the same, and sees me, and lets me tell him whatever I want to.

'I need to report something,' I say. My voice is strong and steady. 'I don't know if I'm in the right place.'

Women say things like *if that makes sense* and add the word *just* into their messages and emails in a way that men don't. I read that somewhere. I do it myself, but I don't feel like I should do it here. I shouldn't do it anywhere. None of us should.

Little Darlings

'I hope you can point me in the right direction,' I say, re-wording. 'It's not urgent.'

No rush, I was just wondering, if you wouldn't mind
No no no.

'By which I mean it's not recent,' I correct myself. The man is nodding just a little, just enough to let me know that he is keeping up, not so much that he is trying to take over or guess.

'It's a crime that happened. Years ago. A good few years ago.'

'When, exactly?' he asks, his eyes still kind.

It strikes me that what is so unsettling about the police station is the fact that it could easily have been a police station from the year 2000. I feel like I've gone back in time.

And maybe that is what strengthens me.

I feel like I am the Cara of twenty-two years ago, going into a police station exactly as she should have done, with a fire in her belly. Or as someone should have done for her.

How many conversations about Taylor Swift tickets have there ever been on a landline?

'When I was ten,' I answer.

Chapter 26 | March 2001 | Chaplin House in the After

Two weeks passed in the After. Charlotte spoke to me when she had to, but she never played with me or came onto the third floor and she never really looked at me, so she had no idea anything was wrong and I didn't have anything left in me to tell her. Audrey informed us one morning that Lawrence had called. He was in London and he sent his love.

'Tell him we miss him!' Charlotte said. 'We can't wait to see him at Easter.'

I didn't say anything.

We saw Uncle Tony for no more than ten minutes in the afternoon when we got home from school, as he was always in a rush to get his lift to the theatre where he was in some new play that had a long name and that I could never remember. He didn't try to speak to me on my own again. In fact, he hardly glanced at me. I noticed that the car hadn't moved since it had been reversed expertly up the drive. The dent had been fixed. It was just there one day and gone the next, but nobody had driven it since. We all walked past it and ignored it. It was part of the driveway.

Audrey's own filming was over and she hadn't been cast in anything else. She was, apparently, writing a play with an old friend of Tony's. She got a lift to his house every morning and was back at dinner time, and seemed full of life after her sessions. She told Charlotte all about it and ignored me because I never got excited enough, which was fine with me.

Still there was no sign of Ronnie.

Little Darlings

Charlotte and I walked to the bus stop by ourselves, so sometimes I would get to break time at school and I hadn't said a single word out loud since the night before. Amelia had become a break monitor, and she walked in circles around the playground with her arms folded now, so I didn't get to play with her even if I wanted to. I ate my lunch as slowly as I could, hoping I could sit in one place in the canteen for the whole of lunchtime so I didn't have to walk about by myself outside.

I had done this one Thursday with little effort. I had eaten half my cottage pie slowly and couldn't face the rest. My tummy hurt and my head hurt, and I thought I was getting sick again. Maybe I could have a few weeks off school, I thought, if it got really bad. I let myself daydream about staying in bed all day and not having to see anyone. I'd even take a horrible cold or the flu again or even the Nem-own-ya everybody talked about. It would be worth it not to sit in my classroom five days a week. But what if Lawrence came home early to surprise us all and he found me alone in the house? That would be worse than school. Much worse. No, I couldn't get sick.

I went into the toilets at the end of the lunch break. I sat down, then froze. There was blood. A lot of it. I just stared at it, not knowing what to do. I heard someone come in, wash their hands. I tried to see through the tiny crack between the stalls if it was Amelia, or maybe Cathy, but I couldn't tell. They left, and then the bell rang. I could hear my heart beating in my ears. If I told someone I was ill they would have to call Audrey, and she would be annoyed with me for spoiling her day, for taking her out of her playwriting.

Then she would want to know why there was blood there, and I would have to tell her, and she would know, and Lawrence would hate me and everyone would hate me.

Students started skipping past the door, going back into their classrooms. If I was late, I would draw attention to myself, and that was the last thing I wanted. It was one o'clock. Only two hours to get through before the end of the day. We were doing science next, a new topic, and that usually just meant listening to Mr O'Shea in our seats. I could do that.

I washed my hands quickly and left the bathroom, managing to join the very end of the line.

I floated into class behind Lindsay like an actress fulfilling a role she knew by heart. This was where Cara Chilver sat in the classroom. This was how she sat, with her ankles crossed underneath her. Yes, Cara Chilver was quiet and shy, but there was nothing strange going on with her. Nothing stranger than usual. She wasn't brilliant at science, but she paid attention and made a good go of it.

I tried to listen, but my pulse was too loud in my ears and I knew my cheeks were flaming, and like the year before, after being with Lawrence outside the shed, I just knew everyone could see it written on my face. And this time it wouldn't just be my face, would it? Everyone would know exactly what happened on the day of the audition. They'd read it on me and see it on me and there was nothing I could do and no way I could hide it.

Mr O'Shea was explaining the new topic and there was something in the air that was different. The other girls at my table seemed to be sitting up a little taller, their faces set and eyes to the front of the room, not giggling or whispering like they usually were. I looked down at my skirt again to make sure I was still safe, then tried to zone back in.

'Basically everything,' Mr O'Shea concluded with a shake of his head and a clap of his hands. 'All the ins and outs. And if you want to ask me anything, these next two weeks will be your chance. At the end, there will be a quiz and a survey to find out how much you know, and deal with anything you've picked up wrongly. We'll have someone in from the Health Services to speak to you as well, as part of this trial. Normally you wouldn't be learning any of this until high school, but sometimes that's just too late. Now, we're going to deal with the big one first, get it out of the way. If you've heard rumours or you've had older brothers or sisters telling you things over the years, I urge you to forget all of that now. In this class, we'll deal with the facts of sex and nothing more.'

There were two or three nervous giggles at that.

I became aware that I was holding my breath only when I started to feel weak. I took a big gasp in that made Lindsay and Jenny snap their heads towards me. They shared a look and an eye roll, presumably at how pathetic I was for being dramatic over this new topic.

Mr O'Shea was handing out textbooks to share between two.

'Page seventy, please,' he instructed, laying a yellow textbook between me and Jenny. Jenny pushed it towards me and stretched herself to her right to share with the others. There was a cartoon man and woman on the front, neither of them wearing any clothes, but with the title of the book – *Growing Up and How We Get There* – covering their middle sections.

'Are we all there? Good. Now, who can tell me – even if you're not sure of the ins and outs of it yet – what the reason for two people, a man and a woman, having sex is?'

Sex. Yes, that was the word. Of course it was. I knew the word, I just hadn't attributed it to myself or anything in my life. I wasn't connected with that word, how could I be?

Cathy Hopkins had her hand waving in the air like she was at a concert. Apparently she wasn't embarrassed enough not to want the class points.

'To make a baby, sir,' she announced, even though he hadn't called on her yet.

'Yes, that's it. Well done, Cathy. Ten points.'

A baby? My heart pounded in my throat. I tried to catch the expressions on the faces of those around me, but most of the girls had their heads in the textbook and all of the boys had red faces and were looking at the floor or laughing. A baby? Did everyone know it was linked to a baby? Did everyone know except me?

Is that what the blood meant?

My fingers stumbled on the pages. I was both desperate to find the right place and sick with dread at the thought of what I might see there. I got to page seventy and my breath got stuck in my throat and wouldn't come out. There were more cartoons on this page, and diagrams too. Complicated shapes and lines with labels, but I couldn't read or pronounce the words. A little box of text at the bottom of the page caught my eye, in a stand-out red colour with a huge question mark next to it.

> *DID YOU KNOW? The age of consent in Northern Ireland is 17, while in the rest of the UK it is 16. It is illegal to engage in sexual activity with anyone under the age of consent.*

I stared at the question mark until my eyes blurred. Illegal? Images of police officers with German Shepherd dogs flooded my mind and I saw myself being led away from Chaplin House – or worse, from school – in handcuffs, with everyone staring at me and knowing what I'd done and what I was. Because everyone would know now, of course. That must be what the blood meant. I'd never known anyone who had had a baby, but a girl who used to work with Mum in Tesco had waved to us across a café one day. She'd had a big bump under her coat. Pregnant. I was *pregnant*.

I couldn't remember how to breathe.

When I became conscious again, I was lying on the floor of the classroom with a headache and a pain in my stomach that were obvious even before I opened my eyes.

'Cara? Are you quite all right? Did you have a funny turn?' It was a man speaking, and for a moment I thought it was Lawrence, and I wanted to jump to my feet and run away as quickly as I could, and I also wanted him to hug me. But it was Mr O'Shea, and he was leaning over me and peering into my face, and instead of egg sandwiches he smelled like coffee, the same way Lawrence

Little Darlings

sometimes did, and I turned onto my side and threw up the tiny portion of cottage pie I'd had at lunch, and the lumps got stuck in my throat and it hurt like acid.

Mr O'Shea told Cathy to run for Miss Tate, the nurse, and I wished for the first time that I was dead. That I was anywhere but lying on the floor of my classroom or, even better, that I was absolutely nowhere, and I didn't have to think any more and I didn't have to talk to anyone or look them in the eye. He was still bending over me, asking me questions over and over, and four girls were crowded around me too, and everyone was staring at me and I still could hardly breathe.

'Oh, sir, look!'

Everyone turned to where Lindsay was pointing, including me. A few drops of blood had dripped onto the floor from beneath my skirt. Lindsay looked horrified, and so did Jenny, but a few of the others looked away, embarrassed, and Ellie Taylor bit her lip at me and tried to look understanding.

'Ah,' said Mr O'Shea. 'Right. Well. Back to your seats, everyone, Miss Tate will be here in a minute. An appropriate day for the new topic, I suppose!'

He was trying to be cheery, but his words echoed in my head like he'd screamed them at me in fury. *An appropriate day for the new topic.* They all knew. They knew what I was and what I'd done. I couldn't even deny it.

Miss Tate took one look at me and said I wouldn't be back to class that day. She asked me if I could stand and I tried, but my legs wouldn't do anything. She put her hands under my arms and started to lift me, gently, and Mr O'Shea came over to help but I flinched away from him and his smell so violently that he actually did one of those double takes they do in films.

With Miss Tate murmuring to me all the while, we managed to make it slowly, slowly, across the playground to her wee tiny nursing building.

'Good thing you weren't in PE,' she said, trying to smile. 'I don't think you'd have fancied the walk between the football pitch and here, would you?'

I didn't say anything, I just let her guide me to a plastic chair on one side of her desk. I let my eyes wander around her tiny office. There was one of those beds below the window that had wheels on it. A rolly bed. The blinds were closed and I was glad. Miss Tate took her own seat opposite me and looked at me, expectantly. I couldn't meet her eye. There were no words for what I'd done. I'd just let her figure it all out.

Lawrence was going to be so angry with me.

'How are you feeling now? It's Cara, isn't it?'

I'd never been to see Miss Tate before, but she was famous around the school for being so young and pretty and lovely if you ever had a headache or fell in PE. She'd been at Holy Trinity herself, 'And probably not that long ago,' I'd heard one of the other girls in my class say. I looked at her in sections and not all at once. Her smooth skin was a bit tanned, so I wondered if she'd been on holiday over half term. Auntie Audrey had mentioned going to The Canary Islands over Christmas, which was somewhere that was full of birds, so I knew there were places that were roasting even when it was cold here. Miss Tate was wearing lipstick, but not like the deep red that Auntie Audrey wore, this one was pale pink and looked beautiful and I made a bet with myself that she would have beautiful eyes too, but I couldn't bring myself to look there. Instead, I looked at her hair, which was clean and in a bun, but the bun didn't make her look like she was bald, the way I looked when Charlotte used to do buns on me, in the Before.

'Yeah,' I said after a minute, realising I hadn't answered her. 'Cara Chilver.'

'Yes, I know your big sister. She's awful fond of you, isn't she?'

Charlotte? Was she awful fond of me? I couldn't remember the last proper conversation we'd had.

'I'm not sure,' I said.

Little Darlings

'Now,' Miss Tate said, leaving the topic. 'Did you hit your wee head when you fainted?'

'I fainted?' I asked, gripping the arm of the chair, feeling the plastic give a little. 'I thought…'

'Yes, I think you fainted. I'm going to check your blood pressure, if that's okay, and in the meantime, you tell me if you think you hit your head. Does anywhere hurt?'

Just every bit of me, I thought. Just every inch of my awful, stupid, ugly body.

The blood pressure check hurt my arm, but it made me feel a bit more awake and alert. My head still hurt, but the pain in my stomach had dulled a little. I was just so tired. I kept my eyes on the rolly bed, imagining I was getting into it and sleeping for a year.

'Wee bit low,' Miss Tate murmured to herself. She leaned over and started pressing gently on my forehead, on my temple. 'Did you have lunch in the canteen today, Cara? You look a bit peaky.'

I'd never heard the word peaky before, but it made me think of the word beak, which made me think of the birds outside my window at Chaplin House. Of the thing Lawrence told me about their songs. They weren't singing to each other. We all just thought they were. That was such a scary thought.

'I had some pie,' I said, feeling it suddenly in my mouth again. 'I threw it up in my classroom. I'm sorry.'

'Don't be sorry,' Miss Tate smiled. 'It'll be cleared up and all. I think you've hurt your head, Cara, I can feel a bump here.'

I sat there for half an hour, my eyes half closed, letting her check me over. She asked me questions in a simple way but she didn't treat me like a child, which was new and which I liked. Finally, she said, 'Have you had a period before?'

I looked at her. I knew what a period drama was but my fuzzy head couldn't make a connection.

'What do you mean?' I asked.

'Ah. Maybe we pulled you out of O'Shea's class too early today.'

Miss Tate slid her chair across to behind her desk and pulled out a pink zipped pouch that looked like one of Auntie Audrey's makeup bags.

'Everything you need will be in here,' explained Miss Tate, and she began taking out the contents of the little zipped bag and holding each of the items up and explaining them to me. I listened only enough to get a feel for it, and then I just let myself look at the colours and wonder what materials they were all made of.

Why was she being so calm? And why did she have one of these pregnancy packs just in her desk drawer? Did a lot of girls get pregnant at school? Maybe it wasn't such a huge deal after all.

'Do you have to tell my aunt and uncle?' I whispered.

Miss Tate paused and considered. 'No,' she said after a moment. 'But I would encourage you to at least tell your auntie about it when you get home. She can help you with any questions and she can buy you whatever you need. But, no, I won't be telling them.'

'They'll notice anyway,' I said glumly, picturing their faces when they noticed the huge baby bump starting to grow.

'Will they?' Miss Tate asked.

'When I have the baby, yeah.'

Miss Tate did the double take that Mr O'Shea had done, then gave a little laugh.

'No, no. Sorry, Cara, I should have explained more clearly. That's not what this—'

'I understand,' I said quickly, just wanting to go home and into my little attic room so I could get under the covers and cry in private and sleep. 'I know.'

'You have to have sex to have a baby,' Miss Tate said.

'Yes. I know.'

'So, you're not having a baby.' She was still smiling as if I was making a cute joke. 'You have to have a husband or a boyfriend, and then have had sex to get pregnant and have a baby.'

'I know,' I said again, not understanding. She had given me the pregnancy pouch and explained what it all meant. Why was she being so silly?

'So...' Miss Tate paused and frowned. 'Well. You can't be pregnant, can you?'

'But the blood—'

'The blood means you aren't pregnant.'

I waited for her to say she was joking. I didn't want to breathe in case that broke the spell. I'd take these few seconds of believing that maybe, just maybe, I still had my secret.

'Then... then what—'

'The blood means you *aren't* pregnant,' she said again, but there was something in her face that was less assured than before, and less jolly. She had a line in her forehead that wasn't there before, and I hated that it was talking to me that had given it to her.

'Why did you think you were pregnant?' she asked finally, leaning closer over the desk. When I didn't answer immediately, she leant closer still. 'Do you understand that you have to have sex to get pregnant, Cara?'

'Yes,' I whispered. The relief was still there, but I still couldn't meet her eye.

'And... and do you have a boyfriend?'

'Sort of.'

'And you've had sex?'

It was called sex, then. It must be. The thing that had happened.

If I had ever imagined this moment, if I had ever daydreamed about someone finding out about my secret, the question was never asked in such a simple way. There was never an easy yes or no answer, when I pictured this moment. It was never a kind school nurse, in a quiet room, just the two of us. It was never straightforward. It could never be over with just a nod.

And maybe that was why. Because the question was already there in front of me, and I just had to reach out and acknowledge it. No words came from me, I didn't have to say it.

So I nodded slowly, and let my tears out, but I didn't feel sad.

It was just happening again, like it had a few times before, where I became aware because of the wetness on my face that I was sobbing for something I couldn't name.

I tried my best to answer Miss Tate's questions, but mostly I waited for her to ask outright so I could just nod or shake my head. My heart was pounding and I wasn't sure why. I thought maybe this was a good thing, but I couldn't pinpoint why I thought that. I had tried for so long, for months, to keep our secret. Had lied and pretended and said nothing so nobody would know, but maybe this pretty woman, an older girl, really, could take part of my problem away from me so I had less of it. Even if I could just speak to her about it every now and then, maybe that would be enough and I could get through.

We had established that the thing that happened wasn't sex. Not quite. But she still seemed very worried.

'And you're sure that's what happened? Exactly as I've described it?'

I nodded.

'And, Cara, who was it?'

I looked at the window, at the rolly bed, down at the arm of my plastic chair. I felt like I would always remember the exact shape of all of them until the day I died.

'Was it someone at home?' Miss Tate asked.

I shook my head so violently I hurt my neck. Maybe I wasn't quite ready for all of this. Maybe I had to speak to Lawrence first, to work out how annoyed he would be by what I'd said already. Maybe there was a plan we could come up with so that we wouldn't go to prison. I saw the huge question mark again. *The age of consent.* At least Miss Tate knew, and once I spoke to Lawrence we could explain what had happened. That it was nothing bad, but that it had to stop and we needed help to stop it. We couldn't go to prison.

'Was it someone at school?'

Little Darlings

I waited, trying to figure out who she could possibly mean. The boys at school were too young for all of that, surely? Then I realised with a jolt that she must mean Mr O'Shea or Mr McAlinden, the male teachers. The smell of coffee filled my nostrils and I felt my stomach contract again, but I didn't want to mess up Miss Tate's nice-smelling office.

'Do you want to tell me, Cara?'

I waited for her to be more specific, both hoping and dreading that she would say Lawrence's name. But then, she probably didn't know who he was to name him.

That's stupid, I heard Charlotte in my ear, *everyone knows who he is. The only reason we're not bullied senseless for being the new girls is because everyone knows we're related to the Wolfes.*

Ask me if it's Lawrence, I found myself thinking, hard. *Ask me and I'll tell you, and together we can figure out what happens next. Please don't make me do this on my own any more. It just got out of hand.*

I felt like I'd been pulled backwards and forwards all afternoon, and I just wanted to lie down.

'I'm so tired,' I said finally, finding courage from somewhere that made me briefly bold. 'Can I have a lie down?'

Miss Tate looked as though she had aged twenty years in the time we'd been in her office, but she did her best to give me a smile.

'Yes, pet,' she said. 'You have a lie down. I'm going to make some phone calls, but you shout if you need me.'

I can't shout, I thought, as I got onto the rolly bed in my full school uniform and my black patent shoes. I didn't even pull back the cover, I just lay down on the crinkly white paper and closed my eyes. *I'm not allowed to make any noise.*

When I woke up, I couldn't work out why there was paper underneath me or why bright daylight was pouring through the round window to my left. There were girls talking and giggling outside the window, so close I could hear them even though the window was closed. They were talking about a test they had the next day and how badly one of them was going to do in it. Before I could pinpoint where exactly I was or how I got there, I became aware of jealousy, deep in the pit of my stomach, that they were worrying about that. I ached to worry about a test with my friends. I ached not to ache everywhere else.

I turned on my side. Miss Tate's office in the tiny building across the playground. I had a period, but I wasn't pregnant. But even though I wasn't pregnant, people still knew, now. The world was different now that I'd woken up. The secret didn't exist any more. I felt numb instead of relief, numb instead of scared.

I watched the clock on the wall. It was just after three, the end of the school day. I watched the hands on the clock go around for an hour, counting the seconds along with the tick, trying to match my breathing to five-second intervals. The sound of the girls outside faded until it was gone completely. I imagined students getting on the bus, getting into their mums' cars, walking home. I wanted to be one of them.

The phone on Miss Tate's desk rang at ten past four, and it made me jump, and I hoped nobody would come to answer it because I just wanted to lie there on my own. In a bed where I felt safe. Nobody came to answer it.

At half past four, I became aware of the need to pee that had been growing for a few hours. I slid out of the bed and tested my legs. They seemed to be working. I lifted the little pink makeup bag from where Miss Tate had left it in that life before, and I took it with me into the small bathroom behind her desk.

I locked the door. Enjoyed the feeling of locking it. A secure lock, not like the flimsy plastic ones on the doors of the school toilets, not like the broken ones on the bathroom doors in Chaplin House. Nobody had ever walked in on me, but I could never relax when I was in the bath.

I unlocked the door, just to make sure I could still get out, if I wanted to, and I felt relief wash over me each time I locked and unlocked it. I was in control of this and I could be safely secured inside, but I could get out any time I wanted.

I slid the lock across.

At five o'clock, there was a knock on the door so tentative that I thought maybe I had imagined it. I didn't say anything and waited. The knock came again, a more definite sound, accompanied by Miss Tate's voice saying, 'Cara?'

I cleared my throat. 'Yeah?' I tried to call back, but I sounded croaky and unsure.

She opened the door, slid inside, and closed it again.

'How are you feeling?'

I sat up so I could look at her properly. I considered her question. Nothing, really. I didn't feel anything. My stomach didn't hurt any more, and even the pain in my head had gone. I felt… tired. I felt exhausted after my sleep, but I knew that was ridiculous and impossible, so I said, 'Fine.'

'Okay. Good. Cara, your Auntie Audrey is here to see you. Is that okay?'

I froze. Auntie Audrey? Here, at school? I had never known her to come anywhere near the school, never known her to phone them or speak to them. I didn't even realise she knew where it was. Had something happened with Uncle Tony? Why was she here?

'Why?' I heard myself asking, but Miss Tate had opened the door again and beckoned Auntie Audrey inside. She let the door close after her with a click and I was alone with my aunt.

Audrey came at me like the tornado in *The Wizard of Oz*. She was all questions and loud and whirling and it didn't feel right and it didn't sound right, and I felt like she was demanding something from me and scolding me at the same time. I didn't know what she wanted so I didn't say a word.

'I didn't understand what the wee girl was saying on the phone,' she said finally. I noticed what felt so unusual: there was no accent.

This was Audrey standing in front of me. And she sounded like my mum, and she even looked a little bit like her. She wasn't acting. For the first time ever I could imagine her the way that Laurie had described her, on a day at the beach what felt like years and years ago. *A carpenter's daughter who fell in love with someone who could take her away from a normal life.* She was a real person.

'She's said the headmaster has phoned the police!' Audrey said. 'Explain what's happened, Cara, now. We can't have the papers finding out about this.'

Auntie Audrey darted past me and stood on tiptoe to look out of the window behind the rolly bed, as if she thought there might be a cameraman and a journalist with their ears up against it.

Satisfied, she turned back to me. 'Explain, please. From the start.'

The start. I thought about what that meant. When did it all start? The answer probably wasn't as simple as, 'That day in the shed'. Maybe, if I acknowledged and accepted my role in what had happened, Auntie Audrey wouldn't be so angry with me. So that meant, surely, going back much further? I saw myself rushing back through time. The shed at Halloween, in the beautiful garden, on the beach, when he had given me my birthday present and I had taken it, when he had held my hand while we watched films, did it start there? Was that when I had done this horrible thing? Or was it even before that, on that first night we met Lawrence, the day we first set foot in Chaplin House?

Charlotte had claimed him as her own with nothing but a look and I had let him fall in love with me. I had laughed at his jokes, had smiled at him and encouraged him. I had talked to him and throughout it all, throughout everything, I had just… let him. I let him do everything. Without meaning to, of course, but I'd still done it, and now he was in love with me. And I had abandoned my sister in the process of letting him. No wonder Charlotte hated me.

'Cara?' Auntie Audrey demanded. 'Why have I just been called away from my *work* on a Thursday afternoon to see to you at school? The headmaster got through to Tony on his mobile who got through to Angus Fletcher *with whom I am in the middle of writing a play* and he was told it was an emergency and I had to go to the school right away. You can't imagine how worried I was when I was interrupted mid-scene to be told that. I assumed one of you had died. And now I hear it's some nonsense. Have you any idea?'

I was saved from answering by another of Miss Tate's knocks on the door. She came in immediately this time, though she looked terrified.

'Sorry to interrupt,' she said, directing this at me and not Auntie Audrey. 'But the police are here now. Mr Reynolds has suggested you use his office.'

'For what?' I asked, shaking my head. I was so exhausted. I was definitely more tired than I'd been before I slept.

'To talk to them and explain what happened,' Miss Tate said. She glanced at the clock. 'The social worker is on her way. Do you want to wait for her, Mrs Wolfe? Or do you want to speak to them with Cara?'

Auntie Audrey looked as if someone had punched her in the stomach, which was exactly how I felt. She was leaning forwards, one arm reaching out towards the wall as if she needed to steady herself.

'What the hell has happened?' she demanded of Miss Tate, her voice sounding like a raspy whisper, like she really needed a drink of water. 'Can someone please explain why the police are here, and what this has to do with Cara? Is this a joke?'

Miss Tate looked at me, but any bravery in me had been all used up and I was completely incapable of saying anything, especially in front of Audrey. There was no way.

'I think maybe Cara should speak to the police when the social worker gets here,' Miss Tate said. 'If she isn't comfortable telling you. But there's been an incident…'

From the handwritten call out notes of PC J Boulton, typed up by DS Jessica Curran in March 2023

Thurs. 15/3/01
Called to Holy Trinity Primary School, Anniskillen, by Joseph Reynolds, HM, at 2.45 pm. Me (PC Boulton) and PC Bronagh Magee attended c.5 pm. 10-year-old girl, Cara Louise Chilver (DOB 05.08.90) of Chaplin House, 60 Bracknamaragh(sp?) Road, Anniskillen, reported to school nurse that she 'had had sex'. Had refused to give name but told us he was her boyfriend. Child seems confused as to the meaning of the word. School nurse (T Tate) v concerned and believes allegation. No further details from child who was v distressed and refused to speak. Interview room 1 booked for 10 am tomorrow (Fri) to give statement. Spoke to Emily Mackintosh (social worker local authority) who will accompany. Contact details for CLC legal guardian + Holy Trinity Primary are below.

Chapter 27 | April 2023 | Back to Chaplin House

Since the crime happened in Anniskillen, the kind PC Miles told me, it will be handled by their police force, and they will be in touch as soon as possible with any further queries. The whole thing took forty-five minutes. I was standing on the pavement opposite the police station less than an hour after I went inside, and I was in another After. A different After.

This one feels better.

We go to the park at the weekend, we laugh at *Would I Lie To You?*, cringing at each other just a little when the contestants swear and praying Daisy doesn't repeat any of it. We book the village hall for Daisy's tenth birthday and invite every child in her class, and bicker about the party bags which can't have any gluten-containing snacks and can't have any plastic toys. All of the parents stay for the party, so we have to run out twice to buy more snacks and more juice, and Steve is quietly annoyed because *it's not how it was in our day, when people just dropped off their children and left for the afternoon*, and because he hates *making conversation with these people*. I'm so relieved that the parents all stay. They should all stay. But then they all spend the entire time calling their children to make them pose for iPhone photographs, and the kids aren't even getting annoyed about it because even though they just want to play, they've never known their parents' faces or affections without a screen in the way.

Daisy is breathless, red-faced the entire time, running between groups of boys and girls, her party hat skew-whiff on the side of her head, looking like someone late for a meeting instead of a girl having a birthday party. But she is delighted and happy, and I know she wouldn't have it any other way. We carry her cake to her without our phones in our hands and Steve squeezes my shoulders when she blows out her candles and murmurs, 'What do you think she wishes for?' and I reach back to squeeze his hand because I have no idea. I'm delighted and overwhelmed by the fact that I have no idea what she might wish for. She wants for nothing.

'This was lovely,' a mum says to me on her way out, steering a Wotsit-faced boy by the shoulder. 'So retro. It's all paint balling and go-karting these days, but this was like going back in time.'

'Yeah, it's what she wanted!' Steve said. 'Just to run about with all her friends. Thank you for coming. Did the little one get a party bag?'

'Is it vegan?'

'Are the Sizzling Steak Wotsits vegan?'

'What, sorry?'

'Yes, it's vegan!' Steve says loudly, as if he hadn't spoken. 'Here you go. Thanks for coming.'

'Say thank you, Lannister.'

'Thank you!' says the boy without looking at us, and they leave.

'Lannister?' Steve whispers to me. 'Is that for real?'

Later that night, my mobile rings with Tony's number. He asks to speak to Daisy and the two of them have a giggly, awkward phone conversation. I hear every word because he is, of course, shouting. After a moment Daisy hands me back my phone and says, 'Great-Great-Uncle Tony has some money for me for my birthday! He wants to talk to you.' And she runs off, delighted.

'That's kind of you,' I say to Tony. 'She's saving up for a mobile phone.'

'She's not getting one!' Steve calls from a different room in the house. I laugh and close the living room door.

'How are you, Tony?'

'I'm well, love,' he shouts back. 'I am well. Listen, I don't suppose you could come down, could you?'

'Down where?'

'To the house. I've a few things of Audrey's for you, and I've a cheque for Wee Daisy for her birthday.'

I hesitate, my fingers feeling ice cold on the phone all of a sudden. I want to ask him to put it in the post, but would that be rude?

Why do I care so much about coming across as rude?

'Okay,' I say slowly. 'Yeah, okay. When suits you?'

'Oh, as soon as possible, really, love. I'm having a bit of a clear out. Next weekend?'

'I think next weekend should be fine. Let me just check Steve has no plans.'

'Oh! I meant by yourself, Cara, love. If that's possible. Not that I wouldn't love to see Steve and Wee Daisy again, it's just…' I hear him hesitating. 'I wondered if you'd give me a bit of a hand with all of her stuff. Just you.'

I've driven to Belfast by myself I want to say. To him or to myself I'm not sure. I've done that. I can drive to Chaplin House.

I've done a lot of things lately that I never thought I could.

'Okay,' I say finally. 'That's fine, Uncle Tony. I'll see you next Saturday.'

The drive to Chaplin House is easy. I concentrate hard, avoid the motorways, and find myself indicating into the driveway before I've even really thought about it. Steve was surprised to hear I was going alone, but didn't ask too many questions. He and Daisy have gone for a picnic.

Tony must hear my car as it pulls up next to the old, abandoned Audi, for he is standing atop the steps to Chaplin House when I click my door closed.

'Hello, darling,' he says. The 'little' was removed somewhere between our little secret and my broken cheekbone.

'Hi,' I say, taking in the navy cardigan, the navy trousers, the navy slippers, the navy shirt. When in doubt about what will match, opt for all the same colour, I suppose.

'I've made a pot of coffee. Will you have some? There's fifteens. Just from the garage in the village but they're lovely.'

'Sounds good,' I say, mustering a smile as if from memory. A reaction to a suggestion from an adult. From an old man, now.

Tony shuffles along the hall and into the kitchen and I follow him, noticing the dust on the sideboards, the dirt on the floor, the smear on the mirror. Tony pours two mugs of coffee, adds a little milk from a glass bottle, and slides one to me across the kitchen island.

The air is taut, like it's too thin for both of us to breathe easily at once.

'Thanks for coming,' he says, and he makes a sort of cheers in the air with his mug, then takes a sip. 'Did the little one have a nice birthday?'

I glance into my mug and watch wisps of milk chasing each other around in a perfect circle.

'She had a great time,' I say. 'Thanks. Just had a party at the church hall. Bouncy castle and games and things.'

'That sounds lovely,' he says. 'Was there much traffic? Saturday mornings can be hit and miss.'

'Wasn't too bad. Do you still get the bus instead of driving?'

An innocent enough question, but it has surprised even me. Tony's pale blue eyes meet mine and look away. His face is sallow, sunken. He looks his age, finally. Like a defeated old man. I try to imagine if he would be cast in anything these days. The last thing I remember seeing him in was another Shakespeare in the Opera House, but that was five or six years ago. I can't even remember what the play was. I didn't wait around to congratulate him afterwards.

'How's Charlotte?' Uncle Tony asks.

'Grand.'

I have spoken to her on the phone a few times since we went

to lunch together. She sent Daisy a card in the post and sent me a text for her on her birthday. It is the most I have had from her in years, and it feels new and delicate, but wonderful. I have never had a sister as an adult. Indeed, Cara Harris has never had a sister before. Not like this.

'Where's this stuff of Audrey's then?' I ask, looking around the cluttered kitchen as if there might be a box labelled AUDREY'S THINGS for me to sort through. 'What was it you wanted me to have?'

Uncle Tony looks down and I see that he is not bald, like I had thought. He has a tiny, perfectly circular patch of white hair atop his head. Audrey would have insisted he wear a hairpiece if she was around.

'I'm afraid I've rather… lured you here under false pretences. I'm sorry. I do have a cheque for Daisy, but I sorted through Audrey's things months ago.'

'Right.' I frown, but my heart is beating quickly, because I have known all along what this must be about. Why he would insist I should come alone.

'Laurie's agent called him a few days ago,' Uncle Tony says. He is still looking anywhere but at me. The top of the oven might have a script on it that he is reading from, his attention is so fixed on it. 'The police have been trying to get a hold of him. He's been in Yorkshire filming for the last six weeks. *Hardacre Abbey*,' he adds, as if I have asked. 'Making a film of it. It'll be out next summer.'

I stare at Tony's little patch of hair and feel a laugh threaten. The corners of my mouth twitch. Of course everything in the world must be related to their films, to their TV shows, to their plays. Times in their lives are not marked by world events or birthdays or even memories, only by premieres and press nights and season finales.

'He's spoken to them and told them he'll be happy to chat to them when he gets back. But they wouldn't tell him what it was about, only that it was… historical. A historical accusation.'

I blink at him. We are both waiting for the other to talk. Steam still rises from my cup. I've been here for minutes.

'You can't look at me,' I say finally. 'But you had no problem looking when I was wee. You were always watching. I always thought you were watching me, but as I got older I realised… You were watching him. Because you knew, didn't you? You knew what he was.'

I see his Adam's apple move. He puts his palms on the marble of the kitchen island and moves as though he is about to start doing press ups. Or as if he is trying to tether himself to the world and not fall off it.

'I never *knew*.'

It is the third time he has said it, the emphasis on the last word all the time. We have moved to sit at the dining table. I have taken the head of the table, but I have moved my chair so it is facing the patio and the trees and garden beyond. Tony is far away, because everyone is far away at this table, the same one they had twenty years ago, but I can tell he is angled towards me.

'I promise you. On Audrey's life. I never knew for sure.'

I think of six different things to say, a hundred different ways I could react. None of them are quite right, none of them are exactly what I want. None of this is how I want it to go.

'How did you know?'

'I didn't—'

'Why did you *think*, then?'

I hear him take a breath, and if I didn't know who it was behind me I'd have guessed it was a feeble old man with a breathing tube.

'He was… married. Before.'

'I know.'

'You know?'

'Yes. Bridget. And her daughter.'

'Yes. How did you—'

'Doesn't matter. Go on.'

'Well.'

I stare out into the garden. The folding glass needs cleaning, but the trees and shrubs are beautiful, and there are pink and red flowers starting to bloom in beds around the edges of the grass. Audrey never mentioned them hiring another gardener: either Ronnie's handiwork has lasted all this time or Tony has tended to all of this himself. A sparrow flies past the patio and up into the huge oak tree. I watch it for a moment. I could be ten again.

'He never introduced us,' Tony says finally. 'We were so close, but then he met this woman and he was... secretive about it. Audrey guessed it was because she wasn't... You know. Up to standard. She didn't come from money, she wasn't particularly educated, she didn't have a *career*. Audrey thought he was embarrassed by her. And she understood that. And accepted that.'

'But you didn't?'

'He told us she had a daughter. He gushed about how great she was. Audrey was horrified that he was taking on someone else's child – he was so young, you see. We wanted him to do so much with his life, not settle down to play daddy to—' He cuts himself off and I imagine him behind me, shaking his head. 'Anyway. We barely heard from him. He didn't get any serious work for... two years, maybe. When he did call or visit, we asked him all kinds of questions, offered him money, offered to come and visit. He wasn't interested. He was keeping us away from Bridget and... the little girl.'

'Aoife.'

'Was that her name? And then they split up and he moved back in and sold their house—'

'He didn't,' I said, unable to stop myself.

'What?'

'He didn't sell the house. The one in Stranmillis. He still had it when I came to live with you.'

'Oh. I didn't realise you... how did you—' Again, he doesn't finish his sentence. The easy, confident Tony, the man with the voice of honey and the irresistible charm, is faltering. Unsure. Uneasy. For maybe the first time ever.

'And he was gutted, when it ended,' he continues. 'She had broken up with him. *She* with *him*. Audrey couldn't understand it. Neither could I. He'd bought them a home, he was wealthy, he was handsome, he was clever... I couldn't think why she'd leave him. It didn't make any sense. And he started drinking, for a bit, once he was back with us, and when he got drunk he'd talk about how much he missed her and how wonderful it had been and... And when I really sat and listened to him, I realised he was talking about the little girl. Not Bridget. The little girl. So then I started to wonder... Just to wonder. Nothing more. And then I forgot all about it. He cleaned himself up, got another part, and moved on. And then you two came.'

I picture two little girls, side by side, looking up at Chaplin House for the first time, gasping at the beauty of the gardens, choosing rooms on the top floor despite the shrieking door, despite the noisy steps—

'I made sure you were never alone,' Tony says. I hear him slide his arm across the table towards me, but I don't look around. 'I made sure of it. He was barely ever there, and when he was I—'

'Watched him,' I say. 'Yeah. Just not closely enough.'

The sparrow zooms out of the oak tree and past the patio door again. I watch her as she lands on the grass and pecks at something I can't see.

'You went for your audition for Eliza Long in February 2001,' Tony says. It's so matter of fact, so easily dropped in, that this does make me turn around. Here is someone else who remembers that day, someone else who thinks about it, maybe.

'You said something to me afterwards like... Like, "I don't want to see Laurie again," or something to that effect. And I felt like my heart was going to explode. I called the director, my friend Neal, and thanked him for letting my niece audition... and he confirmed it. He said your name was on the list and they waited

Little Darlings

for you, but that you'd never shown up. And I realised what I'd done. I'd let him take you away for a whole day. Nobody watching you, nobody there to…'

There are tears in his eyes and his voice is thick, but he's an actor and I've seen him cry on screen a dozen times, so it means nothing to me.

I look back outside and try to find the sparrow, but she's gone.

'After that I knew I had to get you out of the house. I wasn't sure how I was going to do it, but I knew you couldn't stay. Laurie was away after that. Away for ages. And then you had your fall out the big window, and then—'

'I didn't fall,' I say. I crane my neck, looking towards the side of the house. If I stood up, I could probably see exactly where I landed. 'I didn't fall, Tony. I fucking jumped.'

Chapter 28 | May 2001 | Chaplin House, The Big Window

Like the story in the newspaper about Uncle Tony's affair, the day after I went to the police station and into the room with the tape recorder, nothing was ever mentioned ever again. It disappeared like it had never happened. Laurie was still gone, but I could no longer remember where he was, and Tony was gone a lot, but Audrey was at home and Charlotte was there, but none of those things mattered because nobody spoke to me anyway. Audrey left the room when I came in. Charlotte glanced at me sometimes, then looked away.

I wasn't even sure if I was there or not, because nothing was real any more.

I saw Miss Tate at school once or twice and she always ducked her head away. I wanted to tell her I was grateful for everything she'd done, that she'd been kind to me and I appreciated it, but she wouldn't look at me, and that made me think maybe I'd done something wrong or said something I shouldn't have in my police interview, and maybe I'd gotten her into trouble, so I made a promise to myself that I wouldn't ever talk to anyone again. It wasn't hard. Everyone in my class seemed to forget I existed after that anyway, and they only spoke to me if they had to.

I lay in bed for most of the time I was at home, and when I heard the birds outside my window I clamped my hands over my ears and listened to my heart beating and the blood swirling around in my ears, not letting myself think about the fact that the beautiful things were all screaming.

Little Darlings

Time passed.

Flowers bloomed in the garden, even though nobody was tending to them. I thought that was important, and maybe meant something, but my brain was too foggy to know what that something was.

Then Lawrence came back from filming and he greeted everyone with a hug except me, but he did it in a way that nobody noticed, and I was glad. I left them all sitting in the kitchen, listening to his stories, and I went back up to the attic and thought about how good it would be if I could die.

I woke up to rain tap-tapping on my little window and was glad. That usually meant no birds. I turned over and stared at the ceiling and didn't think of anything. I just listened to the rain and breathed.

The door downstairs clicked. I stopped breathing.

Quiet steps.

The door to my room opened and Lawrence stood there, still dressed.

'Cara,' he whispered. 'I've missed you. How are you? You seem upset.'

I sat up in bed and pushed myself back until I was stuck to the headboard.

'Go away,' I whispered, feeling my heart beating in my neck. 'You shouldn't be in here, go away.'

Lawrence's face, lit by the bright moon, fell. He looked so hurt.

'Cara, what's wrong? I'm sorry. I just want to talk to you.'

He came over and sat on the bed next to me. He reached out and stroked my hair, his eyes travelling over my face like he was looking for clues.

'Haven't you missed me? This is the longest we've been apart.'

Not again, I thought. There is no way. This is not happening again.

'I thought about you every day while I was gone,' he continued. He scooted up the bed so he was lying next to me, and he put one arm across my stomach to pull me in. 'But I'm back now. I want things to go back to normal. Don't you want that?'

'No,' I whispered.

This is not happening again.

'Mum says you've not been yourself, but she wouldn't divulge anything further. Is everything okay at school?'

Not again.

He leant in and kissed me and there was a brief moment, two moments, three moments, when I thought it might be easier to let it happen.

Then I jerked backwards and clumsily climbed over him to get out of bed.

'What's wrong?' he asked, concern in his voice. 'Talk to me, Cara, please.'

I stood up and backed away from him. He stood too. He was looking at me. When was the last time someone really looked at me? It might have been nice to be looked at.

But he stared at me like I was the only person in the world, and I didn't want to be the only person in the world. It was so lonely.

'No,' I said softly. 'Not again.'

'I just want to kiss you,' he said. 'That's all. Nothing else.'

'No,' I repeated. 'No.'

I didn't wait for him to respond. I moved backwards until I fell against the door. I yanked it open and made for the stairs.

'Cara!' Lawrence called.

I remember thinking, *He's called that so loudly. Someone will hear and will know he's in my room. That's good. He'll be caught out.*

He'll be caught.

He'll be caught.

My legs moved down the stairs with more speed than I thought, and instead of rounding the corner when I got to the landing, I just kept going. The magnificent back garden of Chaplin House flew towards me, all shadow and fairy lights, and I had just enough time to gasp before I hurtled into the glass and it shattered around me.

Little Darlings

Two seconds of falling, shards of glass and thick droplets of rain coming with me. A bump, then a thump that flung me around, neither of which I really registered, and then I was flat on my back on the patio. The sky was full of stars – or was it glass? – and I thought I even saw a rocket, and I was aware of nothing else at all but the fact that I was so happy, so relieved, to finally be dead.

Chapter 29 | April 2023 | Back to Chaplin House

'You were lucky you didn't die,' Uncle Tony says slowly. 'You hit the little roof over the balcony of our bedroom first, do you remember? I think if you hadn't, you'd have been a goner. I never would have wished those injuries on anyone... but it worked out for the best. I told that woman, the social worker—'

'Louise.'

'Louise. I told her we'd all taken on more work than we could cope with. That we were very sorry, we'd loved having you both, but that we simply couldn't be there to look after you any more. Especially with you not being able to walk for a while. She was a lovely woman, do you remember? But my God, she was so angry with me for it. You could tell. She was the epitome of professionalism, but you could tell she thought it was the wrong decision, choosing a career over two little lives. People don't understand it. Acting, I mean. It's not a choice. It's a compulsion. We all felt that way. And if it meant getting you away from Lawrence, then I'm glad I did it. You thrived, didn't you? So I thought I'd made the right choice. I still think I did.'

I have a strange feeling like I'm not a part of the conversation. It is a feeling I've had many times when I've thought I'm talking to the Wolfes. This dining table is his stage and this is his monologue and I'm not even the audience member, I'm just in the wings, waiting patiently for my cue.

'You've done so well for yourself,' he continues. 'You got your degree, your job with the logo designs and all that, the arty stuff.

Little Darlings

You got married and you had your little one and I thought… Yes. That was the right thing to do. She's fine. She's thrived. I hoped maybe I'd exaggerated what had happened to you. If it was… *that* bad, surely you wouldn't have been so together. You saw Audrey a few times a year, you kept in touch with your texts, sent us cards. You even sent that picture of Wee Daisy when she was born. Audrey showed me it. And that made me think, well… Surely it wasn't that bad. It was Charlotte I worried about.'

Yes, I think, it's always Charlotte everyone worries about. Charlotte whose anxieties are loud and obvious, impossible to hide.

'But now the police want to speak to Laurie,' Uncle Tony says. 'So, can I assume it's you who has called them?'

I turn to look at the old man, his eyes watery but fixed on me, his mouth set. I nod for a few seconds, thinking. He takes a deep breath and lets it out slowly. Then he surprises me by saying, 'This house is worth about £800,000. I had it valued during the week.'

I blink at him, not understanding.

'I have Premium Bonds with a value of fifty grand, and Audrey did too. Royalties come in twice a year, sometimes they're wonderful. My savings have been dwindling over the last few years, with neither of us working, but my pension is healthy enough and I can survive on that alone without Audrey here.'

I stare at him, a peculiar butterfly flapping its wings in my stomach.

'I would be… more than happy to change my will so that when I go, everything goes to you.'

The butterfly beats its wings harder. I might throw up.

'I'd have a caveat that you'd need to give something to Charlotte, but we can iron out the details when the time comes. We can go and see a solicitor next week and sort it all out. You'd be… Well, maybe after tax, close to a millionaire. All I would ask is that you don't… press this. That you don't pursue it. Why now, Cara? After all these years, after all this time has passed? What good can come of it now? And surely it's unlikely that anything would... happen? There wouldn't be any evidence. It was twenty years ago, for God's sake.'

'Twenty-two,' I murmur.

'Exactly.'

Uncle Tony stands up and goes to the kitchen sink. I watch him without really seeing him as he pours himself a glass of water and downs it in two gulps. He pours another and stands with it in his hand.

'Don't make your decision now,' he says after a moment. 'But think on it. It's an offer worth considering.'

'Why are you still trying to protect him?' I ask, and there is no frustration in it, only a genuine curiosity, genuine disbelief.

'He's my son,' Tony says simply. 'In every way that matters, he's my boy. And he had a hard start—'

I'm not sure which of us is the most surprised by my bark of laughter.

'Plenty of people had a hard start,' I say. 'Thanks to him, I did too.'

'He was...'

'Troubled?' I guess, remembering a conversation with Audrey in this kitchen, so long ago it's like a dream.

'Yes. He was. Little Jamie Ward was really a piece of work when he first came here.'

I wait, thinking for one horrifying moment that Jamie Ward must be someone else that Lawrence has abused. And then I understand.

'You changed his name?' I ask. 'But he was five, wasn't he? Isn't that – isn't that strange?'

'Maybe,' Tony says. He turns so we are facing each other, his water glass still in his hand. 'But if you adopted a dog, and that dog had been... kicked and punched and screamed at, had cigarettes put out on its coat, would you want him to remember all of that every time you called him? Every time you said his name?'

I don't answer, staring at him, wondering if this is a hypothetical, or if—

'He's made mistakes, obviously. Lawrence has made mistakes, but he… He tries. I know he does.'

'What about Audrey?' I ask, looking at the seat where she once sat and took my hand and told me she'd love to adopt me, and I believed her, but I didn't really. 'Did she know?'

'Absolutely not,' Uncle Tony says, so loudly he sounds like he's back on a stage. 'She'd have dropped dead. She thought he was the sun and the moon and the stars and every bloody thing. It would have killed her, Cara. It would have killed her, having this come out.'

'Mm.' I consider this and I think he's right. And I think maybe I knew that all along, and maybe that's why it had never seemed like a possibility before, the thought of walking into a police station and saying Lawrence Wolfe's name. Not while Audrey was around.

'I don't know that you ever saw the best of her,' he says. He leans against the kitchen counter and looks at me, a small smile playing on his lips. 'By the time you two came she was obsessed with being anyone but Audrey. Fake hair, fake face, fake lips, fake boobs.' He snorts and takes a sip of his water. 'But the woman underneath, she was amazing. She was so funny. And clever. God, I loved the bones of her. But she was so ambitious, she just…' He shakes his head. 'She kept changing herself so she would look younger or thinner, thinking it would help her get roles for younger or thinner actresses, when in reality she should have let herself grow older gracefully and she would have been cast in plenty of roles that were actually meant for her. Men are lucky. We have no choice but to let ourselves get older.' He turns his glass in his hands, thoughtfully. 'I think she was addicted to the idea of her career instead of the reality of it. She liked telling people she was an actress, and she liked going to events, but I'm not sure how much of that was her and how much of it was… Well, wanting to impress me. Do you know what I mean?'

'Not really,' I say, bored and tired of him and not caring any more if I'm being rude. 'Was there anything of Audrey's you wanted me to look through?'

'No,' he says, his shoulder's dropping a little. 'I'm sorry to bring you here with a lie. I didn't want to make my offer over the phone.'

'I think I'll go, then.'

I stand and push my chair in under the table. It squeaks.

Tony follows me to the front door and stands holding it open as I hoke my keys out from my pocket. For a brief moment, we both let our eyes fall on the Audi, then Tony looks away.

'Let me know what you decide,' he says, cheerfully enough, as if we've been discussing what time to go and see a film at.

I take a few steps towards my car, then turn on my heel, a thought occurring to me. 'If you loved Audrey so much,' I say, 'Why did you have an affair with a teenager?'

'What?' He sounds baffled. Then his face changes and he lets out a sigh. 'Oh. Her. Catherine Bloody Molloy. God, I haven't thought of her for years. Nothing happened with her. I was working on a film with her and we chatted a couple of times. She must have got the wrong idea. Well, either that or she was a stupid little liar who almost ruined my marriage. And my career. She wanted attention, that's all.' He seems to struggle with something for a moment, and then he adds, 'I don't want people to say that about you, but they will. If the papers find out about this… They'll think you're making it up.'

I feel my cheeks redden and hate myself for it.

'That's what everyone thought last time,' Tony adds. I close my eyes, because he's right. They thought I was an attention-starved child who learned about sex in class one day and decided to make up a story about it.

'Cara?'

I open my eyes, but don't say anything. Neither does he, for a moment, and I think maybe he has thought better of saying any more. Maybe he won't say another word. Not for me, not for himself, not for Lawrence.

'There's no evidence,' he says after a moment, speaking slowly, so slowly, in that voice that made him millions and had women – girls – swooning, 'So, what makes you think that it'll be any different this time?'

The same question twice in the space of a month. I have no more to say to him than I had to say to Charlotte when she asked me. I have no answer, so I don't offer him any.

Tears cascade down my face as I drive away from Chaplin House, but I think it's just a reflex; I don't feel especially sad. I think about the name Jamie Ward, and how ridiculous it sounds compared to Lawrence Wolfe. How those two men are different people, and about how important that is.

I park on the street half a mile away from Anniskillen Police Station and allow myself time to dander to it. My eyes are probably still red, but I didn't bring any makeup with me and there's nothing I can do about it. DS Jessica Curran, who has taken charge of the case, will have to take me as I am.

I give my name to the officer on the front desk, the most bizarre butterflies in my stomach, as if I'm about to go on a first date with someone I'm not quite sure of yet. I have to wait only ninety seconds before there is a buzz from the door on my right and it swings open. A pretty, dark-haired woman about my age is standing there. She's not in uniform, but in sensible black trousers, a thin jumper and a long tan-coloured cardigan.

'Mrs Harris?' she calls. 'Hello, I'm Jess Curran. Do you want to come with me so we can have a bit of a chat?'

I nod, the butterflies in my stomach banging into one another and panicking, but I follow her down a cold corridor and into a small office room, not much warmer.

'Please excuse the mess,' she says, hurrying to switch on the light, then using her fist to bash a little white heater. 'Technically this is my office, but I don't get a lot of time to use it, never mind clean it.'

There are empty Diet Coke cans over almost every surface, and the bin under the desk is overflowing with Subway sandwich wrappers. Other than that, DS Curran has a locked filing cabinet, a computer and two monitors, and a tiny window in her office. There is also an old-fashioned spinny office chair opposite her desk, and it is to this she points and motions for me to sit.

'Thank you so much for coming in,' she says as we take our seats either side of her desk. 'Like I said on the phone, I would have come to you—'

'No, it's fine!' I say quickly. 'My husband doesn't know I've... started this. I'll tell him, I just haven't yet. It's not that I don't trust him, I just...'

I am blethering. She nods kindly, and I wonder if her shiny ponytail tickles the back of her neck. She takes a notebook from her desk drawer and clicks a Biro, but she doesn't make to write anything.

'I understand,' she says. 'Well, look. This is an informal chat, really, Mrs Harris. I just want to get everything I can from you. We've already made a few inquiries. We haven't been able to speak to Lawrence Wolfe yet—'

'He's in Yorkshire,' I say. 'He'll be back soon.'

'Oh.' She furrows her perfectly styled eyebrows. 'Are you in touch with him?'

'No! No, no. I saw his dad just now and he told me.'

DS Curran bites her lip. Her teeth are bright white. She must not drink coffee. Maybe if I stopped drinking coffee—

'Okay. It's probably better if you have nothing to do with them for the foreseeable. Until this is cleared up.'

'Sorry,' I say quickly. 'Sorry, I never thought.'

'No, it's okay. We'll be speaking to his dad – Antony Wolfe, right?'

She says his name like 'Ant-o-nee', without the H, and it's

surreal. She has never heard of him, I think. She blinks at me. She has no idea who he is. Even Steve had vaguely heard of him. It's encouraging, somehow. She's going in blind.

'Yeah. Anthony. Tony.'

'Tony. Okay, yes. We'll be speaking to him shortly, after I've got a few more pieces of information from you.'

She has an English accent. A real one, not a put on one like the Wolfes. It's only just registered as my heart has started to slow. She is kind, polite, seems to want to help. Genuinely. I'm so pathetically glad it's a woman.

'So this happened while you were living in Anniskillen, is that right?'

'Yes,' I say. For a split second I feel as though I am ten years old again, transported back into a kind nurse's office, happy to answer yes/no questions. So grateful that I didn't need to colour it, I just needed to provide the outline. Miss Tate, I think with a jolt. The kind school nurse, Miss Tate. Where is she now? Does she still work at the school?

'And you were ten at the time?' DS Curran asks, ripping me from my daydream. Her pen is moving across the page but she is managing to keep enough eye contact with me.

'Yes, that's right.'

'So what year would this have been?'

'It was 2001,' I say. 'It was February.'

'Okay. And Lawrence Wolfe, who is your – remind me?'

'My great-aunt's adopted son,' I say, and it sounds ridiculous and jumbled, like a novelty Christmas song. 'My mum's aunt's adopted son.'

'Mm-hmm.' She is still writing. Her nails are long and painted red. I wish I had enough length on mine to paint them.

'Okay.' She takes a deep breath and leans forward, dropping the Biro. 'And this is the important bit: you say he hit the gardener with his car?'

Transcript of police interview

Transcript produced: 26 March 2023, on request of DS Jessica Curran
Date of interview: Friday, 16 March 2001
Location: Anniskillen Police Station, Room 1
Detective Inspector Y McIvor and Detective Sergeant P Hoey interviewing Cara Louise Chilver. Also present, Emily Mackintosh, social worker

DS HOEY: Now, Cara. You know why you're here don't you? You're just going to give us a bit of help to understand what's been going on. Can you do that for us? Cara, can you speak up a bit, please?

A Yes. Sorry.

Q That's okay. Now, I need you to use your biggest and loudest voice for me today, because this thing here, this big box on the table, it's going to record what you're saying. Is that okay?

A Yeah.

Q Good girl. That's perfect. Now, let's start with the easy stuff. Can you say your full name into the tape for me, please?

A Cara Louise Chilver.

Q Thank you. And give me your birthday, Cara.

A The fifth of August.

Q Yeah?

A 1990.

Q And just because my maths isn't the best, can you tell me what age that makes you, please?

A Ten.

Q That's great. Now, Cara, where do you live?

Little Darlings

A Chaplin House.
Q Where's that? (After a pause) You're not sure?
A No.
Q Ah, okay. And who lives in Chaplin House with you?
A My sister and my auntie and uncle. They're not my real auntie and uncle.
Q Is that everyone?
A Ronnie was there sometimes.
Q Who is Ronnie?
A He was the gardener.
Q And what do you mean they aren't your real auntie and uncle? (After a pause) That's okay. We can come back to that. Does anyone else live with you there?
A No.
Q What about Lawrence? (After a pause) Well?
A Sometimes.
Q Sometimes, okay. Why just sometimes?
A He's always away.
Q Away where?
A Dubai, I think. Other places.
Q He's an actor, is that right?
A Mm.
Q And he's the son of your auntie and uncle, is that right?
A Yeah.
Q So that makes him your cousin?
A I think so.
Q Okay. How do you get on with the people you live with, Cara?
A Okay.
Q You like spending time with them?
A Sometimes.
Q With Charlotte?
A Sometimes.
Q With your uncle?
A Yeah. Sometimes.

Q   With your aunt?
A   Sometimes.
Q   And with Lawrence?
A   Sometimes.
Q   Okay. Now, we had a call from Mr Reynolds at your school yesterday, and I believe you spoke to my colleagues, Bronagh and John, is that right? And you've very kindly come in this morning to tell us a wee bit more in a more formal setting. Thank you for that. We just have to get everything on paper. I'm sure you know yourself from your studying, it's easier to have everything on the page, isn't it? Now, what I need you to do, Cara, is to start at the very start and tell us everything from the beginning. About what happened, what you told Miss Tate about yesterday. Can you do that for me?
A   (No audible answer.)
Q   Cara, if you don't tell us what's happened, we can't help you. We want to help you. You understand that, don't you?
A   (No audible answer.)
DI McIVOR: Cara, do you want to start by telling us what you told Bronagh and John yesterday?
A   (No audible answer.)
DS HOEY: You aren't in trouble at all, Cara. Do you understand that?
MISS MACKINTOSH: Do you want to take a break, Cara?
A   Yes, please.

Chapter 30 | April 2023 | Anniskillen Police Station

I speak to DS Curran for another two hours. This conversation is much more in-depth than the one I had in Dromary, and she asks questions I have to think hard about and some to which I do not know the answers. But by the end, she has my full report. A summary of what happened to Ronnie on the day I was supposed to audition for Eliza Long in Belfast. The day that changed my life forever and, I think, took his.

'He was Ronnie Glover,' DS Curran says. She types something in on her computer and turns the monitor around to face me. It is a MISSING PERSON poster, crudely made, with a short description and a contact number at the bottom. His photograph is photocopied in black and white and shows him in his school uniform. He is a much younger Ronnie than I ever knew. It makes me feel strange that no later photos of him existed.

'Did his grandmother make that?' I ask.

'Think so, yeah. It's not an official police one. People used to bring pictures into the newsagents and they would print them off and make copies. Rosa Hilditch was his nan. She officially filed him as a missing person on Tuesday, 6 February 2001. He'd gone out on the Saturday afternoon and never came home. He hadn't said where he was going.'

'Poor Rosa,' I murmur.

'So I'm assuming the Saturday in question must be 3 February,' DS Curran continues. 'And she came up to Chaplin House on the Monday to ask if any of you had seen him.'

I swallow a lump in my throat. 'Does she still live in the village?' I ask.

I have a strong urge to go and find her house after this, to tell her everything and apologise for not speaking up sooner. The years of uncertainty I could have saved her—

'She died in 2003.' DS Curran is grimacing. 'I tried to find her when you first raised this about Ronnie, but she's gone. Throat cancer. Nasty.'

'So nobody was even looking for him?' I say in disbelief. I feel hollow. I think of the kind young man who picked us up from school and made me laugh and was sweet to me in all the ways I needed, and who was nothing like the monster Lawrence Wolfe.

'I'm afraid not,' DS Curran says. 'And he was twenty-seven at the time he went missing, wasn't considered vulnerable, didn't have particularly steady work or a girlfriend or anything so...' She has moved her screen back around to face her and is looking at it sadly. 'I think it was easy enough for him to be... ignored, if you like. It sounds harsh, but according to the file he wasn't really a priority. Nobody thought he was in any danger.'

By the time he was reported missing, I think, he wasn't.

'One more thing before you go...' DS Curran sounds less assured now. She is still looking at her screen, but I get the impression she is simply trying to avoid looking me in the eye. 'When PC Miles passed this on to me, I started to get together everything I could that might help, and I found—' She looks at me suddenly, and her shoulders are tense. 'Were you Cara Chilver, then?'

Transcript of police interview

Transcript produced: 26 March 2023, on request of DS Jessica Curran
Date of interview: Friday, 16 March 2001
Location: Anniskillen Police Station, Room 1
Detective Inspector Y McIvor and Detective Sergeant P Hoey interviewing Cara Louise Chilver. Also present, Emily Mackintosh, social worker

DS HOEY: Hi again, Cara. Did you get a wee drink and a break?
A   Yeah.
Q   And are you ready to speak with us now, do you think?
A   Yeah.
Q   Okay. So, you told Miss Tate yesterday that you'd had sex with someone. Is that right?
A   Yeah, but…
Q   Okay. And can you tell us who that person is?
A   No.
Q   Okay, that's fine for now. Is it someone you know?
A   Yeah.
Q   Okay. And how many times did it happen?
A   One.
Q   Just once?
A   Yeah.
Q   Okay. We'll call it the incident, okay? And where was this?
A   (No audible answer.)
Q   Where did this happen? This incident?
A   In the bedroom.
Q   In your bedroom?

A (No audible answer.)
Q Sorry, Cara, would you mind saying your answers out loud? Remember, I told you about this wee tape machine.
A Sorry.
Q That's okay. Did this happen in your bedroom?
A No.
Q Was it another bedroom in your house?
A No.
Q Okay.
A There was a rocket on the floor.
Q A rocket? Okay. That's great, you're doing well.
A It was a light. It was supposed to be on the ceiling. A rocket.
DI McIVOR: Sorry, Cara, can you tell us where exactly this was? Was it somewhere here in Anniskillen? We're going to need more than the rocket, I'm afraid. (After a pause) Or can you tell us who this person was that you were with at the time?
A Lawrence.
Q Lawrence Wolfe? Your cousin?
A (No audible answer.)
Q Please don't just nod, say it.
A Yes.
Q So, what exactly did Lawrence do? (After a pause) Cara, if you don't tell us, we can't help you. At the minute all you've told us is you were with Lawrence and there was a light shaped like a rocket. That's not a lot to go on for us to do our jobs, is it?
DS HOEY: Maybe if we just let Cara—
MISS MACKINTOSH: Maybe Cara would like another break.
DI McIVOR: I understand that Cara is upset, but what she is saying is very serious, so she needs to give us something concrete to work with, otherwise we'll have to call it a day.
A Can I go home now, please?

Chapter 31 | April 2023 | Anniskillen Police Station

'Yes,' I say in answer to DS Curran's question. 'I became Harris when I married my husband but, yes, I was Cara Chilver then.' My mouth is dry, suddenly. I know why she is asking. Of course I know. There was never any way to do this, without doing *this*.

'And you were interviewed in March 2001? Also in relation to Lawrence Wolfe?'

Her eyes are brown and the irises are flecked with little dots of black. She looks effortlessly beautiful and put together. Like she has never tried. I know I look tired and fat with bad skin and short nails. I've never looked like her. So why did he ever pick me?

'Yeah,' I say quietly. 'March 2001. Not about this, though. I never told anyone about this.'

'Yes, I can see that.'

'How did you—'

'I mentioned to one of my colleagues that Lawrence Wolfe was the name of the suspect. Your interview wasn't forgotten, it seems.'

I think back to 2001. St Patrick's Day weekend, green bunting in the middle of the village. Coming to this police station, though it was a different building then, has been updated since in a way that Dromary Police Station hasn't. I wonder if the refurbishment was recent.

'My colleague actually tracked down the notes that were made at the time. They weren't digitised or anything, so nothing came up on the system when I searched for Mr Wolfe originally. I think they were in a box somewhere, if you can believe that. In the records room, which is actually in the basement.'

'Like in a film,' I say, smiling weakly. She smiles back, then stops herself.

'I've read your interview,' she says. 'But nothing ever happened, it seems. Never really got started, actually, by the looks of things. But my colleague remembered it.'

'Did she?' I ask. I try to picture the faces of the officers who interviewed me. A man and a woman, definitely. Middle-aged? But everyone seemed middle-aged then, they were probably not even forty. She was younger. He was older. I can't remember their faces.

'He,' DS Curran says. 'DS Paul Hoey. He remembered you.'

'Oh.'

'He seems to think it was…' She trails off, lets her eyes flick to the door as if someone might be about to enter. 'Pushed under the mat. A wee bit. He wanted to pursue it but his superior officer overruled him.'

I blink at her, not understanding.

'He wasn't sure of the ins and outs, but given that the family were quite wealthy…'

She doesn't finish her sentence, just gives a little shake of her head. After a moment, she asks, 'Can I ask what it is that happened to you?'

I've told Aoife. I've told Bridget. I've told Daisy a child-friendly version.

I didn't tell Steve.

I told Steve about Lawrence hitting Ronnie with the car, that day we sat parked next to that very same car outside Chaplin House, the day of Audrey's funeral. That I could tell him about. This was harder to explain.

But is there a part of him, maybe, that knows there is something more to the story?

'Lawrence was… grooming me,' I say. I look at her notebook on the desk in front of her, not trying to read her writing upside down, but pretending that maybe I am. 'It was actually all a big mistake.'

Bizarrely, I give a bark of a laugh, just like I did with Tony. Was that only a few hours ago? If my laugh shocks DS Curran, she doesn't let it show.

'I got my period in school one day,' I explain. 'And I thought that meant I was pregnant. I was only ten. Didn't know, obviously. But I went to the nurse and she probed me with questions and we got our wires crossed a bit and…' I am back in Miss Tate's office. Kind face. The rolly bed. The little makeup bag with sanitary towels inside it. 'I thought maybe I'd had sex. I didn't fully know what it was, but I thought one of the things Lawrence—' I break off. There are words for all of this. I have them all now. I can use them if I want to. But I don't want to. Not on another bright afternoon in another cold office with another pretty stranger, even if this one will try to help me too.

'He groomed me,' I say again. 'Abused me. When I was ten. But it… It's hard to explain. It'll sound ridiculous if I say it out loud.'

'Try me,' DS Curran says. She hasn't taken her eyes off me. Her shoulders are still tense.

'The reason I haven't done anything about it,' I say slowly. 'Is partly because there's no physical evidence, and partly because it… Well, because I'm okay now.'

She still doesn't react. She blinks.

'We went into foster care after we were with the Wolfes because I had an accident,' I explain. 'And our foster parents were lovely. Really kind. None of those horror stories you hear. They were a nice couple who wanted to do a nice thing, and we were well looked after and… and loved, I think.'

In an unexpectedly lucky twist, Louise found us a foster placement only two miles away from where we'd lived with Mum in Oldry. It was like going back home after being on another planet for a year. The couple, the McKays, took us to therapy – though I never heard from or saw Julie again – and they took us to visit Mum religiously. Audrey would phone their landline every other Sunday morning and ask us all the right questions. I think she really did miss us, especially Charlotte. The Sunday phone call tradition continued, and Audrey became the one surviving strand in my otherwise severed connection to Chaplin House. She gave me updates about Tony and occasionally Lawrence, and I included their names when I dutifully sent their Christmas cards... but it was almost possible to pretend it had all been a bad dream. Until I caught sight of the slash on my cheek.

The McKays were already fostering three brothers, all under the age of four, by the time I graduated. They looked after them and loved them and took them to therapy, just as they had done for us, so I wished them all the very best and let them get on with being angels.

'I did okay in school,' I continue now to DS Curran. 'I went to uni, I met my husband, we had our wee girl. I have a nice life. He hasn't... He didn't take any of that from me. He didn't stop me from... living. So I've never wanted to bring it all up. I've got something good. Better than good. Something that he didn't ruin for me and I don't want him to infect it. That probably sounds like absolute nonsense—'

'Not at all.' DS Curran is shaking her head. 'No, not at all. I understand.' She takes a deep breath and lets it out in a little puff. 'Do you want to tell me about it?'

'No,' I say. Then I add, stupidly. 'Sorry.'

She shakes her head. 'Do you want to pursue it?'

'No,' I say. I don't add anything this time.

'Okay. That's fine. It's absolutely your decision. As a police officer, I feel like I owe it to you to tell you that things are very different now, compared to what happened to you twenty years ago. You would be taken seriously. It would be looked into. Properly.'

'Mm,' I say. It's not that I don't believe her. It's that they are only words, and the thing itself is far too scary for me to say anything more, because I have something now that is worth protecting.

'Do you have anything else to add about this?' she asks, she taps her notebook with a knuckle.

'That's everything I can remember,' I say. 'Do you think you'll get a search warrant?'

'We might.' She says it with a sigh and rolls her chair back and stands up. 'Okay. Well. I'm going to give you my card anyway, Cara, so you can phone me if you think of anything else. I'll keep in touch with you about the progress, and if we find anything I'll let you know as soon as I safely can. Okay?'

She walks me all the way out, past the front desk and into the street.

'Where are you parked?' she asks. She takes a box of cigarettes from her cardigan pocket and offers me one. I shake my head.

'I'm just round the corner,' I lie, thinking of my long walk ahead.

'Well, thank you again for coming to see me. I'll do my best with this.'

'Thank you for listening to me,' I say. 'I feel… lighter. Like I've finally done the right thing. I'm just sorry it took me so long.'

She lights her cigarette and inhales, nodding. 'If you change your mind about… about the other thing, will you let me know?'

'Yeah,' I say, looking away from her, feeling suddenly embarrassed by it now that we're out in the open. There isn't anyone around. 'I nearly was going to. I played it out in my head a few times, imagined what it would be like to go into a police station and tell someone the whole truth but I… I don't think it's what I want. I'll let you know if I change my mind.'

'Okay.' She inhales again. 'I know you said he didn't take anything from you,' she continues. 'And I'm delighted you think that, but…'

There is that look again. Steve's look.

'But what?' I ask. I'm not sure I have ever bristled before, but I think maybe I do now.

'But are you sure that's true?' she asks. She doesn't have her head tilted to the side like she pities me, the way Aoife did in Café Nero. She is just looking at me, and we are the same height. With a start I realise that I have the same cardigan as her. It looks better on her.

No, it doesn't. It just looks different and I'm being self-critical.

'No,' I say after a moment. 'No, I'm not sure.'

Chapter 32 | June 2023 | Cherry Hill Primary School

Daisy's end of year play, *The Comedy of Errors at Cherry Hill Primary*, is performed in the assembly hall on the very last day of term. Steve is on leave for two weeks and has been tending to the garden and encouraging me to go with him for evening walks. I have settled back into work and have handed in all of my mock-ups on time, have created a digital advertisement that went humbly viral, and have been given two new clients. I have attended every client meeting that I have been assigned to and have even made CJ laugh twice.

Steve knows I have told the police about Ronnie, and he asks all the right questions and makes all the right noises. I have heard from DS Curran twice. Once was in mid-May, when she let me know they were still gathering evidence, had conducted a few interviews, but hadn't made any discoveries or arrests. The second time was earlier this afternoon.

I haven't spoken to Tony since he made his offer, so I don't expect any updates from him.

Everything is, on the surface, much as it was before my visit to the police. As it was before Audrey's death, even. But I feel different, and I think it's in a good way. I am anxious, certainly, but instead of a faceless sense of foreboding, I feel anxious about something tangible that I could, if I wanted to, talk about with my husband. It is strange to have a problem that I can talk about if I want to. It must be how normal people feel. We laugh at our shows. We even go to dinner in Belfast, the three of us, and I drive and Steve has a few beers. Daisy tells me she is proud of me for driving and even falls asleep in the car on the way home, and that is how I know she feels safe. I don't have to think about which Mummy to be each day. They still look to me to set the mood, but it is slightly easier to smile at them and make jokes and think of puns. There is a tiny bubble in my chest.

The carpark of Cherry Hill is busy, rammed with cars trying to park and families ushering groups of children towards the assembly hall. Daisy has been in school since 9 am, attending her last classes and then rehearsing all day in preparation for the big performance. The night is warm, and the sun still shines as though it's late in the afternoon. Everyone is in summer dresses, long shorts, thin cardigans. The summer stretches ahead, long and lovely, and everyone is talking about it because even though it happens every year, it is always a surprise.

Steve and I find a space to park and walk hand in hand to the hall. We present our tickets – handmade by the P5 class – to a beaming teacher. She gives a little laugh at Steve's pink T-shirt, which today reads HAVE YOU TRIED TURNING IT OFF AND ON AGAIN?, and points us to our seats. Charlotte is already there – early. I am touched and delighted, and we hug and kiss and sit chatting happily – like sisters – until the play starts.

I have never read – *watched*, I think to myself, hearing Tony's voice in my head, *you're supposed to watch a play – The Comedy of Errors* before, so I have no idea how this kid-friendly version holds up to it, but it is funny, in a slapstick way, and the kids lap up the laughter of the audience, and some of them are genuinely very good. With the exception of a slightly shaky start, Daisy gets each of her lines perfect. She could be mistaken for a professional, were it not for the fact that she seeks out our faces after all of her lines and grins and gives a small wave that makes Charlotte and me giggle like children. Steve has to shush us twice, but he is laughing too.

The applause at the end of the play is deafening, and the parents, families and friends of the children all stand up and stamp their feet and cheer. The children on the stage beam back. One girl starts crying, which elicits a collective *awwww* from the audience, and I wonder what it must be like to be in front of all these people. That moment when the nerves and the adrenaline have left your body and all there is is praise and applause and claps on the back. I remember something Tony said to me the last time I saw him, *It's not something you choose, it's a compulsion.* That idea that *you're born with it or you're not, you don't have a choice.*

I think now that maybe Audrey said something similar to me once, a long time ago. But of course, for her it wasn't a compulsion. It was her husband's compulsion, and she rode alongside. I think about Lawrence and the idea of compulsions and wonder if he believes that too.

Jamie Ward never would have been a successful actor.

I shake my head, as if trying to physically rid my brain of thoughts of him. I wonder if I'll ever be in a place where I can choose to forget him.

I think maybe I will, someday.

There is an end-of-year party after the performance, and some of the parents help to carry in tables of diluting juice and biscuits while the little actors go back to their classrooms to change.

'There she is!' Charlotte cries, as Daisy and her classmates rush back into the hall. Some of the adults start clapping again, as the mass of children separate off to find their families. Daisy comes towards us beaming ear to ear, her whole face pink. Charlotte finds her first and wraps her in a hug.

'You were the best one on the whole stage,' she whispers theatrically into Daisy's hair. 'I'm so proud of you. I've been telling everyone that will listen, Emilia is my niece.'

Daisy giggles and hugs her back.

'I messed up my very first word, did you not hear that? Mummy, did you hear I messed up the first word I said?'

'I didn't notice,' I lie. 'You were fantastic. You did such a good job. Did you enjoy it?'

'Yeah!' Daisy says breathlessly, accepting a hug from her dad. 'We have another performance tomorrow afternoon for the local old people's home, Auntie Charlotte, and then that's it all over.'

'Retirement home,' Steve and I say in unison. 'You were amazing, Dais,' Steve adds. 'I got a bit choked up at the end.'

'Must run in the family, this acting bug,' Charlotte says.

'Mm,' I say.

Daisy drags Charlotte off to meet her friends, and Steve gets chatting with another dad that he used to work with, so I reach into the pocket of his hoodie and take his keys, then motion to him that I'm nipping out to get my jumper from the car. The hall is getting colder as the sun is starting to set outside.

I have taken ten steps in the direction of Steve's car when a pair of headlights flash twice at me. I glance over towards the big white car, reversed into a disabled space near the reception building, and give a little half wave and a smile without really looking. It must be one of the other parents. I continue towards our car.

The lights flash again.

'Cara?'

The driver has put the window of the car down to call to me and I look around.

The BMW that nearly killed us en route to Audrey's funeral.

That number plate, LAW 0LF3.

And the Wolfe himself behind the driver's seat, his eyes boring into mine.

'Come and talk to me,' he calls. 'Five minutes.'

I stand frozen, Steve's keys in one hand. The hairs on my arms stand up. My bare shoulders are cold, even in the warm night.

'Five minutes,' he repeats. He glances at the door to the assembly hall, then back to me. 'Please.'

My grip tightens on the keys. Women are told to walk at night with their keys poking out from between their knuckles. No, actually. Women are told not to walk at night at all. Little girls are

Little Darlings

told not to get into strangers' cars. Stranger Danger. Strange men. Bad men. Nobody warns them that sometimes it's just men.

Twenty-two years have passed.

I am not the same person I was then, when I did anything he asked.

And yet…

My feet want to move towards the car. My brain is screaming at me that no, there can be no reason for him to be here. No good one. But I am curious. Maybe it's Tony, I think dully. Maybe he's died.

'Please, Cara,' he says.

I take one step towards his car. Then another.

I keep the keys in my hand.

Chapter 33 | June 2023 | Cherry Hill Primary School, carpark

I open the passenger door and climb up to sit down. The car is higher than ours. It's so unnecessary, I think. The car is warm, but unpleasantly so. Like he has been sitting in it with the heating on.

I glance at him and can't read his expression. His skin is smooth and tanned, not a wrinkle in sight. It is ridiculous and quite unfair that I could probably pass for older than him.

He is wearing a white shirt, three buttons open, and tan-coloured trousers and shoes. His hands are on the steering wheel and I know he is trying for casual, but he is gripping it just a little bit too tightly, and his jaw is set so I can't see his teeth, and that is rare for him.

'How did you know I would be here?' I ask, looking straight ahead at the door to the assembly hall. It has been propped open with a fire extinguisher. No wonder it was getting chilly in there.

There are people in there. I am safe.

'Your little one told me this was her end-of-year play, remember?' Lawrence says. 'At the funeral.'

'How did you know what school?'

'I didn't. Looked up primary schools in your area and checked online. *The Comedy of Errors at Cherry Hill Primary* was plastered all over the school website, with the time and date.'

'Right.' I swallow. 'Should you really be looking at primary schools online?'

I feel him looking at the side of my face and know I am blushing. I force myself to look at him, and he is smiling slightly. It is not me who should be embarrassed. Why am I blushing?

I know you said he didn't take anything from you… but are you sure that's true?

How different would I be if I wasn't defined by a cold day in February?

'No idea what you mean,' he says, his voice so low it's a rumble. 'I needed to speak to you and Tony wouldn't give me your number. I'm going to ask you this once, Cara, and I want you to be honest with me: how worried do I need to be about the police?'

The seat below me is heated. He has heated this seat, knowing I would be getting in. I hate that he can read me so well. What was stopping me from ignoring him and going back inside?

'What do you know so far?' I ask lightly.

'I've been questioned once,' he says, leaning back in his seat. He is going for lazy, casual. 'They've asked me about *Ronnie*. You remember him, don't you? He was our gardener. He upped and left one day without a trace.'

'The day you hit him with your car, funnily enough,' I say softly.

'I wasn't sure you remembered that,' Lawrence says, with something else in his voice. Admiration, maybe? I don't have time to work out what it is, because he adds, 'That was a big day for you.'

My breath comes too quickly and I work hard to steady it, gritting my teeth.

Are you sure that's true? That lie you've told yourself?

'I think you're confused,' Lawrence continues. 'I think your memories are getting all mixed up. You were very emotional back then, don't you remember? You were very upset about your mum. How is she, by the way?'

'Dead,' I say, as simply as I can, unwilling to give him the satisfaction of my seeming upset.

'Oh, yes. Audrey did tell me, I forgot. Pity. Well, anyway. I told the police all I could remember and they seemed pretty satisfied. They spoke to Tony too. He backed me up. I'm sorry to say it, but we both had to play up to it a bit. Exaggerate how... messed up you were. They believed us, though. Of that I'm certain.'

'My word against yours,' I say, shrugging.

'Exactly. And without any evidence...'

'Evidence, evidence, evidence,' I say, shaking my head. 'That's all anyone cares about. Your dad seemed to think there was no point in me bringing up anything from the past because there was no evidence... Even Charlotte said I should let sleeping wolves lie, really, because there was no proof.'

'Sleeping wolves lie,' he says, smiling. 'Very clever.'

'Thing is, neither of them knew that what I was going to the police about was what happened with Ronnie. They both assumed it was... something else. I'll be honest, at the start, that's what I thought too.'

'That's what I'm asking you,' Lawrence says. He folds his arms in front of him and leans back in his seat. 'How worried should I be? Should I have a solicitor? If the papers find out about this—'

'Your next premiere might be delayed,' I say sadly. 'Yes, what a shame. I don't know how you would get over that.'

He gives a snort of laughter and looks at me, his brow furrowed.

'You're very different,' he says. 'I'm not sure I like it.'

'My answer is I don't know yet,' I say, ignoring him. 'It depends how they get on with the investigation into Ronnie. If they find evidence... if they find his body—'

'I'm telling you,' Lawrence says, his voice louder, a hint of a temper creeping in. 'There's no body to find. He's out there somewhere, doing people's gardens or washing windows or God knows what. You'll see.'

'I'm not ten years old any more, Laurie,' I say softly.

'More's the pity,' he says. He is staring at me the way he always did. Like he is starving and all he wants is me. His eyes bore into mine, and in spite of what I said, I do feel like a child again. Small and unimportant. Too young and too naïve and too little for this big game.

I look towards the door to the hall.

Charlotte is there, staring at the car, her mouth open. She narrows her eyes at me, a question, and I shake my head.

No, I'm fine. Don't intervene.

He sees what I'm doing and looks over himself.

'Ah, there's Charlotte. I must offer her a lift.'

'She's staying at ours tonight,' I say, feeling a pathetic hold over him. 'Don't bother.'

'I'll throw in a bag of coke with the lift and I know who she'll pick.'

I have nothing to say to that, so I don't respond. Charlotte still looks concerned, but she doesn't approach. She just watches from the doorway of the hall, her arms wrapped around herself.

'There is evidence,' I say at last.

He turns his body towards me. 'Go on.'

'Just a bit. Just one thing. But it might be enough to get a proper investigation going, apparently. The DS looking into it called me today to tell me.'

'And what is this magical evidence?' he asks. He still sounds amused.

'Ronnie's Walkman,' I say. I look at him, wanting to enjoy his reaction. He blinks and shakes his head.

'What?'

'The Walkman he always had. You remember it. It was the newest model at the time. He never had it off him. You remember?'

'Yes...' Lawrence's eyes are narrowed, moving, re-living a memory I can't begin to imagine.

'I took it off him,' I say. 'After you hit him, I took it. I have no idea why. I just did. And I hid it in the wall in my bedroom in your dad's house.'

Lawrence's smile is fixed tightly on his face. 'Right. Well.' He glances at his phone, which is held snugly in a holder on the dashboard. 'They're not going to get a search warrant based on your word, are they?'

'They didn't need one,' I say. 'They just asked to come inside. Earlier today. And they found it. And it's covered in Ronnie's blood.'

Lawrence's jaw moves.

He smells the same as he did. Issey Miyake aftershave, I think suddenly. I haven't thought of the name of it for years. Debenhams. Walking through the men's section with my mum in the Before.

'It's enough to suggest he didn't simply wander off into the sunset without saying goodbye,' I say. 'It's enough for them to take it seriously. To really look for him.'

'It's nothing,' Lawrence says finally. 'That's not proof.'

'Your dad tried to tell me that you'd sold your house in Stranmillis,' I say, thinking out loud, something suddenly at the forefront of my mind. Something that has been trying to get through for weeks, but that has always been just out of grasp. 'Why would he do that? Why would he drop it in casually that you'd sold that house? He must have known you hadn't, because, if you had, where was the money to show for it? He didn't know I'd been there with you.' My voice threatens to waver on this last, but I don't let it. 'He thought he could convince me it had been sold years before. Is that where you put him? Is that where Ronnie's buried?'

For a moment, I think he isn't going to respond. Then he lets out a laugh that is lyrical, and genuinely full of mirth.

'That imagination of yours, Cara. I have absolutely no idea what you're talking about. Now, I think Charlotte wants you. She looks worried.'

I look back to my sister, who hasn't taken her eyes off me, and who looks ready to run towards us at any second.

'You really think she didn't know about us?' Lawrence asks.

I focus on breathing. In, hold, out. It's easy, I do it all the time. Why does it feel so difficult?

Little Darlings

'She didn't,' I say. 'You hid it well.'

'You're even more adorable than I thought if you really think Charlotte knew nothing. Why do you think she's stayed so close to me all these years?'

'You're her cousin,' I say, just a trace of doubt creeping in. 'And you helped her out.'

'She's keeping tabs on me,' Lawrence says, and his voice is drawling, lazy again. 'She makes sure none of my partners ever have kids. I've even caught her checking my phone history once or twice. As if I'd be so naïve.'

'She didn't know,' I say again. 'And you don't tell me how I feel any more.'

He nods slowly and seems to consider this.

'Why me?' someone asks, and it's me who has asked it, but I don't remember forming the words.

'Why you what?'

'Why me and not her?'

'Oh.'

Lawrence looks between us. My pretty sister, her summer dress hanging at her knees, her colourful baseball trainers, her curls neat tonight. Then me, in my greying white vest top and jeans that dig in. He lets his gaze settle on the scar on my cheek and it tingles.

'Audrey had already claimed her, I suppose,' he says finally. 'She was going to make her into a little mini-me. Dress her up and play with her, make her into the teenage daughter she'd never had.'

'And I was left?'

He moves his hand as if he is going to take mine, and I flinch. He seems to think better of it and lets his hand slap down on his own knee.

'I really loved you,' he says after a moment. 'Whatever you want to call it… I would have married you.'

I open the car door and put one foot out. It doesn't reach the ground, just hovers in the air, high above it.

'Forgetting this nonsense about Ronnie, should I have my solicitor on speed dial?' he asks, and is still trying to sound amused. 'Just in case you change your mind and decide to tell them about... about our relationship?'

'Yes,' I say. 'I think you should.'

'Simon Hadley is the best criminal barrister in this country,' he says simply. 'He was there last time. Before. When you... said those things. Audrey called him and made him aware of the situation but...' He trails off, looks out into the darkening carpark like he is looking for someone. 'Well. Didn't need him in the end, did we? I never even met him; I only found out what had happened months later. After you had your little accident and moved out. Simon made his money easy that day.'

'You paid off the police so they wouldn't look into it.'

'I did no such thing. I didn't even know about it until later. If anyone was paid off, it wasn't by me.'

'Tony, then?'

The corner of his mouth twists up and I see there is a tiny gap between two of his teeth at the side. I have never noticed it before. He makes a noise that could be hesitancy or could be tentative agreement.

'Well, it doesn't matter who paid whom. The police had nothing to go on, anyway. Only the words of a confused child. Nothing would have come of it. They didn't believe you.'

I realise with a strange disconnect that I have played this scene in my head a thousand times. I have lived this, this exact moment, countless times. In some ways, I have been confronting Lawrence Wolfe for twenty-two years. But in all the fantasies, in all the daydreams, I was angry. I screamed at him; he was frightened by me, terrified that he was about to be caught. He felt guilty, felt horrible. He apologised. He begged me not to turn him in. In my dreams, I make him afraid. I make him so afraid of me.

But here we are, the closest we have been since the night in my bedroom, and my thoughts fuse together and I see the green inflatable chair and hear the birds screaming outside, and the rain, and smell the damp in the Jack and Jill bathroom. This is the closest we have been since the moments before I threw myself at the glass window and let myself fall towards the flower beds below like I was nothing more than another shard of glass raining down. But here, instead of being afraid of me, he is calm. He is amused, taunting me with those huge eyes, grinning at me with those perfect, feminine lips. And I am afraid. I am afraid. I am thirty-two and I am afraid. I am a mum and I am afraid.

I tell myself I am safe.

I am, of course I am.

The door to the hall is still open; people have started walking back to their cars, all within shouting distance. Charlotte is right there.

But there were always people right outside. They were all there.

I am safe from him now only because of the inevitable fact of growing up. Some women find it so cruel – haven't I myself bemoaned the horrors of finding wrinkles? Felt the stab of hurt that comes with realising I can't comfortably lean over to tie my own trainers any more?

But being older means I am safe.

I have never realised before how wonderful it is, how beautiful.

He will not hurt me because I am a woman now, and it is not women that he hurts.

He leans towards me, dark eyes glinting, careful to keep his expression neutral in case anyone is watching from outside. 'So, what makes you think it's going to be any different this time?' he whispers.

I feel my shoulders sink. The same question Charlotte asked, the same one Tony asked. The one I have no answer for.

The light is fading around us outside. The sky is bright pink.

I have to get back to Steve and Daisy. Steve and Daisy. Steve. Steve.

Hannah King

I step out of the car and go to close the door in his face, but then I look back at him, my answer suddenly there, fully formed and honest and alive and true.

'Because this time nobody is going to shut me up,' I say.

Chapter 34 | June 2023 | Dromary, County Down

The huge BMW drives off so quickly and with such a loud rev of the engine that several parents emerging from the assembly hall glance at one another with their eyebrows raised.

'What was that about?' Charlotte asks, panic in her voice. 'What's wrong?'

'Nothing,' I say, and I think on some level I mean it. 'Nothing is wrong. He wanted to know if I was going to tell the police about... you know.'

'So he knows you've told them about Ronnie and the car?'

'Yes, they've spoken to him already.'

Charlotte lets her breath out in an unsteady sigh. 'Okay. What did you tell him? Are you going to tell them anything else?'

Daisy's best friend, Ellen, comes out of the hall with her parents, and my conversation with Charlotte is cut short with having to congratulate the little girl on her performance – already I can't remember whom she played – and make small talk with her mum and dad about how big they're all getting, and how there's a quare stretch in the evenings. They finally bid us goodbye and Ellen skips towards their car.

If Lawrence was still parked out here, would he have watched her?

My stomach does a back flip.

How many little girls has he watched in the years since I jumped from the window?

Has he ever done more than watch them?

'So?' Charlotte says, her eyes darting around. 'Are you?'

I give her a shrug that feels pathetic and entirely inappropriate for such a huge question. In some ways, this is bigger than me. In some ways, it's not my own personal secret to keep. I think of him on the primary school's website. Another back flip.

I have been so preoccupied with playing my part as Mummy, as Cara Harris, that I have left it so late to worry if there were other girls.

'I don't know if I can,' I say to Charlotte, my mind racing. 'I want to but I… What about Steve? What about my life? It's going to disrupt everything. And it's not the kind of thing you can just keep secret, once you start it. It's Lawrence Fucking Wolfe for God's sake. Everyone would know. That's the first thing they'd think of when they saw me. I start that ball rolling, nothing's going to be the same again. And it might be for nothing.'

'Not for nothing,' Charlotte says, her eyes bright. 'And I'll stick up for you this time. I'll tell them I lied before. I'll say I knew all along. I'll back you up'

'But you didn't know,' I say. 'I don't want you to lie.'

Charlotte looks at me for a moment, opens her mouth as if to say something, then closes it.

'They might get him for Ronnie,' I say, nodding as if I believe it. 'Whatever happened the next day, somebody is bound to know something. The car had to be fixed, the body has to be somewhere. The evidence is there, they just have to find it.'

Charlotte nods, but I can tell she doesn't believe me. Who is going to remember a car they fixed twenty-two years ago?

I go to re-enter the hall, but Charlotte takes my hand and pulls me back.

'Wait,' she says. 'What if I did it?'

'What if you did what?'

'What if I went to the police and said it was me that he… abused.'

I stare at her, not sure if I'm understanding.

Little Darlings

'You could tell me everything, I could learn it off by heart. Like a script. And I could say it was me. Then it's not your life that gets disrupted, but he still gets what he deserves.'

A huge group of people come out of the hall, and we have to squeeze together to let them through. For a moment, with her hand clutching mine and our heads close together, we could be children again. A big sister sticking up for a little one. Protecting her against the bad man.

'You said yourself,' Charlotte says when the group has passed. We are still standing close together. 'There's no evidence of any of it; just your word. So if it was my word, it won't matter. Nobody knows any different. Steve doesn't need to know a thing.'

There is a bubble in my chest and I can't name it.

Something has shifted.

Has Charlotte really been keeping tabs on Lawrence? I wasn't worrying about the possibility of other girls… but maybe she was.

'There you two are!' Steve comes out of the hall, hand in hand with Daisy. 'We wondered where you'd got to. Shall we get a move on? It'll be dark soon. Want to get our own little Anne Hathaway home!'

Daisy giggles and takes my free hand in her free hand, so the four of us are moving in one long, ridiculous, snaking line. Steve laughs and Daisy laughs, so I do too, so Charlotte does too. Charlotte squeezes my hand and I squeeze hers back, and it used to mean something, when we were very young, before our lives went off course, and it means something now, but I don't quite know what.

Charlotte goes to sleep on our sofa, and Daisy, too, is out like a light. Steve falls asleep immediately, like he always has, because he is a good man with a clean conscience.

I lie awake and think about all the things that could have been. If, if, if.

If someone else had adopted Jamie Ward, if Audrey and Tony hadn't given him such a stupid and pompous actor name. If he'd been good at maths instead of drama, if he'd had a normal job.

If we'd been put in foster care from the start, or even if we'd been left alone to raise ourselves. Even if we'd been adopted by a couple who were physically cruel, that would have been better.

If Mum had taken the day off work when it was so icy. If she'd never slipped and smashed her skull on the ground.

Jamie Ward never would have had a chance of doing what Lawrence Wolfe did, would he? Someone like Jamie Ward wouldn't get away with what Lawrence Wolfe did. Jamie Ward would be found out or, even better, people would be keeping an eye on him, and they'd know never to leave him alone in the first place.

Lawrence played his part so well, I think, turning over in bed.

But I played mine too, without knowing it.

I was the girl who was obsessed with him, who adored him, who told him he was wonderful and looked at him constantly like he was a magnet. Lawrence Wolfe's adoring fan. And I had kept my mouth shut, hadn't I? For a long time I had taken my role seriously, done my best with it. And that first time, on Halloween, outside the garden shed… Hadn't I enjoyed it? That I had something over Charlotte. My stomach flips now, thinking about how delighted I'd been that I had something she wanted.

For a moment I am alone in my bed in Chaplin House and I feel… marked. Touched and unclean, lording my kiss with Lawrence over Charlotte but knowing somewhere in my gut, in the very makeup of my soul, that it was wrong. More than wrong. Sensing danger, but unable to describe it. I had asked for it. Wanted it.

I think about Jamie Ward. His relationship – because that is what it was, wasn't it? – with me.

Of him on Cherry Hill's website. In the carpark, looking at the children.

I think of Charlotte's offer, of how she is willing to give up everything, to lie for me.

That is what seals it.

I have a sister who is willing to protect me. Too late, maybe, but it still means something.

And I make up my mind to help the little girl who is still stuck in the attic of Chaplin House.

It doesn't matter much what happens to him, I think, as I slip out of bed. It's not about him any more. This is about me, and about my family and about what I want.

I unplug my phone from its charger and tiptoe towards the bedroom door. I look back at Steve, his chest rising and falling dependably. Strong.

And there will be consequences; of course there will. But there will be consequences if I do nothing, too.

I want to do, for the first time, what *I* want, when it comes to Lawrence Wolfe. Not what Bridget Spears, a stranger, wants me to. Not what Charlotte has suggested. Not what Tony has begged of me. Certainly not what Lawrence wants.

I open the back door and close it after me.

It is cold now, and I shiver as I search through my contacts.

DC Curran doesn't answer when I call – of course she doesn't; it is so late, and she has a life – so I leave her a voicemail. I have never left a voicemail before, but I am strong and I am an adult and I am not afraid.

'Hi, it's Cara,' I say, my voice steady. As an afterthought, but with a spark of happiness, I add my married name. 'Cara Harris. I've had an idea about a house where you might look for… for Ronnie…'

There is a high-pitched squeak from above me and I glance up just in time to see a bat zipping across the navy sky and into the night beyond. I make a mental note to ask Steve what their squeaks mean. He'll know.

'It's in Stranmillis. If you give me a ring back, I'll talk you through exactly where it is,' I continue. 'And I've thought about what you said about the other thing and… Yeah. Let's do it.'

EPILOGUE
May 2001 | Chaplin House

One Sunday morning – or, really, the deep black depths of the night before it – Charlotte decides she will make up with her little sister. They have been behaving strangely around one another for days, weeks – it hasn't been months, has it? Has it been since they came to Chaplin House, nearly a year ago? Barely speaking, arguing when they have spoken, but even Charlotte has to admit that it is boring not speaking to Cara, and she feels guilty for ruining Cara's good new Christmas paints.

Cara has been pretending she doesn't even see Charlotte recently, and Charlotte knows she deserves it for the way she's treated her. Her sister has been walking around the house like a zombie, not looking at anyone. Even in school, if Charlotte sees her, Cara is just staring at the ground or walking around by herself.

She will apologise and get into bed next to her sister and they will talk about their mum, because Charlotte is pretending she has forgotten, that she has adapted so well into this new life with its colours and its beauty and its easy, carefree money, but she thinks about the little terraced house every day, and if she can't have her mum, the least she can do is have her Cara.

Their mum would be ashamed if she could see them now, Charlotte thinks. Barely acknowledging each other. Would she even recognise them? Cara has just been so different since they arrived at Chaplin House, even more so these last few months. And Charlotte knows she has changed too. She likes the confident,

Little Darlings

popular girl she is becoming… but she hasn't left much room to be a sister, and that doesn't feel fair.

Laurie has returned home today for the summer, his work complete, and it would be nice if everyone could just get along again. Maybe he would push them in the hammock again soon; the weather will be warm enough in a few weeks.

Charlotte slips out of bed and crosses the silent hallway. The moon is high and bright through the windows on the landing and it guides her way. Rain lashes against the roof of the house like static from a TV, and it makes her feel like she is in a film. This would be an important scene.

She eases open the door to the attic rooms. It doesn't make a sound any more, not like the shrieking it used to make. The tortured girl in the attic. Charlotte is annoyed with herself that she scared Cara with that. She'll tell her tonight it's all made up, just in case Cara still believes it. She might even offer to move back upstairs. Yes, she'll do that. It would be nice to share the attic again.

Charlotte takes a moment to gaze out of The Big Window. The garden is dark like a cave, the moon showing her only the tops of the trees. They're swaying in the wind. She gets a sick feeling in her belly and decides she doesn't like being so high up. Maybe she is a little bit afraid of heights.

There is a noise from above her and she turns her head to the attic. Just a bed spring. Just Cara turning over in her sleep. Then she hears a murmuring. Cara hasn't talked in her sleep for years, has she started again?

Charlotte ascends the final few steps. She hesitates outside the door, then pushes on the wood so it opens just a crack. She freezes at what she sees. A sight that she will think about daily for the rest of her life. The window of Cara's bedroom allowing the light of the moon to illuminate the bed perfectly, as if an artist or a photographer had set it up that way. And no sleeping sister nestled safely under her sheets, but two figures. Curled around one another. Or – is that quite right? Not curled around one another. Not really.

Charlotte holds her breath and realises they are talking quietly to one another. Or at least, Lawrence is talking to Cara. Charlotte's heart beats fast and loud in her ears, because she can't be found here. She knows she is not supposed to see this.

And Charlotte learned about puberty the year before, the stupid roadshow that toured the schools and did a survey at the end, and she knows about feelings and urges and she knows the facts of life and the birds and the bees, but she doesn't quite know the name for when the people involved are your ten-year-old sister and your twenty-six-year-old uncle of sorts. She won't know the name of that, of him, in fact, for another three years, when a girl in her class makes a comment about the nine-year age difference between her parents and refers to her dad, jokingly, as one. And then things will start to click into place, things that Charlotte will both choose not to think about and be unable to press from her mind.

But not now.

Because now, in the early hours of Sunday morning, she feels sick.

With anger.

She has been betrayed by her own sister, who is pretending to be afraid of Lawrence Wolfe but who really, secretly, nastily, invites him up to her bedroom when she thinks nobody is watching. They are spending time together without her, giving one another presents, meeting up at night in secret just so Charlotte can't join in.

But Charlotte will be watching from now on. Charlotte will always be watching.

She lets the door close, silently, and tiptoes downstairs.

That's why Lawrence had the door oiled. For her. Maybe it was Cara's idea. They have both been lying to her, they have both betrayed her.

Little Darlings

Well, let them have each other.

Charlotte has just gotten back into bed and pulled the covers up over her head when there is an almighty crashing sound from somewhere above her. Glass breaking, she thinks.

She whips out of bed and into the hallway, her feet moving as though she is on roller skates, just in time to see the door to the attic open and Lawrence rushing out. He stops dead when he sees Charlotte and they look at one another for two, three seconds. He is fully dressed, though creased-looking in a way that Lawrence Wolfe never is. He has come from her sister's bedroom. Where he was talking to her sister, and leaving Charlotte out.

There is movement from behind the door of Tony and Audrey's room, noises of confusion. Lawrence glances at their door, looks at Charlotte again, then runs downstairs.

'ARE WE BEING BURGLED?' Audrey cries.

Their door opens and they both stumble into the hallway.

'What was that?' Uncle Tony demands. He is in his pyjamas. Grey flannel. She'll remember that image.

'I don't know,' Charlotte stammers.

'Down here!' Lawrence's voice comes from somewhere downstairs, and Tony runs to follow him. Audrey grips Charlotte by the arm and looks into her face, her own shiny and bright white with a face mask. She looks like a clown.

'ARE WE BEING BURGLED?' she screams. 'I HAVE TO KNOW.'

Charlotte shakes her off and sprints down the stairs after Uncle Tony.

There is the ambulance. Audrey's tears. The bright lights of the hospital. Thinking Cara is dead. Then, knowing she will live.

There is a long day of sitting in a hospital on an uncomfortable chair while the adults take it in turns to sit with Cara and talk to the doctors and make phone calls. Charlotte and Laurie are left alone only once, and he looks at her, but neither of them says a thing.

Audrey takes Charlotte back to Chaplin House in a taxi and they eat a slice of toast with butter – Charlotte has never seen Audrey eat butter before – and Audrey mumbles something about how Cara must have been sleepwalking and shakes her head sadly and they both go to bed.

Charlotte doesn't sleep.

She hears the grandfather clock chiming two in the morning and three in the morning, sleep not coming, thinking about the way Cara's body looked, smashed on the concrete under The Big Window, next to the flowerbeds. How it felt when she thought Cara was dead.

And then she lets her brain go further back, to the pair of figures on Cara's bed in the moonlight. She doesn't understand.

Were they a *couple*?

No, of course not. That was ridiculous.

But they were clearly very close. They must not even like Charlotte.

And she is sad for her sister, because she must be in pain, but somewhere deep inside her – deeper than she has ever delved before – there is the anger. She is angry. Angry that they've played her like a fool. Cara pretended she was scared of him, she tried to get him into trouble with the police, and all the while…

She curses the pair of them and hates her sister and hates Lawrence and hates everything and everybody else.

And even when she learns the names for things, and even when her subconscious brain begins to add together the things that she has seen and heard, she will refuse to believe. For a long time, she will blame her sister and blame Lawrence in equal measure for how unhappy she feels.

Often, she will think back to the police interview before St Patrick's Day weekend. How nobody had told her anything, nobody would answer her when she demanded to know why she wasn't allowed to go to drama after school, why instead they were driven to a police station the next day. They spoke to Cara, then

Little Darlings

Audrey, for over an hour. When Audrey came out, Charlotte went in. Audrey's face – Charlotte would never forget it. Nobody could act that shocked, nobody could. She will recount to herself – over the years, not quite yet – what exactly she said, but the truth is she can barely remember. 'She loves Laurie, she adores him, I have no idea why she would say this,' something like that? One thing she does remember saying, over and over again, 'Laurie hasn't done anything wrong. I don't understand what you mean. Cara just wants attention.'

How good it had felt, all the officers' eyes on her while she talked and talked. She got into it. Her first role, the one that pivoted her life. The anguished older sister, fearful and confused over the lies her baby sister was telling. And she must have played it well, for they all believed her. Even the social worker. They nodded sympathetically; they passed her tissues. She pretended to blot her eyes with them but realised she didn't need to pretend, she was crying. She could cry on cue from then on. It would come in useful.

The irony, she would realise when she was older, much older, of accusing Cara of wanting attention when she herself had loved every minute of being in the police station.

She'd believed what she was saying then. Hadn't she? She'd trusted Lawrence completely, trusted her sister less so. Knew for certain there could be no truth in what Cara was claiming. There was no way Laurie had *hurt* her. That was for sure. Cara was lying. She had to be.

Although…

There were the touches, Charlotte would think suddenly, while she was crossing the road outside a bar in Belfast at the age of sixteen. He was very physical with her.

She hears the grandfather clock striking four and turns over in bed, eyes wide open and staring, angry, angry, angry.

There were the presents he bought her, she'd reason, aged twenty, swallowing an ecstasy tablet for the first time.

The grandfather clock tells her it is five o'clock in the morning. What is Cara doing in the hospital? Is she asleep? Is she in pain?

On her twenty-first birthday, she will see Cara and they will chat for hours, almost like they are normal sisters celebrating. Then she will go to a nightclub with a group of her friends and she will wake up the next morning with no idea what part of the city she is in, and no purse and no keys for her flat, and she will think all day about Cara falling – *jumping, it must have been jumping* – out The Big Window, and she'll go to the pub and top up from the night before, just to forget.

She turns to lie on her back and stares at the ceiling and thinks about Lawrence being on the bed with her sister and talking to her and telling her secrets and she wants to punch him, and thinks that maybe she wants to punch Cara too.

What happened up there last night? One minute they were talking… the next Cara was lying on the concrete below.

Had he pushed her?

No, he would never do that.

So what was it?

'*She's obsessed with him.*' That was something else she said to the police. That Cara was obsessed with Laurie. More irony, another lie. It was she, Charlotte, surely, who was obsessed with Lawrence Wolfe. Who had been from the moment she met him.

Aged twenty-three, lying with her cheek on the dirty tiles of an unknown bathroom, she'll remember the image of them both in Cara's bed in the moonlight, and she'll force herself to sit so she can throw up into a stranger's toilet, unsure if it was the drink or the memory.

All of that will come later. The guilt, the horror of what she's done, or not done. She'll stifle the feelings with drugs, and she'll let it work.

And Cara will seem fine, after all. She will do well. She will get her degree, she will marry, she will have a child. She'll do all the things they were both supposed to do. So Charlotte will let her live her happy life and remove herself from it and not try for any of it herself because she knows, deep down, she doesn't deserve it.

And she won't tell anyone about how sad she feels, about how guilty. About how much she hates herself. She will have no one to tell but Cara anyway, and Cara doesn't deserve to worry about Charlotte. Charlotte had never worried about her.

She will stay in touch with Lawrence. She will never be quite sure why.

Yes, he is a useful person to have around. He has a lot of money and he is generous with it, with her. Why is that? She will ask herself but never be able to think of an answer. Sometimes, when she is very drunk, she will want to ask him, *Do you know that I know? What do I know? Is it true, this thing I think I know?* but she never will because she is a coward, and if she doesn't know the answer she can pretend that he likes her, that he thinks she's funny, that they're friends.

Or maybe she has just always wanted to keep an eye on him. To protect another little girl from harm the way she didn't protect Cara.

She will be certain, always, that there was never anyone else. There couldn't be, she has made sure of it. Just Cara.

How ridiculous, that word *just*.

But no, for now it is anger.

Light is blazing through the curtains of her bedroom, now. They are going back to the hospital first thing to relieve Tony and Lawrence. To play nurse to Cara.

The grandfather clock strikes eight in the morning and Charlotte gets up out of bed, ready to play her role.

We would like to extend our thanks to the police officers and clerical staff of Anniskillen Police Station for kindly supplying transcripts and case notes to aid us in preparing the script for our upcoming documentary BIG BAD WOLFE: STORY OF A BEAUTIFUL MONSTER.

– True Story Production Studios, September 2027

Acknowledgements

My first thank you is to my brilliant agent, Charlotte Seymour, who has championed Cara's story from the start and was hugely helpful in the early drafting stages. Thank you also to Anna Dawson, who is endlessly accommodating of my questions. I am very grateful to have you both on my side.

A huge thank you to Carolyn Mays and the team at Bedford Square for the vast amount of work that has gone into getting *Little Darlings* ready for publication. I am glad that this novel has found such a good home and has been so well looked after by such a professional and talented editor and team.

I am also very humbled by and grateful for the support from the booksellers, readers and other authors who make my own author life so enjoyable. I appreciate every rating, every review, every recommendation, every message.

Thank you to my best friend, KP, who read *Little Darlings* in one go and sent me the best voice notes of my life at two in the morning. I am forever grateful for your biased enthusiasm, your help with the social stuff, your passion for books, and your laugh.

Thank you to my mum and my dad and John. We are the best team.

But John, most importantly, you're welcome.

About the Author

Photo credit © Karen Proctor

Hannah King is a writer from Country Down, Northern Ireland, where she lives with her partner and their dogs. Her first novel, *She and I*, was critically acclaimed.

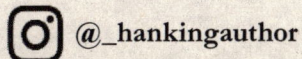 @_hankingauthor

NO EXIT PRESS
More than just the usual suspects

— CWA DAGGER —
AWARDED BEST CRIME & MYSTERY PUBLISHER

'A very smart, independent publisher delivering the finest literary crime fiction' **Big Issue**

MEET NO EXIT PRESS, an award-winning crime imprint bringing you the best in crime and suspense fiction. From classic detective novels, to page-turning spy thrillers and literary writing that grabs the attention. Our books are carefully crafted by some of the world's finest writers and delivered to you by a small, but passionate, team.

In over 30 years of business, we have published award-winning fiction and non-fiction including the work of a Pulitzer Prize winner, the British Crime Book of the Year, numerous CWA Dagger Awards, a British million-copy bestselling author, the winner of the Canadian Governor General's Award for Fiction and the Scotiabank Giller Prize, to name but a few. We are the home of many crime and noir legends from the USA whose work includes iconic film adaptations and TV sensations. We pride ourselves in uncovering the most exciting new or undiscovered talents. New and not so new – you know who you are!

We are a proactive team committed to delivering the very best, both for our authors and our readers.

Want to join the conversation and find out more about what we do?

Catch us on social media or sign up to our newsletter for all the latest news from No Exit Press.

f fb.me/noexitpress   𝕏 @noexitpress

noexit.co.uk